THE
TARINN
FABLES

Nuvummburtee

KRIS GODWIN

Nuvummburtee
Book Two of the Tarinn Fables
Print Edition ISBN: 978-0-6482585-4-4
eBook Edition ISBN: 978-0-6482585-5-1

Cover by Amygdala Design.
http://www.amygdaladesign.net/

A catalogue record is available at the National Library of Australia.
https://www.nla.gov.au/

For the family... and thanks to you, for sticking with the journey!

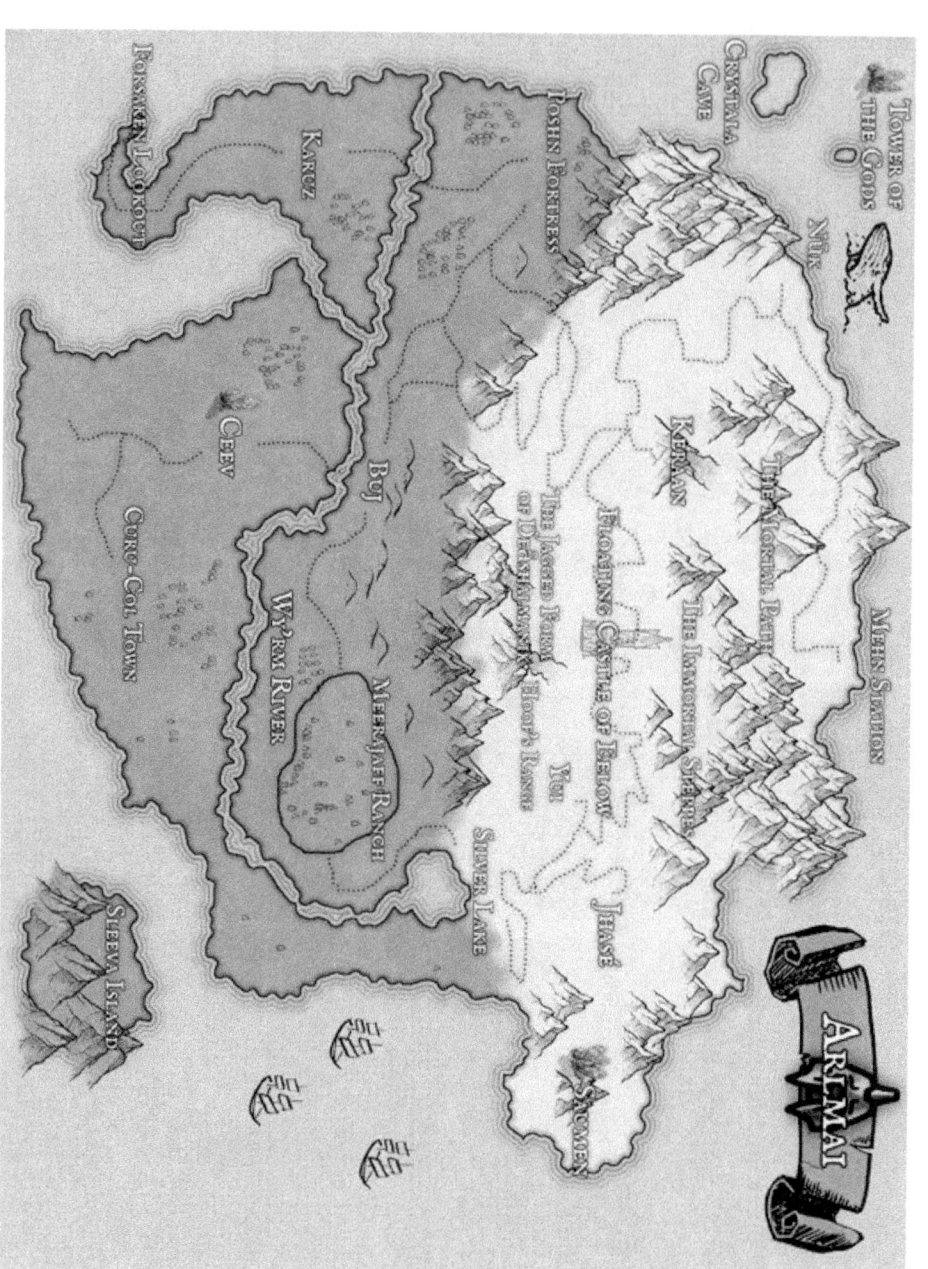

PROLOGUE

Kwennsefulass.

That was his name.

He did not know what it meant. But he liked it. It soothed his soul; its characters deeply hewn into the holy emerald of his necklace. It was a word that bought some semblance of identity to his blank being – for that's what he was.

Blank.

Like a music sheet devoid of its melody, or a canvas bereft of its painting, 'Kwenn' was a man with no meaning. No history and an uncertain future both haunted him in equal measure; much like the scar that seared his cheek.

Still, he coveted that scar in a way… it gave him a morbidly warm reassurance that he was a real person with a real past.

But…

He was *not* a real person. He knew that now.

* * *

It all started on that fateful day, in the Forbidden Forest.

He had awoken upon the matted, vine-covered ground; his

unfocused gaze penetrated by sallow beams of sunlight that seeped between the oppressing, twisted tree branches. His mind was one of nothingness; a void that desperately tried to piece itself back together. But that simply would not happen. He tried so hard to *remember…* but he couldn't.

He didn't know where he was, or even who he was. It seemed like years ago when he woke, but in truth, it had only been a few hours. The man had arisen from what seemed like an eternity of nightmares and untold horror – none of which he could remember. Much like his own identity.

As he slowly entered the world of reality, he felt a massive pain on his right cheek, as if someone had sliced him open with a dagger. This was odd, considering the fact that there was a mysterious sword lying right next to him, gleaming brilliantly in the morning sun. It had a dark lime handle with maroon ends, and a solid gold finger guard that was encrusted with a magnificent blue stone.

This weapon left the perplexed man awestruck, and when he absentmindedly reached for the handle – and clasped it – he felt a surge of power that replaced his cheek pain with an even greater hurt. He tried desperately to let go, but the sword would not allow it. It wanted the grief-stricken person a taste of true power, and true consequence.

Suddenly the pain stopped, just as quickly as it began. Gasping, he released the sword gradually as fire seared its way through the rest of his body. For some inexplicable reason, however, he felt refreshed – like shedding an old skin.

Out of the blue, he felt incredible.

Clasping his chest to feel his rapidly beating heart, the breathless man noticed that he had another mysterious item – a necklace – a square shaped, emerald coloured necklace. It had a simple, peculiar design, and one finely engraved word; 'Kwennsefulass'.

That was his name.

Well… at least, that's what he was called. He wasn't sure what the word meant, but he was nevertheless dubbed 'Kwenn' somewhat innocuously by that girl from the inn… Jeleenn Ironmonger.

It was from that fateful meeting where everything was set into motion – a chain of events that forever changed the lives of many, many people.

Jugo – Jeleenn's father and owner of the Queezy Fennick Inn. A silently grieving man who gave up his only son to save the world.

Ilod – The wise old Numanta master who would follow his friend Jugo to the ends of the earth.

Lord Sterlio – An enigmatic merchant with the power to control the dead.

Trebor – The shadowy warrior.

Panin – The humble guardsman of Gen who lost his comrades to a horrifying attack on his town.

Puul – The ambitious young Numanta with the responsibility of leadership thrust upon him.

Oviinia – A hapless scientist inexplicably bound to Kwenn's destiny.

And of course – Jeleenn. The young woman with the weight of the world on her shoulders. The young woman who threw-off the shackles of a sheltered existence in the pursuit of a greater responsibility.

The young woman who was ultimately taken.

Taken by the monster – the one who called himself 'Hekor'.

And it was this monster who spread his vile influence across the peaceful island of Shali. Starting with the portside village of Gen, before moving north-west to the river town of Gimlum, and then finally encroaching southward to the small city of Henra, the dark influence moved. In each location, the devastating attacks were foreshadowed by the same, unnatural signs; animals that lose all sense of purpose, a broiling storm that *took away* all water, hellish flames that enveloped all… and then, the shadows.

Those shadows. With relentless mirth, they slaughtered anyone who came between them and their precious quarry.

And that quarry was children.

Or at least, a special *kind* of child. For Gen, Gimlum, and Henra were not ordinary townships. Each of them were founded as protective beacons for three sacred sites – sacred sites which held mysterious, ancient power. Ras Temple – located on the Isle of Sechon. The web of rivers known as the Tilth. And the enigmatic Magick Shrine, which was protected by the supernatural 'Lethe Scud', as well as the Conquest Mountains. It was in this earthly triangle of spiritual influence that suffered Hekor's wrath, for it was said that the chosen child was hidden within its unseen boundaries. And it was this child who would soon be unveiled as the greatest hope against the oncoming tide.

The Invisible War.

But... *what child?* No one knew... except for one man.

Kwennsefulass.

An anomaly. The one who should not have existed. But yet, he did. He lived. He learned.

But... he was *not* a real person. He knew that now.

CHAPTER I

How did it come to this?

He thought about it long and hard, yet he was still utterly bamboozled.

He could not move. Could not talk. Nor could he even breathe – at least, it seemed that way to him.

He was just a passenger; a spectator to the awesome show that played before his unmoving gaze.

Schools of fish; hundreds – nay, *thousands* – their pulsating masses dancing in the crystalline lights. With a unified mind, they darted between crumbled, barnacled remains, as their scaly bodies reflected intense reds of countless spectrums. The sharpness of the lights hurt his eyes… but he embraced it, all the same.

Octopuses slithered along the glittery sands; occasionally casting furtive glances at him, which betrayed their unexpected intelligence. Munching on shellfish, they would squeeze themselves inside glowing cracks within the surface. Where did they go? Was there some sort of eight-limbed civilisation that lived beneath his prone form? Why couldn't he go with them?

Fleeting familiarity with a life long past would sometimes dart through his consciousness. He had a family – he was *sure* of it. Were they still there? Did they miss him? Pangs of utter loneliness crept up though his belly, but, over time… over a long, long time, he felt change. In his bones, it vibrated, as his face grew warm with the cloud of tears that silently flowed.

The change became greater. Bubbles were everywhere; caressing his body as things became foggier.

He could not see now. All was grey. His existence was now chaos; *noise* became his new reality, and it utterly terrified him. The tears got hotter and hotter, and – suddenly realising the existence of his mouth – he tried to scream in agony, but nothing came of it. He fell back into the darkness once again, as hands reached out to him.

Before all was nothing once more, he heard a woman's soft voice… **Nuvummburtee.**

＊ ＊ ＊

Ya'k-lum thought hell had finally frozen over; which was quite an accomplishment, considering how cold this land was.

Finally, for the first time in his miserable life, something exciting was *actually* happening!

It was as if *Qual-nu* himself gave him a sign. It was time to leave the frigid burg of *Jhasé*, and venture out into the big, wild world. His elders would *regret* the countless thrashings they gave him over the years for his supposed 'blasphemy'; they clearly angered the God of Misfortune himself! Poor Ya'k was always the scapegoat – he was *just* as devout to his faith as his kin – it wasn't his fault that he was more… *modern thinking*, than the entirety of his stuffy village.

Carving a piece of wood in both excitement and anxiety, he looked down at his best friend, Jana. Wagging her shaggy tail, the blue dog studied him with inquisitive eyes.

"What?" he replied to the gaze. "You'll get dinner later. I'm thinking, okay? This could be either the best day of my life, or the worst."

Indeed, she knew what was up. The pup always had a knack for reading the young man's innermost thoughts; though he was never exactly subtle about it. Oftentimes, it was when he wore his emotions on his sleeves that got him into the most trouble – even *he* had to admit that his mother would have been justified in kicking him out of the house ten times over.

A commotion pulled him away from his existential crisis. It was time.

It really *was* like a dream, and he still couldn't believe that it had happened.

In the wee hours of the morning, the entire village was roused from slumber by Tak'funt, who arrived early from the annual pilgrimage to *Silver Lake*. Clearly, he had travelled non-stop, and the fact that he was so far ahead of the rest of the group was alarming. Much hand-wringing occurred. Had some horrid disaster struck? Were they attacked? An avalanche?

Nay, something far more unusual had happened.

As his kinsmen gathered around him to hear his strained tale, Tak'funt relayed a most peculiar happenstance; on the eve of the *Ceremony of a Thousand Chaos*, a mysterious beam of light shot forth from the depths of the Silver Lake, causing glassy waves to envelop the Mercanian peoples. The elder *Angakkuq* deemed this a miracle, and advised a priest and a warrior to journey to where the light had erupted, using a canoe built from blessed bark.

They did so, and what they found defied all expectations; below the shimmering surface was a body.

The bespangled night sky was one with the lustrous water, and the cadaver was like that of a divine being emerging from the ether. A male, he had skin as white as pearl, and was garbed in simple attire, like that of a peasant. He looked youthful in years, and atop his head he was clad in an odd helm; one that had a ruby jewel placed right in the centre.

Barely containing their religious fervour, the two emissaries pulled the man from the depths. What they discovered next, truly convinced them that this was a sign from Qual-nu.

He was still alive.

Warm to the touch, it was as if the frigid temperatures had no effect, and that the submerged saviour was merely sleeping.

Suffice to say, once ashore, they had tried to revive the man. He had stirred and groaned, but would not fully come to consciousness. A great debate raged regarding what to do next. Some folk wanted to stay at the lake, and wait until their new charge had awoken. Others wished to take him back to Jhasé, so that they may provide better care there; though arguments raged that they would be selfishly keeping this divine secret from the other villages. In the end, the Angakkuq decided on the latter option, so that they may weigh their options and not act in haste.

Ya'k-lum shared his peoples' disbelief, excitement and trepidation toward the story. Yet, he knew it to be true, as the trail of tusk torches had been lit to signal the arrival of the procession.

Now, a couple of days had passed, and Tak'funt's words were coming to fruition. They had arrived. It was a nice clear afternoon, with cool breezes bought on by the mauve canyons, as the fiery Sollus beat down upon them. Usually, after the Silver Lake ceremony had concluded, the entire village was supposed to disperse in order to undertake the annual *Hunt of a Thousand Chaos* – where all but the lame, elderly and expectant were required to each slaughter at least one Bloodless Boar.

Ya'k always hated it, and was relieved to see that it was to be delayed by a week.

More time to come up with a convincing illness. My 'black plague" from last year wasn't good enough...

Jana barked, and he came back to the present. The holy pilgrimage was back. At the front, as ever, was the old *Angakkuq Trafr'ad*, waving his crimson lantern – and at his side, was the smoky direwolf Amarok. Both of them were ancient in years, but showed no signs of failing health. Behind them were the village priests and warriors – one of whom was Ya'k's own father.

Everyone gathered around them in hushed tones, as they exchanged pleasantries and hugs, as well as hot bowls of soup.

Ya'k and Jana jogged forward, the frosty dirt crunching beneath their feet. His long ginger ponytail swayed – sometimes reaching around to smack him in the face.

Spattering the rogue hairs out of his mouth, he ran right past his elder brother *Ya'k-lutt* – whose arms were outstretched in preparation for a happy reunion – in favour of glimpsing the new 'arrival'.

Not surprised to be embarrassed yet again by his petulant sibling, Ya'k-lutt shook his head in silent despair. His sister – a warrior priestess named *Ya'n-loo* – placed a sympathetic hand on her brother's burly shoulder. "And he wonders why he's never invited..." she breathed in despair.

"Even the dog's happier to see us" Ya'k-lutt grunted.

Truthfully, Ya'k-lum hadn't noticed his elder brother and sister. He was too fixated on the man. The one that now lay before him, fast asleep, like the princess from the fairy tales.

"Is that him?" he whispered in amazement, as the tired Ya'k-lutt trudged behind him. "Great to see you too, little brother" he replied wearily. "And yes, that's him. Don't even *think* about touching him. I mean it."

He bent down to ruffle Jana's furry skull, to which the hound lolled its tongue happily.

Now that the guy was right in front of him, it was suddenly all too real. He squinted to get a better look, as the villagers carted him into one of the cabins. Draped in skins, his white face peered from the bundle – as peaceful as one can be. His head glinted with the silver of his helm, as the sun reflected the brilliance of the ruby.

It *really* was... real!

"Really?" Ya'k-lum rounded on his much-bigger brother. My whole life, you chastise me for not being faithful enough – and now that I show unquenchable interest in the *emissary of the gods themselves*, you ban me from learning more?

"*One* god" Ya'k-lutt growled. "*Our* god. *Qual-nu.* This must be record time. I've only been back a few moments, and I already want to strangle you."

"Oh, let him enjoy his excitement" Ya'l-lum laughed as she approached her brothers. She was clad head-to-toe in the blood-flecked fur of the great *Yolder Beast*, as was customary of her status. She was only a few years from being a full red magi – a *Sollikane*. "Who knows, maybe when he awakens, little brother here can have a fulfilling life as a man-servant!"

Ya'k-lum scoffed, trying not to show the stinging effect of his sister's words. "Jest all you want. I'll let you know that, while you were gone, I composed *three* poems that I've sent to the university already! I'm waiting to hear back – and I'm expecting a *big* offer this time!"

They could have laughed or scoffed at their brother's boast right there and then – but really, all they could do is shake their heads sadly. For indeed, Ya'k-lum was a talented wordsmith with a large imagination at his disposal – and they loved that he had such a passion that kept him loving life. They only wished that he would funnel that passion into the community and his faith. Their elders always scolded the poor boy – a lot worse than they themselves could ever do.

"Wonderful" Ya'k-lutt countered. "I'm off to take a bath. It's always nice to come home to you, brother." He turned to trudge away, before rounding back at Ya'k-lum. He pointed a huge finger at him. "And as I said. Do. Not. Go. Near. Our. Guest."

Ya'l-lum simpered, and she ruffled his tangerine hair. "Seriously pup, please listen to us. The last thing we need is you incurring the wrath of a divine being."

"*Fine.*" He groused. "Jeez, I'm not *that* much of a pain, am I?"

Tonight, he was *absolutely* going to go near their guest.

* * *

The Fiery Orb of Fertility had said farewell to Jhasé for another day.

As the sun's last petering light bathed the hamlet in scarlet, the moons were already out in full glory, as the first hints of glinting stars attempted to break through the rusty sky.

A fairly isolated community, Jhasé was one of the many small communities that peppered the Merca Lal Mountains, which dominated the island of Arlmai. It was in these regions that most of the old ways of the natives still thrived; their worship of Qual-nu remained unchanged for centuries, despite the attempted encroachment of the *Pisistratie* and their attempts to 'enlighten' the denizens of the Four Sister Isles.

The moss-covered homes were now alive with activity, as most were now preparing their feasts and finishing up their toils. Bushy goats bleated and danced amongst the rocky outskirts, whilst the local hot springs slowly filled with aching bodies.

The chapel's braziers gushed with the hallowed red fire – a concoction that only the most senior of Sollikane knew how to create. The only 'ingredient' that was known to outsiders was that the light of the sun Sollik was needed – but since it was that time of the year when the Blood Sight of Redemption slept, the flames were incredibly rare and valuable. The building itself was the only stone structure in the entire township, crafted as it was from the mountains themselves. Though modest by the standards of a city, it still commanded awe and respect by the people – as did the local Angakkuq, Trafr'ad.

Perched on the windowsill of his attic room, Ya'k-lum was bursting at the seams. Sollus seemed to take forever to go away, and to whittle away the minutes, he scribbled on a piece of paper.

Fat fat fat, too much fat. Fat fat fat
Starvation
Fat fat fat. There is too much and he knows it fat fat fat fat fat fat
Bones
Laaaaaaaaaaaaaaaaaaaarrrrrrrrrrrdddd fat fat fat faaaaaaaaaaaaaaaaa
aaaaaaaaaaaaaaaaaaaat

Chew chew chew chew chew swallow
Gone

He grumbled. It's not very good. He tried to evoke a literary sensation between the minimalist descriptor of emptiness, contrasted with the poetic 'waste' of needless, ugly words that intended to elicit anger from the reader. A commentary on society's imbalances and greed.

Eh, I suppose I've written worse.

His house was rife with activity, as dinner was being made. His siblings were talking loudly, as the scent of root vegetables made him hungry. Grimacing at the idea of once again sitting down with his bratty younger sisters and his sanctimonious parents, he nevertheless pondered whether sneaking into the church was truly a good idea.

He had done it before – but it did not end well. Trafr'ad had thrashed the adolescent Ya'k-lum until his backside was as red as the flames that framed the violet-stoned building. He didn't even remember *why* he had attempted such a daring feat in the first place – probably to see one of the altar girls he crushed on.

Similarly, he didn't exactly know what he would do once he had infiltrated. He planned on getting a good look at the mysterious man, maybe even touch his fancy helmet.

He huffed in frustration, as Jana's nails clicked along the steps outside his room.

What is my life? Plotting and scheming just to fondle some sleeping beauty?

He had to leave Jhasé. He was tired of being the town jester. His entire life, everyone made fun of him and called him a screw-up. 'Little penguin' they dubbed him, because he was as graceful and dignified as a fat, waddling bird.

To hell with them. God of Misfortune, huh? Well, maybe Qual-nu won't mind if I conjure a little chaos of my own?

Yeah, that sounded good. Get in and get out. No-one would know he was even there...

* * *

There were porcelain faces. All of them; staring at him with black, abyssal sockets.

Terror plunged its freezing, jagged bladed into his ribs, and he screamed – but he had no mouth.

He was one of them now; eternally marching in low vibrations. His reality was naught but oppressive density – he disappeared within himself, as his very consciousness was caged like an animal.

Welcome to the end of the world.

It was forever – but, at the end of that forever, was another life. He broke through the wall of his very truth, and what met him on that other side was light. Light. Happiness. Family.

Life.

Those ghosts that pressed upon him now smiled – but it was not ghoulish. No fear permeated his new heart. They were now happy. Healthy. They clasped him in a warm embrace, and laughed.

They were his brothers.

They explored meadows. They rough-housed. They joked and chided one another.

They celebrated their humanity, and doted upon their younger sibling – a little boy who represented a new beginning. A seedling that was to be treated with tenderness.

They were fiercely protective of him.

Overseeing them all was their mother. Her immortal face creased in joy and contentment, as her stellar gown flowed like liquid diamond.

Another forever spent together... but, why did it end? Was it *supposed* to end?

They were torn apart. Against their will, they were forced to see beyond their walls – at the putrid death and decay that was always there, just beyond their periphery.

His face was blistered and battered, and his unceasing deluge of wailing and blubbering shredded apart his mind, as he saw each one of his family members fall.

He had come full-circle, as he slowly sunk back into the pit. The last thing he ever saw was his own face, screaming in rage and utter despair.

It was a nice eternity, while it lasted…

* * *

His skin was *burning*.

Taking his first, true, honest-to-goodness breath, his lungs nearly exploded, and he gasped and gaped like a beached fish.

As his sight began to work once more, his world came back into focus. He realised he was sitting up in some sort of cot.

His own panting was causing his head to throb, like drums bashing within his temples.

Without thought, he reached to his head, and his brow creased in confusion, as he felt something metal and thick.

"Wha… where… am I… who…" he croaked.

He saw movement. Like a dumbstruck chameleon, his eyes both took their time to focus on it, and saw that it was a person. A young man, jumping around in a panic. Loud, panicked words spewed from his mouth, but his hearing was still muffled.

"What…" he uttered huskily.

Biting his fist in clear hysteria, the man looked around, as if expecting unwanted company.

He wore a simple brown outfit, albeit thick with fur. Slightly pudgy in build, he had dark skin, which was contrasted by bright orange hair that almost reached his rear, as well as the crimson coloured mark that surrounded the left side of his face.

"I said, keep it down! Please!" he whispered harshly. Getting down on all fours, he bowed his head to the smooth, shiny floor. "Oh damn damn damn… what have I done?! *I'm* done! *Done!*"

The helmed man stuck his fingers in his ears, and tried to clear them. "What... what is this? Where am I?" he asked once more. His senses got sharper by the second, and he saw that he was inside a small room. Lit by candles all over the place, it was toasty warm, and the flames highlighted the ornate visages that jutted from the walls; visages that were quite ugly... all horns, tongues and beady eyes. Smoky scents filled his nose, and stuck to the back of his throat. Hanging, old-looking scrolls flapped from the wafts created by the frenzy of the flailing man, as he gritted his teeth in a desperate bid to stay quiet.

"I gotta get out of here" he whispered. Thrusting his hands toward the bedridden soul, he gestured downward. "Just... go back to sleep, eh? Forget I was ever here... uh, see ya!"

Bowing his respects, he started to tip-toe towards a door. Presumably the way out.

"Wait..."

There was barking now. Outside.

"Damn it Jana!"

"Jana?"

"My dog... just, shush! Lie back down!"

Movement outside the room could now be heard, the *click click clicking* of nails on a hard floor, and hard breathing.

The man squeaked, and collapsed to the ground like jelly. "*Amarok!*" he wheezed, on the verge of a panic attack. "*I'm dead. Dead!*"

Crawling like a worm, he slid around the other side of the bed, and put his head to his knees.

He snivelled pathetically.

What in the hell is going on?

Reaching over the edge of his cot, he stared quizzically at the sobbing mass.

"Uh... what's your name?"

"Wh...what does it matter? This time tomorrow, they'll be celebrating my funeral..."

"Just tell me!"

Rubbing his eyes, he craned his neck to look up at him. "... Ya'k-lum. My name's Ya'k-lum..."

"Okay... *Ya'k-lum*. Can you tell me where exactly I am?"

"Y, your in Jhasé."

"No idea what that is."

"In the Merca Lal Mountains?"

"The *what?*"

"Y, you know – in Arlmai?"

The man shook his head in utter puzzlement, and he felt something run down his neck.

A necklace dangled.

Ya'k-lum seemed almost convinced he was being mocked. "Come on man! Arlmai, of the Four Sister Isles! How *long* were you under that lake?"

He caressed the newly-discovered piece of jewellery, almost as if he suddenly became unaware of his new friend and his ongoing stress assault. The necklace was simple and rectangular. A colour of chestnut bronze, it bore a symbol of lines on one side – and on the other, was the engraving of one word.

Nuvummburtee.

"Wait... lake?" He turned his attention to Ya'k, who was staring at him in veneration. "What lake?"

The dog outside woofed again, and Ya'k winced. "The... the Silver Lake" he whispered harshly, in a desperate attempt to get his cohort to understand the seriousness of his current predicament. "That's where you were found! Under the waves! *Still alive!*"

He couldn't quite put his finger on it, but something about those words spurred old imagery to run through his head; memories of lying in the depths for a long, long time... forgotten by all but the bubbles...

"Still alive..." he parroted.

Ya'k-lum planted his knees to the ground, and leaned his forearms on the bed like an excited toddler ready for a grandparent's story. "Yeah, still alive. Tell me... are you... were you really sent by our god?

Qual-nu? Why are you here?"

"The hell's a Qual-nu?"

The young lad's eyes grew three-times larger, and looked as though he had been stabbed in the ribs by an assassin. His mouth tried to find the words. Stuttering and stammering like a fool, he shook his head in an attempt to shake out any cobwebs that might have caused him to mishear.

"Q...Qual-nu? Our god... you know? The God of Misfortune?"

"Sorry, can't say I've ever heard of him."

The poor boy looked like he was about to have a total meltdown. Rubbing his fingers to his temples, he moaned softly, as if everything he had ever known just came crashing down.

"I... I... Ooooohhh... Oooohhhh nnnnnoooooooooo... no no no no no no no... This can't be happening..."

He flopped onto his back, and breathed hard and fast. "You've done it now Ya'k-lum... You've gone and bloody done it now!!! Sneaking in the church... disturbing a holy being... make him lose his memories... I am... I am... totally and utterly done. I. Am. Done."

He began to whimper and kick his feet like a baby.

The dog barked again.

"Shaddup Jana!!!"

He screeched, having realised what he had just done.

The door to the room burst open, causing the candle flames to whip into an inferno. A massive, monstrous wolf snarled and snapped its gigantic, frightful jaws. Its eyes beamed with a devilish glow, and it had immediately set its sights on Ya'k-lum.

Barely fitting through the door frame, it stepped forward – and the young man screamed like a girl.

Realising its master was in danger, the dog outside barked madly.

"Shit!" the man in the bed yelled. He did *not* expect that. Frantically, he threw the covers off himself, and swung his legs to the side. It was only then that he realised that he didn't fully have the strength to stand, and so he too fell to the floor.

The beast chomped its jaws, and each of its dagger-sized teeth was coated in drool.

"What on earth is all of this racket?!"

A crumbly voice reverberated throughout the walls, and the wolf did not go any further. It stared wrathfully at Ya'k, as an ancient man appeared beside him.

Looking more like a preserved corpse, he was garbed in a lavish cardinal vestment, and his skin was almost completely covered in unusual patterns. His white hair threaded around itself; looping upward like a blooming flower. His eyes were closed, but this did not seem to hinder him in any way, as he shambled unhindered along the beast's flank.

Upon peering into the room and seeing the dishevelled bedding and hectic rustling, his bushy eyebrows ascended. "You... what is *happening* here?"

As the sounds of snivelling floated into the ether, two faces peered over the edge of the bed.

The old man gasped, which caused his eyes to actually open, revealing the pearly gaze. "You are awake!" He coughed, stooping over and leaning against his pet for support.

"An – Angakkuq!" Ya'k-lum slowly emerged, showing concern.

The wolf growled, warning the young intruder to keep his distance.

"*Ya'k-lum!!!*" the Angakkuq cursed, as he wiped his mouth. He thrust out a bony finger like a sword. "You! What in all that is profane *are you doing?!*"

Ignoring the youngster's frenzied blubbering, he then lowered his probing digit, and slowly turned his non-sight to the other figure.

He wasn't exactly inconspicuous. The glint of his helm was reflected by the dancing candles, and the ruby jewel glowed with an inner light.

It was only now, that he himself discovered the existence of his headgear, and he uselessly pawed at it like a cat with no claws.

Pursing his cracked lips at the undignified scene before him, the elder rubbed the wolf in reassurance, and it seemed to calm down.

"Hmph. It seems you are awake, friend. That, I clearly can see."

Ya'k-lum hid behind his helmeted cohort, and shook his head so fast that his jowls clicked.

"L, l, look... Angakkuq... I'm sorry! Please! I... I didn't mean to cause any harm! I was overcome with curiosity!!! You know how I get!"

He spluttered out an unconvincing chuckle, causing the wolf to bare its own smile.

A smile that said *just give me the word, and I'll eat him right here, right now.*

Ya'k-lum was off on a tangent now. The cogs were visibly turning in his head, as he boldly tried to weasel his way out of his certain doom. His eyes lit up, and once more, he ducked behind his human shield, before whispering in the poor guy's ear.

"*Please! You gotta get me out of here alive. I... I... you! Yeah! You! Promise that you'll protect me! Please!!!*"

He grimaced, feeling Ya'k's breath run its way across his face. "What?"

"*The Angakkuq thinks you're a divine being!*" he hissed in response. "*Just, come on! Please! Just promise me divine immunity! It doesn't mean anything... I just wanna get out of this building alive. I want to live!*"

He screamed this last part, before being shoved away.

Seriously? Divine being? God damn it...

"Fine" he grunted. Slowly raising to his wobbly feet, he staggered slightly, and looked at the wolf and the old man.

"I don't know what is going on here" he began, before weakly palming his helm again. "Ugh. Anyway... let's all just relax, hey?" Outstretching his hand in a peaceful gesture, he asked. "Can I ask you your name, sir?"

Almost as if he was having trouble processing the farce that was playing out before him, the ancient, robed man bowed with nary a kink. "My name is Trafr'ad, and I am the Angakkuq of the village of Jhasé. This here is my loyal friend, Amarok. The guardian of Jhasé, and the latest in a long line of direwolves that have – ahem – *seen to business."*

With an inhuman rigidity, like that of a puppet, he turned his head back toward Ya'k-lum, who ducked once more.

"And what should I call you, if I may ask?" Trafr'ad returned with a smile.

The man was taken aback. Such a simple question should have such a simple answer... yet, he had nothing. Furrowing his brow, he became chafed at not even *thinking* of remembering.

My... name. Wait... what is my name?

He was pretty sure he had one once... maybe...

He pulled out his necklace once more, and ran his fingertip over the engraved word. That strange, strange word.

Could it be?

"I think my name is Nuvummburtee. Can't be sure, though."

* * *

Nuvummburtee and Ya'k-lum sat.

The main hall of the temple felt cavernous, despite not being very big at all. He guessed it was that shape of the building – with purple-looking stone pillars holding up a domed ceiling that left a major hole open in order to let the stars shine inward.

Flakes of snow fell downward, and all were sucked in by an invisible force that gently created a spiral of white which descended into a pit of fire, producing hot water which gathered inside the cracks and crevices of stone murals and cause jets of steam to shoot from the mouths of the many strange gargoyles that dotted the walls.

Despite the blazing braziers that attempted to warm the building, Nuvummburtee was anything but toasty.

The woollen blanket that enveloped him did little, as his chill came from within.

Staring into the glittering night above, he was wonder-struck – yet filled with a hopelessness that only came with the feeling of being totally and utterly lost.

Ya'k-lum, however, was straight up cold. He had expended the entirety of his energy in his desperate attempt at self-preservation, and, against all odds, he had succeeded.

Almost falling unconscious upon the end of the ordeal, he still couldn't believe he had pulled it off. Nor did Jana, judging from the dog's quizzical face as she lay at his feet.

It was either the lowest he had ever sunk – or the most brilliant move he had ever concocted in his short life. He took advantage of an amnesiac – probably one from the *heavens* – and convinced him to grant him immunity from Trafr'ad's undoubtedly-lethal punishment.

This Nuvummburtee character clearly did not need to protect Ya'k-lum, nor did he seem to particularly care about him being wolf food; but Ya'k did what he did best; he whined and cried until he got what he wanted.

Desperate for the madness to end, Nuvummburtee – or 'Nuv', as Ya'k decided to call him – made Trafr'ad promise that he would forget about the boy's transgression. Live and let live.

The Angakkuq gave an evil grin when he accepted, which should have alarmed him, but as of this moment, he simply did not care. He had survived.

Now though, he was perhaps in for a far worse fate. His elder brother and sister were with them now, flanking the two as they tried to keep the night's events hidden from the townsfolk.

Chaos was the last thing they needed.

Ironic, considering who they worshipped.

"You may have conned your way out of the Angakkuq's grasp" his sister Ya'l-lum hissed in his ear, "but you haven't escaped *us*. Mark my words, this is probably the *worst* thing you've ever done!"

Ya'k-lum swallowed. "All I did, sister, was wake up a man. That's it." She looked like she was about to thrash him, and he winced. Looking at Jana, and then Nuvummburtee, she relented.

Muttering a mantra, she trudged off.

"You got some balls" Ya'k-lutt rumbled, puffing his chest out. "If our esteemed guest weren't here, I'd--

"Enough."

Trafr'ad entered the hall, followed by Amarok. The direwolf's breath reverberated off the walls, causing Jana to lay down in submission. Ya'k-lum wanted to do the same.

The Angakkuq shuffled to face his audience, and slowly sat on one of the pews. For a long time, he did not move nor speak, and Nuvummburtee wondered if he had passed away. His theory was quashed, as the ancient priest pulled out a long stick, before placing one end in his mouth. A small flame sparked from his thumb, and he lit the other end, before blowing a bluish smoke.

It smelled sweet, and tickled the back of Nuv's throat and eyes.

"So" Trafr'ad began, after a few puffs, "you do not remember who you are, or where you have come from?"

"No..." Nuvummburtee responded quietly. "I think... I vaguely recall being underwater... that's about it." He bowed his head, almost ashamed to admit it.

"Intriguing" the Angakkuq mumbled. A young woman tentatively stepped into the fray, as she carried a tray of hot, steaming cups. Like Ya'k-lum, her hair was tangerine in shade, and was bundled upwards much like her ancient master.

"Come forward dear" Trafr'ad said, sensing her presence though his heavy lids. "Would you like something to drink?"

"I'd love to! I'm parched" Ya'k-lum perked.

"*Not you.*"

"Oh."

Nuvummburtee took the hot mug, and thanked the girl. She smiled back, and then looked at Ya'k. She almost shook her head in exasperation, as if she too was used to his shenanigans. She resisted however, and proceeded to hand his older sibling their own beverages.

Nuv took a furtive sip, and instantly fell in love. This was the best thing he'd ever tasted!

Or... may as well be the first thing.

It was frothy and nutty, with a sweetness that melded harmoniously with a bitter, spicy taste. The priest explained that the concoction was known as *kakawa*, and was a popular recipe all throughout the mountains. He seemed perturbed by his guest's lack of knowledge regarding such a simple thing, let alone his utter ignorance regarding the Four Sister Isles and Qual-nu.

Rather than being disappointed, the Angakkuq seemed even more fascinated by the youngster's condition.

After all, he *was* found at the bottom of Silver Lake. During the Ceremony of a Thousand Chaos, no less.

It *had* to mean *something*.

"You are no mere vagabond with a swollen brain" Trafr'ad declared confidently after taking a long swig of his kakawa drink. "I do not know what all of this means, exactly, but I do believe we will find the appropriate answers."

Nuv was comforted by the words. A sadness washed over him, and all he desired was to curl up into a ball and cry. Despite the warmth that ran through his belly now, there was a gaping emptiness that made him feel... hollow. Not a real person... and it didn't make sense to him.

He wondered if he had friends or family that were out there right now, desperately searching for him. He looked at the direwolf that slept at the foot of the pulpit, and then Ya'k-lum's furry companion. Did he have a similar creature of his own? A cherished pet that missed him right now, at this very moment?

He immediately banished the dark scenarios from his mind, and forced himself to think of the present.

Now that he was calm, and his bones no longer felt they were rattling, he clasped his palms around his helm. The metal was cold on his skin, and he hoisted upward.

It came off without trouble.

Beholden looks of astoundment surrounded him, as long, dark hair fell down his shoulders. For the first time, he saw for himself the very thing that made those around him gawk.

At least it wasn't something on my face.

"Well, that was easy" Trafr'ad chuckled, as smoke shot from his nose. "That does seem to confirm my suspicions that the helm you have there is enchanted in some way."

Nuvummburtee rubbed the back of his neck, and stared into the ruby that ensnared him in its gleam. "En...enchanted?" he whispered.

The old man regaled him with the entirety of what had happened since finding him at the base of the mountains, with Ya'k-lutt and Ya'l-lum chipping in details; including the fact that they could not remove the helm themselves, no matter how hard they tried.

Trafr'ad explained the traditions of Jhasé. As part of the wider societies of the Merca Lal Mountains, they were the native peoples of the island of Arlmai. As part of their culture, they worshipped Qual-nu – the God of Misfortune, and the creator of the land itself.

They were one part of the Four Sister Isles; which, along with Arlmai, was also home to the islands of *Shali, Miiri* and *Liniii*. These other lands had their own religions and customs, including those from outside the wider world. There were differing belief systems, as manifested by the different types of mages – but all co-existed peacefully with each other, even though some bitterness and resentment remained from many of the natives of the islands, who still viewed themselves as being 'invaded' from foreigners and false gods. Once upon a time, there was even fanatical infighting from within the archipelago itself.

Regardless, Jhasé was a traditional village with simple values, and whenever outsiders made contact, they were welcomed with open arms.

Every year, there was the Ceremony of a Thousand Chaos. An annual pilgrimage that takes a select group from every village southward to the Silver Lake; a holy sight where the waters are blessed from the 'cloud snow' that cascades from the *Floating Castle of Eelow*, which is said to be a gateway to heaven.

As the oldest settlement of the mountains, and home to one of the three 'sacred sites', the inhabitants of Jhasé are the first to venture to the lake. A group of Sollikane mages – led by the resident Angakkuq – make the journey during the *Blinking of the Eyes*, another annual event where the suns trade places, and the forces of nature in the world are altered for twelve months.

Nuvummburtee had absolutely no clue what any of this meant. These people may as well have been speaking gibberish. Gods? Islands? Blinking eyes? He was a stranger in a strange land, and the only form of vague familiarity he felt (or at least, a facsimile of the feeling) were the two trinkets that were already on his person.

His only worldly possessions.

Inhaling the last of his stick, Trafr'ad crunched the remains with his yellow teeth. "It was at the lake, where you were found. Or, to be more accurate, where you called for us. We barely had time to make our preparations, when a beam of light burst forth from the waters... and, well, you can probably guess what happened next, hm? It was then when we found you – even as deep as you were, the divine waters made everything clear, and you my boy, were as clear as the sunrise. Alive and well, against all odds."

"Alive..." Nuv murmured. "How?"

"That... we can only guess. As I said, your helm seems to be enchanted in some way, so I am hazarding a guess that it played a part."

Ya'l-lum stepped in between the two, and nodded toward the head wear. "If I may be so bold, Angakkuq... may I ask permission to study the artefact? Maybe we can glean something from the type of metal and jewel, as well as any magical residue."

"I have no objections, Ya'l-lum. But it is not mine to hand over!"

Nuvummburtee shrugged his shoulders. "As long as I can get another cup of that kakawa stuff, then we have a deal."

CHAPTER II

They were like clockwork. Tinker-tailor toy soldiers that lined up in a rigid formation, their inky-black armour absorbing the transient light that surrounded them. Even their weapons, as sharp and cold as they looked, refused to illuminate.

They were ghosts.

Yet, ghosts still felt things… did they not? They lamented past lives and wallowed in sadness and despair. They were still *souls*.

But these *things* did not even do that. They simply followed orders, with no will of their own. They were unnatural, and did not belong in this realm – nor any other. They were a perverse meeting of magic and technology; resulting in an abomination that not even the once-great Pheekonshenee people would have tolerated.

At least, she hoped so.

When her brother made them take off their helms, she recoiled in soul-wrenching horror. Her heart crumbled into dust, and she could no longer stand on her own two feet. She wept for them, and her tears fell like glittering diamonds.

He talked, but she couldn't hear his words. All she could do was quaver in disbelief, and try her hardest to *not look*.

For it was not their emotionless faces that devastated, nor their inhuman bodies.

It was their *eyes*.

They were eyes that did not belong. Eyes that contained the sheer oblivion of non-existence, and looking into them threatened to drive her mad.

Over and over again, she asked herself, was this really what the Pheekonshenee *were*? Did they twist everything around them into affronts of nature?

Did they mock the gods with their very existence?

No... no, she refused to believe it. Whatever these things were, they were not Pheekon. They were a beautiful and enlightened people.

They were not this.

This was her brother Joner.

* * *

"What did you do, Joner?!" Jeleenn wailed as she slumped to the leafy ground.

Her brother's green gaze looked upon her with sympathy. Clad in puce-coloured set of armour that danced with violet tinges, he looked every bit the fairytale prince. His long cape seemed as though it was crafted with fine-looking flower petals, and his flowing silver hair was flecked with feathers that dangled over his shoulders.

He tried to place a hand on her shoulder, but she slapped it away.

"As I said, I am finishing what the great wizards started. I am uniting everything. I am bringing it all back together once more. So many wonderful facets of the universe have been split apart due to ignorance and prejudice. The magi exist because of differing ideologies, when in fact they are all one and the same. For eons, the gods they so blindly worship have fractured Tarinn with their selfish desires. The Pheekonshenee knew this, and they were wiped off the face of the earth because of it!"

He gingerly caressed his rejected palm.

Jeleenn could only shake her head in incredulity, as her eyes betrayed the look of a sibling who saw nothing but madness in her kin. "You… *what are you saying Joner?* That you are, what, trying to bring back the Pheekon? And you're doing this by snatching children and laying waste to everything? *You destroyed my home!!!*"

She jumped now, and madly swung at her brother. Without changing his expression, he calmly held her at bay with unnatural strength.

"*No.* The Pheekonshenee are relics of the past, only kept relevant by the dusty teachings of the Numanta. I am taking what they accomplished, and bringing it full circle!"

With a vice-like grip, he twirled his sister on the spot, and forced her to look upon his army.

In desperation, Jeleenn tried to avert her watery gaze, but she couldn't help but look upon their appalling splendour.

They all now stared right at her.

"I hate everything man has created" Joner growled. "The wars. The greed. The self-absorbed ideologies. With the *Eidian*, I have access to the bridge between the two worlds. With the power of the *Arche*, I have mastery of space and time itself. And now, I possess the technological secrets of the *Pheekonshenee*… soon, I will merge all… just as it was meant to be!"

Jeleenn tried not to shrink away from the wicked eyes that now focused on her shrivelling soul. They all seemed now to get closer every time she blinked with burning tears. "But… why the children?" she demanded through grinding teeth.

He let her go, and she fell once more.

Joner did not move, but Jeleenn could see his face darken, and his gaze crackle with fire.

"*Mother's* full-blooded offspring, just like she always wanted…"

He laughed with malice, and turned to walk away.

Rage boiled in Jeleenn's blood; the ire of unknowing threatened to overwhelm her, and she tried desperately to swallow it back down. For a second time, she climbed defiantly back on her feet, but refused to scream or yell.

"*What do you mean?*"

He stopped, and a furious wind gusted around his feet, causing a wave of red leaves to undulate outward. This time, Jeleenn held her footing, as she dug her heels defiantly into the spectral ground. She chilled at the thought of turning her back on those *things*, but she had to stop herself from being a meek quarry for every vile thing she encountered. She was *not* afraid.

"I *said*, what do you mean?!"

Joner did not turn. "I have told you more than you can process" he stated without emotion. "Father is coming, and I want to be ready when he arrives."

Jeleenn's heart pounded. "D, Dad?! How? Why?"

Her brother tilted his head to the side, but refused to look her in the eye. "Hekor has seen it. Him and that accursed old Numanta friend of his. Time is irrelevant to us. We already know."

He waved his arm, and suddenly, Jeleenn found herself in a large room. Before she could process what had happened, she looked around and saw an ornate cradle with great golden bed-posts on either side. Surrounding it were sandstone walls that pulsed with a cyan radiance and strange masks leered downward with unsettling grins. In her head, Jeleenn began hearing the soft – yet discordant – plucking of harp strings.

"You can stay here, if you want" Joner revealed.

She shivered, and looked quizzically at her new surroundings "If I want?"

Her brother smiled. "This realm is not the same as yours. It can be overwhelming if you try to fight it, so don't. This is only the shallow layer of the invisible kingdom, and those that have arrived beyond comprehension may cause a… discomforting impression. But please, do not take offence to their actions."

An exasperated look washed over Jeleenn's features. "*What?*"

In return, Joner seemed apologetic for a moment. He bowed, and waved a flippant hand. "Again, I do not want to burden you with too much information right now, sister. Please, just do me a favour and rest. Is that asking too much?"

All over again, anger bubbled from within her, and she wanted to strike down this young man whom she thought dead for so long. She hated his offhand demeanour, and the way he slandered their father and everything he stood for. Instead of being happy that they were now back together again, Joner was instead a bitter and disturbed megalomaniac.

She wanted to say this to his face, but somehow could not muster up the courage. Why, she could not guess… maybe it was the power he projected. Maybe it was his crazed rhetoric. Or maybe… just maybe, it was simply because he was her family.

"Okay" she said with resignation, "I'll do what you ask."

He closed his eyes and tilted his head, obviously happy. "I've had servants draw a bath, and there are fresh clothes for you. They have been there for quite a while now… quite a while."

He turned to leave, his footsteps not making a single sound.

"The children in those cells" Jeleenn asked in one final attempt for answers, "what's going to happen with them?"

But he was gone.

She was alone. Alone in this accursed place, without any hope of escape. She had no idea if she would see her home again, and she closed her eyes tightly to stop the tears from gushing. She tried to gulp down a lump that formed in her throat, but all that flooded her mind were those *things*. Those unfeeling, soulless personalities whose ghostly faces represented the very worst of Joner's insanity.

She couldn't help it. She began to weep, knowing now where *he* came from.

Those pale faces of Joner's duplicates.

Of Kwennsefulass.

* * *

The blade balanced perfectly.

On her palm, it was as still as death itself. The complete absolution of its own universe; a black hole of inescapable inevitability. It did not move – everything moved *around* it.

As usual, *Remana tol Dwen* had crafted another work of art. The obsidian sword looked like the Grim Reaper, to continue the protracted death analogy.

Satisfied, she wrapped the weapon, and placed it with the customer's order. It would fetch a princely price, but people didn't come to the town of *Nūk* if they weren't willing to spend big.

Settled comfortably in the far north-west of Arlmai, the place was utterly unremarkable in every way. A chilly coastal municipality, it saw not much besides trade in exotic seafood and artefacts from the *Crystala Caves*. Lodged at the back-end of the Four Sister Isles, it wasn't far enough to be at the edge of the world, nor was it the greatest place to journey to the far western seas, such was its protected armour of innumerable icebergs that downed many a ship.

Unremarkable… that was, until Remana tol Dwen arrived.

An orphan adopted by the town's blacksmith, she was an incredibly remarkable child. Tall and powerful, she quickly developed an aptitude for her family's business in crafting weapons and tools of every conceivable type, with every possible metal and mineral. Likened by her community to the dwarves from the fairytales, only 'stretched thin', word of her gifts spread like wildfire.

Which was apt, as she herself never knew the hellish agony that came from the infernian element.

Working in blazing conditions that would cause any other smithy to recoil in blistered terror, her coal-dark skin was immune to any and all flames. Nary a bead of sweat would drop from her nose, as she surrounded herself in environments that would otherwise incinerate the world around it.

Realising that they truly had a special daughter, Remana became something of a treasure to her town, and as she grew, so too did her ruthlessness in business.

Of course, when one had such a powerful gift, it was natural to seek out answers – to find out where they came from. She had fully intended to explore the world, and find her true birth parents; but her life – *this* life – got in her way.

And it was a life that grew like a beanstalk; an anarchic force that rippled the earth around it. Seeing her as the golden goose, her father nurtured and encouraged her to take full advantage of her gift, by becoming the best forger in all the land.

Journeying across the Merca Lal Mountains in search of the deep volcanic underworld that lay beneath, Remana fully embraced her destiny, and her father's dream became hers. Truly, she was just happy that she belonged; that she was loved, regardless of her background or skin colour.

Nevertheless, this was an arduous time in her life. Whilst her brother manned the family business back home, she and her father soon realised that they had vastly underestimated the peril of their trek across the freezing, jagged mountains. Though believing their intentions to be harmless, they encountered resistance from the land and its peoples, as they were marked as pillagers concerned for only riches.

Though perhaps true to an extent, the hostility they had faced from the snow-born villages served only to light a fire underneath their feet – and *this* was a fire that burned her greatly.

After hearing of a legendary deposit, her father had traced its origin, and was truly convinced that it actually existed. As the months passed, a rift began to widen between the two, as desperation and starvation cracked the foundations between father and child.

Eventually seeing him overcome by his greed and madness, Remana became the victim of his escalating abuse, as he seemingly became possessed by the mountains themselves; channelling their rage directly through his weakening body.

These were the longest days of her life, which ended one foggy morning, as she had found his body; succumbed to frostbite, and with his face twisted into a perpetual state of sorrow, his tears caking his blue face.

She herself deteriorated beyond her own recognition, and everything was a blur in her memory… until her life was irrevocably changed by an old man.

Somehow, by some divine intervention, he had found her alive. Nursing her back to health, he had told her things… things that she could no longer recall. On some days, she was convinced that he was merely nothing but a dream, an emaciated, bony figure that seemed incapable of moving; let alone dragging her body through such brutal conditions. Yet… here she was, alive. The most vivid thing she had remembered during this time was a searing, white hot pain in the middle of her head, as well as an overwhelming urge to find something… or some*one*. It was as if she merged with the island itself, and that the old man unlocked something in her… a new will. A new resolve.

Her first clear recollection after this was being found by a *Meerajaff*; a large, bipedal green mount that nudged her prone body with its flat face, before she gathered the strength to mount it. She was surprised by its placid nature, and eventually found that it belonged to a rancher in the south, as the best whooped and clucked as it took her back to his farmstead.

It was after recovering her mind and body, that the first day of her new life began.

After a laboured journey back to *Nūk*, she broke the news to her devastated family. Enraged at her return, she had eventually learned that she and her father had been sent on a wild goose chase by her adopted brother, who fed the fake legend of the deposit in order to take over the business himself, and in the hopes that they would both perish in the mountains.

He had always hated her, and in their absence, he struck up a deal with a group of murderous corsairs – along with Nūk's leading shippers and vendors – to use the town as a den in exchange for protection and redistribution of treasures.

Her heart had never felt as shredded as it did. She had lost her family. Her mother had wasted away and died from grief at her son's actions, and people whom she thought were her friends and teachers had betrayed both her and her community.

She was almost killed, if it had not been for the resolve of the mayor and a few loyal elders and townsfolk, who saved her life, before loudly protesting what had happened to their home. They had had enough, and began rioting against those that had stolen so much from them. The pirates that were present brandished their blades, and the two sides clashed in a bloody battle.

With the fury of the suns above, Remana tol Dwen slew her brother in the very shop that they had grown up in. His blood stained the walls and the furnaces, which blazed white hot with the life of Arlmai.

Bursting from every opening, the righteous heat shot forth, and devoured any with evil in their soul.

Fleeing in terror, Nūk's foes plunged into the freezing tide – and from that moment forward, Remana tol Dwen would be the protector of her people.

That was a couple of years ago now, and in the present day, she often thought about her actions. If she could have done anything differently… if everything that had happened was her fault. Regardless, Nūk was still alive. Those that had lost their lives that day… she had thought about them constantly. But… nothing could be changed. She forced herself to move on, and helped to rebuild the town into something bigger and better.

She had changed. Indeed, after the battle, she remembered wandering the streets in shock, before seeing her reflection within a shattered mirror. Branded into her forehead was a strange symbol, and she had known… that it was that old man who had given it to her.

What did it mean? For her, it was emblematic of a new birth.

And begin she did. She took charge. Within her gut, she knew the world was on her side… that whoever blessed her with such a physical ability knew that she would be destined for something great.

"*Is* this great though?" She muttered to herself, as her silvery eyes scanned the rack of recently-built swords.

Crossing her sinewy arms, she looked out the window. Nūk was practically unrecognisable from what it once was; yes, the town now had more to offer than rare artefacts and exotic seafood… she had achieved her father's dream. She was the greatest blacksmith anywhere, and she didn't need any hocus-pocus, fairy dust minerals to make it happen.

It didn't take long for the impeccability of her work to be noticed by outsiders. No matter what she crafted – be it a simple nail or a lavish claymore – it was done with both inhuman speed and quality, and it attracted many from far and wide.

In such a quick time, her home became a trading hub that buzzed with the rarest metals and jewels. So many people travelled – not just from the other islands, but from across the treacherous oceans – just to utilise the services of the 'Cerberus Girl'.

Merchants came to her with ancient blueprints and ingredients. Navy vessels wanted special ship frames. Even the occasional knight would ask for armour alterations – and their armour was utterly sacred to them.

She found herself needing to expand her business quicker and quicker, as well as learning the different methods and styles that came with such a mind-boggling amount of products. Yet, she absorbed it all. No challenge was too insurmountable for her skilled fingers, and within a few more months, her shop… her *family's* shop, had expanded into a shipyard and a full-on emporium.

As remarkable as Remana was, even *she* had her limits. Soon, the number of requests and orders came far too fast, and as such, she had to swallow her pride, and employ staff and apprentices to tackle the easier tasks.

Still, they could not do what she could. Her customers knew that, and now she was becoming a victim of her own reputation and success. She found that being hands-on was far easier than actually *being* a businesswoman.

Not to mention, the rapid expansion of Nūk had begun to cause some grumbles from her old elders and friends, as the increased presence of unsavoury guests, businesses and industrialisation has made it harder for the children to be safe in the streets, and for smaller shops to stay afloat.

Still, with so much money coming in, they weren't about to kick up a stink.

Remana smirked humourlessly, as she spied one of her workers swearing after kicking her foot against a crate laden with cannonballs.

Money... it always comes down to money doesn't it? Why does it change so many people?

"Hey, Yui!" she shouted from the window, "be careful! Don't damage the merchandise!"

She saw the girl give her a dirty look, before continuing her work.

Sighing, she tried to block out the sounds of progress that pressed against her building. Of sawing and hammering. Of bellowing and laughter. Of hawking and haggling.

She wanted to retreat into her private furnaces and work in peace. No-one was allowed in these chambers – they were specially-built for her use, and her use only. She was always experimenting with the structural integrity, trying to push the flame resistance of the stonework further and further. She had recently been doing extensive research in flame retardation, in the hopes of creating a room that could withstand the heat of hell itself.

Progress was slow, though. She never knew how her parents did it – how they juggled the books, whilst keeping their sanity.

There was a knock at the door, and Remana sighed again. It was Utis, undoubtedly here to chastise her for not doing paperwork.

"Yeah?" she called, not bothering to move.

"Ma'am!" came a soft voice from outside. "You've got a g, guest..."

She opened the door, and was faced with a thin man with large spectacles. He was holding a large folder thick with paper. He looked white – even whiter than usual.

"A customer?" she asked. She didn't need to hear the answer. No-one these days wanted to visit just to enjoy her company.

"Y, yeah..." Utis said, his voice shaky.

Remana cocked a red eyebrow. "Utis? Is something the matter?"

"You need to go see him now... he says he's a pirate. And that he'll burn the town to the ground if you don't!"

"The hell?"

Remana shoved the poor aide aside, sending his papers flying. She marched toward the front area of the main shop, and saw a well-dressed man reclining on the waiting couch. A wide captain's hat was placed beside him, its colourful plumage of feathers flapping in the breeze that wafted in from the saloon-style opening. His gold-encrusted fingers held-up a book that hid his face.

She cleared her throat. "Excuse me, is there something I can help you with?"

He lowered the reading material, and she was met with the handsome visage of an older man – perhaps in his forties. His long brown locks framed his head, and he smiled.

Raising to his feet, he was certainly clad like a pirate. He wore a doublet of silk, and a tunic that seemed to sparkle with bits of reflective, glassy beads. His shoes were covered in a bluish-fur.

"So!" he began, "This must be the Cerberus Girl, whose reputation has been slowly carried by the sea breezes!"

"It is" Remana replied. "And whom do I have the pleasure of speaking to?"

He tossed the book aside and bowed. "You can call me *Archie. Captain Archie. Captain Archie Shorn.*"

"Captain... Archie Shorn" she repeated. "I'm Remana tol Dwen.

The master smithy of Nūk. How can I help you?"

"So polite!" Archie recoiled in mock shock. "I had heard the Cerberus Girl was a rough and tumble master of all that she surveys… though from looking at you, I wouldn't be surprised if that was the case, eh?"

Remana was instantly put-off by the man's demeanour. She had met a lot of quirky characters over the last couple of years, but this guy… there was something definitely off about him.

"I've been known to crack a head or two" she replied sarcastically.

He laughed in a forceful, almost mocking manner. "That so? Nice… nice. So, yes. As you can probably tell, I've come far in pursuit of your services. You see… I represent a very wealthy client. This… client of mine, they wish to make use of your particular talents." He sniffed loudly, and seemed to cast his gaze briefly at one of the windows of the building.

"I see" she replied flatly. "What is it that you would like done?"

She was uneasy. The man before her looked to be on edge, and was desperately trying to cover it up with his smooth acting.

The captain scrunched his face, and muttered to himself. "Your little assistant man… the four eyes. He's gone and got the authorities, hasn't he?" Like an inquisitive cat, he stretched his neck and once again looked outside. "Damn it… I had to run my mouth."

She silently thanked Utis for his quick thinking, and promised herself that he would get a raise. The man was meek, but boy, he was smart when he wanted to be.

"I imagine he has" she said, taking care not to appear intimidated. "He said that you were a pirate. Is that true? Hey, we can still do business, there's no need for any trouble."

Archie tightened his lips, and turned his attention to the woman once more. "Mmmmm… good to hear love. 'Cause *this* transaction is about to get a little messy."

With a flash, the man reached into his coat, and threw a spherical object at Remana.

She lost all of her senses, and she couldn't recover them fast enough. As her mind resorted itself, she realised that she was being held by strong, flailing arms.

With a dry yell, she kicked and scratched at whatever was on her, and she heard a gruff curse. "Get off me, you bastard!"

Erratic voices filled her ears, and she soon realised that she was being tied down. Her vision returned, and she had a prime view of the stone flooring.

"You could've waited until we got her to the bloody ship before we nicked 'er!" bellowed a man above her.

"Oh, *I'm sorry*" roared another man, clearly the captain, "what was I supposed to do, wait until the guards come bustin' through the door?! Are the boys ready?"

"Yeah" the other man grunted and spat. "Don't worry about 'em, they got it all down pat."

Remana heard an explosion outside, and screaming. Tears gushed from her face, as she was transported back to the horror and bloodshed of two years ago. Images of her brother's lifeless, white face blazed in her hot eyes, and she tried everything not to sob as the invaders manhandled her.

Everywhere she went, death seemed to follow.

She knew now that this bastard attacked her with some sort of concoction. Her face was on fire, and she felt like she could barely breathe. She tried to scream her throat out, but there was... nothing. She was limp. Just like that, they dominated her. She didn't even have the *chance* to fight back.

How... how did this happen...

* * *

She was being tossed aside. Like a ragdoll, her limbs flailed without bones, as she was slammed against the black walls. Again and again and again...

Make it stop...

She came to, and her arms were in agony. Her shoulders felt like a pincushion, and her wrists burned.

It was dark. She was bound. Her stomach flailed, and her murky thoughts finally pieced together that she was on a ship.

She had been on a few smaller vessels in her lifetime; but this was new. She was swallowed whole by a behemoth – a small piece of flesh that rattled about intestines of steel, wood and salt.

"Wakey wakey, eggs n' bakey" said a man's voice.

Grinding her teeth into dust, she tried to lunge forward, but ended up vomiting instead.

"Ah, crap!" the man said again. "Damn... not all over the floor... geez..."

The hot liquid surged through her, and splattered at her feet.

After evacuating her stomach, a metallic door creaked open, and a warm, calloused palm pressed against her cheek.

"Damn it all!" he swore, with a surprising hint of empathy. "I'm gonna have words with Gurt... those god damn chillies are too much..."

He seemed to leave. Her sight became accustomed to the darkness, and she now knew that she was in a cell.

A brig.

After a few moments, the guy was back, with a couple of others. They entered the cell, and cleaned her up.

"Sorry love" the same man said again. "Gurt's recipe and the cradling of the waves... hell, just pull my fingernails out instead. More humane!"

She saw an older gentleman, with a large moustache. Though details were hard to make out in the dimness, she noticed that he had an eyepatch.

A pirate all right...

"Where... where are you..." she croaked.

"Just drink the water, love" he ordered. A cup pressed her lips, and the lukewarm liquid felt like the elixir of life for her body.

"Cap'n's comin'" one of the other (considerably younger) men said.

Again, there was shuffling, and another figure made his entrance. Lighting a lamp, Remana could see the smarmy expression of the same person who invaded her home with his lecherous presence.

"Sleeping beauty is up!" Archie guffawed, before lighting a couple of other lamps. "Badger" he nodded toward the older man, "I've got this."

"Aye" he replied. He turned to his charges. "Stay here with the cap'n."

They saluted, as he trundled off.

Archie sighed loudly, and handed the lamp to one of his swabbies. He leaned casually against the metal bars, as if he truly had no compunctions about the crimes he just committed. "*Righto.* Now now, where do we begin, hm?"

"I can tell you how it ends..." she hissed with her scratched throat.

He chuckled, much like a pompous aristocrat would. "Don't take it personally, Miss Dwen. Look... let me set your mind at ease, eh? At least one thing you don't have to worry about; none of your friends or family are dead, savvy? Me boys, they made a lot of noise, and blacked a few eyes – but all in all, your emancipation went smoother than a wet duck."

She was almost ashamed about feeling a sense of knee-buckling relief, only because *his* words were the catalyst.

"You're lying" she growled.

He looked almost disappointed. "I do that a lot. I built a house of lies. Or, 'House o' Flies', as I like to call it. But look, I'm telling the god's honest truth here. You don't have to believe me, but you should, since it'll make this whole thing a lot easier for ya."

She pursed her lips. "And what... is this *thing*? Slavery? Selling me to the highest bidder? Kill me, because my talents have caused an upset in your little pirate communities? Or is it... revenge? Because we ended your buddies' pathetic worm lives a couple of years back?!"

She coughed, and her gut strained against the fits.

Archie Shorn said nothing, clearly reading her intently. He fiddled with his ear, and mumbled. "Like I said, I have a wealthy client. It's remarkably simple. They want you. I retrieve you. They pay me. There's really nothing more complicated than that."

"They pay *us*, er, right cap'n" one of the boys squeaked.

"Shaddup."

Remana couldn't help but laugh. In a way, she bought this on herself. After her life-changing journey with her father and her war with her brother, she had changed. She became a woman unafraid of death, and was almost arrogant in her dismissal of any potential danger. She supposed it was a way to cope with just how damaged she really was on the inside… but regardless, her reputation ballooned way too fast – and everyone in Nūk suffered for it. This was bound to happen sooner or later. She got too big for her boots.

She sneered, and bellowed every threat she could muster toward the man.

Archie's cage was not rattled in the slightest. "I'll let you cool down a bit, before we reach our destination. It's going to be a bumpy ride."

With arrogant pomposity, he bowed, before snapping his fingers. "Trully. Sniffer. Keep her ladyship company. Don't let her out. Good lads."

The two minions saluted with an 'aye aye', and when the captain exited, they immediately sat down and began playing cards.

* * *

The frigid waters churned; their slushy waves rippling like the ebony skin of writhing mambas under the twilight skies.

Tupeen and Arntus had risen together as expected, the moons' combined light bathing the ship in a bitter-sweet burnt glow. Soon, Sarm would follow, creating a richer rosy gloss over the western seas.

The deck rocked from side to side, as the rough-as-guts crew ran like ants all over the vessel; barking and swallowing orders.

Captain Archie Shorn marched across the *Life of Lyra,* as her polished floor boards glistened like lava in the lights of the lamps and braziers that sprinkled across her haughty frame. His first-mate Badger was at the wheel, spinning it with a deftness that only came with a lifetime of familiarity.

His big blue moustache wiggled in the wind, and with foresight, he turned to greet his captain without any prompt.

"How's the girl?" he quizzed, as he handed back control to his superior.

"Mad" Archie replied. "Feisty. I like her."

"Don't get too attached" Badger scolded, squinting his singular eye. "We'll probably be at the sea floor before you two can get hitched."

Archie laughed. "From what? Nūk's wrath? Or the *curse?*"

"Both, probably. That was a ballsy, reckless move, Archie. We coulda lost a lot of men back there."

"But we didn't" he replied with a tad more thoughtfulness in his voice. "I knew we could do it. That's why we did it. No-one's expendable to me... you know that, Badger."

The elder man sighed. "Well, regardless. We'll probably be dead soon enough."

Archie ignored the remark. "Anyone following us?"

"Not in the immediate area. The coastline's out of view now, but I reckon they've launched a reatlia... retally..."

"*Retaliatory.*"

"Yeah, that. They've got a couple of good vessels there that could probably pursue us. Especially since the town's cash-cow is now gone, they'll be pulling out all the stops to bring 'er back."

The captain snorted in derision. "Nūk's no navy port. They've always been a little cluster of buildings that got their wealth from scavenging. Remana tol Dwen hasn't changed that. They're busy counting their riches, and wondering how much they should spend on privateers – well, the privateers that can be arsed, that is."

He pulled out a compass, and stared at it intensively. Though he spoke with confidence, Captain Archie Shorn couldn't help but be *slightly* concerned. Badger wasn't just being his usual worrywart self; the crew faced a very real danger – and he wasn't even thinking of their pursuers.

"How long we got 'till we reach the tower?" Badger probed.

"About half a night, as the wind blows. At most, we'll be there at sunrise."

"He better be right about this" the moustached man growled. "I don't care *how* much he's payin' us… we're risking everything on a bunch of old legends and wives' tales…"

"I know, mate" Archie shook his head. He was so tired of having this argument. If it was anyone else, they would have walked the plank ages ago. But he respected the old fart way too much. He almost *liked* him… but it didn't matter. If they managed to pull this job off, each and every one of them could retire comfortably. Their client had only paid them half of what was owed, and already, they were *swimming* in it.

And for once, it *wasn't* salt water.

"Well, whatever" Badger huffed. "It'll be a sight t' see it with my one eye. I never thought we'd make it so far across this old world. How're we gonna get the broad to cooperate?"

Archie pressed his lips together, deep in thought. "Don't sweat it, I got it all down pat. We meet our illustrious benefactor at the tower. He'll know what to do. We just have to get there, without any misfortune befalling us."

If he had only known what was to come, he would curse himself for saying that.

* * *

Sweat beaded on Remana's forehead. Despite it getting colder and colder, she felt hot from within. She tried everything she could think of in order to break from this accursed cell and throttle the two boys standing guard over her.

One was clearly a bit dim; the other, seemed almost rat-like in his cunning. Though, she had to admit, they didn't seem all too malicious. They were barely older than teenagers, and seemed more fascinated by her presence, than outright hostile.

Over the next couple of hours, they made small talk. They were unable to give her the silent treatment, but were still smart enough to be cagey when required.

She lost all track of time. She couldn't decide whether she had been kept prisoner for years, or mere minutes. The swaying of the ship created a bubbling sickness within her, and only helped to thicken the oily dread that pumped through her veins.

She had decided that she was going to attack the next time they opened her prison. She was going to bite, scratch, spit – it didn't matter. She was utterly devoid of concern for her own wellbeing. They could run her through with every blade they had… she was going to kill each and every one of them.

Even the kids in front of me? Yes, even them.

Her thoughts only grew darker as the brig got colder. She calmed herself. She had been in worse situations before, and she had come out alive. A bunch of scurvy-ridden men weren't going to be the death of her, that was for damn sure.

Remana sat. Her eyelids became heavy, as her stomach clenched from trying to keep herself steady. The murmuring of her caretakers was occasionally punctuated by a sigh or snort, and she fell into a waking sleep. She became caught between two worlds, as her mind wandered the astral plane of dreams.

She saw a man before her. His face was unseen, and a flash of red assaulted her eyes. She saw stardust, separated by nothingness, before churning seas gave birth to new lands. Beings danced in the eternal light, as enlightened people took these lands between their fingers, and moulded them like clay.

The dancing beings knelt down and sobbed, and all was stardust once more. She saw a small figure; lumped over. He crawled into a little hole, and shut himself inside with a giant boulder.

Aodh...

Screaming pierced her heart, and she gasped as her eyes returned to the land of the awake. She was on the floor, and in her unthinking state, she became aware that she was no longer in a dream. Wood, metal and embers rain down all around her, and she ached from being tossed against the metal bars. Deafening wind tore at her skin, and water drenched every inch of her.

She forced herself to get up, and in her shock, she finally realised that something had ripped a hole within the side of the ship.

Her legs were wobbly, as her entire world seemed to twist and turn. Her hearing became lost, as the howling of the sea was joined by the hair-raising bellows of... *something*.

The shrieking gale threatened to tear the flesh from her bones, and she tried desperately to croak out a call for help. Beating her to the punch, was one of the swabbies who stood guard just moments prior.

"Someone!!! HELP!!!" he cried out in terror, as he pulled his friend's bloody body across the drenched floor.

Bellows and cannon fire now clouded over her head, and another impact rattled her skeleton and thrust her heart up to her gullet. The two boys were tossed aside like paper, as more men now entered the brig amidst the anarchy.

"Secure anythin's you can!!!" one of them commanded. "Anythin's flammable, got it?!"

Remana bellowed out to them, but she was ignored.

As the pirates jumped around the brig like frenzied, clockwork elves, Remana witnessed one of the most horrible, awesome things in her life, as a gigantic spear or horn burst through the walls, impaling one of the crew, before thrashing and destroying everything in its path. It then withdrew, carrying the corpse back out with it.

A high ringing was all she could hear, as she crumpled to her knees in utter horror and awe.

With every effort her slack body could muster, she turned her saucer-sized gaze toward the cell door. It was twisted, creating *just* enough of an opening for her to escape.

Her body acted without thought. She jammed herself through the jagged remains of the metal. It cut against her thighs, and ripped her trousers. She did not feel pain; only anger toward the fact that her flesh was impeding her progress.

She made it out. She fell to the wet, bloody deck like a newborn calf, and refused herself any time to recover. Sloshing through the vile liquid, she crawled with every burning muscle in her body.

She bumped head-first into a pair of shins.

"Damn it! *Of course* you had to escape! Just my luck!" Captain Archie Shorn roared, as he grabbed a handful of Remana's oily, knotted hair.

She screamed, and grabbed his legs. With every last drop of strength, she lifted him off his feet, and slammed him straight into the depths of Davy Jones' locker.

She was blinded by darkness and water, but that didn't stop her mounting him, before mashing his smug face like dough.

Her unbridled joy of feeling her knuckles crushing against his skull was short-lived, as both of them were thrown sideways by another impact; a mass of limbs and debris slamming against the walls.

Remana felt nothing this time, as she was already on her feet. Her furnaces were blazing once again, and she only had one goal in mind.

To eliminate the squirming man in front of her.

She got agonisingly close, before more of his lackeys emerged. Pointing and yelling, they then rushed her as they clumsily drew their blades.

Grabbing the nearest hunk of solid object she could see, she threw it with a force that completely blindsided the nearest pirate, smashing him against the face and dropping him.

The other two were quickly caught off guard, and like a silty tidal wave, she rushed with a gale force that buckled their ankles. With a flurry of kicks and scratches, her visage was of a demon, as she held back both men at once, before using the tight corridor to her advantage by slipping between the two bellowing figures, and striking them in their heads until her hands shined with claret.

There was no style. No eloquence. She was a rabid creature that refused to be put to sleep. She had lost herself. Amidst the total anarchy that rained above, she stood over the groaning figures. She had one of their swords in her trembling hand, and raised it in order to deliver the mortal plunges.

She was trapped in a pitch black hell, and her soul had burned away; its embers hissing away as they hit the cloudy, briny drink. This was her only way out.

Yet… something stopped her. A shaft of light bore its way through her sagging heartbeat, and a spark of humanity made her drop the cutlass.

"Stop!!!"

A voice… was it… her father?

"Stop!!! Please!!!"

No… it was Captain Archie Shorn. The blood of his face glinting in the water's moonlit surface, he was on his hands and knees, and we swayed back and forth like a sick dog.

Whatever battle was raging outside, felt distant and faint now, and Remana could only hear the pitiful man's gasps.

"Please…" he begged, "Don't kill him. Don't kill them. It's the last thing I need right now…" He hacked violently, and the ship responded in kind, as it quaked with another impact.

She fell again, but kept a tight grip on her blade. She could not believe the gall of this mongrel, to try and play the sympathy card, now that things weren't going his way.

You bastard.

She lunged at him, before he had a chance to pull one of his devious tricks, and pressed the blade against his neck.

"You son of a bitch!" she snarled. "Give me one good reason why I don't stick you like a pig, right and right now!"

The man gritted his teeth in pain, and raised his hands. "You… I don't have any reasons. Well… one reason, I guess. Look, you can kill me now if you want. No-one would blame you." He coughed again, but tried to keep his vain composure. "But, as you can see, my crew isn't doing so well at the moment…."

She was tired of his voice. "What the hell is happening?!"

"We're being attacked, as you can so plainly see." His words quivered. "Some… some of my mates are dead. Not a good day. Not a good day at all…"

"Good" Remana hissed, "you can join them."

Yells of agony filtered their way downward, and Archie's gaze looked genuinely tortured. "Like I said… you can kill me now. But it's going to do you no good. Slaughtering my entire crew won't do you any good, neither… we're trapped."

"Imagine my dismay" she replied with venomous sarcasm. "I'm not your crew. Whomever's attacking you will plainly see that. I'm going to chop your head off, and hop off this floating trash heap. Sorry, *mate*".

Archie grabbed the blade with his bare hands. And crimson droplets fell from his palms. He tried to laugh, but again, the frog in his throat wouldn't allow it. "That's not going to happen! We're not being attacked… by another ship."

"What? Then who is it?"

"Not *who*… but *what*."

The ship cracked all around them. Before they could say another word, their innards burst with hell's trumpets, as another impact to the ship rocketed their bodies into the darkest pits of the abyss.

* * *

The first thing Remana tol Dwen could recall was heaving her guts up. Again.

She was mildly interested in her body's ability to act completely independent to her own conscious thoughts. She would have further stewed on the subject, if she had not been in such sizzling harrow.

It became bright. Too bright. Stars danced before her, as a hot, stabbing sensation clawed at her side. Sightless, her rattling hands instinctively searched for the source – before they found another pair of hands.

"Don't move" Archie said quietly, in a craggy voice that sounded like it came from a geriatric.

"What–

"You've been impaled. A huge chunk of wood. Just… sit still."

She began to see clearly. She was out in the open. The salt of the sea burned her sinuses, as droplets and splashes of water poured around them.

The ocean stretched out before them. It seemed to have a mind of its own, as it lapped the gnarled and jagged wreckage, like the feelers of a catfish. She realised that she was still on the ship, and whatever had struck them, had rend a massive hole in its side.

"We're… we're still floatin'" a weak voice spoke from behind her. He sounded like he was about to break down in tears. "We're still floatin'…"

The moons shone down upon them. She could see so much now. Any other time, she would have marvelled at the beauty of the constellations and the Great Ring that streaked across the amethyst sky. She would have shed a tear or two of her own in happiness.

Not in pain.

Archie and another of his (presumably last) pirates slowly pulled out the splintery object, and her neck bulged in utter anguish. She would not give them the satisfaction of screaming.

Blood gushed from her abdomen, as the two men swore, before trying to do everything to fix the wound.

She felt the hot liquid run down her side, and mix with the dark still water. She wanted to curse a blue streak at the men who were 'helping' her, but she bit her tongue.

And she tried not to do it *literally.*

"Yeah, we're still floatin'..." another man said. She thought it was the older man, the one Archie called 'Badger'. "We ain't dead yet, y'hear? Don't go breaking down on me. That's an order."

A weak 'aye-aye' was the only response.

All around her. She heard the cries of many men. Some must have been dying. Others were undoubtedly wishing they were dead.

"What's... what's *happening*" Remana hissed, as she resisted the urge to choke the life out of the captain.

His face was a mess. Yet, his eyes were bright with an unyielding determination and rigidity that was a characteristic of a strong leader.

He did not speak.

"Answer me" Remana ordered.

"Yeah, answer her!" Badger suddenly shouted. "Come on Captain, tell her everything! Ya may as well, since we're all fish food!"

"Not now" Archie said.

The older man seethed, before ordering the remaining crew to gather up whatever weapons they had left.

"Yes, *now*" she echoed the first mate. "Tell me now, you--

She howled, as the other pirate cleaned her would with some sort of concoction. She tried to take a swing at him, but Archie held her arm.

"All right!" he growled in her ear. "Calm down! Alright? Let Gurt work his stuff. We're being attacked, okay?"

"By... what?!"

"Some sort of sea beast... the guardian, I'm presuming."

Her fist was still clenched. "The guardian... of *what*?!"

A look of desperation crossed Archie's face. Remana knew that face. She had seen it so many times. It was the face of guilt.

"I haven't got time to explain... it's going to come back. It won't stop until it finishes us off... look..."

He let go of her, and fell on his backside. "Look... I'm not going to beat around the bush. I need your help."

She cackled, and it felt like shards of glass jolted through her stomach. She coughed and wheezed, as the man known as Gurt nervously held her still.

Remana pushed him away, and slid her back to the nearest wall for support. "You… understand what you're saying? How much of a god forsaken idiot you sound like right now?"

The seas rumbled, and everyone began to yell.

"It's coming back!!!" someone in the upper decks screamed.

"I've got no time to argue!" Archie barked, as he pounced awkwardly to his feet. "We can sort out everything later, but I'm *not* letting any more of my men die, you hear me?"

His voice dripped with malice. "Either help us, or don't. Either way, I'm going to kill this thing, and send it to hell, where it belongs!!!"

A few of his followers whooped in response, energised by their leader's words. They began to yell and curse, desperate to keep the crippling fear of death at bay.

"You heard the man!" Badger boomed like thunder. "Everyone, get to defensive positions! We are the *Zircon Halibuts*!! Remember where you all came from! What you all endured! I dunno about you, but I ain't letting some fish be the end of me!!!"

She had to admit, she was impressed by their fortitude. What seemed like a dead, floating husk showed a spark of life, as the ship was alive with renewed activity. Lights were re-lit, and the thumping of armaments being reloaded was like a drum beat.

I guess I have no choice. What else can I do?

"Damn it" she spat. Clutching her wound, she staggered after the captain.

* * *

It was cold.

Maybe it was the fever brought on by her injury, but her sweat masked just how far they were from Arlmai.

Icebergs were becoming more frequent, and the ocean looked

thick with slush.

She trailed Archie Shorn, as he tried desperately to walk with a stiff back and an even-stiffer upper lip.

It was obvious that he was hurting bad. Remana wondered why he even bothered. These were a band of cut-throats – not the navy. They probably couldn't have cared less about their boss' prim-and-proper demeanour.

"Okay, captain" she began, "you want my help? First thing's first, who paid you to abduct me? Why?"

Archie's shoulders stiffened in clear frustration. "An answer for an answer. Deal?"

"Fine."

He turned to her. "I only met him once. A real regal sort of bloke. Said he needed to find a group of certain special folk. You were one of 'em. He put out the call. We answered."

"What was his name?"

"He only went by 'Mr. Telos'. Not his real name, I imagine. Now, you answer me this; are you fit to fight?"

She finally got a good look at her injury. It was wrapped, but she had no idea what kind of internal damage there was. For all she knew, he was slowly dying.

"I've had worse. Do you have any idea what is attacking us?"

Archie resumed walking. "Some kind of horned beast. A giant. I can't believe it's real..."

"What do you mean by that?"

Again, the ship was hit. The impact wasn't as hard as before, but it still caused them to fall into each other's arms.

They both pushed each other away in disgust.

"We have cannons, stinkpots, grappling hooks, knipples and harpoons" he continued, as he went up a flight of stairs. "Do you know how to use any of them? Can you craft something?"

"Yeah sure, I'll light up my workshop right now and whip up a giant, exploding weapon of mass destruction" she bit back.

They reached the upper deck. It wasn't as mangled as the main body of the ship, but it was still chaos. Remana finally saw everything around her – and realised that they were heading further and further into the ice.

"Where the hell are we going?" she shouted over the whipping winds.

"Through the wall of ice" Archie replied. "To the *Tower of the Gods*."

A massive screech came from below them, and stopped Remana's heart. There were few times in her life where she had been so utterly terrified; and in a way, she marvelled that there were still things in this world that could *still* instil such terror within her.

"The Tower of the Gods?!" she screamed. "Are you insane?!"

She could not believe her ears. The Tower of the Gods was a place draped in myth and legend. A sky-borne citadel that was supposedly located north-west of Arlmai, it was said to be surrounded by an impenetrable circle of toothy ice and rocks, and guarded by a mythical creature known as *Dun*. It was said to be the reason why the village of Nūk was founded, and was ingrained into the minds of every man, woman and child. The reason for its existence was often debated, but all believed that it was constructed from the god Qual-nu, and was one of the most revered places in the world for the red robed Sollikane.

Remana still had vivid memories of elderly mages coming through the town in order to sail forth to the place. So many privateers, merchants and navy vessels would refuse them, but according to some naive treasure hunters, there *was* a way.

None ever came back.

The captain laughed quietly to himself as he took the wheel from his helmsman. "Probably" he replied with a haggard murmur, "but nevertheless, even *insane* people know when they have a key. And we've got one."

Before she could get another distrusting word out, Remana desperately gripped the nearest thing her hands could reach, as the bottom of the ship grazed an unseen object.

"Iceberg, cap'n," one of the pirates called out.

Archie nodded. "It's now or never."

He pulled out something from his pocket; a compass. Made from red ochre wood, it glowed ominously in the pale moonlight. He then dropped it to the deck, before crushing it under his heel.

It popped, as Remana looked on in utter bewilderment.

As if it could hear the object's destruction, a mighty roar once again echoed throughout the seas, as their monstrous pursuer made it clear that it was still circling its prey.

Everyone on board trembled in fear, as it seemed like their very souls were sinking deeper and deeper into the black, frosty hell that eagerly awaited them.

"Stay on your guard!" Archie shouted, as he stood unyielding with stubborn determination.

Even Remana was almost driven mad with cold-sweat. She couldn't quite believe that this man before her was so strong in the face of a horrific death.

Oh god, he really is crazy isn't he?

Lifting his boot, shards of glass and splatters of mercury rained from Archie's sole. Shaking his leg like a dog, he carefully picked up the mangled compass.

"Here" he said, handing it to Remana.

She was speechless. And thoughtless.

"Uh… thanks? Wh… what am I supposed to do with this, exactly?"

Yep, he's crazy.

The captain wiped his hand on his coat, before closing his eyes. He breathed deeply, almost as if it were to be his last, wonderfully salty breath. "You want answers? Well, here you go."

He pointed towards the sea. "You were a pain in the arse to find, Remana tol Dwen. But we did, and we're here. We're on the verge of total annihilation. My beautiful ship is nothing but a skeleton… and I've lost quite a few good men. It's been a lousy day, if I'm being totally honest with you."

"Yeah, and all of it could have easily been avoided!" She snapped back, as the vessel hit another chunk of ice. She waved the broken compass in front of his dishevelled face. "Just what the hell is this supposed to be for?"

"We don't have much time left" he continued. "Look, the man I told you about. Mr. Telos. He claimed that he knew a way to get to the Tower of the Gods. It required two ingredients. A world-weary compass… and you."

She coughed, as pain again made its annoying presence known."*What?*"

More impacts thudded against the hull, and the captain cringed. "Look, like I said, I'll explain everything once we get out of this mess. But, love, you just need to trust me! If you don't do what I say, we're all going to die before dawn."

She prickled at him. "Don't call me 'love'!"

Another roar from the deep. Another wallop. They were becoming more frequent. The ship was being torn limb from limb, as all the men around her began to moan and mewl, despite their best efforts to put up a brave front.

Somehow, in spite of everything, she felt genuine pity and sadness for them. They risked everything for this mad bastard of a 'captain'.

She sighed. "Okay, *Archie*. What do you want me to do?"

He tightened his lips at her scathing tone, but held his tongue. "There *is* a way to get into the tower. To get out here alive. We needed a compass that had been all over the world, and we needed… well, we needed what was called *Aodh*. In other words… you."

That word… Remana felt like she was hit in the chest with a hammer… but… why?

Aodh.

"Keep going" she ordered.

Archie grabbed the wheel once more, in a meagre attempt to navigate what was left of his pride and joy. He continued. "Somehow, some way, you can open the path. I guess that's why my client wanted you so bad. Why he paid so much… according to his instructions, once our vessel was to enter a point of 'no return', I was to destroy the compass, and give it to you… Aodh. From there, you are supposed to navigate to the bowsprit of the ship… and…"

"… and? And *what*?"

"… and then you need to cut your palm with a shard of the broken glass. Then, the way to the Tower of the Gods will make itself known."

He then presented a serrated piece to her, and it shined like a serpent's fang that dripped with venom.

I cannot believe this is happening right now.

She was wounded. Sick. Battered and bruised. Stuck on a floating coffin as it slowly sank into frigid seas, whilst being stalked by a ferocious, hungry monster of the deep. And the very rat that put her in this situation in the first place, is now asking her to perform some sort of asinine ritual to open a path to a location… a location that is merely the stuff of fables. A location that… only she can get to? Because some rich criminal said so?

She shook her head and laughed. She snatched both the compass and glass piece from Archie, as the vessel was wracked with spasms. She nearly fell overboard, but was caught by the strong arms of one of the crew.

"The Lyra's in 'er death throes" he lamented to his captain, as he released the woman. "'scuse me impatience, but whatever we gotta do, we better bloody do it now."

Another howl from the blackness beneath them. The hunter could not get to its prey, and it was angry.

Thunderheads slowly surrounded them. The crisp light of the moons began to fade into nothing, as The Life of Lyra ground and splintered against the solidifying waters. As below, so did cracking and booming beckon from above; and they were now caught between the fury of both heaven and hell. They were the last cinder of life left, and it was only a matter of time before they were snuffed out; crushed into complete oblivion by their hubris. Their arrogance in challenging nature. They would now pay the ultimate price.

The hoarfrost moved fast. Things began to degrade inhumanly quickly, as the men all around her slowly turned grey and lifeless. Echoes of the mountains avalanched into Remana's mind, and peeled back her skull with sharp precision. She remembered her father. Her mother. Her brother... and the transient, ghostly old man that saved her.

"Okay" she uttered with croaky besetment. She curled her lip toward Archie, making her hatred toward him evident. "Fine! Sure! Great! Let's do this! The sooner I entertain your delusions, the sooner I can die."

Captain Archie Shorn smiled, showing a grisly bleached grin between blue lips. "Thatta girl."

CHAPTER III

Nuvummburtee.

That word meant nothing to him, nor did it to his keepers. A name? A place? A title? It was an unknown label written with common characters; a tongue that was both familiar and balderdash. It could have been some sort of ancient language of a people long-gone, or even a confounding code that was meant to be cracked... but it was his. And that is who he now was.

A young, handsome man with pale skin and soft blue eyes, he certainly stood out from the people of Jhasé, who looked upon him with wonder. When he stepped out of that temple for the first time, his squinting gaze was met with the reverent stares of many people. Some bowed, whilst others seemed more wary of his arrival.

Was he truly an emissary of their god? For what purpose?

He felt utterly naked and helpless. He felt like they expected him to perform miracles, or proclaim a holy message that would change all of their lives.

But there was nothing.

As the days went by, the excitement waned. Word of the arrival of the 'Ember Mind' soon spread across the Merca Lal Mountains, as Angakkuqs from other settlements came far and wide. They ogled him. They asked him the same questions. Over and over. Some were satisfied. Others clearly were not. Much debate raged between the Sollikane, with many wanting to further examine the Silver Lake, whilst others wished to hold a colloquy at some mysterious, far-off location.

Nuvummburtee felt like he was being assaulted from every angle. Like a butterfly, he was being crushed by overly-possessive hands; hands that were also pulling his limbs in all directions. He spent a couple of weeks acclimating himself to the village. The days brought with it crisp blue skies that brought many of the moons into sharp focus, as the sun brought warmth and life to the frosted soil. Like glass, the nights were beautiful, but could be sharply unforgiving. One could get lost in staring at the constellations and auroras, but if not for the safety of the volcanic springs and the fires produced by the people, death surely would come swiftly for those who wandered into the icy wilds.

It would have otherwise been a lonely and sad experience for him, were it not for one person.

Willing or not, Ya'k-lum became Nuv's caretaker. The duo immediately became fast friends, as the young local was eager to make the new guest feel at home. The energetic youth seemed to be the only one in Jhasé who treated Nuvummburtee like a normal person, and not some sort of curio.

They both received sideways glances by the others, who shook their heads in silent disapproval. Ya'k-lum laughed it off, and taught his new pal to do the same.

"I'm somewhat of an outsider here, too" he had told Nuv one day, as they sat in his small room. He had eagerly shown him everything he knew about Tarinn, as well his own written works. "Honestly, I cannot wait to get out of here."

He would often talk about his hopes and dreams, as well as speculate endlessly about Nuv's own past.

This was a man who truly knew nothing, as if he were a newborn.

"But" Ya'k-lum said, as he played tug-of-war with Jana, "it's not like you sprouted from the ground like a potato!"

Indeed, the entire mystery fuelled the wordsmith's imagination, and he would eagerly peruse the ancient texts in the temple.

Old man Trafr'ad even seemed to welcome this. Perhaps he viewed Ya'k-lum's excitement as a renewed sense of religious duty.

As time went by, things began to settle. It was clear that no great event was to occur any time soon, and business resumed as normal. The people began to treat Nuv as one of their own. Not wanting to be a burden, he contributed and learned everything he could. He went on hunts with the men, whilst the women taught his how to properly prepare the wide range of food that could be harvested from the region. He spent his evenings studying Sollikane lore, though he as by no-means a magi. He understood very little, but came to understand the beliefs held by these folk.

Though labelled as a god of 'misfortune', Qual-nu was by no means evil. The creator of the island of Arlmai, as well as the red sun Sollik, also known as the *Blood Sight of Redemption*. A lot of the philosophies were hard to grasp, but he was one of the originators of the Four Sister Islands – along with *Lamun, Tson* and *Shalisshakin*, who respectively created *Shali, Miiri* and *Liniii*. They were the islands of water, earth and wind... and Arlmai was fire. It was written that these places were the entryway to worlds beyond, that they represented Tarinn... and that the Tarinn 'flowed forth' from them.

"We are taught that Qual-nu is our fire" Ya'k-lum explained, "we are born from the chaos and will go back to the chaos. The thrill of the hunt. We make reality our own. *Kia*.'

Over the past millennia, faiths from foreign lands tried to usurp the natives, leading to war between the mages. The monotheistic Pisistrati'e slaughtered many, and gained a presence in the lands – including the Four Sisters. In more recent times, the Numanta have also spread their profane, godless beliefs of ancient civilisations and insular philosophies.

"Ancient civilisations?" Nuv asked.

"The Pheekonshenee" Ya'k-lum replied in a low tone, as if he were afraid someone would hear. "I heard bits and pieces about them. Apparently they were a people that had technology and ideas the were far, far beyond our own. The white robes... the Numanta, they say that so many of the world wonders of Tarinn were actually built by the Pheekons. They say that the gods don't exist! As you can imagine, they painted a pretty big target on their back. That was ages ago though, everyone is pretty friendly now."

When not spending the nights reading by candlelight, Ya'k-lum and Nuv would enjoy the hot springs; especially to heal their aching muscles after a day of chores. Ya'k's siblings would eagerly join, pestering their brother as they cooked meat sticks in the broiling waters and asking inane questions and postulating theories about Nuv's helm.

For that silver piece of headwear was just as perplexing as the man himself. Upon handing it to Ya'l-lum for examination, the woman gasped and dropped it to the ground. She could not lift it, nor could her brother. It had been spellbound in a way that only Nuv could carry it around, and as such, there was no danger of it being pilfered.

"If you put it on a cart, would the cart buckle?"

"What if you used it as a ship anchor?"

"What if you ran into a wall while wearing it? Would the wall break?"

"Ember Mind! More like Ram Head!"

"*Ram Head! Ram Head! Ram Head!*"

They all laughed and joked, and really, for the first time he could remember, Nuvummburtee was at complete peace with himself. Was this his new life? If so, he certainly wouldn't complain. Whatever or wherever he had come from, it was becoming more and more inconsequential. The meaning of his life was here.

* * *

What is the ember?
   That spark? That shine?
   His weathered eyes wrinkle
   Laughter sings from between gates of pearl
   No tear-drops here
   Only when the life leaves the beast's eye
   It's own ember gone
   Hot wine flows. Cover his hands and washes his sins
   The ember sparks
   Breathe in
   The ember blazes
   Breathe out

* * *

"I'm just saying," Ya'k-lum huffed, as he tried to get his striding friend's attention, "there's only so much I can write about while being stuck here. I need to spread my wings! There's only so many times I can compose a soliloquy based on bloody snow. Literally. *Bloody. Snow.*"

"Mm-hm" Nuvummburtee replied.

Months had passed since he had been brought to the village of Jhasé. He had made a home here. He was one of them. He was no longer a "dribbling mongoloid", as his supposed best mate put it.

So, why now? Why was the Angakkuq calling him to this meeting? Did he finally find something about who he really was?

He had to admit, he was nervous. Why? Is this not what he wanted?

He scratched at his beard.

I don't know what I want… because I haven't wanted *anything.*

The dusky sky darkened quickly. Its dying radiance bouncing off the plum-coloured bedrock, as a herd of golden elk could be seen shooting through the trees in the distant forest.

A sign of bad weather…

"Thanks. You agree, then" Ya'k grunted.

"Sorry" Nuv shook his head. "I'm just wondering what's going on. You think it's got something to do with that thousand hunt festival?"

"That's not for months yet."

"He doesn't want me to... be a magi? Maybe that's what it is?"

Ya'k-lum growled. "How should I know? Let's talk to the old man and see, shall we?"

He rapped on the wooden doors, and swung nonchalantly on his heels. He cleared his throat, and smelled his breath.

Nuv smirked. "Scared?"

"Of *what*?"

A young girl answered. Irn'luv; a Sollikane-in-training, and Ya'k-lum's unrequited love.

"Hey guys!" she said cheerfully, undercutting the solemnity required for someone in her position. "You're early. I was just feeding Amarok. Come on in, I'll let the Angakkuq know you're here."

She was certainly easy on the male gaze. Her large olive eyes were easy to get lost in, and her tall frame gave an air of 'high priestessness'... as Ya'k-lum described it in his typically-erudite way. The same dulling of the mind was on display now, as he grinned stupidly, before shuffling his way inside.

Nuv followed, politely scraping his boots on the threshold, before gesturing his respects to Qual-nu.

This place never failed to bring him a sense of comfort. For the first few weeks of his new life, he had lived within the dorms – really, a small basement with a few beds intended for visitors. It was cosy enough, but soon got awkward when his personal space became akin to a way-station, as a regular flow of travellers would disturb any form of privacy he had. Sure, it was an irregular occurrence, but the novelty of making home in a board wore thin very quickly for him, and so he eventually moved in with Ya'k-lum.

In an incredible gesture of kindness, the townspeople had actually built the two men a home. Nothing extravagant, of course, but it provided a veritable haven for two individuals who found great companionship and a common ground.

They both felt like outsiders.

Insiders on the outside? Outsiders on the inside?

Sure, they were members of a close, god-fearing community. They were loved and appreciated (at least on *some* days for poor Ya'k-lum), but, at the end of the day... they were different.

Still, if either of them were given grief over it, Ya'k-lum's mum was always there, ready to thrash them with her demonic wooden spoon. That's when she wasn't fretting over her son, often visiting them with bundles of food and clean clothing – much to his great embarrassment.

Now though, Nuv was the one experiencing discomfort on behalf of his buddy, as he once again tip-toed around Irn'luv whilst trying to conjure pathetic small-talk.

Amidst the steamy atmosphere, Trafr'ad emerged, like a phantasm. Amidst the pale, rose light of the fledgling moons and the flickering sconce, it would have truly been a frightening sight to an outsider.

And that was *without* the four-legged behemoth that oft trailed him.

The duo bowed deeply, and the ancient priest dismissed them with a gentle wave of his skeletal hand.

"Right, I'm off to sate the beast" Irn'luv told them, "and yes, Angakkuq, the meat's plenty warm."

"Good" he replied, "poor Amarok's old belly can't take it like it used to. The old boy lost another tooth, too. I'll have to check if his chompers are getting cleaned properly. His breath is terrible!"

"I'm telling you" the girl mumbled as she grabbed a massive, steaming bowl from one of the seats, "a fibrous soup. That's what he needs..." she continued to mutter as she exited in a puff of pinkish mist.

"Oh...uh...I can help, if you like?" Ya'k-lum called weakly, after she was well and truly gone.

Nuv rolled his eyes.

"No" Trafr'ad said. "I need you, Ya'k. Both of you" he coughed, and pulled out one of his smoking sticks. "Follow me."

The two youngsters exchanged quizzical glances, and shadowed the shuffling magi into his small office.

Ya'k-lum's visage changed drastically, and it took Nuv by surprise. His face was utterly dazed, like a stunned deer. "I've... never been in here before" he said quietly.

The room was crammed full of shelves, books, papers and scrolls. Bright, colourful figurines overlooked the trio from every crevice, and jars of spices, organs and skeletons dotted the walls. Pagan symbols criss-crossed the ceiling, and they seemed to move and warp, as if morphed by unseen heat-waves.

The Angakkuq motioned them to sit. They parked themselves on two wicker chairs that sagged comfortably under their weight, and their host produced two mugs of kakawa. They sipped furtively, whilst doing their utmost best to not pollute the sombre quiet with their slurping.

"Nuvummburtee" Trafr'ad began, as he sat on the opposite side of his stone desk whilst blowing smoke "I have called Ya'k-lum and yourself here tonight. As you can no doubt ascertain, this is no mere social call."

"Yes Angakkuq" Nuv replied impassively.

The wizened cleric continued. "Since your arrival so many months ago, there has been so much. Who are you? Where did you come from? What did all of this mean? Indeed, it was a turbulent time for both you and our people... my, who could forget the fuss raised by myself and my contemporaries." He chuckled. "Again, my apologies for making your life such hell."

Nuv shrugged. "No worries. Really. It's only natural to want to look underneath every stone for answers. Heavens know *I* certainly wanted them."

"And... you still do?"

Nuvummburtee tried not to show any emotion. *Why is he saying this? What is this all about?*

"... sure. Of course. But, I must say, I've been very happy with how I've been welcomed in Jhasé. I've learned so much, and not a day goes by that I don't thank you and everyone else for it."

Once more, Trafr'ad crowed, his bones practically rattling. "I am happy to hear it. After all, the strange happenstance of your discovery was not something that I could exactly ignore and forget. And as such... I have brought you boys here to tell you... that you are going away."

Ya'k-lum almost choked on his drink. "E, excuse me, Angakkuq?"

Trafr'ad was quiet for a moment, deep in thought. Nuv almost thought he had died, but then, like a lizard, he sucked in his smoking stick and began crunching on it. Once he was done, he breathed deeply. "Yes... yes, it is time. Nuvummburtee and Ya'k-lum, what I am about to tell you is something that very few in the history of Jhasé are aware of."

Nuv grew concerned and anxious, but avoided interrupting. He nodded, indicating his full attentiveness.

The magi continued. "On Arlmai, there are three locations. Locations that have been kept under protection for centuries. They are known as the *Sacred Sites*. These are places of power; power that is rich, like a vein of gold... each of the Four Sister Isles have them. The Tower of the Gods, protected by Nūk. *Ceev*, protected by *Curu-Col Town*... and *Saumen*, protected by Jhasé. They are the trinity of flame... and they may be the key to your identity, Nuvummburtee."

Nuv didn't know what to think. There was emptiness where raging ideas should have been.

"Why..." he mumbled, "why are you telling me this now?"

Trafr'ad caressed his spotty chin. "To be quite honest with you, it took me a while to come to this conclusion. You must understand, not even the other Angakkuq of the mountains know of the sacred sites. Yes, they know of the locations themselves – but not of their true purpose. I, however, do. The secret of Saumen has been passed down the line of Jhasé's leaders for generations... and the message has always been crystal clear. The sites exist as an awakening."

"An awakening..." Ya'k-lum reiterated in astonishment. "For what?"

"That, I am not so sure" Trafr'ad admitted. "The prophecy has always been open to interpretation. But it is nevertheless a duty that has been upheld with utter gravitas, and I cannot help but think that you may have something to do with it."

He pointed a crooked finger at Nuv. He now regretted using his helm as a paperweight for Ya'k's works.

"That... me? *I'm* somehow part of an ancient prophecy?" he replied with doubt. "I mean, sure, the circumstances of my... er, *discovery*, was unusual... but couldn't we just chalk that up to good old fashioned sorcery?"

Trafr'ad frowned. "Trust me, my boy, it was anything but. I have been waiting. Waiting until you were strong enough. Wise enough. That you have learned about our ways. Our relationship with the mountains. You are ready. You must go to Saumen."

Thunder boomed in the distance. The golden elk always knew.

* * *

"This... this is real, isn't it? We're actually doing this?" Ya'k-lum sniffed, as he tried to balance his immense backpack on his shoulders. "I can't believe it... I knew it Nuv. I knew you'd change my life."

The sun Sollus leaked through the craggy peaks of the distant mountains, casting the valley in long steaks of cool shadows. Dawn had arrived, and with it, azure skies, newly recovered from a night and day of dry thunderstorms. Flecks of olive and burnt ochre forest scattered like herbs across the tundra, and curlews sang with deliberate scarcity. The Great Ring was a silver line that split the atmosphere in two, and a few stars tried to cling on the remaining life they had left.

Nuvummburtee breathed deep. "Yeah, this is real. You always said you wanted to leave. Well, you got what you wanted, mate!" In truth, he was a lot more nervous than he probably should have been. Of course, he had been outside of the village before. The hunts he undertook were gruelling, taking him far from home; both in the grass and mud of the lowlands, as well as the arid white of the north.

But, until just over a day ago, he had no idea that this 'Saumen' place existed. What kind of place *was* it? He and Ya'k were forbidden from mentioning it to their friends and family, which caused a great deal of stress for his poor friend. Though he was quite excited to venture to this forbidden, mysterious location, he struggled greatly in coming up with a convincing lie to tell his kin.

Only his sister Ya'l-lum was privy to the truth, as she was chosen as the next Angakkuq. His brother Ya'k-lutt also knew, and in time, so would Irn'luv. Despite this, all three of them were forbidden from accompanying Nuvummburtee and Ya'k-lum, with Trafr'ad adamant that the two must accomplish this task on their own.

Was this a test of their worthiness? Did Nuvummburtee live among the people of Jhasé, learning their ways of life, just so he could be ready for the day he was to strike out on his own? To leave?

Was it today?

Though the storms receded, Nuv's own mind was cloudy. He felt like he had just awoken from one of his rare night terrors, and tried vainly to recall the terrible imagery that assailed his senses. It was hopeless though, and he refused to let his demons shatter his chipper veneer.

"I still don't think they will buy it" Ya'k-lum warbled with uncertainty. "Us? Going on a 'spiritual' hike? The Angakkuq saying we both need to 'broaden our horizons'? It almost seems like he's leaving the village dunces to die in a forest..."

"It's really not far from the truth" Nuv observed with a forced laugh. "Aside from the 'dying' bit, that is. Though... you know this could be really dangerous, right? Do you have everything you need?"

"Yeah" Ya'k droned. Nuv could tell his friend was apprehensive of the potential dangers they faced. They were told that there indeed was a path to Saumen, so at least they wouldn't be wading blindly through thickets and being beset by wolves and boars. However, the way was still supposedly treacherous, with a lot of cliff faces and easy-to-miss clues that led them in the right directions.

Despite this, Ya'k-lum was eager for the adventure.

They stood on the periphery of Jhasé, facing their goal. There wasn't much land that way, but it was still an easy area to get lost in. They had said their goodbyes to their family and friends, and promised that they would return safe and unharmed in a few days.

Ya'k-lutt stood with them, ensuring that they would be sent off safely. The warrior voiced his displeasure at letting the two inexperienced journeymen go off on their own, and tried his damnedest to convince the Angakkuq of accompanying them. It was all in vain, and he was convinced to let his kid brother go.

"Okay" he snorted. "Now remember. Cross the plains in the north-east, until you reach the mountain line of three. Find the hidden path under the centre peak, using the *berrie-berrie moss* as your guide. Once through, *only* traverse by morning twilight, using the shadows to find the correct way through the winding canyons. During the rest of the day, look for blooming *magama flowers*, and follow their pointing petals. Eventually, you will reach Saumen."

He squinted his weather-beaten face at Ya'k-lum, not even trying to hide his despair. "Got it? Have you written it down?"

"Yes, yes" he replied irritably. "Don't fret, brother. I know you don't want to see me dead. You love me way too much."

Ya'k-lutt bared his teeth. "*No-one* will see you die out there."

"Nice."

The large man placed a palm on Nuv's shoulder. "He's your responsibility, now. Watch your backs out there. You've spent time with us. You know what dangers lurk out in the mountains. You're a fine survivor, Nuvummburtee. But, *be careful*, and come back in one piece."

Nuv looked at him square in his stern gaze, and felt the warm respect and pride flow from him.

"I will."

* * *

The Merca Lal Mountains. Nuvummburtee liked to think he had become intimately acquainted with the snowy ranges, glades and rivers that provided the nectar of life to so many communities across the north. Yet, crossing through a doorway to somewhere he had no idea existed… it was a humbling feeling. To take two steps to the side, and wind up in a completely foreign land. It was a specific moment, when he snagged the invisible line that separated *his* world to the rest of *the* world. A change in the air. That indisputable sense that he *properly* arrived at a new land away from home.

Ya'k-lum had to have been experiencing the same sensations. He could read it in his friend's body language; the wide-eyed stares, the smelling of the air… the lack of complaining.

The pair had debated on bringing Jana along for the trip, but decided against it, despite the dog's attempts to guilt them by way of pathetic, watery stares. Her grovelling distressed them greatly, but they had no idea how perilous the journey would be – especially with talks of treacherous cliffs. Ya'k-lum would have been a paranoid wreck, constantly shouting at the pooch if she strayed more than a foot away from them, lest she be sent plummeting to her doom.

No, it was easier if it was just the two of them. Even a pack mule was impossible to bring, as they didn't know if it would have fitted in the secret mountainside passage, let alone navigate gracefully along the rocky terrain.

So, they travelled light. And Ya'k-lum's definition of 'light' was having Nuv lug all the heavy stuff. Cooking utensils. Rations. Water. Rope. Anything and everything… including every curse word Nuv knew.

Still, he managed fairly well. His time in Jhasé made him strong, both in mind and body – and despite his doughy appearance, Ya'k-lum was no slouch either. He could hunt and forage when he wanted to, which was something they most likely needed to do whilst on this trip.

Nuv carried two ulus. Though affectionately known as 'woman's knives', Nuv grew a knack for using them in every conceivable way, from skinning game and preparing food, to chipping ice and skimming for roots. He was even taught some combative techniques from Ya'l-lum and the elders of the village, much to the men's amusement. He also wore his helm, which could only be a boon on a long, cold journey. It was very much a symbol of pride.

The normally-pacifistic Ya'k-lum also packed his own tools of destruction. A long snow knife made from bloodless boar horn, as well as a bola; two heavy weights attached to cords of fur and tendon – used for catching animals by tripping them up.

Like any youth, the first time catching and killing a living thing was a harrowing experience for both Nuv and Ya'k; hearing a beautiful creature's cries of agony as they plunged the sharp knife in their throat… feeling the life drain away… the resentment shown toward their elders, as they displayed a cold uncaring disposition. Of course, like any man or woman forced to choose between eating or starving, it slowly got easier over time; like a callous, the two of them quite simply toughened up, and lived life the way it was meant to be lived – the way of the Merca Lal Mountains.

A life of respect toward nature, and the bounty she brings amidst the chaos.

After whispering their prayers to Qual-nu, they made their way across the plains, weaving between the wooded areas whilst maintaining their singular direction. Progress was slow, as there were no clear paths to follow, and Nuv was not overly familiar with the area. Ya'k-lum had a little more experience, as he had foolishly ventured in the forbidden areas alone many a time, mostly to hide from his responsibilities and find motivation for his poetry.

He cheerfully regaled Nuv with his daring exploits, whilst pointing out various factoids regarding the local flora.

The small-talk helped to pass the time. It really seemed like they were the only two people in the world; very few signs of life could be observed, save for a few darting hares and whisper-quiet condors. The mauve mountains glistened as the sun illuminated the land, and before long, began to redden and set by the time they had found the triple-peaks.

They were very clear against the tangerine skies; an earthen crown that pierced the clouds and cast the woods below them in shadow. Ya'k-lum recalled only seeing them twice in his life, and wondered why they did not have a name – or why his people rarely ventured this far, preferring instead to make their living from the south.

"These look like foreboding lands" Nuv observed. "Not as rich in resources. There don't seem to be any hot springs, either. It's like this entire place is a half-finished painting."

As night fell, they made camp in a small copse. Blue, poisonous mushrooms ran through the grey tree trunks like ribbons, giving off a soft radiance that, when added to the flames, sweetened the smoke and kept away any potential predators. Though elusive, there was no doubt that predators prowled beyond their periphery.

"Yeah" Ya'k replied, between mouthfuls of herb bread dipped in soup, "I always thought the same thing whenever I ventured out here. Like, maybe this Saumen place has something to do with it? A sacred sight? There's probably a magic barrier protecting it. We'll disintegrate as soon as we cross it, I'll bet."

"*You* will" Nuv teased, "you'll be my scout, after all. I'll just be a few paces behind. Don't worry, you'll get a *great* funeral."

Ya'k squinted in detestation. "Gee, thanks pal." He lapped up the remainder of his meal, and stared at the bejewelled sky. "Really though, I'm kind of nervous... *excited*... but nervous."

Nuv furtively sipped his broth, and stared unseeing into the flickering flames. "Yeah, I know what you mean. Me too... but really, what'dyou think will happen? A part of me can't help but think this is all just a wild goose chase."

"What, you think the old man is wasting his time sending us out here?"

Nuv shrugged, before quickly glancing at the silver helm that sat next to him. The ruby within it warmed his heart more than soup or campfires ever could…

"No. Even if this leads to nothing…. I'll be glad we made the journey."

Ya'k fell backward, and made himself comfortable. Cupping his hands behind his head, he closed his eyes. "And if it doesn't? What happens then? If you had to… would you leave?"

"One thing at a time" Nuv shook his head. He drank the last of his soup, and immediately followed it with a chilled kakawa. Following his friend's example, he laid himself across his fur bed, and lost himself within the infinity of the night sky.

"One thing at a time…"

* * *

The thee-pronged mountain (or, the 'Merca Lal Fork' as Ya'k-lum called it) was truly a lot bigger than it had seemed from a distance.

As it increased in size and detail, it seemed to stretch further and further away from them as they marched.

The land grew thicker and thicker with brush, making it harder to make significant progress. Occasional whips of birds and nattering of animals pierced the chilly air, as the Sollus was obscured by the leafy ceiling that closed in above their heads. Branches swayed and cracked like snapping bones, and the winds whistled their faint eldritch music between the trees.

Surprisingly, some semblance of a path could still be seen – no doubt a relic of a bygone age. It came and went in patches, though the two men were still thankful for its existence.

They tried keeping to their north-easterly course, but it was hard going. Nuv was wary that the ancient road was deliberately trying to deceive them, perhaps eventually leading them in the wrong direction, but so far it seemed to guide them straight and true.

Well, not so much 'straight'...

The two passed the time by singing songs and playing games, whilst trying not to let the overwhelming fear of being mauled by wolves overcome them. By midday, they had sat to feast on a couple of hares they had caught.

Luckily for them, the skies remained clear, with rays of sunlight trickling down from between the mossy leaves. Between mouthfuls of stringy meat, Nuv tried to help Ya'k in creating a new composition for their little adventure, but truthfully, he was more interested in watching a nearby ant colony.

After an unholy amount of time coming up with a word that rhymes with 'frost', Nuv was eternally thankful to Qual-nu for giving him the patience for not using his helm to headbutt his friend repeatedly, before dumping his body where no-one will ever find it.

For the remainder of the day they continued, as Nuv desperately pleaded for Ya'k to accept the word 'cost', and be done with it. Of course, *mister writer* was having none of it, insisting that 'cost' was too obvious a choice.

Finally, he relented, only because he was too hungry to carry on. The ground became more rocky, as the woods began to open up once more. Nuv was wise to stick with his gut, as the path they had been following did indeed veer off to the north during the last stages of their trek. Whether a deliberate misdirection or not, he would never be able to tell, but he did wonder why someone would create a clear-cut path to a 'secret' entrance in the first place.

Either way, they had avoided a disastrous detour. Almost as if congratulating them for passing a test, owls hooted in great numbers; their yellow eyes shining in the growing dim of the afternoon dusk.

They had approached the foot of the mountains, its icy crags providing an inauspicious welcome. Both Nuv and Ya'k wondered how long it had been since the last people had arrived at this very spot. Years? Decades? Centuries, even? Saumen was supposed to be hidden from the world, and they had the privilege of visiting it.

It was such a simple concept to understand, yet, now that they were getting closer and closer, the feelings of awe became greater and greater. Nuv felt like he was one of the ants that he had so blithely watched with omnipresence. It felt... scary?

No... more like... intimidating. As if he was expected to undertake a great responsibility. To stop messing around with self-indulgent fantasies of having a 'family', and to get serious with accomplishing his mission... the mission was born to do.

What... why am I feeling like this?

Feeling a headache coming on, he removed his helmet, and let the cool breeze flow through his long hair.

"Nuv?"

"Eh?"

Ya'k-lum had been talking to him. "I said, let's turn in for the night. No use in finding a secret path in the dark."

Nuvummburtee nodded. "Right, true enough."

Again, they made camp. Sitting around a small blaze, they had parked themselves in the cosiest rock groove they could find. Their backs against the stone for extra security, they discussed at length their plans.

Nuv was concerned about the time they would waste in finding this passage. They were supposed to use the berrie-berrie moss as a guide; which was easy enough, albeit an unusual method. A bright pink strain, it only grew for a few days around the Blinking of the Eyes, and as such was incredibly rare and valuable... yet, they were told it was present here all year round. Nuv had only ever seen it cultivated by the people of Jhasé for use in medicine and cooking, and even then it was very delicate to keep alive.

He wasn't sure how long it would take. He assumed it shouldn't be more than a day. What worried him the most was when they would actually *find* the entrance; their explicit instructions were to only traverse the shadows during morning twilight. It was an incredibly short window of time, and if they arrived too early, they would have to waste an entire day and night just to wait around like dummies.

Of course, Ya'k-lum himself found the prospect of sitting on his arse doing nothing quite enticing.

It didn't help worrying about it. What mattered is that they had a clear objective to follow for tomorrow, and that was enough for Nuv.

Pulling out a single-stringed lute known as a *kelutviaq*, Ya'k-lum strummed a few ditties, as Nuv sang along. It put his mind at ease, and before he realised it, he had fallen fast asleep to the twangy lullaby.

* * *

"Is this it?" Ya'k-lum called out, as he poked the fuchsia morass with a stick. He scrunched his face in concentration, tongue poking out from one side. "Yeah! I think it is!"

"You said that the last two bloody times" Nuv grumbled. He trudged over. "First, it was a group of fungi. Then, it was a vomit of some description."

"Heh, I was just messing with ya" Ya'k chortled.

Any concerns Nuv had in finding their way too quickly were tossed out of the window. It had taken the entire morning to find their first clump of berrie-berrie moss, and even then, they weren't sure where exactly it was pointing them. They debated endlessly regarding which way to go, and Ya'k-lum then threw a further wrinkle in the plan, when he decided that maybe the moss literally pointed in the direction they were supposed to go – and that they were too dumb to see it.

Nuv was angry both at Ya'k and himself. He told himself he was overthinking it; he refused to believe that he was so dim that he couldn't follow such basic instructions. Literal *children* could do it... why couldn't *they*?

If someone told him he would reach his breaking point simply because of a clump of damned moss... well, he would probably believe them, honestly. Not the cold. Not the dark. Not wild animals. Not starvation... no, it was *goddamned moss*.

So far, this was only the third collection they had found. Nuv roared in frustration causing a flock of birds to cry in response. "To *hell* with this! And to hell with *you!*"

He pointed a shaking finger at Ya'k-lum, which made his friend double over in laughter.

Nuv pulled hairs from his beard to distract him from his evil thoughts. "Well?" he huffed, "Is it or isn't it?"

"Yeah" Ya'k replied, wiping away a tear. "It is. Three down, fifty six more to go."

"Don't even *joke* about that."

Ya'k shook his head, like a parent humouring their cranky offspring. "Come on buddy, don't be like that. I think we're making good progress, personally."

"Say that again when we step right off a cliff."

To Nuv's point, their terrain did indeed become more perilous as they went on, which hopefully meant that they were making progress. Throughout the day, every smattering of berrie-berrie brought with it sharper rocks, narrowing paths and higher drops. A couple of times, both of them almost lost their footing, as the ground suddenly gave way from beneath. As they got closer and closer to the Merca Lal Fork, they could no longer delineate between the three peaks and their bases; and took great care in making sure they were still in close distance to the centre mountain.

Taking swigs from his water skin, Nuv began to sweat from the workout, and similarly noticed Ya'k huffing and puffing with every careful step. Snow fell lightly around them, and they both hoped it wasn't a sign of something heavier. Qual-nu willing, they would find their way before sunset, as there was very little space to camp out, let alone find shelter in case of a blizzard.

Though Qual-nu *did* thrive in chaos...

Wolves howled in the distance. Not a good sign. Fortunately, as the day waned, it became clear they were headed the right way. It seemed both Nuv and Ya'k were right; the moss literally pointed to where they had to go, with the 'arrow' head growing stronger than the 'tail' of the accumulation. Like matted fur, each growth billowed sideways toward the correct bearing.

This both fascinated and even disturbed the travellers – moss was supposed to face northward, yet somehow, each bunch they found grew facing toward the next, regardless of the sun.

Something was literally affecting the laws of nature. A tinge in the air left a copper taste on the tips of their tongues, which got stronger as they got closer to their goal. A stillness created a disagreeable quiet throughout the deeper crevices of the mountain ridge, which strangely seemed to sing louder and louder in their ears as the day waned. There was a heightened awareness in their hearts; an awareness that sang a song of a forbidden world which pressed against their bodies, pushing them away… but at the same time, enticing them. Urging them onward, step by staggered step, to discover a realm that existed beyond their own life sphere.

Sunset cast a gloom across the land, making them feel small as they scurried along the rocks like desperate ants. Nuv knew they were getting close now, and his heart's pounding was like thunder in his ears, as he gasped in bedazzlement as rosy streaks of light crackled alongside Ya'k and himself; both welcoming and congratulating them for reaching the end of their perilous journey.

No longer playing coy, the berrie-berrie moss came alive in the weak coral daylight, fracturing the land with preposterous speed and tenacity as it climbed the mountainside, before swirling inward like a whirlpool. In a trance, Nuv and Ya'k watched with bewildered stillness, their jaws dangling, as a passageway unveiled itself before them in a melody of falling rocks and an avalanche of rubble and snow.

"Are… are you seeing this?" Ya'k-lum gawked, letting his rucksack fall to his feet.

"Yeah… I'm seeing it" Nuv confirmed. "This… I'm guessing this is the secret path, huh?"

* * *

She floated in the cold void.

Remana tol Dwen was sinking downward… or was it upward? She had no sense of gravity, and it was good. It was one less thing to worry about, and one more thing to make her smile, as death's comfort bought tears of relief in her dulled eyes.

She vaguely recalled what brought her here… something to do with a ship? Being kidnapped? She didn't care… it was time to let go… to go back to her beginning…

Not yet, Aodh!

Leave me be…

No! No! Not yet! Darn fool girl! You think I'm gonna let you die?! After wasting my time bringing you back? After I fed you the best fish soup I ever concocted?! Pshaw!

Come on Saumen…

No! No 'come ons'. You are the fire of Qual-nu! What would your papa say, seeing you like this?

You old fool… everyone dies… even me….

His disapproving, wrinkled face met hers. Amidst the broiling of bubbles, his massive silver beard moved of its own volition. His craggy, black skin would have been almost invisible in the dark, if not for the fire coming from his bloodshot eyes.

I know… but your time isn't now. Sorry, pretty lady! The boy is coming. You need him, and he needs you.

Boy?

Her head exploded in agony, as light filled her skull, and felt like it would melt her skin. A hand passed through the man, dissolving his image, before gripping Remana by her wrist.

Just grab it… may as well see what happens next…

She squeezed in turn, before her body was pulled into the world of the living. An incomprehensible noise shredded her ears, as daggers of accursed air forced their way down her gullet, rending her lungs in a worse pain than any poison could accomplish.

She gasped like a fish, as her body convulsed from the cold of the slurried waters and rushing winds. She stuttered the worst curse words she could think of, before she was thrown toward solid, crunchy ground. She looked upward, to see the gurning face of Badger, before he tossed a woollen skin over her.

"She's alive!" he boomed, before scooping her up.

She tried everything in her meagre power to kick and scream, but her bones were frozen. Yells and wails echoed all around them, as her saviour trudged with heavy, sinking steps toward the source of the chaotic noises.

Teeth chattering, she tried to get the lay of the land.

What she saw was… actual *land*.

They had made it. She knew it. They had somehow, by some miracle, made it to the Tower of the Gods.

She could scarcely recall what had happened… she did what Captain Archie instructed her to do… to perform the ritual… the spell… whatever the hell it was… in order to open the way. To stop the deep-sea beast from having them for dinner. She now vividly recalled the sharp sting on her palm, as she cut herself with the broken compass glass, before the hot blood ran down her arm, and splattered on the wooden surface of the ship…

Then, nothing.

She moaned, and smelt smoke. Her abdominal muscles wrenched from the uncontrollable chills, as the blue-bearded behemoth of a man lowered her gently beside a roaring blaze.

"Broad's alive!" Badger shouted again. "I dunno how, but she is!"

Without so much as a warning, a gush of liquid surged from Remana's throat. She coughed with ferocity, before weakly demanding to know what happened.

"It's a mess..." the first mate whispered, whilst palming her back. "Don't rub your hands together, love. Sucks the heat from your organs."

She did as she was told, and with cadaver-like eyes, she weakly looked around her.

They were indeed shipwrecked. In the foggy distance of the early morning light, the remains of the ship was barely more than a pile of matchsticks on the rocky shore; as debris littered every single area she could possibly see. Figures could be seen bellowing and shouting, as dead bodies were lined up further inland. She couldn't see more than a dozen men; the dead far outnumbered the living, and she couldn't help but shed tears for their fates.

Why? She didn't know, nor did she question it. Seeing them now, crying in despair until their throats were raw... even Badger, as his voice warbled with grief, tried to process just what had happened to his best mates and family.

"The... the thing you did" he continued, kneeling beside her "that... I don't know what that was... but when you cut yerself, your blood shot forth like a friggin' arrow, and it lit up like a piss stream of lava... I never saw anythin' like it before."

She looked at her shaking hand, incredulous. The small slit was purple against her pale-brown skin.

"And it hit an invisible wall" the man continued with shock, "and the entire horizon just shattered like glass, and before I knew it, you were flung from our hands like somethin' or other plucked you from the sky, and threw you across the sea, toward that damned tower! I didn't have much time to dwell on it, because everything just... just went to hell... the Lyra... she was speared again by that beast... and... I'll be damned, it *actually* pushed us toward the island, before flinging us like we were no better than snot!!!"

He spat, rage welling in his husky tone. He breathed heavily and loudly through his nose, and Remana was genuinely worried that he would strangle her.

"Are you well?" he finally asked, much to her relief.

"I th, think so" she whispered. She felt her side, and winced greatly, as her wound felt like stinging nettles were growing from her ribs. "I… I didn't ask for this. Any of this."

"I know, love, I know."

"Is Captain Archie–

"Yeah, he's here. He's alive. But I'm not sure how much longer." He growled, and stood tall. "Stay here and warm up. I'm gonna find some water and supplies."

He was gone like a ghost. With a limp, he scurried amongst the icy rocks and crunchy shell-covered shoreline, barking with as much meagre vigour he could muster.

All around her, was nothing but desolate land. The weak flames were her safety net amidst the mist, and others too, took solace. Three other men were in bad shape, suffering from broken legs and hypothermia, and their moaning made her feel sick.

Why should I be worried about the well-being of pirates? Because right now, they're just men… men in pain.

The one with the broken leg stared at her with utter contempt, whilst the other with the shakes was too busy trying not to freeze to death. The third, a young man barely out of his teens, was dark-skinned like her, and had a bandage wrapped around his head, and didn't seem to know where he was.

I wonder if he's one of my people… or from another in some far away land.

It had to be some sort of divine intervention. She could not see any other reason why she still lived, and this enraged her. Why did she deserve to live, whilst others around her drowned like rats? Was it because of her special abilities? Because she was destined for greater things? Some sort of grand plan?

She rubbed her forehead in agony, and looked. She knew it was there – the Tower of the Gods. It buzzed within her heart; a calling that urged her forward… something was *there*.

For a flitting moment, utter terror seized her. Before she could recognise it, it was gone, and in its place was a burst of hatred that pulsed toward the figure that loomed toward her.

Captain Archie Shorn.

Framed by messy brown hair, his face was gaunt and lined with defeat. In one of his hands, he clasped a telescope, whilst in the other was a flask.

She hoped it was water, and not something with *spirit*.

"By god, you're alive" he said with no emotion, before kneeling and handing her the flask. She took it, and in return, socked him in the face.

Without a noise, he fell backward and rolled. She thought she had killed him for a moment, before he sprung to his feet, and dusted himself off. Without a word, he trudged back to her, and sat down.

She took a furtive sip, and was relieved to taste water that wasn't filled with salt for once. "Congratulations" she hissed, "you got what you wanted. I hope your benefactor pays you handsomely."

Staring into the fire, Archie rubbed his jaw. "It wasn't supposed to happen like this… "

"It *did*."

They sat in silence for a long time. Remana hoped that the man truly did not have a conscience, because if he did, he would be enduring a living hell right about now, with the weight of so many souls upon his shoulders.

"It's all my fault."

She was about to sneer in agreement, but held her tongue. If he wanted to, he could decide to end her life at any time, but judging by the disaster they were in, there were more pressing concerns.

She sighed, relishing the last drops of the nectar-like liquid. "I don't know what you want me to say. Was this not part of your plan? To get me here? What was *supposed* to happen?"

Suddenly, the man's face twisted into something horrible. Any trace of his good looks completely vanished, as spat, swore and smashed his utensil against the ground.

"NOT THIS!!!" he screamed, pouncing to his feet, "They're all dead! EVERYONE! I'm going to kill that son of a bitch! He told us it was going to be safe! He... he..."

As quickly as he exploded, he sank to the ground like a rock. Instinctively, Remana caught him in her arms.

"Capn'!" the man with the broken leg shouted.

"Uhhhh... I'm fine" he mumbled, pushing himself away from the woman. "I'm fine. Just tired."

He spat again, before hiding his face with his hands. It was clear to her that he wanted nothing more than to curl into a ball and weep.

It wasn't humorous. She gained not an ounce of satisfaction from it. It was a sad sight... and she was sad for him. He was broken. A captain that failed his crew. A captain whose greed and hubris cost him everything.

Badger could be heard shouting somewhere off in the distance. It meant nothing. He was deaf to everything. The ocean swirled, as if mocking them with its lapping waves, and as far as she could tell, it was the only natural sound that made itself known. The island was otherwise eerie in its silence, and she worried if that meant a lack of game. Even gulls were absent, though with all the commotion, she hardly blamed them if they just decided to flee.

How long has it been since people stepped foot here? We must be the first in a long time....

She didn't want to assume the place was empty though. Who knows what lurked amidst the fog? She shuddered to think, and tried to place her mind firmly into more immediate matters.

"Archie" she said, breaking the pitiful spell he was under, "tell me. The man who hired you. Tell me everything."

CHAPTER IV

To the layman who somehow managed to escape the realm of the faerie, many plaguing thoughts and emotions haunted them for the rest of their short lives.

Like a waking dream, they often longed to return to the esoteric land of milk and honey, without really understanding *why*.

Though they eventually reintegrated into the common decency of society, and did all the *proper* things a *proper*, law-abiding citizen would do, they would nevertheless be nagged by an invisible force that forever looked over their shoulder, as it grinned in cheeky glee.

These people, touched by the other world, would forever belong to *them*.

Sure, they would marry. They would have children, grandchildren, and great grandchildren. They would live successful, fulfilling lives and become beacons of inspiration and joy to those around them... but it would all be nothing but a façade.

Because, in truth, they never came home.

They saw *it*... and they *cannot* unsee *it*. It consumes them. Day in and day out; that intangible *otherness* that exists *just* beyond the periphery of human comprehension. The type of otherness that can only be glimpsed in the dead of night, when all is still, and everyone is in the land of nod. The type of otherness that can be touched by the fingertips after years of inward reflection and spiritual isolation.

The type of otherness that *finally* shows itself after death.

The further humanity moves towards enlightenment and the lifting of the veil, the further away it drifts. For eons, this has been the rule of the world, and it is only in their final, gasping moments do these people finally understand this.

The Wizards of Chanthalaroos. They knew, of course. They *always* knew, but they were always too afraid of fully embracing it. That's what led to their ultimate downfall, but – just like the denizens of Tarinn they had ruled for so long – they too, saw the light only when their time had finally come.

They truly were their people's kings.

Once upon a time, though, humanity wasn't so dead. The Pheekonshenee, hallowed be thy name, lived life as it was meant to be lived. They knew that God was within… yet…

Where did they go?

Even as malleable as time and reality was to him, Joner could not find them again. Only relics; technology that merely served as proof of their existence. Whatever had happened to them, they were hidden even from what was invisible itself.

Still, the magics of the magi were fine substitutes, he had to admit. As blind as they were at times, even *they* possessed some understanding of the universe. The green Eidian tribe always knew of the wonders of the fay, as did the white Numanta of the Pheekons. Little did they know, for all of their pointless platitudes and poisonous organisational mentality, that they were in fact, two sides of the same coin.

Really, *all* of the robes were. The dogmatic grey *Pisistratie*. Their 'evil' foil, the red *Sollikane*. The pacifist, apathetic blue *Solluskane*. The pagan orange *Solenirkane*. The philosophers and singularitism of the black *Titanicae*.

The Titanicae…

And of course… the violet *Arche*. Long extinct from Tarinn… but not of this existence.

It often amused Joner. To see the world so *close* to the precipice… yet, so unbelievably *far*.

For him, there was no better representation of all of this than his very own mother and father.

Queen Bean Si and *Jugo Irononger*. One, the last of the elder folk. The other, a humble mortal.

Both of them, stabbing him in the heart.

Of course, if you asked them, their intentions were *only* of the purest and most noble. A half-man bastard, Joner was obviously unwelcome in his rightful kingdom, but being an infant, he had no idea of the suffering his dear old mum caused until *much* later in his non-life.

Growing up with his father, his life could not have been better. The son of a great hero, he benefited from the love of his peers and of countless adventures; making a name even for himself within his small circles. A kid hero, as it were.

Even as his father remarried, what should have been a shock to his perfect life was made even better with the birth of his little sister.

Jeleenn.

But then… that day.

"NO!!!" *Jugo screamed, as he hopelessly ran his hands through the grey ash.* "Not like this!!! NOT LIKE THIS!!!"*Now, they couldn't reverse the effects of the Pheekon machine. The world would remain in a state of flux before it eventually collapsed on itself, killing everyone and everything. Unless, the 'chosen one' fulfilled his duty. Unless, Joner sacrificed himself for the sake of all.*

Joner laughed, and the halls of The Great Castle of the Leaf jingled in mirth.

That day was when everything came crashing down… yet, a new megalith was built in its place, before the moons could cast their glow on his pale ghost.

* * *

The morning crawled along the Merca Lal Mountains; its pale, bony fingers of light defrosting the black night.

A biting wind sang throughout the high valley, escorted by the rattling of the green nut stalks that collected throughout the crevices of the land. Nuvummburtee told his body not to shake, but it disobeyed him, and so did Ya'k-lum, who was busy relieving himself over their camp fire.

"No-one's watching" the huffing boy assured whilst shaking his leg. "We gotta be quick, brother. The morning twilight beckons!"

Nuv wasn't so sure. Ever since they reached the secret entrance yesterday afternoon, he was on edge, with the overwhelming feeling of being scrutinised by the hills themselves. He did not sleep a wink, and was now really feeling it. Tiredness charged at him like a raging bull, but he shook it off as best he could. Slipping his helmet on, he noted that it felt particularly warm this morning, and it lit a symbolic flame in his belly – one that was thankfully free of Ya'k-lum's vile influence.

His smoky breath breaking the heavy air, Nuv looked vigilantly toward the entrance; a small hole barely larger than a door, and still framed by the writhing and luminescent moss. It waited impatiently for them, and he had to admit that this too contributed to his restless night. The spectral, pinkish glare should have been a welcome night light in the brutal wilderness... yet, it bothered him, penetrating his tightly-closed eyes, forcing him to cover under his blanket like a frightened child.

It felt like the ghouls were going to grab me… the sooner we leave this place, the better.

A low humming reverberated in their quavering legs, and echoed from the darkness of their destination. Nuv wasn't sure… but it felt like it had a rhythm?

"D'you hear that?" Ya'k-lum breathed, hands on his hips and eyeing the entrance like a carpenter examining a crooked window. "Come on, we better do this!"

"You're certainly brave this morning" Nuv observed in mild

surprise, as he followed his friend. "You sure you didn't hit your head or something?"

Ya'k-lum looked forward, and then back to his friend. His face was that of someone about to dive into icy waters. "I'm *terrified...* but I'm trying not to think about it. We're here, and there's no backing out now."

He's right.

"You first, Nuv."

Bastard.

Scratching his beard, Nuv shrugged, and strode confidently through the path.

He wasn't sure what to expect, but nothing happened. It was a short corridor, dotted with honeycomb holes in the 'ceiling', which let the sun through in wispy rays. Fat bats could be seen hanging in their slumber, and were marked with cute pink fluffs on their chests. Nuv did not know their breed, but hoped to Qual-nu that they weren't aggressive.

"Wooooww" Ya'k-lum gawked from behind, as he shuffled in after. It was a tight fit with all their bags, but moving was manageable. "I can't believe this was here all this time... like, untouched. We must be the first people in donkey's years, Nuv!"

Nuvummburtee looked at the floor of bat guano that flickered like crystal in the light. He pursed his lips. "Yeah, I think we are."

Aware of the limited time they possessed, the two walked briskly, praying that they wouldn't cause a commotion amidst the winged denizens. Aside from the occasional fluttering and squeak, it was relatively calm, aside from feeling *something* patter on his helm, making Nuv cuss.

"Don't slip" he advised his rear guard.

Ya'k-lum held his breath artfully in response, trying not to inhale any unpleasants.

They quickly made it to the other side, exiting into a strange gorge that was covered in both berrie-berrie moss and a similarly odd, pinkish grass that was dotted with tiny flowers and large grasshoppers. The air smelled of a musky odour which carried throughout the snow-covered peaks, whilst the glowing eyes of wolves darted with agency, their nimble figures barely seen against the rocky terrain. The moons were still quite visible, refusing to give up the sky to Sollus, as the celestial face-off was obscured by jets of steam that hissed from the craggy ground.

Both Nuv and Ya'k just wanted to drop everything and spend the next few hours staring slack-jawed at the beauty that stretched before them, but the clock was ticking.

"Th, the shadows" Ya'k-lum jabbered, poking his mitten at the nearest black mass. "Look!"

Unlike their arduous trial with the moss, following the twilight shade turned out to be a very clear undertaking; albeit one that was even more perilous.

The gloom cast from a dead tree nearby coiled like a snake around them, and once more, the measured, subterranean thumping was heard.

Ya'k-lum made an embarrassing noise as he jumped, before the shade straightened, creating a clear path for them to follow. However, that path seemed to climb near-vertical walls, as well as hover over large drops.

"You can't be serious!" they both gasped in unison.

"Well, it was nice knowing you, Nuvummburtee!" Ya'k-lum trumpeted, as he turned to go back. Nuv grabbed him by his long weave before he could go any further, and pushed him forward.

With unending protestation, Ya'k led them both onward, with Nuv holding his friend's belt firmly, in an amateur attempt at playing mountain climber. Enveloped within the unnatural, wavy umbra, they inched forward as briskly as they dared. Their heavy boots crunched along the frosty grass and dirt, as the leaping insects chirped like birds amidst the readily-approaching dawn. Their laboured breaths sounded in perfect harmony with the occasional drum beat that stalked their frightened forms. Time seemed to crawl to a halt, with the perpetual half-light stubbornly refusing to make way for the new day.

Nuv wondered if he was going mad, and Ya'k's disconcerting silence only helped fuel the suspicions which wore out his thoughts.

"We can't go any further!"

"What?"

After what seemed like a sluggishly long time for such a short distance, they approached a cliff face. Their writhing guide continued upward, completely dismissive of the laws of gravity.

"I said we've come to a dead end" Ya'k grunted, pulling Nuv's cold grip off his rear. "What now? Do we wait for the sun?"

"It's… taking an awfully long time" Nuv observed, looking to the relatively bright eastern sky. "Surely we're not expected to *climb*, right?"

"No way, not with all our stuff" his friend laughed unconvincingly. "N, no. Of course not! Surely not! They can't be *that* sadistic… right?"

Nuv wasn't sure what he meant by 'they', but he craned his neck to look at the mountain's side, and was suddenly hit with a strange hunch. It was a gut feeling that made no sense whatsoever… yet, goosebumps ran up his arms… almost like the excitement from the satisfaction of *knowing* something. His body reacted in a curious way, but his brain was still trying to untangle the message…

How… wait… why am I feeling this?

"Ya'k" he began, tearing his gaze away from the uncompromising hurdle, before grabbing his chum by the shoulders. "I think we can go up! I'm sure of it!"

Worried about the slightly crazed look in Nuv's sharp blue eyes, Ya'k-lum recoiled slightly. "Uhhh, what are you talking about?"

"I've just got this… feeling. It's strange… like, whatever is guiding us… it's speaking directly to me… in my soul… I can't explain it…" Nuvummburtee shook his head in frustration at his inability to properly articulate himself. "Like, the land itself is inside my head."

Ya'k-lum stared without any emotion, as if he was too tired to even put on the *pretence* of being disturbed. "Uh huh. The land."

Tightening his lips in a counter to his friend's passively condescending attitude, Nuv raised his foot, and planted it on the rocky wall.

"Nuv, what are you--

His askance was cut-off by a dog-like yelp, as Ya'k-lum leaped high enough that even the giant grasshoppers looked upon him with envy. Landing on his backside, he stared with astonishment as Nuv began to walk up the cliff, his body completely sideways and unperturbed by any and all laws of reality.

Holy hell, it worked!!!

From his point of view, Nuv's entire world flipped, and *he* was the one that was standing upright, and *Ya'k* was the one jutting from a wall like a quaking bug. "Ya'k!!!" he shouted, excited and ecstatic. "Look!!! I think it's some sort of trick! There's nothing to worry about!"

Smiling like a dope, he held out his hand. "Come on!"

Rising shakily, before hiking up his pants, Ya'k-lum hesitantly grasped Nuv's strong palm, before being hoisted into a strange, new world perspective. He gasped, and his legs wobbled once more. "I'm gonna be sick!" he croaked, before latching on to his partner like a child. "E, everything's sideways! What… what's…"

He threw up.

Dodging the splatter with finesse, Nuv held steadfastly to the disorientated man. "Are you okay?" he asked with concern.

"Urf… yeah, I'm good."

Wiping himself off, he dared himself to glance once more at the topsy-turvy mountains and canyons, and the sky that was now *in front* of him.

"This… this is incredible" he whispered. He then looked to Nuv with a look of concern that genuinely surprised his friend. "Nuv… how… how did you know?"

The helmed man adjusted his rucksack, and looked toward the pale moons that marked their destination at the 'top' of the mountain. It almost seemed like they were walking towards heaven itself.

"I don't know. Let's move."

Trudging towards the wild blue yonder was a far more terrifying task than it initially seemed. As they got further and further, snowfall came towards them, biting their faces and obscuring their vision. On their left, were the remnants of nightfall, as stars blinked away one by one. On their right, Sollus just hung out of view, waiting for them to finish their ascent.

They were sure of it. Time had stood still.

Nuv advised Ya'k to avoid looking upwards or around, lest he turn to a pile of jelly. He did as ordered, but was nevertheless stiff as a board in his strides. He was petrified by the cloudy sphere that stretched all around them, even as the occasional mountain goat bleated its reassurances to him.

Despite the relative ease of following the straight and narrow, their path was still tough, with uneven and bouldered terrain that was loose, which caused debris dislodged by Nuv's feet to 'fall' toward Ya'k, much to his spitting chagrin. The winds picked up as they ascended, hurting their ears and deafening them more and more, as their legs pained from their unforgiving and extraordinary road.

As they got closer to their goal, the trail began to slope downward, and both were relieved to see some semblance of 'walls' emerge, protecting them both from the weather and the intimidating kingdom of the clouds.

They had now developed a lifelong phobia of falling endlessly into the sky.

"It has to end soon. It's gotta!" Ya'k-lum puffed, pathetically drinking the last drop from his now-frozen skin. Nuv stopped dead in his tracks, and he nearly crashed into him. "What? What are you doing?"

"Shhhh" Nuv commanded, raising a fist. "Hear that?"

Amidst the gales, they tried to listen. Their hunting instincts kicked in, and they both crouched – at least, as best as their gear would allow. Ya'k tugged on Nuv's pants, "*What?*" he whispered.

Nuv raised a finger, and pointed. Loud shuffling could be discerned from the howling gusts. Something *heavy* was climbing the mountain beside them, and was just out of their view. Grunting and babbling bounced off the crags, and seemed to get closer, as both men silently drew their weapons. Its heft caused a small rock slide, making it growl angrily, before it shuffled just above the natural facade.

Everything became dead quiet. They knew it was there – and *it* knew *they* were there.

Nuv and Ya'k were ready. Petrified, but ready.

Nothing happened.

'Is it gone?' Ya'k mouthed in silent terror.

They waited a bit longer. They figured that both the crevice they were holed up in, as well as the everlasting shade that drenched them, kept them well-hidden. However, Nuv did not want to take any chances.

So, they waited.

After a bit longer, they were prepared to move, when a *massive* shape jumped between the opening above them. They couldn't see any details, but it was colossal, and sped away with frightening speed and quiet.

They waited again. Only this time they had no choice, for they were rooted to the spot. After a while, they plucked up the courage to continue on, and their insides twisted with the agony that came with facing one's own mortality.

The only time Nuv had been that scared was when he had been attacked by a bloodless boar; goring his legs from underneath him, and overpowering his weak body like it was nothing. Thank Qual-nu that he was not alone that day, but it nevertheless took many arrows to fell the beast. In the end of the scuffle, he had been left with scars that had yet not fully healed to this day – and most likely never will.

It sent his guts plummeting to think what would have happened if such a scenario were to repeat itself, only for the beast to be even *bigger*. Would the two of them be able to take it down, if push came to shove? Mercifully, they would never discover the answer, as the monster had seemed to completely vanish off the face of the mountain.

They both exhaled long and slow, their utter relief nearly making them crumble.

"*What. Was. That?*" Ya'k wheezed, shaking from the frigidity of the changing wind.

Nuv shook his head slowly, and pierced his friend with a gaze that said 'this whole thing was a terrible idea. A terrible, terrible idea.'

* * *

They had reached the top.

The world slowly reorientated itself, as they walked a clear, paved road that curved them over the bluff of the mystifying mesa, before reaching a summit that led to a domed ridge that almost looked hand-carved.

The writhing shadow that acted as their guide slithered away from underneath them, leaving a trail of fiery buds that exploded in the sunlight.

Magama flowers. The final escort.

They decided to take a rest. The wonders they had been exposed to over the last couple of days had almost struck them dumb. Illuminated pink moss. Moving shadows. Time standing still. Walking up walls like a couple of geckos. And now, before their very eyes were red-yellow blossoms that unfolded across the cold, unforgiving rocks like sorcery. On top of all that, the sun was moving again, almost as if it was rushing itself towards noon.

Starting a small fire, they both grounded themselves back to normalcy with a cup of steaming tea.

* * *

As the last remnants of the surviving corsairs gathered around the hearth, they licked their wounds and took stock of whatever remaining supplies that remained. Tensions were high, and Remana tol Dwen wondered if she was about to witness a mutiny.

No such thing had occurred, though screams, shouts and curses were as common as the glassy air itself. They demanded answers.

They all listened to Captain Archie Shorn with puncturing glares, as he passed around a surviving bottle of rum.

"Men" he began, attempting to muster some authority in his voice, "I know. I know you hate my guts right now. I know you blame me for the deaths of our brothers. Of the destruction of the Lyra." His lip quivered at that last statement, almost as if he lost a child. "I blame me, too. I am responsible. As the captain, I can't *not* be. And now, we're in the fight of our lives. A fight to survive."

The mood was tense and still, broken up by the occasional cough or wheeze.

"First of all, before we address more practical matters, I owe you all – and Miss tol Dwen – an explanation. To frame the situation, and to put this all into context. At least, give me this right, before you decide to lynch me."

Murmurs arose, before Badger shushed them. Only the tides refused to remain quiet.

"So, as you all know, we received a contract. One that was almost too good to be true – and, I guess it was. We, the *Zircon Halibut Gang*, had just finished a job smuggling spices and weapons into southern *Tapl-Tapl*, along the archipelagos. It didn't pay as much as we were expecting, and we were starving. Though piracy has been on the decline over the last couple of centuries in the south-western oceans, it seemed like our services did not increase in value for our more wealthy and desperate clientele. You can imagine my surprise then, fellas, when someone called upon us; someone who would change our fortunes drastically."

Taking another swig, he passed the bottle to Remana.

"I know a lot of you weren't privy to the specifics, so I'm letting you know now. When we were shored in Tapl-Tapl, and were about to scope the west, I was visited in a tavern by a man who called himself 'Mr. Telos'. He was an affluent sort, skin smooth and white as pearl, as if he'd never seen a hard day's work in his life. Shock of white hair, and pretty like a broad! He even put *my* good looks to shame, honestly. It was clear he was swimming in it, but it made me curious as to why he had shown up in a dive like the one I was in."

"He approached me for a job. He was adamant that it would not be easy, but it would be worth it. Apparently, he had bad luck in the past with other crews, but had heard of our reputation, and was willing to spend big. The way he talked and carried himself... I thought he was a mage of some description, and my suspicions were proven correct, when he transported us to an amazing hall the likes of which I'd ever seen... it... it was like in the middle of a fairytale, lads. The land of plenty, and all that. The fact that he managed to teleport me like this when Sollus was still in effect, told me that he was *extremely* powerful."

"And you trusted him, cap'n?" a young fellow asked incredulously.

"No" Archie said, squinting. "No, son, I didn't. I never do. But it was obvious this was someone not to be trifled with. Someone higher on the food chain. Of course, I was curious as to why someone like him needed sea dogs like us, but when he told me his story, well, I just couldn't resist, especially since you boys needed food on the table. Desperately. Basically, it was a 'retrieval' mission."

"Kidnapping, you mean" Remana grimaced.

"Yeah" Archie nodded. "What, you think privateering is all harmless fun? It has a dark side, one that pays well."

"Don't lecture *me* on *privateering*" the woman growled. "You rats have been a plague on my home for way too long, and that of so many others."

"A discussion for another time" the haggard captain replied evasively. "Anyway, what Mr. Telos was after was a special group of people. Women, specifically. Women who were allegedly gifted, and represented an immense value to him."

Remana looked both disgusted and stunned, and felt as though she was on the verge of weeping. Archie cut her off before she could wail at him, "Yes. I know how it sounds. At first, I thought it was some perverse thing. Like, he wanted a harem or collection of toys or something… but, he was quick to dispel this notion. He was adamant that his request was for an incredibly important cause, and that many deaths would ensue if these girls weren't found."

Remana felt the colour drain from her skin. "*What?*"

"Yeah, that was my reaction too. He said he had spent years trying to find them. There were four in total, and that they could be located anywhere in the *entire world*. According to him, they were the products of something inhuman… a great evil."

"And you *believed* him?!" the woman spat, irate.

What in the hell is he saying? 'Inhuman'? 'Evil'?

"I believed in the money!" Archie shouted, whilst shrinking away from her righteous wrath. "The four women were known as *Vatn*, *Acasta*, *Vayu* and *Aodh*. One of them, Vayu, had already been found and was under his care. Another, Vatn, had been located once upon a time, but was lost during an attack. The other two had yet to be discovered. Our job was to locate Aodh. You, Remana tol Dwen, are Aodh."

She couldn't hide it any more. Tears poured from her bloodshot eyes; her cheeks embracing their salty heat.

That name.

"How…" she rasped.

How did this mongrel know more about her than she did herself?

"It was not easy" he said softly, taking another self-loathing sip of the rum. "Telos said the four of you came from the Four Sister Isles, but he always thought you'd be hidden in the far corners of Tarinn. Not right *here*…. not right under his nose. We managed to find you after word began to spread about the 'Cerberus Girl', and how she would play with fire like it was nothing. It took us two years."

She looked to her palms. Cracked, pale and splattered with droplets, she suddenly grew disgusted with herself. Her hubris. Her flaunting of her gift. She couldn't understand...

Who... who am I? What *am I?*

"F... fire?" she repeated between sniffles.

Archie nodded. "What made you girls special was your innate connection to the four elements. Fire, earth, wind and water. Of course, I was dicey about the whole thing, but I humoured Telos, and the more he talked... well, the more I became convinced that the words that came out of his mouth weren't the ravings of an eccentric sorcerer. There was a conviction in his words... like, he was trying to *save lives.* I dunno... but in the end, I was drawn in, and I took the job."

Trembling, the woman got to her feet.

"*Saving lives?*" she hissed.

Archie turtled again, fearing another strike. "Yes!"

"Does this look like *saving lives* to you?!" she screamed, waving her arms around.

The others didn't know what to do. They stood, their arms crossed and their heads bowed.

"What about this tower?!" she questioned, pointing to the barely visible monolith that hid the mist. "Was this about *saving lives,* too?!"

Archie adjusted his ratty coat, and sat upright, confident that he would not once again feel her fist to his face. "The Tower of the Gods," he explained, "was – as you already know – where we were supposed to take you. I don't know why, but apparently it's known as one of the 'sacred sites' of Arlmai, and there are three on the island. One of them is in the east, and the other is in the south... and you are the key to 'unlocking' them."

"*Unlocking* them?"

Enough was enough. This was beyond satire at this point. She was caught up in the plot of a deranged magician and a bunch of utterly gullible pirates; and because of their lunacy and stupidity, people were dead. And soon, they would *all* be.

Pursing her blue lips in both pain and ire, Remana shuffled and adjusted her position, so that she was practically touching the waning flames. Staring into the flickering light, she wanted nothing but to dive into the meagre inferno, and merge her very soul with it. She longed to fly amidst the freezing winds of the northern seas, piercing the frost with her unceasing embers like a phoenix of the skies.

The captain sounded as if the very words he spoke pained his tongue. "Yes. I know. Gobbledygook. Stuff from a fanciful imagination. But that's what Telos said. And his words came with coin, which was good enough for me."

"'Sacred sites'" Remana repeated scornfully. "This just gets better and better." Running her warmed palm over her side, she scrunched her face upon feeling the tender muscle.

"You shouldn't be movin' so much" Badger advised, tossing the last of the dry driftwood into the shrinking hearth.

"That's fine, because *none* of us will be!" one of the men snapped, followed by a sharp look from the first mate.

"Okay Archie" the woman said quietly, tying her long red-black hair in a knot in a meagre attempt to keep her hands busy from committing evil deeds. "What else? Is that it? I'm a fire elemental of some description... a pretty magician told you to find me and my 'sisters', on whom the fate of many lives are held... and I have to 'unlock' a trio of 'sacred sites'? Is there more to this utter lunacy?" Her voice cracked, not because she hated and disbelieved the story she was being told – but because, somewhere within the depths of her stomach – it somehow rang true.

Why? Because Captain Archie Shorn said *that* name.

"I'm now inclined to believe it's *not* lunacy" he retorted, waving his hands around like a frantic exile bobbing in shark-infested waters. "*This*" he spat, with a sudden accusing inflection "is all too real. You're not the only one who has suffered here, *Miss tol Dwen!*"

She allowed her face to remain emotionless. Though underneath the skin, it felt like ugly maggots threatened to burst forth. "I see that" she sneered. "My condolences."

A wind howled through the lifeless reef, sending chills up and down every spine. The fog waned ever so slightly, giving more definition to the massive spire that almost seemed to reach over them, like a curious giant. Clouds broiled and darkened, signalling further unpleasantness.

"Neither way" Badger grumbled, "we *knew* what we were gettin' into. There's no time nor place to start arguin' or turnin' on each other. We need to do somethin' *now*. About food and shelter. And maybe a way off."

Archie snorted. "Optimistic, my friend. But you're right. We're *all* not gone yet. Look... Remana--

She glared.

"*Remana*" he repeated defiantly. "We can all fight to the death at a later time. It's clear we've both been played... some more than others."

"What's that supposed to mean?"

"Nothing. I mean... look. Things have obviously changed. Come with me to the tower. Maybe we can find something there."

"Treasure? Or a place to dump my body?"

He stifled a laugh, and realised it came off more unsettling than he intended. "The former, hopefully. But a way out of here would be good too."

* * *

On the plateau, they slept soundly. The heavens cradled them in their sparkling embrace, as the cinders of the expiring flames ascended like will'o wisps into the inky abyss.

Dreams nor nightmares plagued them until the hoary morning light, which once more exposed the burgeoning magama flowers and their road of tangerine. Despite their bloodcurdling run-in with *something* yesterday; they oddly felt at-ease. Even though such a creature would probably have no trouble backtracking and locating the hapless duo, they knew they were protected.

It was an illogical confidence that would have easily gotten an experienced hunter into a lot of trouble in the wilds – never mind two youngsters caught out in the open, in a strange and unfamiliar land. Perhaps it was the sight of fauna that frolicked freely amongst the frosty rocks, eyeing them with curiosity as they went about their lives. The azure mountain goats seemed unperturbed even at this height, their bleats playing back-up vocals to the fluttering of cloud-dwelling dragonflies and the trills of umpteenth species of birds.

Quickly downing some lukewarm porridge with berries and nuts, Nuv and Ya'k-lum made-off on their final stretch of this most unusual journey, as they traipsed along the relatively simple path. 'Relatively' was the key word, as it still was not easy. They were high up now, which brought with it thinning air, as well as more opportunities to plummet to their doom.

Using sturdy walking sticks they managed to scrounge up, they weaved around rugged spires and precipitous chasms, and ducked under gnarled, greying trees that dripped scarce dawn dew on their heads. Poke weed used every opportunity available to cover their pants in pointy cobbler's pegs, causing one of them to pick the other clean, much like monkeys and their fleas. From the exotic lands of Lamunenkée, Ya'k learned, there were primates of all shapes and sizes, from thimble-sized marmosets, to giant gorillas that could uproot entire trees.

"Imagine running into one of those" he drawled, squinting as the sun bounced intensely off the blazing clusters that beckoned them onward. "Imagine if it palmed your noggin. I can't think of a worse fate."

"Hm" Nuv replied in his nonchalant way. His mind wandered towards the horizon, as Sollus peaked between thick, swirling clouds, and phantoms of the moons could scarcely be seen amongst the baby-blue sky. The gentle snowfall halted, allowing them better visibility, which ended at a flat ridge. Could that be Saumen? Surely it shouldn't be much further...

After noon had broken, they had reached an obstacle. A wide, deep obstacle.

Chilled and breathing shallowly, they literally skidded to a halt and attempted to gasp.

Before them stretched a colossal gorge, easily fifty yards across, and at least twice as deep. Mist or steam billowed from the deep darkness below, almost obscuring another unthinkable test of faith.

The path of flowers continued on, in mid-air, all the way to the other side.

Ya'k swore, before cackling in hysteria. Kneeling as close as possible to the edge, Nuv's belly turned as he looked into the abyss, and saw nothing but brief shimmers of liquid in the wavy, pallid tide. Reaching into the ground, he tossed a handful of dirt over the invisible, floret-covered walkway, and was mildly jolted at the sight of it scattering as if it hit solid ground.

Sighing in resignation, he turned to his best friend, smiled and shook his head.

"I hate you" Ya'k-lum scowled.

With almost no hesitation, the luckless lyricist overtook his friend, and planted a boot on the unseen footing. Nuv held him in place, just in case his buddy's confidence sent him falling into the underworld.

"L… like jumping into a cold pool" Ya'k gulped, his eyes bulging. "See? Just gotta go for it, Nuv. Trust in the process…"

"The process" Nuvummburtee groaned, his heart jumping from Ya'k's oafish brazenness, "is not the same as walking head-first into danger like a dope!"

"Oh, it's okay when *you* do it" he countered, squirming in Nuv's vice-like grip. "Look! It's fine! How else are we gonna pass, huh?"

Nuv knew Ya'k-lum was right. It was obvious what they needed to do. Still, he was angry at his recklessness – perhaps unreasonably so. Maybe Ya'k was tired and wanted to go home, and his fatigue chipped away at his worried temperament, which resulted in a new-found bravery. Or was he trying to prove something to Nuv?

Nah, I'm not that egotistical.

Sucking air through his teeth, Nuv peered over Ya'k's shoulder, and saw his hoof planted firmly against nothing. Reluctantly letting him loose, he then shuffled lamely (but ever-so necessarily) until he was peering over the edge once more. He planted a palm next to Ya'k's shaky leg, and pushed.

"I can't believe it… it feels so strange! Like, it's nothing. Neither warm nor cold. The closest I can describe is like thick glass!" Brushing the dirt around even further, he estimated that the walkway was about six feet across. He reached for a magama, and picked it. It faded to ghostly grey almost instantly, and he let it go.

"A test of faith" Ya'k-lum proclaimed, as he assuredly stepped his other foot outward, so that he was now standing in mid-air. "I'm lucky I can't see the bottom, because if I could, I think I would be… done."

Nuv shook his head in marvel.

"Nuv?"

"Yeah?"

"I think I was a tad too brave. I can't bloody move. Hold my hand."

Nuvummburtee sighed again.

* * *

Merca lal, oh Merca lal
> *Pearls of teeth, biting the heavens*
> *Gnawing the Ring*
> *Biting cold to the root, and under that, under under so deep, is broiling and bubbling*
> *Life between these two worlds, and the twosome and their two worlds*
> *Amidst the crunching, calling and creaking*
> *Following the pink; the motherly sprouts guiding them from the womb and into the devil's pitchfork*
> *The premature life, the fledgling light, dim and wavy*
> *Guided by the dark, the serpent, whispering sweet nothings*
> *Merca lal, oh Merca lal*
> *Ascending amongst the pearls of teeth, biting the heavens*

Black on the left, white on the right
Jewels above, and the gnawed Ring
Life between these two worlds, and the twosome and their two worlds
Emergence! Lo! Fire! Awaken! Life is real, and it smells of flowers!
The nectar of living, of faith and of conviction.
All the way to the old one
Merca lal, oh Merca lal
Sinking down, under the pearls of teeth, biting the heavens

* * *

Their feet were swollen and sore, and their joints ached. Weary in both body and soul, they descended the ancient stairs, their laden forms illuminated by braziers of red flame, making their shadows dance along the carved stone walls that ran with rich veins of silver that swirled; tricking their heavy lids with moving images of foxes and elk that ran alongside them.

Strange wooden charms clonked and clacked with gusts of both cold and hot air, altering the tonal pitch of the cave with a melodious aria that heralded their arrival.

Skins of every conceivable shade and size lined the entrance to a large chamber, and wafting from it was a cured, smoky stench that sizzled their wet eyes, and was made all the more intense by the pungency of herbs that unexpectedly made their bellies growl with an audible intensity.

"It never fails" laughed the ancient being that sat cross-legged before them. His skin was as black as ebony, and his massive beard covered most of his body, its tangled form curling around him many times over, as it billowed with countless small jets of exhaust; much like chimneys from a tiny city.

His eyes were large, inflamed and terrifying, and seemed almost crazed. His face looked like that of a frostbitten corpse.

"Welcome, you two. I am Saumen."

CHAPTER V

How did it come to this?

He sat there.

Within the hallowed halls of Gen's temple, all was quiet. With a caginess that permeated their sublime movements, fireflies roamed the small chapel. Their rainbow emanations dimmed shyly, as if they still mourned the chaos and devastation that blighted their small town not too long ago.

Effigies of revered figures looked on with a sombre air, as the light of large candles flickered thanks to a ghostly breeze.

Was it the spirits of Gen's departed? He didn't know.

He didn't know much any more. He thought he was finally getting a hold of his twisted world – that the answers were at last becoming clear.

But this… *this* shattered everything.

It lay there, like the corpse of some sort of martyr. Shafts of soft jade moonlight filtered through the shattered sky roof, before bathing the figure in its incandescent glow.

Though it was shrouded by a dirty blanket, it still seemed to mock him with its very existence.

After all, it was the body of Kwennsefulass.

At least... that's what he thought. But... *he* was Kwennsefulass. Wasn't he?

Yes, of course he was. His own necklace said so. The word was right there, engraved into the emerald.

So... then who was laying here before him?

He didn't know what was more distressing; the fact that this man was in every way his equal – or that the body wasn't one of flesh and blood.

"You need to get some sleep."

It was Ilod. The elderly Numanta mage who was master of the temple. Though defiled by the same dark shadows that pillaged the town and stole its children, Gen's church still lived. It was a little worse for wear, but after some maintenance and a holy cleansing by the few that remained in the town, it was at least a little closer to resembling its original splendour. Though the Pheekonshenee were not gods – the Numanta still revered them. An ancient race who mastered technology and spirituality, it was these people who served as the foundation of the world today – and *not* the gods – as the other mage classes believed. Of course, this has historically caused friction between the white-robed Numanta and the other religious colours, but today, they live in relative harmony. On the island of Shali, the Pheekons were the most revered of the 'old ones', along with *Lamun* – the Goddess of Reincarnation and deity of the blue *Solluskane* magi.

In ages past, further conflict arose from the spread of the monotheistic worship of *Veronususs* of the *Pisistratïe* Grey Robes from the north, clashing with the native beliefs. That was a long time ago, however, and all religions now co-existed in peace.

"I can't sleep" Kwenn answered quietly. He rested his chin on his closed fists, as he stared intently at his motionless doppelganger.

Ilod shook his head sadly, and placed a warm hand on Kwenn's shoulder. "Well try then. Or go outside for some fresh air."

Kwenn looked up at the older man's face. His dark skin gave away his native background of the Four Sister Isles, and his trimmed beard was as white as snow. What always took Kwenn by surprise were Ilod's bright blue eyes – eyes that seemed ageless and abyssal in their intensity. No doubt they have seen a lot of astonishing things in their lifetime.

He didn't answer. Looking back at the cadaver, Kwenn mindlessly stroked his necklace. This time, it provided no warm reassurance.

Folding his arms into his mink robes, Ilod sighed and began to wander around the room, before stopping at a statue of a woman. Half of her head was smashed to bits, but her slender form was otherwise intact. In one hand she held a small book, whilst in the other, she clasped a scroll. The two items represented a juxtaposition between the authoritative rule-of-thumb (the scroll), and the bountiful, untamed frontier (the book), whilst the woman was the physical embodiment of the motherly energy that permeated society – a supportive matriarch, or a stifling dream-crusher – depending on one's view.

"There are two sides to every story" Ilod proclaimed as he sadly looked upon the carving. "Two faces on every coin. Black and white. In this day and age, it's a rule that many have forgotten."

Kwenn turned his head slightly. "What do you mean?"

"There is an old saying in our order; 'the world is built upon two truths'. There is one's truth... and then there is the other."

The Numanta smiled without emotion, and directed his azure gaze toward the shrouded body. "Without going into too much detail, it basically means that you should never be constrained by your own truth... that you should always look beyond your own preconceptions."

Kwenn was silent.

Ilod continued, "What I am saying is that this... *situation*... the truth may not be what you think it is."

"What I 'think' it is?" Kwenn replied in an irritated tone. "Please Ilod, enlighten me... what do I think *this* is? Because I would damn sure like to know!"

Ilod simply looked at him coolly. "I think you *do* know, Kwenn. So tell me."

He didn't expect that. A brief thought passed through his head; that Ilod was playing with him. The mage after all had somewhat of a twisted sense of humour at times…

"I think" Kwenn began with a flustered tone, "I think…"

He didn't know what to say.

What *could* he say? So much had happened… the attacks on Gen, Gimlum and Henra. The taking of Jeleenn and the children. Joner.

Joner…

The child of Jugo – and Jeleenn's brother. It was he who was the key to all of this, Kwenn pretty much knew that now. What Jugo and Ilod had told him was almost beyond belief…

Jugo had heard enough. He strode to the wizard, and stuck the tip of his blade against the leering old man's forehead.

His voice trembled. "Don't you dare say that! Tell me! How do I stop this?! How do I save Tarinn?!"

Uilosees smiled. "You know."

With blinding quickness, he grasped Jugo's blade, and thrust it into his own heart.

With a cry of despair, Jugo watched helplessly as the wizard fell. Slain by his own hand.

Trebor caught the old man in his arms, but it was too late. Beams of holy energy escaped from Uilosees' body, before his corpse crumbled into dust that fell through Trebor's fingers.

Just like that, it was over. The ruling Wizards were all gone.

"NO!!!" Jugo screamed, as he hopelessly ran his hands through the grey ash. "Not like this!!! NOT LIKE THIS!!!"

Now, they couldn't reverse the effects of the Pheekon machine. The world would remain in a state of flux before it eventually collapsed on itself, killing everyone and everything.

Unless, the 'chosen one' fulfilled his duty.

Unless, Joner sacrificed himself for the sake of all.

Joner; the little boy that had committed the sin of simply being born. He was the profane offspring between the human and the invisible. Kwenn wasn't given the entire story, but Joner's mother was supposedly a being of the faerie – a being known as Queen Bean Si.

He could scarcely believe it. But that wasn't all – there was also Oviinia Trundle, the woman who was incredibly bound to Kwenn's fate. Why? She was just a marine biologist, who loved the creatures of the deep blue. Yet, like him, she was plucked by the cruel hands of destiny; and it was that destiny that led the spirit of the young boy Rayn toward her, as well as acting as a channel for Kwenn's memory reclamation.

Who is she?

* * *

The body that was hauled aboard the *Sterlionic Fortress of Wonderment* was Kwenn's equal.

It had the same visage. The same build. Yet, it had no scar. Nor did it possess an emerald necklace which provided some semblance of identity.

This doppelganger shook Kwenn's very foundations… yet still, that was not the most disturbing thing about it.

Because this was not a body of flesh and bone. It was one of…

Well, Kwenn was still trying to figure that one out.

It wasn't *real*. From what the enigmatic merchant Lord Sterlio could ascertain, the corpse was one of metal and material. Of gears and whirring cogs.

It was an automaton. A toy. A puppet.

Kwenn couldn't help but laugh. It was the kind of chuckle that belied the sheer unbelieving of an absurd situation – a situation that seems like it was designed by some sick and sadistic god.

It was the kind of chuckle that came from fear.

Still, if there was one thing Kwenn had learned over the last few weeks, it would be dealing with fear. He thought of everything he had been through; the tribulations and sufferings he endured at the hands of villains like Hekor and Wilko... not to mention his own personal demons.

So, this is just yet another thing to add to the woeful pile, Kwenn thought with grim casualness.

Still, he wasn't the only one going through a tough time. He constantly had to remind himself that there were many other people who had suffered tremendously.

He cast his gaze onto the shrouded body again, and shuddered. He had almost forgotten the presence of the Numanta mage who stood over his shoulder.

"So tell me" Ilod once again asked, "what do you think is *happening* here?"

Kwenn sighed. He wasn't in the mood to be put under... a microscope. Is that what Oviinia called them?

Still, he relented. "I think... I think I came from something twisted. I know that now. I... I'm an abomination."

Ilod shook his head sadly. "Really? How so?"

Tears suddenly welled-up in Kwenn's eyes. "Come on! Isn't it obvious by now? Hekor, Joner... *everything*! I was obviously a part of all of this – but something went wrong! I can just... *feel* it. I feel like... like I shouldn't have existed in the first place!"

His heart pounded now, and saying it all out aloud upset him a lot more than he thought it would. His voice cracked, and he covered his face in slight embarrassment.

The magi tilted his head slightly, seemingly unmoved by Kwenn's emotions. "Okay then. So what do you *know*?"

This again...

"What do you *mean*, Ilod?"

The elder man began to stroll around the hall, obviously anticipating such a response. "What do you *think* I mean?"

Kwenn suddenly found himself getting angry, and now simply wanted to go back to bed. This was the wrong hour for deep philosophical discussions...

"I'm tired" he said abruptly, before wiping his face and rising to his feet. "I'll tell you in the morning."

Ilod breathed and smiled warmly, resigned to the fact that he would not get any more out of his charge this night.

However, Kwenn paused in the small entryway of the hallway. He did not turn.

"I know" he said, with a little more strength in his tone, "that no-one is going to stop me from making things right."

Ilod nodded, apparently satisfied. "Then *that's* the truth you need to hold on to."

Kwenn went to bed.

* * *

The twin suns began to glow over the port town of Gen.

Solenir; The White Flame of Emotion, and Sollik; The Blood Sight of Redemption bathed the wounded settlement with their incandescent light, as its remaining denizens emerged from their quiet houses for yet another day of living.

Gen wasn't exactly a thriving metropolis before the attack – but with the town's children now gone, and many of the townspeople killed by Hekor's evil forces – the township was now a mere shadow of its former self. Still, things were slowly getting back to normalcy, and there was still some hope that the kids would eventually come back home.

Despite the wicked fires, greenery began to thrive once more, which did wonders for the spirits of the people. It also helped knowing that they were not alone in this struggle, as the towns of Gimlum and Henra were also going through a tough time. After all, all three places shared a special connection.

Gen was the settlement that protected Ras Temple, one of the three 'sacred sites' that existed on the Isle of Shali. As such, there was one time of the year when the town was transformed into a bustling hive of activity; and that was when pilgrims (and the merchants that followed them) made the journey to Shali in order to further their enlightenment, and it was known as the Festival of Life. Whether that would be a monk on a journey of self-discovery or an apprentice mage looking to further their rank, the Four Sister Isles was the place to be.

All this happened during the annual 'Blinking of the Eyes', wherein the solar transition marked the movement of Tarinn away from the 'order' of the gods (Solenir and Sollik), toward the 'chaos' of nature (Sollus; The Fiery Orb of Fertility).

Whether by coincidence or not, Kwenn had 'awoken' and found Gen during the waning hours of this revered phase. At the time, he didn't really notice the changing of the suns, as the light they cast was more or less the same, regardless of the colour. It genuinely shocked him when Jeleenn pointed it out to him for the first time.

'I never notice the little things' he would often tell her sardonically.

He hoped he would get to tell her again.

The Queezy Fennick Inn was still a quiet monument to the hustle and bustle of that celebrated time, as well as standing as the shrine of Gen's last stand against those atrocious fiends. The building's windows were no longer boarded, but the interior was still cold and quiet with the nameless sadness that still crept along the earthy walls. Still, a warm energy slowly came back to the old structure, thanks to the return of its owner; Jugo Ironmonger.

The grizzled innkeeper was still understandably withdrawn due to the disappearance of his daughter, but he was still protectively caring for his fellow Genites, not to mention noticeably more open toward Kwenn.

The man was once a great hero, who had to make the ultimate sacrifice in order to save Tarinn. Going through something like that must have weighed heavily on his mind every day since, and Ilod told Kwenn that Jugo fled back to his home of Shali in a desperate attempt to escape his past, taking his little daughter and starting anew in the town of Gen. Soon after, the Numanta followed suit, believing that it was his destiny to go and find his friend. Still, the innkeeper never forgot his old life, and constructed a simple grave in remembrance for his son, Joner.

Officially, the inn was open for business once more, but the only people staying at the establishment were a couple of merchants who generously offered their help to get the townsfolk back on their feet. One of these merchants was Lord Sterlio, who was more than happy to help his old friends. It was the least he could do, after the unpleasantness with Wilko and the pirates.

Likewise, the port was mostly devoid of activity. The grey waves slowly slushed against the wooden piers, as the remaining vessels slowly bobbed in synch with the gulls that squawked overhead. It was a peaceful site, especially for Kwenn and Oviinia, who sat at the edge of a dock while eating some lunch.

After returning to Gen, the group talked at length about what to do next. It was generally seen that the best course of action would be to journey toward the Magick Shrine, as Kwenn felt he needed to do. Little by little, his memory was coming back to him, and he was convinced that the mysterious sacred site was the final piece of this great puzzle. Everyone was in support of this move – however, much debate had arisen as to *how* they would get there.

The shrine itself was located south-west off Shali's shores, and there were only two visible ways of getting there. One was to climb the treacherous Conquest Mountains, which was the 'official' way of getting there. The second was to simply sail there, and risk the ire of the 'Lethe Scud'; a brain-rattling fog that turned sailors around back where they came from.

Neither option sounded particularly enticing.

"Maybe the fog will make way for us?" Oviinia ventured, as she tossed a pear core in the water.

Kwenn looked at her disapprovingly. "I don't know. I guess it's possible. If I'm meant to go there, then there obviously has to be *some* way in."

"There is" the bespectacled woman corrected him, "it just requires the absence of the fear of heights…" She thought for a moment, and shivered, "… and the fear of falling onto jagged rocks."

Kwenn shook his head. "Surely climbing those mountains can't be *that* hard, can it?"

Oviinia sighed wistfully. "Don't ask me. I'm a water person. *Not* a mountain person."

"Jugo and Ilod must know."

She shrugged. "I guess… though wouldn't Sterlio have some sort of black magic to counter this 'Lethe' thing? If we used his boat…"

Kwenn found himself smirking. "You just want to use his boat to find more strange fish. Go on, admit it."

The biologist laughed. "Yeah… well, you got me. I couldn't care less what everyone else wants to do; I just want to get back on that vessel!"

Kwenn scratched his scalp. "Heh, I can't blame you. That Lord Sterlio is something else. To tell the truth, I'm a little scared of him."

He wasn't lying.

Still, as frightening as the merchant may seem – he definitely did seem to have plenty of tricks up his sleeves. Maybe Oviinia was right? Maybe they *should* just sail on through?

"Don't worry Kwenn, I am too."

His heart almost leaped from his shirt. Puul had sneaked up on him.

Oviinia was also startled. "Don't *do* that!"

The young Numanta bowed his head slightly, but didn't bother to hide his smile. "Apologies. I just needed to get a breath of fresh air. Cleaning that temple is taking a lot out of me."

He gingerly folded his robes, and sat beside Oviinia.

"Not used to housework, eh?" She teased.

He simply bobbed his head. It was the bob that said 'no, that's not it, but whatever'.

"Where's Panin?" Kwenn asked.

"He's at the barracks… there… there aren't a lot of them left."

Kwenn understood. Almost all of the town guardsmen were now gone, with only Panin and one other older man left. The man – a mentor of Panin's – took it upon himself to help rebuild Gen. It was said that even mayor Deret leaned on him for moral support. Gen was all they ever knew, and they'd be damned if they were going to let it die on their watch.

"He puts on a brave face, but Panin is… he's hurting. Especially now that Jeleenn is gone…" Puul quickly corrected himself, "I mean… she's not *gone*. We'll get her back. And everyone else."

They were silent then, as thoughts wandered back toward the gravity of the whole situation. It was like a magnetic pull; a constant struggle to avoid sinking into despair and melancholy. Oviinia tried to steer the subject into more pleasant territory. "So you and Jeleenn have been friends since childhood, huh?"

Puul nodded. "Yes. Our parents – Panin and I – they died when we were young. Ilod took me in, and Lumiin of the guard began to train Panin. Apparently, I was always adept with magic; even as an infant, I would glow in order to keep the darkness away and to protect my brother from the monsters."

The woman laughed, but in an affectionate way. "Puul the glowing baby!"

The Numanta closed his eyes, and bowed his head. "I was quite the attraction, apparently." He began to chuckle, too.

"Did…did Jeleenn ever talk much about Joner?" Kwenn asked hesitantly.

Puul shrugged. "Not really. Panin and I didn't even know he existed until we were in our teens, but that memorial has always been there. Panin and I, we were two of the few to have seen it. She trusted us, like we trusted her. We basically *were* her brothers. Still, she remembered him vividly, despite only being so small when he perished."

There was an awkward silence after that, with Kwenn silently contemplating – as he was wont to do. He then asked, "The Magick Shrine Puul. How do you think we should go about this?"

The magi stared blankly, before wiping the ocean spittle off his face. "If mayor Fultyne was still with us, I would have suggested seeing him. His family, after all, was chosen to protect the shrine… but now that he and his family are gone… who else could possibly know the secrets to the sacred sites? Deret is the only one left – and he is not concerned with anything else besides Ras Temple."

Kwenn rubbed his temples. Why did everything have to be so *complicated*?

"What about Gimlum?"

"Huh?" Kwenn turned to Oviinia.

"Gimlum." She repeated. "The Tilth was one of the sacred sites… yet, you never set foot anywhere near there. *I* brought its secrets to *you*."

Kwenn scratched his nose. "Uh huh."

"Well, how come?" She rose to her feet now, as if to emphasise the importance of her message. "The same with Ras Temple. It was *me* that channelled that power. *Me. Why*?"

Sitting down and staring up at her, Kwenn looked very much like a wide-eyed child who was unceremoniously accused of misbehaving. "Um… I don't know…"

She crossed her arms. "Well, for whatever reason, the gods have decided to 'bless' me with this gift, so there has to be a reason, right? *I* was the one that survived Gimlum, and *I* was the one that Rayn chose to speak to. So, what if *you* aren't supposed to recover your memories, Kwenn? What if that's what *I'm* supposed to do, while you are tasked with doing something *else*?"

Now Kwenn got to his own feet. "I… I don't know. What else *am* I supposed to do? Are you suggesting that you should go to the Magick Shrine yourself?"

"Maybe. Why else am I tasked with being the errand girl? What's the point of me coming along with you when you get your mail? To make sure the address is verified? *Come on…*"

Now Puul jumped up. He stuck his finger in the air and began twirling it, as if he was brewing an idea. "So what you're saying, Oviinia, is that Kwenn is supposed to be doing something else? Something else that is of equally high priority?"

Kwenn echoed the Numanta's thoughts. "Yeah, is that it?"

Oviinia took off her glasses and shot the both of them an exasperated look. "Look. Kwenn's memory was fragmented for a reason. And that reason is usually something to do with great danger – and great importance. Kwenn knows something – and that *something* is valuable enough to be hidden in such a convoluted way."

She looked straight into his eyes. "Valuable enough to fall into the wrong hands."

"Like Hekor" Kwenn finished. "But… when we met. He didn't recognise me. He had no idea who I was."

"Wait" Puul chimed in, "you think that's why Gimlum, Gen and Henra were attacked? Because they were looking for Kwenn's memories? Then why did they take the children?"

"I don't know, Puul. I'm just connecting the dots, like you do. Filling in the blank spaces. Maybe I'm way off base."

Kwenn thoughtfully rubbed his chin. *No Oviinia, you're not. It all fits.*

He gripped his necklace, and closed his eyes. *Is that really why they killed so many people? Just for my memories?*

And what about that fake body? My body? Where does that come into this?

Oviinia seemingly read his mind. She spoke softly, as if she was afraid of upsetting him. "And Kwenn. You're supposed to be some sort of duplicate of Joner. And now we have a corpse that is a duplicate of *you.*"

Kwenn caught his breath. "I know."

And my mother… I can feel her spirit calling to me. But, I can't recall her! I can't remember who she is!

Puul looked at both of his friends. He was the first one to say it aloud.

"I think Joner is still alive."

* * *

Jugo Ironmonger wiped the counter with his *rutra*-soaked cloth, and slowly savoured the musky aroma that emanated from the ginger wood polish. It smelled of old times – good times. Of times that would return, once he was done with restoring his home.

He wondered if Ilod felt the same way, as the Numanta was similarly busy with his church. As opposite as they seemed on the surface, the two men were remarkably alike. They shared the same values, the same world views, and the same family. Sure, they had their differences, but really, they were kindred souls. Jugo often thought – and not without a shred of gratitude – how amazing it was that he and his friend were still close, even after they had lost so many other companions over the years.

Dian, for one…

He should have been surprised when the kids told him that Joner was still alive. He should have cursed, bellowed and bodily thrown them out of his inn. He would have been right in doing so, too. Imagine *saying* something like that to a parent! That their dead child was still alive!

But, he didn't.

He didn't, because he knew. Deep down, he always knew; and seeing Kwenn for the first time simply made that belief into a chilling reality. He thought that finally admitting it would lift a heavy burden off his shoulders, but it was in fact quite the opposite. He felt more weighed down than ever before, with a cold pit in his stomach that only came with a hideous acceptance of committing a ghastly crime.

And no matter how much he tried to justify it, Jugo had done exactly that.

A few ornate lamps shimmered warmly, as the wide windows of the front entrance allowed the healing rays of the suns to fill the main room with light. Dust particles danced much like the fireflies of the night, and the ornate artwork that covered the wall seemed to possess a renewed energy.

There was still a fair bit of work to do, though. The thought of those vile monsters touching his building was almost too much for Jugo to handle, and it seemed as though no amount of scrubbing and polishing would ever remove the taint of their demonic fingertips.

Still, he could only do what he could.

He was overjoyed that his two helping hands – Truil and Wedani – were still here with him. They protected the Queezy Fennick in his absence, and were like family to him. Truil was Wedani's mother, and Wedani herself was Jeleenn's best friend. After Truil's husband was killed in the attack, she and Jugo both saw the inn as a haven from the losses they had endured.

"Jugo" Truil said softly as she placed a hand on his broad shoulder, "stop wiping that counter. Say something."

He sighed, and did what she said.

"What do you want me to say, Truil?"

"I know this… all of this has been painful. God knows I know. But you need to face this head on. We all do. We can't keep on acting like this… like nothing has changed. It has changed, Jugo. And it will *keep* changing until this all ends."

Jugo pursed his lips, and put his hands on his hips. He felt tears welling up from behind his eyes, but stopped them before they materialised.

"I thought it *did* end. For so many years, I tried to come to terms with that. God, I tried so damn hard, Truil. You know that."

"We're *all* coming to terms with our tragedies. You must remember that! You need to face this, not just for yourself, but for *all* of us."

She was right.

We really are all in the same boat, aren't we?

He clasped her hand into his own, and smiled unhappily.

It was time to call a meeting.

* * *

Kwenn looked around the Queezy Fennick.

Aside from the lack of patrons, it was just like the day he had first arrived here. Once a ragged stranger in a peculiar town, he marvelled at how far he had come; and how much things had changed since Jeleenn had generously handed him that first bowl of beef stew.

Night had arrived, and the curtains were drawn in an attempt to block the prying eyes of the nine moons. Lamps lit the bar with a homely luminosity, though Lord Sterlio had taken it upon himself to donate a couple of strange globes that radiated with "a light that changes and adapts depending on the accumulated energy of a room." It was beyond Kwenn's understanding on how they worked – but they nevertheless did emit a sombre auburn. Puul fancied it as a 'flame of determination', which settled Kwenn just fine.

Aside from the young magi and the weird merchant, joining him were Panin, Oviinia, Jugo, Ilod and Mayor Deret. It was all very hush-hush, as Jugo reasoned that there was always a chance of being watched by unwelcome eyes.

A wise assumption.

Considering what happened earlier on during the day, he was surprised to see Jugo so calm. No… calm wasn't the right word. It was more like… professional. As if a militaristic spirit had possessed the innkeeper, and ordered him to get business *done*. No more emotions and no more crying.

It was an attitude that spread like wildfire between all of them, and Kwenn felt rejuvenated, and he felt his morale increase a thousand fold. Everyone agreed with this sentiment, as hearts began to burn with a fortitude that had not been felt in a long, long time.

Kwenn was the one who told Jugo about Joner, and he felt this was the turning point for the grizzled man. After all, one can only feel helpless for so long, before saying *enough is enough*.

Ilod was first to speak, and he was *straight* to the point.

"So. Magick Shrine. This is where we are going, yes?"

He looked to Kwenn and Oviinia, who both nodded.

"At least, that's where *I* definitely need to go" the woman clarified.

Kwenn still wasn't sure. Oviinia felt that he needed to go somewhere else, to deal with more pressing matters. But, where? What? There was nothing he could think of!

"And you believe you should go alone?" Ilod quizzed.

She looked at Kwenn apologetically. "Well, not literally. But I just can't shake this nagging feeling about the redundancy of having Kwenn *and* myself needing to go to the same spot."

She did have a point there. Why *was* Oviinia needed to help Kwenn reclaim his memories? Why couldn't Kwenn just do it himself?

Panin leaned forward with intent. "Maybe Kwenn needs to find Hekor."

No one spoke. That name bought a chill down everyone's spine.

Puul chimed in, "Well, there is Camo Temple, up north. That was one of our options, remember? We still haven't heard from Trebor, or indeed *anyone* from that region."

Ilod nodded. "Yes... that is a good idea. We have no clue about the other islands, too. For all we know, they could have been attacked as well."

"Are there any other sacred sites on those islands?" Kwenn asked.

"Yes" Ilod replied with a hint of dread. "There are."

"Which only strengthens my argument" Oviinia declared. "Why on earth would they *not* attack those places?"

Jugo raised his eyebrows at her. "So, what, you think all this isn't restricted to Shali?"

She seemed to mull it over in her mind, before replying with a firm "yes".

"I hate to ask this" Puul challenged, "but why do you think so?"

Oviinia seemed to smile slightly. She was aware that she and Puul had developed some sort of fledgling 'intellectual' rivalry.

"Because, we can't afford to *not* think it so. That's why. Either way, I think Kwenn should head north."

"Do I get a say in this?" Kwenn asked indignantly.

Oviinia winked at him. "No."

Well, fair enough.

"If you believe this to be the best course of action" Ilod inquired as he folded his arms into his robes, "then how do you think you will be able to make it to the shrine? Because if you are going to climb those mountains, then I am afraid I am out."

Oviinia kept smiling, before putting her arm around Lord Sterlio.

"What, me?" Sterlio stuttered, as his one good eye bulged. "I have never attempted to brave the terribleness of the Lethe Scud, milady! And for good reason!"

She wasn't convinced. "Come *on*. You mean to tell me that there's nothing in your big bag of tricks? Somehow, I don't believe it."

Ilod's eyebrows quirked slightly, as if he knew the woman had a point.

Jugo chuckled too, as if he also agreed with the strong-headed scientist. "I don't either. C'mon Sterlio, I *know* you can get to the shrine with ease. Don't be a chicken, mate."

The merchant hissed, which made Kwenn's insides jolt a little.

"*Fine*" Sterlio sulked through gritted teeth. "Once again, *I* have to come to the rescue. Peer pressure strikes again!" He placed his effeminate hand on his forehead in melodramatic fashion, almost like he was threatening to faint right then and there.

Kwenn looked to Oviinia, "Are you *sure* you want to do this?"

Was *he* sure, himself?

"Yeah" she reacted simply. "Call it a gut feeling, or whatever. But Kwenn, if the worst happens… at least one of us will still be alive."

That surprised him.

"What? None of us will die, Oviinia. That's simply not an option."

Was she scared? Was she trying to protect him? Or was it both?

"The boy's right" Deret said as he firmly clomped his ale on a table. "*Too many* have perished already. If these fiends really *are* after even more sacred sites, then I'll be damned if they even reach the shores of our neighbours. They tried to desecrate *my* family's legacy; I'm not letting that happen to anyone else. They may have gotten Fultyne and Yuligh, but they didn't get *me*."

Kwenn had a feeling that the mayor had started drinking earlier.

"What do you propose?" Jugo asked.

Deret sighed. "I won't pretend that I can do much. But I *can* spread the message about those monsters. Thankfully, I have already done so quite a few days ago. I sent one of my very good friends – a fisherman named Chundra – on an urgent mission to notify the authorities in Miiri. With him, I entrusted my most precious possession... the seal of my family. I hope he made it in one piece..."

The innkeeper approved. "Knowing Chundra, he probably completed his task *and* sampled the local delights. The guy knows what he's doing, always. You did the right thing, Deret."

"Isn't that the cur who once tried to sink my Fortress...?" Sterlio mumbled to no one.

"Good" Ilod nodded, ignoring his friend. "So Kwenn, do you agree with all of this? Will you head to Camo Temple up north?"

Kwenn didn't want to overthink it. He was tired of weighing every possibility and worrying endlessly about what ifs – it was time to take some action.

He breathed deeply, and took in the musky aroma of the inn. "Seems like everyone's made up their mind. If Oviinia insists... then yes, I'll go to Camo Temple."

He paused. "But..."

There was still the matter of that...*thing* that still lay within the church.

Kwenn struggled to mention the subject, but nonetheless managed to cough it up. "The body in Ilod's temple. What do we do with it?"

It was at this point where glances wandered, and feet shuffled. It seemed like no one wanted to speak up. Finally, Sterlio broke the silence.

"I have a proposition."

CHAPTER VI

Its arms lay across its chest in peace.

No-one dared to speak too loudly, nor disturb the perfect serenity that was once again shrouded in the jade light of Suuran, Tupeenn and Lotup. Their presence in the starry sky even overwhelmed the great ring of Tarinn this night, as the fledgling greenery around Gen danced in the windless dark.

Everyone now stood in solemnity, as Lord Sterlio leaned over the faux Kwenn corpse in fascination. Every once in a while, he would tap his black eye with a *clink*, before muttering to himself. Around the body, the merchant's 'family' was placed delicately; that is, the grotesque shrunken heads with various knick-knacks jammed into their eye sockets.

After what happened with Wilko, Kwenn knew very well that these little shrivelled skulls were anything but dead; he still had nightmares about the way they flew in the air as they devoured the twisted Henran sergeant.

Now though, they were as still as… well, death.

Sterlio had also asked Puul for the Pheekon artefact that he had purchased from him earlier, its flawless platinum glinting astonishingly within the moonlight. Puul ascertained that it somehow roused the spirits of the dead, which resulted in their communication of the slain monks of Ras Temple.

For such an incredible object, Kwenn was baffled as to why Sterlio parted with it. However, all eventually became clear when the merchant had performed a double-turn by betraying Wilko. He saved them all by thinking ahead.

Other than cash, it seemed like Lord Sterlio lived for the dead.

Maybe the dead help *him make money?*

"Are you sure this'll work, Sterlio?" Jugo whispered. It can't have been easy for him, seeing *two* Joner impostors – particularly one that looked like the product of some perverted doll-maker.

Because that's what it is. A doll.

Initially, Ilod wanted to pull it apart; to see what was *inside*. But whether out of respect to Kwenn – or for some other reason – he decided to delay such a move.

That was probably wise. Kwenn doubted he would have been able to handle such a sight, let alone Jugo.

"Truthfully, I don't know" the merchant admitted, "but if there *is* a way, then this is it! Stand back, all of you."

They all did as commanded, as he placed the Pheekon artefact onto a stool, before tapping his fake eye again.

Amazingly, a small beam of light then shot out of his face, before making contact with the book-shaped object.

Puul gasped, before looking to Ilod. The elder Numanta simply nodded.

What on earth?

The artefact began to illuminate with strange symbols, before it started to pulsate. Smiling, Sterlio then picked it up, before waving it over the corpse.

"Ahhahaha… I thought so" he chuckled in mirth.

"What?" Oviinia breathed in awe.

"Our fake friend here… it seems as though he has a basis in Pheekonshenee technology." Sterlio concurred with himself, before carefully putting the artefact back down. His gaze lingered on it a moment longer, before he forwarded his attention to the main attraction.

"I must warn you all" he said solemnly, as the mirror-white relic continued to thump, "this may be distressing. I'm telling you all now, yes."

Jugo approved. "Go ahead, Sterlio."

Kwenn began to sweat. He went to wipe his brow, before realising that Oviinia was clutching his hand tightly. It surprised him slightly, but he felt a warm feeling from the grip.

I know... I'm scared too.

Spinning on his heel, Sterlio suddenly produced a long, thin object. For some reason, he then snickered, which gave Kwenn the creeps.

The merchant then began to wave it about, as low chants began to come from each of the shrunken heads.

"Is he... conducting?" Kwenn heard Puul say to his brother. He wasn't sure what that word meant, but he began to notice the undead murmuring take on a rhythmic beat. The heads began to shake and vibrate, before they took off and floated around Sterlio like some kind of petrifying – yet meticulous – whirlwind.

Kwenn's heart thumped like crazy. He was terrified of what was about to happen, yet he couldn't take his eyes off the spectacle. His head began to spin, as he pulled Oviinia in closer to him. It was almost like a reaction without reason, and somehow, he knew she felt the same.

With a crack of ethereal light, the body jerked and seized, before opening its eyes.

Its mouth opened wide on jaw hinges, yet no voice could be heard. It twisted its head to and fro, as if it tried to shake away the blindness that it carried over from the other side.

Kwenn was crying now, though he barely noticed. He tried to look at his friends, but found himself unable to tear his blurred gaze from this horrifying scene.

Sterlio placed his bejewelled hand onto its chest, before tapping his eye once more with that thin thing he had in his other palm.

"Speak" he said with firmness.

The Kwenn clone calmed, yet still moved with an erratic, jerky motion. It finally fixed its renewed sight on the merchant, and gazed at him without as much as a blink.

It did not move a muscle.

Again, Sterlio tapped his eye. "Speak. Can you do it?"

Kwenn heard the cogs whirring within this… thing. He couldn't help it. For some inane reason, he sobbed and buried his face in Oviinia's shoulder.

"Kwenn…" she could only say softly.

He didn't know why. It was those *sounds*. It was like they mocked his very existence. They laughed at him – and whoever crafted them, *they* laughed at him too.

After an interminable amount of time, the mannish facsimile slowly turned its head, before rising into a sitting position. There was no struggle, and no gesture that indicated that it was a living thing.

It really *was* a machine.

And it looked *straight* at Kwenn and Oviinia.

"Can you walk?" Sterlio asked, and not without some astonishment in his voice.

It seemed to ignore him, before slipping off the table one foot at a time. It wobbled slightly, before standing as straight as an arrow. Its gaze on Kwenn and Oviinia did not break.

"Do you have a name?" Sterlio questioned.

Slowly, it turned its gaze onto the merchant.

It stared. And stared some more.

"Er" was the only thing Sterlio could say, before the machine struck him with a vicious blow.

The man careened like a spinning top, before landing amid the wooden benches.

Sterlio's family hissed in anger, but they then simply fell to the floor and clattered about.

"Sterlio!!!" Jugo yelled.

Again, the machine turned its gaze toward Kwenn with what sounded like the venting of *steam*, before striding toward him with purpose.

"Hold him down!" Jugo shouted once more, as Panin and Puul dived toward this new threat.

They each clasped an arm, as Kwenn was frozen in shock and fear.

"Get a rope!" the innkeeper told Ilod, as he bounded toward the twins' aid. He tackled the automaton to the ground, as he barked at Kwenn to help.

Kwenn shook his head, snapping himself out of his daze. He let go of Oviinia, and grabbed his sword. He kept it nearby in case something bad would happen.

Of course, something bad *did* happen. It always does.

He wasn't sure what he was going to do. Would he impale his own... what, brother? Cousin?

What the hell was this thing?

Still, he had to do *something*. He pinned one of its feet down, and thrust his blade into its calf. He cringed, expecting a blood-curdling cry, but none came. Realising that the thing didn't even slow its thrashings, Kwenn stabbed repeatedly, until its foot came completely off.

Even though it was a danger, he still felt awful for doing such a thing. He moved over to the other leg, before Ilod thankfully bounded in with a large coil of rope.

"Don't mind me... I'm fine..." Sterlio's voice emanated from somewhere in the seats. "Just a little brain damage... I'm good..."

* * *

"Well, *this* was a bloody grand idea!" Jugo growled as he paced back and forth.

He furiously smoked a pipe, as the Kwenn-clone writhed in silent protest. It did not seem to notice its recent dismemberment, as it tried vainly to escape its bondages.

It still gazed at Kwenn with malice.

"It *was* a grand idea, thankyouverymuch!" Sterlio babbled as Puul applied some sort of ointment onto his face. He waved the young magi off, and pointed to his rear end, "Never mind my delicate features, young master Puul! I do believe I have a broken tailbone! Fix it!"

"He is fine, Puul" Ilod said somewhat heartlessly. "Come over here and take a look at this."

Unquestioningly, and patted Sterlio sympathetically before walking over to his master.

"Wait! My grievous injuries!"

"You are fine. Put a sock in it" Ilod ordered. "Puul, what do you think of this?"

The young apprentice stopped, and warily eyed the object Ilod handed to him

It was the severed foot.

Reluctantly, he handled the extremity, and examined the open 'wound'.

"Sterlio, you said this…*thing*, was Pheekonshenee? That it was crafted by the ancients?" Puul asked aloud without removing his gaze from the object.

The merchant grunted. "Yes. The artefact recognised it as such."

Puul looked to Ilod, who shook his head.

"This does not look like any Pheekon make I have ever seen" the older man revealed. "It is as if… it is a hybrid of different technologies. It… it truly is *fascinating!*"

"I agree" Puul added.

Kwenn sat on a stool, with his face buried in his hands. His mind was an utter blank. He couldn't bring himself to stare at that squirming monstrosity, nor could he find the energy to converse with his friends. He just felt drained.

"So what does that mean?" Oviinia mumbled, as she placed a comforting arm over him.

Puul looked at her – then him – before addressing the both of them. "Well, um… it means that this… *automaton* is not of Pheekon origin. Truthfully, I don't know much more than that…"

Puul then looked to his master, who shook his head sadly.

"Initially, I would think such a machine would be the result of the technologically advanced Gamsay-Rumm… but this is *different*. It is no mere puppet, it has a lifelike demeanour of, of…"

"Of Joner" Jugo finished. "Of Joner, and of Kwenn."

Ilod accepted the conclusion. "I believe magic is involved. What kind, I am not sure."

Forgetting his mortal wounds, Sterlio let slip his entrepreneurial side, "So… it would be worth quite a bit, eh?"

"Maybe to the right person" Jugo grunted.

"What do you mean?" Kwenn mumbled.

Ilod was quicker on the draw than the younger man. "You mean… *they* will come and try to reclaim it?"

His friend shrugged. "I dunno. I doubt it was cast into the sea on purpose…"

Kwenn felt uncomfortable when Jugo referred to the machine as *it*, but he quickly got over it. "So… what? You think Hekor will come back? Do you think we should… should…"

Kill it?

"I don't know *what* we should do" Jugo completed the dreaded thought, "but either way, we can't sit here and mull it over too much longer."

As usual, he was right. They couldn't do much as of right now. There was no talking to this robot – that much was painfully clear. Maybe if they had all the time in the world, they could slowly teach it to feel love, and maybe *then* they could have a nice chat; but that was simply not possible.

Not while everything else was falling down around them.

"So we should leave him here?" Oviinia demanded, perhaps slightly harsher than she intended.

It still glared at Kwenn.

"I would *love* to examine it some more" Sterlio offered. "Provided it is... *incapacitated*."

"No go, mate" Jugo shook his head. "You're taking the girl, and you're headed to the shrine. First light."

Sterlio shrugged. "I could take it with me."

Kwenn expected Jugo to dismiss the merchant once more, but the innkeeper was instead silent for a moment.

"We can't risk them coming back to Gen" Sterlio pushed.

The odd man had a strong point.

Jugo looked to Ilod, who simply closed his eyes and bobbed his head.

Not much spoken communication was needed between the three old friends, that much was clear.

"Okay" Jugo relented. You take it with you. Try to get as much information from it as you can, Sterlio."

Oviinia swallowed, and the older man seemed to notice this. "Don't worry Oviinia. There is no safer place than the Sterlionic Fortress of Wonderment."

She smirked, and pushed her glasses up. "Since you said that with all the seriousness in the world, I'll choose to believe you."

Kwenn was still shaking, but he knew this was the best course of action.

"So that leaves me to head north then" he confirmed.

"Not alone" Puul nodded. He looked to Panin, who mimed his brother's gesture.

Kwenn couldn't help but smile. "Okay then. First light."

* * *

Solenir peeked over the horizon.

It was grey and overcast, but the White Flame of Emotion tried its hardest to crack through the clouds with its pale presence. During this moment, it looked like veins of silver that ran through dark rock, as flecks of metallic light indiscriminately covered Gen. Soon, the Blood Sight of Redemption would follow its fiery brother.

Everyone stood now before the Sterlionic Fortress of Wonderment, as it slowly dipped in a rhythmic way. The boat was both outrageous and fascinating in equal measure, as its very presence filled the surrounding air with a charge of electricity that was normally reserved for the domain of the departed. The skeleton of a mighty shark formed the base of the perplexing cabin, and a monstrous seashell was clomped on top of the fearsome remains. Around the craft were carvings of creatures of endless variety, as pink and gold motifs shared prime real-estate with barnacles that brightened everything with a kaleidoscopic light.

Kwenn was *extremely* aware of the contrast between the ship and its drab environment.

Oviinia stood on the deck now, looking very comfortable with her surroundings. The woman felt completely at home on the water, which was just as well, considering her profession.

"To me, the water is the only constant in my life" she had told Kwenn, "yet, it's never afraid to move."

He had thought deeply about those words, and realised he would miss her greatly. It was somewhat of a revelation, considering he only knew her for a very brief time. Yet... he couldn't help but feel like she was her oldest and dearest friend. He was completely comfortable around her, and even grew to anticipate their time spent together. It was the way she talked, the inflection of her personality, how her steadfast demeanour seemed to accentuate her kindness towards everyone she met.

And now, she was leaving.

It was easy to assume that they would see each other again; that their separation was merely the result of inconvenience. But the more he dwelt on the reality of everything, the more he feared that he would finally lose someone.

Would that someone be her?

Already, Kwenn had almost shaken the hands of death quite a few times. As far as he was concerned, this was a war; and sooner or later, there would be casualties.

As usual, he buried those vile feelings deep down. He couldn't let himself succumb to them. Not any more.

After the chaos of last night, Jugo told everyone to go get some sleep, as he, Ilod and Sterlio 'handled' the not-quite-Pheekon machine. At any other time, Kwenn would have protested and argued until he was blue in the face, but quickly realised just how tired he was. He trusted them to do the right thing (whatever that was), and as a result, he was surprised to awaken to a sleeping twin.

He wasn't sure how they did it, but it was just as lifeless as when it was first fished from the briny depths. Sterlio assured him that it wasn't dead, but merely slumbering, which was good enough for Kwenn.

He helped them wrap it in a cloth, before warily placing it into a trunk which was locked with a massive silver key. Sterlio then assured them all that 'they' would keep an eye on it, and Kwenn guessed that the eccentric man was referring to his undead family.

No matter how friendly they were, those little heads still freaked him out.

Still, their power gave him some comfort, as Sterlio and Oviinia were undoubtedly about to undertake a dangerous journey.

"So... I guess this is it" Oviinia said flatly as she rubbed her spectacles with her cream coat. She smiled warmly.

"Yeah. For now." Kwenn tried desperately to sound unemotional and disinterested.

"Kwenn..." she began, before trailing off.

He put his palms on her shoulders, and had no qualms in doing so.

"Look, Oviinia..." he began, "don't... no matter what happens, you can always count on me. Panin and Puul, too. You know that, right?"

She clasped her small hand on his forearm, and looked into his eyes. His heart skipped a beat.

"Yeah, I know. It's been a crazy few days, huh?" She laughed softly and awkwardly.

"I dunno about that. Monsters, pirates, robots... it all seems like a normal time to me."

They then both chuckled, and Kwenn noticed that tears began to run down her face. She wiped her eyes on her sleeve, and blushed.

"God, look at me. Why now, of all places?" She continued crying, but still laughed.

Kwenn felt his own eyes water, but swallowed it down. She was right; why *now*?

The boat's steam-powered engine sputtered and it began to lurch out of the rocky cove.

"Try not to torture him too much, Oviinia" Puul waved with his long sleeve, "and be careful."

She nodded, and punched Sterlio on his golden sleeve. He grimaced.

The craft entered the sunlight, and a strong wind bought good tidings for the day's travel. As Sterlio steered his vessel in a southern direction, Oviinia leaned over the side and waved dramatically.

"You boys stick together, you hear me?!"

She stared straight at Kwenn.

"And don't... don't go dying on me, you hear?"

He nodded slowly, as they all waved. The Sterlionic Fortress of Wonderment got smaller and smaller, before it eventually vanished around the side of the island.

They were gone.

* * *

Sollik was finally up, yet Gen remained enshrouded in clouds.

Still, revitalising wind continued to blow amongst the small buildings, as droplets of rain began to splatter on the green, stubbled ground.

Kwenn had packed provisions that were supplied by Jugo and Ilod, and felt his stomach knot unexpectedly at the thought of actually going back out into the world – a world that hadn't exactly been kind to him.

Still, he knew he could count on Panin and Puul. The brothers were just as determined to end all of this as he was, and they had both proven themselves to be amazing friends. Puul's leadership qualities and wisdom had proven to be invaluable, which was undoubtedly thanks to Ilod's mentorship. Having a Numanta mage was a great comfort to Kwenn; especially if they were in any way like the elder magi.

Panin was also as dependable as ever, but Kwenn had noticed that the young man had grown quiet over the last couple of days. He had thought of asking him if anything was wrong, but decided against it. For all he knew, it was simply the guardsman's way of coping with everything that had happened. Still, to see such a talkative guy reduce himself to only a few words every conversation was quite troubling. Perhaps it had something to do with Jeleenn's absence?

We will *find her.*

Either way, he was ready. The three of them stood at the entrance of Gen, once more facing down the Forbidden Forest. The dark woods looked particularly unwelcoming on this day – especially considering the emptiness of the small, seaside town. To Kwenn, the dripping trees seemed to slowly encroach on the quiet households; as the man-made structures kept the surrounding wilderness at bay.

He was lost in deep thought, when mayor Deret walked up to them. He looked as though he had just woken, what with his indigo robe and straw sandals.

"Where do you fellas think you're going?"

Puul quirked an eyebrow, "What do you mean, sir?"

He cleared his throat. "There's been a change of plans."

"Eh?"

The older man tilted his head, motioning them to follow him. They all headed toward the northern end of town. This was a quiet area that held a small sandy spot, and it was a place Kwenn had only visited once since stepping foot in Gen. It always felt like a hallowed cove; one that was devoid of human activity. The ground beneath his boots was soft with rain, and storm birds sang from behind the edge of the forest. It was here he saw Jugo and Ilod, both of whom were standing in front of a small fishing vessel. He wiped his soggy hair from his eyes, and glanced at the dinghy with curiosity.

"What's going on?" he asked.

"Change of plans" Jugo replied.

"I already said that" Deret huffed. "Can I go and perform my mayoral duties now?"

The innkeeper crossed his shiny arms and nodded. "So, are you heading to Sechon?"

The mayor's face changed. "Yes… I need to. I don't care what you all think. It was *my* responsibility to protect Ras Temple, and I failed."

Just like that, he walked away, without saying another word.

Panin and Puul looked at each other. "What was that about?" the Numanta queried.

"Do not worry about it" Ilod dismissed. "You three are not going through the forest this day."

Panin thrust his hairy chin toward the boat. "So I noticed. What's this about?"

Jugo jumped on the boat with a surprising agility, and pointed a thumb behind his shoulder. "Me and Ilod were talking it over, and we decided that the best way to Camo Temple is through the Great River."

The Great River?

The Great River was a massive, snaking body of water that cleaved the island of Shali in two. It separated the land into its northern and southern regions, before ending in *Toldin Dam* in the west. Kwenn had read about the iconic waterway in one of the books in Henra's Temple of Veronususs, and knew that Oviinia crossed it on her arduous journey from Gimlum. There were two bridges that crossed the monolithic stream; a trade route, and a traveller's road – and apparently, the direction of the water changed throughout the year.

He guessed it was a good idea. After all, the river ran right by Camo Temple, and such a large body of moving water would serve as an immense deterrent to any evil creatures of the fay.

"I was hesitant to go with this route at first" Jugo continued, "'cause I supposed that unseelie eyes would have been watching it."

"*I* supposed that" Ilod amended.

The innkeeper grunted. "Right. Whatever. Point is we don't think you boys can afford to spend so much time dilly-dallying on the road. Not with so much at stake."

Puul shook his head. "So, we're going on a boat now?"

Panin followed his brother's concern, "I dunno about that..."

Ilod put his hands on both of their chests. "Do not worry. You two will do fine. You have been through a lot, and this least of all will beat you."

For a second Kwenn was confused, but remembered that Panin and Puul's parents had died during a boating accident. Perhaps they were uneasy about sailing a vessel by themselves? He certainly couldn't do it, that's for sure...

"You're not coming, master?" Puul questioned anxiously.

"I am afraid not" the Numanta said regretfully. "Jugo and I have our own business we must attend to."

"What's that?"

Jugo jumped off the swaying craft. "We're not just gonna sit idly by and let the world fall around us. This is just as much our fight as it is yours."

Kwenn was curious, even though Jugo spoke sense. "What are you going to do? I thought there was nothing else we knew about. No other leads..."

The magi bobbed his head slowly. "You are right about that Kwenn. But what we have ascertained, above all else, is that we are dealing with the invisible realm. And the greatest authority *on* the invisible realm is the order of the green mages – the Eidian."

The Eidian...

Puul had told Kwenn that the head enclave of the Eidian mages was in fact located on the Four Sister Isles; on the northern island of Linniii. It was known as the *Great Castle of the Leaf*, and the order claimed ownership over the entire land. Apparently, Linniii was seen as the guardian of the peninsula – certainly to some chagrin of the Numanta and the Pisistratie mages. Still, after the great wars of the past, the magi collectives thankfully learned how to respect each other and get along. The supreme overseer of the order of green mages was Dian, who was another old friend of Jugo and Ilod's. She was said to be an extremely powerful woman; one who possessed an unmatched connection to the fay realms.

"I have a bad feeling, in my gut" Jugo muttered as he looked toward the rolling sea. "I think they're in trouble. The lot of 'em."

Ilod continued his friend's train of thought, "And if that is the case, we may very well be journeying into the belly of the beast. We cannot risk taking you boys with us, and losing everything in the process. All of us, together... it feels unwise."

Puul bowed his head, clearly bothered by this. However, he understood his master's wish, as did Panin and Kwenn.

"Okay" Kwenn declared with self-assurance, "then let's do this."

With that, the three young men climbed aboard the vessel, and prepared to depart. They said their farewells, which were short and not entirely emotional. They all knew it – this could be the last time they ever see each other – but they refused to acknowledge such a grim truth. They knew that they would see each other on the other side, because there was simply no other alternate outcome they would accept. Jugo would see his daughter Jeleenn again, and Ilod would reunite with his pupils. The children that were taken by such cold hands would return to their families, and Oviinia would go back home to Arlmai. All will be well once more.

The boat began to creak and moan, as Panin took to the stern, his eyes bright with determination as his brown hair wafted in the cool morning winds. Puul saluted with a sacred Numanta gesture as Jugo and Ilod slowly shrunk within the distance; along with their home. And really, Gen was Kwenn's home too, and his heart suddenly hurt at the sight of the receding coastline.

Yet, they will all come home.

… Even me?

CHAPTER VII

He was starting to get used to this.

The bobbing of the viscous waves. The slightly off-balance inertia. The salty taste in the air. The splashing wetness on his forearms.

Yep, Kwenn concluded that he rather liked being on boats.

The rain still fell in gentle mists, and stormbirds warbled among the craggy coastline. It was quite serene in a way – a direct contrast to the grimness of their immediate reality.

Gen was gone now, as the three young men directed their vessel toward the straight which led into the Great River – otherwise known as the Cleaving River. Kwenn could physically feel the current tightening under his feet, as it began to steadily flow into a focused waterway.

He had half-expected to see other boats during the hour it took for them to approach the river's mouth, but none were sighted. That worried him slightly, considering how much of a merchants' haven the river was.

Could the entire island be in jeopardy? Has everything already been ransacked beyond all recognition?

Not that he *would* recognise Shali in the first place. All of this was just as new to him as it was for Panin and Puul, who both spent most of their lives in Gen.

"Are you doing okay?" Kwenn asked Panin, noting the man's rough time during the trip from Ras Temple.

Gripping the wheel, he nodded. "Aside from the creepy scarecrow I saw, I'm doin' okay."

Drat. Must've missed that.

Puul was sitting cross-legged on the bow, as he rifled through various things. The way he balanced looked incredibly precarious, but the Numanta assured him it was his own way of not 'letting his fears get to him'.

"I hope that scarecrow isn't a portend of things to come" he muttered as he sniffed a piece of coral. "This weather isn't helping either."

Kwenn breathed deeply, and stretched loudly. Joints cracked in protest, before he pretended to check the small sail that fluttered in the strong wind. "So, how long will this take?"

Puul tied the coral to his staff with what looked like a string of grass, and smiled. "I knew you'd ask that. Ilod said the river changes throughout the year, with water flow being particularly steady just after the Blinking of the Eyes. It's not as fast as it could be, but he believed it should take a few hours to arrive at Camo Temple. Proved the rain doesn't get too bad."

"What if it does?"

The Numanta cupped some of the drizzle in his hands, and drank it. "I guess we'll stop at one of the checkpoints."

"If they're still standing" Panin amended with a growl.

Kwenn wrapped a skin around his increasingly-cold body, and tilted his head toward the mast. "I hope you know how to do that, because I sure don't."

"Eh, kinda" Panin said with a distinct lack of concern. "We'll figure it out."

Kwenn sniffed. *Great.*

He wondered how Oviinia and Sterlio were getting along. The suns were up now, and he guessed they would be well on their way toward the Conquest Mountains. His belly knotted in concern, but he took a deep breath, and tried to forget about any perceived danger they were in. He couldn't help them now.

To keep his mind off such unpleasantness, he withdrew his blade, and began polishing the mirror-like surface of the steel. This thing certainly got him out of some jams, and he was always thankful for that. Its hidden power took out the deranged Sergeant Wilko, and – despite being described as "toy-like" by Ilod – he felt protected with it in his hands. He was slightly worried that he would take off a hand or two because of his inexperience, but really, the thing felt like an extension of his own body. He sensed that he needed no training – though he was careful not to let such arrogance take hold of him. Fortunately, he hadn't had the need to use it for a one-on-one duel to the death... again.

I really hope that doesn't happen...

After being lost in thought for a while, he caught Puul in the corner of his eye, as the mage leaned over the side of the boat.

"What are you *doing*?" Kwenn probed.

"Fishing" he replied.

Whether he was serious or not, he couldn't even begin to guess.

The Numanta planted the head of his staff in the bubbly water, and began to chant some strange words. A green glow then emanated from the waves, before he pulled the arcane stick back on board. The coral that had been tied to it now enveloped the entire weapon.

"Wh... what did you do?" Kwenn asked, impressed.

"A warding spell" Puul nodded, happy with himself. "I'm channelling the natural energy of these waters for protection. The spirit within Shali's coasts will serve to reassure both mind and spirit, especially for my brother and I. We are of this land, so the effects will be potent indeed."

Now that Puul mentioned it, Kwenn couldn't help but ask; "Hey Puul... is Panin okay?" He ignored the magi's remarkable display, and tilted his head toward the younger brother.

Puul's smile vanished. He followed Kwenn's gaze, and lowered his head. "You've noticed, huh…"

Kwenn shrugged. "Well, it's just that he's been withdrawn lately… I wasn't going to say anything, but…"

The twin waved a ringed hand. "No. No, you're right. Yes, I talked to him about it. So have Ilod and Jugo. The loss of Lumiin and his friends in the guard has begun to take an effect, I think. That, and with Jeleenn…"

Kwenn looked to Panin, who wasn't paying any attention to them. It pained him – much more than he thought it should – to see him in such a sombre mood. True, he didn't know either of them for very long, but he reckoned he knew them long enough. They were his friends, and he liked to think he was theirs. After all, they'd been through a lot together.

"He shrugged it off, of course" Puul continued. "Honestly, I haven't seen him like this since our parents died. We were only young, but I still remember it so vividly."

He looked to his brother, but seemed to stare through him. "It seems death just loves following us" he proclaimed, without forsaking his scrutiny.

"But Jeleenn isn't dead, is she?"

Puul closed his eyes, and nodded. "No. She isn't. And no one else will perish, that I will vow."

He reached into one of his large pouches, and produced a small vial of a strange grey powder.

"Here, take this."

Kwenn took the bottle, and cast a curious eye over it.

"It's ash. From Gen. And Henra."

He wasn't sure what to make of that. His heart wavered with shock and a little bit of disgust.

"What… why are you giving me this?"

Puul looked at Kwenn with a solemnity that was seldom seen from the normally casual mage. "Kwenn, as a Numanta, I believe the teachings of the Pheekonshenee, and one of the things *they* believed in was the power of the mind. Not just logic or creative thinking, but raw emotion. It envelops us, and imprints itself onto the very fabric of our reality. And it's not just people; every living thing influences our world – even the earth itself."

Kwenn wasn't sure what he was getting at.

"To the Pheekons, technology and spirituality were one and the same. That there were no gods that gave us such gifts… just us. Just the universe. These ashes… I've been keeping them, because to me, they represent everything. They are the symbol which ties all of this… me, you, the darkness, Hekor, Jeleenn, the children, the countless deaths… they are all soaked into that earth, like blood and tears on a battlefield. I think if we can get some ash from Gimlum, then we could have ourselves a very, very powerful tool."

He began to see what the mage was getting at. Somehow, ash from the three sacred towns of Gen, Henra and Gimlum could form a potent brew. For *what*, he couldn't begin to guess, but considering how magical this island seemed to be, Kwenn supposed anything was possible.

"What kind of tool?" he asked with a cocked brow.

Puul gripped his craggy staff tightly. "Certainly no-one at my level could produce. I believe maybe a Pisistratïe grey robe could create a powerful offensive spell from it. I don't think we'll find any *Solenirkane* or *Titanicae* around these parts."

"The *what*?"

"Never mind. Just keep that vial with you. Will you do that?"

Kwenn shrugged, and nodded. He slipped the morbid thing into his backpack.

Though the rain refused to let up, it was still smooth sailing toward the river. Occasionally, the three men would glimpse pink dolphins that would swim alongside their boat, much to their delight. The land began to rise significantly along their side, as the mottled coast transformed into a massive cliff face that disappeared into the cloudy sky. There were quite a few caves dotted amongst the rocks, and even a few houses that were perched precariously over the splashing waves. Despite being furnished with decorative mementos, there were no signs of life.

"Who lives there?" Kwenn wondered, before biting into an apple.

Puul shrugged. "I have no idea. Fishermen?"

"Ghouls" Panin smirked ever so slightly to himself.

"Ghouls don't live in houses, Panin" his brother muttered in silent frustration.

"These ones do" Panin quipped. It was obvious he was just annoying Puul due to boredom.

Ignoring him, the Numanta wrapped his robe tightly around his shivering body. "They must deal with the merchants that travel around. Curious, you'd think there'd be people to greet us."

"Maybe word has spread about the attacks?" Kwenn offered.

Ilod nodded introspectively. "I suppose. I think we should just keep going, at any rate."

They eventually approached the Great River, and Kwenn felt a tinge of excitement. It was much more immense (and intimidating) than he imagined; its swirling waters gushing within the monolithic maw that now stretched around them. It was like the entire island was split in half, because it essentially *was*.

Shali was separated by north and south, with the top part housing a more rugged landscape, thanks to the *Fennick Caves* that dotted the land. Apparently they were home to mysterious three-legged creatures that seldom made contact with the outside world. So rarely have they been seen, that most people were convinced that they did not exist; and that they were merely an excuse by the Eidian mages to keep undesirables away from the mysterious rites they held therein. Either way, the caves were protected by the law of the land, and very few were allowed to visit. Not that many could, as the caves themselves were protected by the treacherous *Muhal Rocks*, and the magi settlement of *Tse Canyon*. The best way to travel the terrain was supposedly the rideable creatures known as Meerajaff, due to their muscular, clawed legs.

Kwenn's mind spun after being told about all of this. There was so much wonder to the world! He seriously wondered if his brain could pack so much knowledge, let alone actually go and *see* such miraculous things for himself.

Maybe one day...

Such fanciful notions would have to wait for now. He kept his eyes peeled for any activity around them; other boats, mainly. Hopefully friendly. He *really* didn't want to encounter any more pirates.

"There" Panin pointed as his other hand gripped the wheel. "I see something! An outpost, I think."

Kwenn squinted, before making out a vague shape of a building in the watery haze. As they approached, more detail came into view, including a wooden gate that blocked the entrance to the river. Its orange and red colouring stood out like a sore thumb, but Kwenn supposed that was the point. There were quite a few boats docked in front of what looked like an inn, its garish advertisements flapping in the wind, as candlelight was visible within its windows.

"Wonderful, a warm place" Puul sighed. "You think it would hurt too much if we stayed here for the night?"

Kwenn had to admit (somewhat guiltily) that the Numanta was on to something. He quickly abandoned such thoughts, though. They would not stop until they reached Camo Temple.

But still...

"I guess it can't hurt to find some answers" he offered. "Is this place safe?"

Panin nodded. "Yes. The merchant trades of Shali are pretty relaxed, yet professional. Still, I wouldn't be too complacent. I've seen some shifty characters come through Gen."

Taking note of the guardsman's advice, Kwenn began to make out the main sign of the establishment; *The River's Mouth Inn*. It didn't sound too sinister, and it was undoubtedly a hive of information. He began to wish that Sterlio was here with them; *he* would've known who to talk to.

"Greasing palms" as Panin termed it.

Unfortunately, they were on their own. Three young, naïve men who were up against everything the world could throw at them. A daunting prospect, indeed.

Panin barked at Puul and Kwenn to lower the sales, nervousness evident in his voice. Kwenn didn't have a clue, and simply followed the magi's lead.

"I *think* this is how you do it" the Numanta said more than once.

Thankfully, the mast wasn't very big, and they had it down fairly quickly. Wiping wetness from his face, Kwenn could now see a figure standing on the pier. It was a woman, and she was directing them to the dock.

"Don't crash" Puul ordered his brother.

Biting his lip, Panin twisted the rudder with rigid determination. He may as well have been directing a dreadnought, for all the strain he exuded. It was an animated sight, though Kwenn sympathised greatly with his friend.

After an agonising crawl toward the sweet, oh-so solid dock, Kwenn grabbed the anchor and tossed it overboard. No one told him to do so, which worried him slightly. However, he wanted to take the initiative, and feel *useful.*

The lady didn't yell at him, which was a good sign.

Landing with a satisfying *splash,* Kwenn nodded at Puul. The magi patted him on the shoulder, and told his brother to relinquish control of the vessel.

Panin sighed, and nearly collapsed.

"It wasn't *that* bad" Puul scolded.

Kwenn couldn't help but laugh. He jumped onto the wooden platform, and tied the boat to a large metal hoop. He stroked his chin for a minute, and concluded that he did not in fact screw everything up.

Thank god.

The woman – a golden-haired, dark skinned native of the island – crossed her tattooed arms and wrinkled her bejewelled forehead.

"This your first time, fellas?"

Puul leaned on his staff like a winded, elderly man. "How can you tell, ma'am?"

She gave the Numanta a wry look, and pulled out a small leather book. "So, what's your business today?"

The three men quickly exchanged glances.

"We're heading to Camo Temple" Puul confirmed with a nod.

The woman scribbled with an inked plume. "I see. Are you aware of the tightened security measures that we've employed recently, due to attacks suffered by Henra, Gimlum and Gen?"

For a fleeting moment, Kwenn panicked. Did he have something to hide?

No... no, I don't... do I?

Before he could fumble his way toward an answer, the magi spoke again. "Yes... we... we come from Gen. We were in the attack."

Panin gave a cursory look to Kwenn, and he knew exactly what the guardsman was thinking.

I guess we're just going to tell the truth, after all... but how much of it?

The woman paused her writing, and gave them a sympathetic look. "Oh, my apologies. I hope you understand, but we can't make exceptions. Shali is enduring a crisis at the moment. Henra is under a temporary leadership, and trade is under strict control by checkpoints throughout the island."

Puul glanced back toward Kwenn and his brother, and nodded in reassurance. "We understand. We don't have anything to hide."

She smiled. "Good. If you wish to visit the inn, then you must leave your weapons with the guards. We'll also have to keep them if you plan to stay overnight. I believe there's still a couple of rooms available."

Kwenn nervously rubbed the back of his neck. No-one besides

himself and Oviinia could wield his sword, which meant he was unable to enter the inn.

Dammit, I'm hungry.

"I'll stay out here then" he told Panin and Puul. "You guys go inside and get supplies. Is that alright?"

The twins agreed, and headed toward the toasty building.

* * *

The River's Mouth Inn was the Queezy Fennick in all but name.

Like a hammer, memories of their childhood hit the twins with force, as musty incense surrounded them, and the aroma of ale filled their nostrils. A massive marlin was displayed over a stone fireplace; its strangely glittering scales flooding the building with starlight.

Spotting a group of guardsmen having a drink at a corner table, Panin motioned his brother to follow him.

The guards – two men and a woman – wore bronzed outfits similar to Panin's, with the notable difference being the navy blue gauntlets and greaves that signified their positions as guardians of the Great River.

Evidently, they had just finished a shift, as their mirth could be heard from the main doors.

"What are we going to ask them?" Puul quizzed as his eyes wandered toward the menu, "I mean, we don't want to put ourselves in any danger…"

Panin waved a gloved hand, causing smoke to waft in swirls. "Relax. There's no harm in getting the lay of the land, bro."

Before they could make their introductions, the guards saw the brothers approach them, and raised their mugs in greetings.

"Ho! What have we here? A fellow peacekeeper and a Numanta!" the strong-jawed women spoke first. "What can we do for you on this day?"

Panin saluted. "Ho there, fellow warriors of the law. My brother and I are travelling to Camo Temple… and, well, we were wondering about a few things."

One of the men used his boot to push a chair out for Panin to perch himself on. "Sit down mates. You want a drink?"

Smiling, Panin nodded, and accepted the offer. "Sure, that'd be great! My brother'll take water."

"There's plenty of water outside, y'know" the second man chuckled, "and ya don't have to pay for it!"

This brought forth laughter from everyone, which was met with an emotionless expression from the magi. "I'll take note of that" he replied sarcastically.

"Go on, sit fellas" the first man said again. "What do you wanna know?"

"Well" Panin began, "as I mentioned, we're going to Camo Temple. We're from Gen, you see…"

Each of the guards nodded, and raised their mugs again.

"Aye, sorry about what happened" the woman apologised, before taking a swig of her drink. "We hope you fellas are doing alright down there."

"Cheers for that" Panin said, thankful for the thought. "Yeah… we're slowly getting things back together. Slowly. It's tough going."

"I can only imagine, mate" one of the men tilted his drink toward him. "A lot of things have changed lately. All over Shali, things've been chaotic. People are scared for their lives."

"You heard about Gimlum and Henra?" the woman asked with sadness in her blue eyes.

Panin was quiet for a moment. "Yeah. Yeah, we have. That's why we're heading to Camo Temple. We're seeing if we can help in any way… my brother here is the apprentice to Ilod."

Puul sat unmoving. He wasn't sure if his brother was giving too much way – or too little.

She raised a red eyebrow. "Oh? *The* Ilod? Well, hopefully you can help figure just what the hell's happened out there. Those poor kids have to be somewhere…"

Shadows crossed the brothers' faces.

"And those attacks" she continued, "they just stopped… everyone's been on edge ever since. The whole island's commerce has ground to a halt."

"This place has never been quieter," a waitress interrupted suddenly, as she placed more tankards on the table, "though things have been slowly getting back to normal. Do you want anything to eat?"

Puul took his drink, and got up. "I'd like to order a few things for the road, ma'am."

Nodding, she motioned for the mage to follow her back to the counter. He bowed to his guests, and awkwardly followed in the woman's footsteps.

"He's your brother?" the other guardsman smirked. "That's a new one! I never heard of a grunt having an egghead white robe as kin!"

Panin shrugged. "I dunno. I guess I just didn't care about magic all that much. Or the Pheekons. Who knows, I probably got some sparkly fireworks hidden under my own fingertips."

They all laughed, and drank deeply. It was the small comforts that really mattered.

Wiping his mouth, Panin looked back at Puul, who was chatting with the staff. He imagined that his brother was doing a little investigating of his own. He was crafty like that.

"Has anyone suspicious passed through here?" he asked without tact.

They all rolled their eyes.

"Pretty much every merchant or traveller that passes through here has their quirks" the woman scoffed. "Some of them are downright queer; especially those from the far off lands."

"The mages and scholars aren't so bad" the second man added, "you get all sorts of types in Gen, don't you?"

Panin stared into his ale. "Yes… mostly during the Festival of Life… and the attack happened soon after that."

They all looked at each other.

"You think someone who visited your town caused its…"

"Destruction? No, no I don't."

Panin knew who was behind it all. It was Hekor. But of course, they didn't know that. He had to be careful in not spilling the entire bag of beans.

I'm not used to this…

The woman drank again, and looked toward the roaring fire. "What makes you so sure about that? Rumours're going around that the assaults were done by magicians. That's how they were able to pop up outta nowhere."

The Gen guardsman shrugged. "I don't know. I just… I just think it was something else. I don't see why anyone would come all the way to our little island just to raze towns and kidnap children."

An unbelieving look washed over her face. "Sorry mate, but I don't buy that. It's a big, nasty world out there. A big nasty world that has a million reasons for trying to crush our home."

She had him there. What could Panin say to that?

He pushed his questioning a little further. "Do you guys know why the towns were targeted? Have you heard anything?"

The woman shrugged her broad shoulders. "Mostly hearsay. We've only had a few folks come through here since everything happened. We had a messenger from Henra, and a merchant from Gen who confirmed the news… but apart from the whispers of our patrons, nothing much else."

"Whispers?"

One of the men chugged his beverage, and planted it on the table with a thud. "Scary stuff, fella. That there's an army of darkness runnin' about, and how demons are swallowing everything in fire."

The second gentleman mimicked his partner's gesture. "Yeah. I even heard that there was a group of crusaders who helped some Henrans survive. Just real, outlandish stuff!"

Panin felt his heartbeat thump just a little bit harder.

Really? He can't be talking about us, *can he?*

In truth, he was slightly disappointed by the lack of new information. These people didn't seem to have much bearing on just what was happening out there. He supposed he couldn't blame them, but at the same time, such quietness chilled him to the bone. If the entire island was under siege… sure, that was something he could've at least understood. But it seemed like the attacks, the abductions, the murders… it seemed like that they never even happened.

Of course, that wasn't the reality. He knew about Kwenn. About Oviinia. About how Jugo and Ilod indirectly influenced everything because of what happened to Joner… And the Wizards' plan of unifying Tarinn and the Invisible Realm. He still couldn't accept that he and his brother were embroiled in all of this, nor the fact that Jeleenn was taken to god-knows-where.

Jeleenn… I hope you're hanging in there, wherever you are.

Puul worried about him. He knew he was acting a little more withdrawn lately. It was because he was scared, plain and simple.

"Really?" he replied in faux surprise. "I guess with whatever's happening out there, there's bound to be some crazy stories that sprout up out of nowhere."

"Who knows if they're true or not" the man continued, as he pulled out a pipe and clasped it between his teeth, "but knowin' this place, it probably is, and then some."

"What do you mean?"

Blowing smoke in the already-musty air, he shook his head. "You know, fella. The Four Sister Isles are soakin' in magic. Who knows what can spring up outta the ground? For all we know, evil is right under our boots!"

The woman punched him in the shoulder. "Rubbish! Don't say that rot."

He curled his lip, whilst caressing his arm. "Hey! Panin here said so himself. He doesn't think they came from the ocean, and neither do I. We all know these islands are full of weird stuff."

"Show some respect, Nutim" the other man admonished.

"Eh? Oh… sorry fella. I didn't mean to make light of it all…"

"No, it's okay" Panin responded. "These questions need to be asked. Which is why I'm going to Camo. Hopefully the monks there have been in contact with the magi, maybe even the Eidian in Linniii."

Jugo and Ilod will be able to talk to them. I hope they get there as fast as possible

* * *

Kwenn lay on his back, as he quietly enjoyed the pitter-patter of the rain as it hit the roof of the boat's storage tent. Well, 'roof' was somewhat of a misnomer; in actuality, they were animal skins stretched to and fro, and they bobbed in the gentle wind.

He felt himself going to sleep, when he finally heard the footsteps of Panin and Puul approaching the boat.

With them was the woman he had met a short while ago, and they all conversed.

"We're back" Puul declared pointlessly.

He handed a large sack to Kwenn, and he could smell the allure of baked goods inside.

Must be lunch time by now…

"Good luck on your travels, boys" the muscular lady said, as she once again scribbled on some papers. "I hope you find what you're looking for up at Camo Temple."

"Thanks" Panin replied, as he chucked a second bag at Kwenn. "Hopefully, we'll get some idea as to what's happening out there."

She slipped her plume behind a bejewelled ear, and closed her book with an exaggerated clap. "You'd better. There are a lot of people out there who deserve answers."

I'm assuming that book is waterproof, Kwenn pondered, as he took a long whiff of the second sack. Dried meat. Nice.

* * *

The torrent of heavenly water was unceasing, which made visibility a woe. Not to mention the assault on the ears as countless droplets battered the river, churning the greyness like the world's biggest soup.

Soup. Ugh, I can't believe I'm still hungry.

The three men had debated on waiting the rain out, but decided to push on. Panin reasoned that the snaking river shouldn't have been too hard to navigate. "If we see a cliff face, just move in the other direction" was his expert nautical advice.

Puul could only groan at that.

Indeed, Kwenn was surprised at how high the 'walls' had become. They disappeared into the soupy sky, and he would occasionally spot houses perched within the rocks. Some of these homes would show light within, and he had to wonder if their occupants were even aware of the attacks.

And then he remembered. This is a massive *river*. This was probably the safest place in all of Shali. His mind lingered back to the events of Henra, and how the dark fairies *hated* running water. Somehow, their foul powers had managed to evaporate whatever streams were present in Gen, Gimlum and Henra – but clearly this cleaving river was simply too much for them.

This got him thinking about the significance of this area, and he shared his thoughts with the twins.

"I've been pondering that myself" Puul muttered, to the surprise of no-one. "Remember what I said about the sacred sites?"

Kwenn nodded, and cast his mind back to when they were on the Isle of Sechon…

Puul reached into his robe, and produced a map. He unfurled it, and pressed it onto the soft grass. It depicted the Isle of Shali.

He then pressed a finger on Gimlum's location. "Oviinia" he began, "you came from here. From Gimlum" he raised his digit slightly, "and here is The Tilth. One of the sacred sites that held Kwenn's memory. One sacred site, and one settlement that was attacked."

He then moved south-east to Gen.

"Here, we have Gen. And east of that, *we have Sechon and Ras Ruins – the second sacred site. Again, we have that, and another town that was burned."*

Kwenn had a feeling he knew where Puul was going with this. His heart beat slightly quicker.

His eyes followed Puul's unclean extremity westward to Henra.

"And we have Henra. The third place that suffered. And the third place that also has–

"The third sacred sight" Kwenn finished.

Puul nodded as he gazed into Kwenn's eyes. "Yes."

Oviinia knelt beside Kwenn, and quietly thought this all over herself as she looked at the sheepskin paper.

"Second opinion?" Puul asked the woman in a slightly impish way.

She tried to come up with a witty retort; but failed. "That's a heck of a coincidence" she conceded.

"That's not all" the magi continued, "take a look at the placement of the towns on the map."

Kwenn and Oviinia did so; though he failed to see the significance.

She however, did not. "They're based on the points of a triangle!" she exclaimed, astounded.

Now that she mentioned it, Kwenn could see it. Gimlum and the Tilth were north, Gen and Ras was south-east, and Henra was south-west.

"Your triangle" Kwenn remembered.

"Yes. And do you know where the centre of that triangle was?"

Kwenn closed his, and tried to think hard. He failed.

"I don't know. Where?"

The magi waved his coral-bound staff off to the side of the boat. "South of here, somewhere. According to the map, it was in the middle of some plains, where nothing resides."

At the wheel, Panin laughed with a mouthful of bread. "No bro! We're not diverting our journey! Not again." He swallowed. "Especially not for some hunch. We're going to Camo Temple, come hell or high water." He looked up into the sky, and squinted. "And if this rain keeps up, these waters'll become high indeed."

Puul frowned. "What's the point of a geographical triangle, if not to investigate it properly?"

His brother shook his head. "No way. I've seen your 'triangle', Puul. It's not even perfect. It's wonky. You're grasping at straws on this one. You're just seeing things you want to see."

A look of indignation washed over the Numanta's features. "*Excuse me!* This is more than some half-hearted case of pareidolia, thank you very much."

Kwenn blinked. "Para… what?"

"Seeing stuff that isn't there," Panin explained. "That's right, mister smarty pants; I *know* what that word means. Don't you even try to lord your intellect over me."

Puul crossed his arms and pouted. "It's not your intellect that amuses me. More like your inferiority complex."

"Only thing that's inferior is your stupid belief in dead people that never even existed."

Kwenn was getting nervous now. The barbs were getting sharper and sharper.

He could see that Puul was steaming, which was uncharacteristic of him. "As opposed to whom? Real live people? The real live people that couldn't even save Jeleenn?"

That was it. Panin released the rudder, and rounded on his brother.

"I'd like to see you try and save yourself!"

He marched with purpose toward Puul, fire in his eyes.

Kwenn had to do something. He jumped in between them, and held his palms up.

"Okay, that's enough guys! Let's calm down!"

The boat swayed, causing Kwenn to lose his footing. Panin could have just as easily knocked him out of the way, but decided to show some restraint. Funny how rage masked Panin's crippling seas sickness.

It was an intense moment, and Kwenn's heart thumped a lot more than he expected. He never saw them like this. He figured they were stressed about this whole thing, and some of that tension finally bubbled to the surface.

The two of them stared daggers at each other, before Puul relented, and retreated inside the storage tent.

Panin removed his helm, and smacked it onto the deck. It rolled, and landed in between some bags. He went back to the wheel.

Well... that came out of nowhere.

What had happened? First thing, they were talking as normal... and then suddenly, they were at each other's throats? Is this what siblings did?

Steadying himself on the wet surface, Kwenn grabbed the side of the tent, and began to stagger toward Puul.

Before he could though, a shout emanated from the magi's location.

Gulping in surprise, Kwenn coughed and hacked, before the entire boat became illuminated in a sapphire light.

"What the hell is that?!" Panin yelled.

Suddenly, the Numanta jumped into view, before pointing a ringed finger.

"Kwenn! Your sword! Look!!!"

He went inside where Puul had come from, and spotted his blade. On the golden finger guard was the blue jewel, and it pulsed like a star in the night sky.

Without giving it much thought, Kwenn reached out, and clasped the weapon.

A whiteness blinded him, and he felt his arm move on its own accord. The sword. The sword had come alive.

He vaguely heard the voices of Panin and Puul before his vision came back to him.

He was on the deck, his arm thrusting the blade out toward a section of the cliff side.

The rain had suddenly stopped, and before any of them could say another word, Kwenn's sword shot an extraordinary beam of azure toward the rocks. Hotness flooded his arm, but he couldn't let go!

Like a wind tearing through it, the foggy atmosphere lifted, revealing an astonishing sight.

The azure ray had hit a monolithic stone entrance, flanked by a golden pier.

Before their disbelieving gazes, the ancient-looking doorway became flecked with creeping blue light, as it ran through the ornately carved rock like liquid.

Losing his footing on the soaked deck, Kwenn toppled backward, and was caught by Panin.

"Where... how..." the guardsman babbled.

Blinking several times to clear the spots from his vision, Kwenn tried to get up, but looked like a flailing beetle on its back. The Numanta stood over them, and assisted.

They all looked toward the rocky cliff where the excitement had occurred, and could see that the mysterious gateway was now glowing with a hum that reverberated through their bones.

Puul shook his head. "Kwenn, what did you..."

"I didn't do anything!" Kwenn spat. "It was the sword!"

"What is this place?" Panin wondered.

"Only one way to find out" the mage decided. "Sorry Panin, but it looks like we're taking another detour after all."

His brother showed no expression.

As the rainy mist began to clear, they manoeuvred their vessel toward the beautiful-looking dock. Now that the torrential downfall ended, Kwenn began to see so many things that were masked by the bad weather; water run-off gushed through their craggy surroundings like mini waterfalls, as birds sang in glee, now that it was safe to come out. They seemed unperturbed at what just happened.

"It's one bloody thing after another with you, isn't it?" Panin griped.

Kwenn didn't blame him. "Sorry. If it turns out that I'm a secret prince, I'll be sure to give you a nice slice of land."

"Deal. And none with rivers. I've had a gut full of 'em."

Kwenn snorted accidentally.

"What?" Panin said.

"You sound just like Jugo when you're cranky."

He ignored him.

As the crew of three bobbed and inched their way closer, heartbeats got faster and faster. There was no telling what they would find. As he grunted with every rotation of the paddle he held, Panin's question kept running through his soggy head.

What is this place?

"Hey!" Puul called from the other side of the vessel. "Look at the water!"

Following his advice, Kwenn could see hundreds of dark objects begin to surface from the gushing waters. They looked like...

"Turtles!"

"Indeed!" Puul shouted again. "I think this is a good omen!"

Kwenn was in awe. He beamed with wonder like a child, as their leathery guardians flanked them in all directions.

"Oh my god, this is amazing!"

Even Panin seemed more cheery, as evidenced by the complete lack of 'turtle soup' quips.

Some of the shells were small, whilst a few were utterly enormous. Either way, they were remarkably silent, and they eventually disappeared as they approached the gold pier.

It was such a small moment, but it made all the difference. It made them feel that not *everything* in this world was out to get them.

Still, the mood became solemn once they disembarked.

"There's no-one here" the Numanta shivered. "No houses. I don't see why this place exists. It's not on any maps I've seen."

Though looking majestic from afar, the dock – whilst still impressive – showed signs of wear.

"It doesn't look like anyone's been here for a long time" Panin added.

Though they could still hear the sounds of nature, everything seemed a little more muffled the closer they got to the glowing doorway.

They climbed up some simple sandstone steps, and a cold breeze assailed them. The day was getting long, as each man silently wondered if they'd spend the night here.

They were now bathed in the eerie glow, and it brought no warmth. Indeed, it felt like they were wading through an invisible lake, and once they passed a certain threshold, the ground rumbled through their boots. Sand and dirt began to fall , as a shaft of darkness before them grew wider and wider. Instead of a stale, ancient gust, the three men smelled the distinct odour of a beach.

The door was open, and they went inside.

CHAPTER VIII

The Sterlionic Fortress of Wonderment.

That moniker made more and more sense the more Oviinia Trundle thought of it. It really was a fortress, and it really did house a wide array of fantastic things… though some of those fantastic things were downright scary, such as Sterlio's family.

She supposed that's where the 'fortress' part came from.

After the gaudy steamer left the cove of Gen, the duo circled the south-eastern coast of Shali, which took them the entire day.

Somewhat remorsefully, she admitted that a part of her was still scared of the strange man. She knew such fears were unfounded, especially after she discovered that he once actually saved the world from utter destruction… but he was so *creepy*. He looked weird. He acted weird. And he was surrounded by *weird* things.

She knew it was a prejudiced attitude, and she was ashamed. During her research days, she met many colourful characters that roamed the blue, and they were some of the best people she'd ever met. Sure, there were a lot of bad apples too, but she'd learned a long time ago that a book cannot be judged by its cover.

Then she saw Sterlio yell at one of his shrunken heads, and she immediately forgot all that.

Still, despite all of this, and against every expectation, Oviinia Trundle found herself greatly enjoying Lord Sterlio's company.

She wasn't sure if that said more about him or her, but nevertheless, she was utterly fascinated with him.

The Sterlionic Fortress of Wonderment chugged and puffed with a single-minded purpose; a purpose that was perhaps even *more* important than the delicious glint of money.

Such a purpose rarely existed in this world... but Oviinia liked to think that the entrepreneurial heart of Lord Sterlio hid a sliver of goodness... and it did. Despite his unsettling demeanour and queer appearance, the merchant was a noble soul – and when push came to shove, he was always willing to lend a svelte, helping hand. After all, he *did* once help save Tarinn.

Could've fooled me...

His uncanny abilities scared her witless. She couldn't help it. The way he communicated with the dead was like being stuck out at sea with a mad scientist; one who performed profane experiments whilst cackling maniacally.

Yet... at the same time, she found such madness almost irresistible to her scientific mind. She was pushed away by Sterlio's eerie manner, yet couldn't help but be pulled in by his *uniqueness*.

He was certainly polite, and his ship was stuffed with the most fascinating of trinkets. As a marine biologist, she was in heaven. Not only did she have the opportunity to survey the surrounding waters, she also found many jars of exotic specimens crammed away in his stuffy shop.

On top of all that, there was the ship itself. The shop was framed by the skeletal remains of an immense water beast, whilst his living quarters – carved from a giant shell – was precariously placed on top.

Well, it certainly *seemed* precarious. God knows how it stayed up there.

Of course, she *had* to know the origins of these marvels, and she pestered the poor man endlessly.

"My dear, the origins of the Sterlionic Fortress of Wonderment are both humble and explosive" he said cryptically. "It would take us eight and forty days for me to do such a tale the justice it deserved."

She was already regretting this trip.

"Come *on*, am I getting blood from a stone here? I've never seen remains like these before! I'll be the toast of Arlmai! They'll name a university after me!"

"I wasn't aware there were universities on the Four Sister Isles."

She sighed loudly, and weaved the fishing rod to and fro. She sat on the side of the boat, her bare legs dangling off the edge. Sure, this was a dangerous mission that meant life or death... but no-one said she couldn't decompress between destinations. The way she saw it, relaxing was essential to keeping a healthy mind. Luckily for Oviinia, her work *was* her way of relaxing

"They'll *build* one, and I'll be sure to name a wing after you!"

The merchant closed his mouth and slowly narrowed his eyes, as if recalling a painful memory. "Already happened once. Never again."

Oviinia could help but laugh in frustration.

Really?

She was lucky it was spitting rain, because she would've been hot with anger.

She changed the subject. "So, you say this ship has such a long history. How long have you been doing this? You know, being a travelling businessman."

Clutching the intricately carved rudder, Sterlio scrunched his face in thought. "Hmmmerrr... well, I suppose it's been quite a while now, my dear. This is a family business, you see? I've been hawking and trading ever since I was in nappies. I think I sold *them*, too."

She shivered, and wondered if Sterlio meant his 'family' family. Those horrible little heads that were thankfully asleep somewhere out of sight.

"Really? So... uh, if you don't mind me asking. Does everyone in your family become... er..."

"Chopped, pickled and stuffed? Why, yes in fact! It's a tradition of my people!"

Erk... why did I ask?

For such a chatty man, Sterlio was incredibly vague about his background. Oviinia spent the next few hours poking and prodding, and only managed to learn that he came from the land of Lamunenkeé, and met Jugo and Ilod about twenty years ago. She couldn't guess his age, though, or if he had any *living* relatives. She also enquired about his abilities, but was of course non-specific in his explanations.

Still, it was possible he was simply too preoccupied in opening up. After all, they were heading straight into a place where sailors dare not go.

"So" she began, as she reeled in another empty line, "what's going to happen when we get closer to this 'scud'? Should we be preparing for anything in particular?"

The merchant stroked his pinkish facial hair, clearly deep in thought. "I don't know, to tell the truth. I've never ventured toward the Magick Shrine, nor have I ever dared to. Unfortunately, my family cannot provide the appropriate answer to this conundrum..."

That wasn't promising. She remembered reading a few things about the Lethe during her studies years ago, but couldn't remember much. She was never too interested in the supernatural... she didn't even believe in it once upon a time. To her, ghosts were simply energy, ghouls were diseased flesh-eaters, and goblins were semi-intelligent creatures. The Four Sister Isles were deeply rooted in fairy tales... yet she always fancied that they were just a combination of explainable phenomena, orally-passed stories, and good old fashioned bull-spit.

She looked out toward where Shali would be. It was now too far away to be seen in the mist, and a feeling of true isolation suddenly enveloped her body.

The last couple of weeks though... they nearly shattered the foundations of everything she knew. Or, everything she *thought* she knew. So much had been turned upside down, and she was barely capable of processing it.

She didn't tell anyone, but she began to wake in panicked terror during the nights. The knowledge that there was more to this world than what she could see made her quake in her boots. Why? She had no earthly idea.

Yet… the thought that there were *things* out there; *powerful* things beyond human comprehension, it very nearly made her lose her mind in fear. She wasn't sure if it was a problem with her specifically, or if it was simply human nature.

If the gods were to walk Tarinn tomorrow, would people cheer and celebrate? Or would they collapse in horror as they finally learned the secrets to the meaning of existence?

It was this that kept her up most nights. She kept it to herself, not daring to share the burden with her friends. They were suffering enough, without having to worry about her existential crisis.

Strangely, she became more drawn to her passions, finding comfort in their warm reality. As the big things became less real, it was the small joys that became more tangible. Her work wasn't just enjoyment or escapism – it became more and more her true meaning of life. Once upon a time, she was sceptical of the idea of spiritual contentment through a hard day's work. She shook her head at the idea of 'regular' folk who were satisfied with a mediocre existence.

But, every day, she became more and more convinced that they were the smart ones all along. That true happiness can be found in the *here* and the *now*, and not some ill-defined notion of the cosmic.

It was something that kept her grip on reality. She needed a constant; an unmoving stone in a gushing river that wants to sweep her away into nothingness.

God, my parents don't even know what's happened to me… I hope they're okay.

Her adoptive folks lived on the Wy'rm River in Arlmai, so she hoped that they would be safe from harm. Still, after what happened in Gimlum, she assumed nothing. After all, the crossing rivers of the

Tilth did nothing to protect the town.

Once this was all done, she vowed to return to them.

"Did you hear me, dear?"

Oviinia blinked. "Huh?"

Sterlio tapped his black artificial eye, and waved an effeminate hand outward. "Look."

Closing in on the vessel, was a huge, deep blue whale. Noiselessly, it glided through the grey water, and Oviinia couldn't help but smile. A real, happy smile. She managed to touch its cold body, before it sank back underneath the water.

She took it as a good omen. A *real* omen.

The merchant nodded with some unknown satisfaction.

"Remember that creature, my dear," he said softly. "Remember, and don't let go."

* * *

They were looking over her.

Tall, angelic figures whose eyes held so much knowledge. So much power. So much compassion.

So much sadness.

She wasn't sure. Was she supposed to be afraid? To scream out and thrash in terror?

No, she didn't see any reason why.

Why?

That was the question she kept asking. *Why? Why? Why?*

She felt like she was getting those answers, but couldn't quite unpack them. The knowledge was like a liquid that dropped on her forehead…

Drop. Drop. Drop.

She couldn't see, but she knew the beings smiled. Sad smiles… but smiles nonetheless.

* * *

The interior was something else.

As Kwenn's eyes adjusted, he made out smooth, rounded surfaces that glistened with wet. The rocky bumps were all kinds of aqua shades; blues and greens that were peppered with stalks of coral.

Streams of water ran down the walls, as motifs of golden bulls looked as though they were moving behind the liquid distortion.

Panin cupped his gloved hands in one of the torrents, and drank.

"Wowza! It's cold! And good!"

The three men walked slowly down a long, winding path that led further in. They descended a winding stairwell that seemed carved from the natural stone, and were surprised to see another door, flanked by braziers of blue fire.

Dozens of little crabs scuttled at the sight of the trio of intruders, as Kwenn could vaguely hear muffled music.

Is that my imagination?

Again, the door was golden, with an incredibly detailed mosaic. Foreign text was carved into the display, and Puul gingerly ran his finger over the cold metal.

Philosophy

Analogy

Metaphor

Wit

Psyche

Only these, the deep thoughts of every mortal, the pondering of possibilities, the acceptance of change. Only these were needed to sustain the holy ones – the chosen children – from damnation and pain and loss. Only these were needed to keep Tarinn alive and thriving.

"It's Pheekonshenee text!" Puul breathed in excitement. "It's one of the Numanta mantras!

Panin crossed his arms. "So, this place was built by the Pheekons?"

The mage shook his head and furrowed his brow. "I… don't think so? This doesn't seem like a Pheekon kind of cave... it seems a little too... rustic."

"Primitive, you mean."

Puul shrugged as he searched for more details. "I guess. It seems to be... hang on." He knelt down, and tapped on a section on the door. "Look! Can you guys make it out?"

Kwenn directed his gaze, and squinted. At first, it was hard to make out, but he finally noticed that the carvings were actually an illustration. He could see the shape of a sun, and a figure holding it aloft with one hand, whilst it used the other to tip out a pitcher of water. It looked lithe and feminine, so he guessed it was a woman.

"It's Lamun" Panin guessed.

"Who?"

"*Lamun*. The Goddess of Reincarnation, and of the sun Sollus" Puul divulged. " She is worshipped by the Solluskane, the Blue Robes."

"Huh." In the very centre of the door, Kwenn saw a strange, thin hole, flanked by eight elongated divots.

I wonder...

He withdrew his sword.

"It's worth a try."

Without a word, the twins stepped aside, recognising what Kwenn was trying to do.

Gently, he slid the blade into the slot, and was caught by surprise, when the door *snatched* his weapon.

Letting go in fright, he looked with fascination, as the blade disappeared within the golden slab. The handle jutted outward, and began to twist slowly, as the blue jewel glowed once more. The divots seemed to come alive, as they lifted off the wall, and bent around the pommel like gnarled roots.

"*Incredible*" Puul whispered.

Whether due to clever mechanisms or some kind of magic, the divots revealed themselves to be the limbs of a golden octopus or squid, as its beak looked as though it was gnawing on Kwenn's sword. The saucer eyes of the animated creature looked around, before closing. The sword popped out, and Kwenn took it back.

Panin laughed in excitement. "Well, that was something."

A seam split the door, and it began to open.

They ventured inward, ready for anything – at least, anything they could try and imagine.

Of course, nothing could have prepared them for what they encountered deep within the island of Shali.

The music Kwenn had heard before came from within a circular chamber that was inexplicably flooded with sunlight – at least, sunlight that was warbled by the surface of invisible water.

The glittering blue tendrils illuminated what looked like a small altar, which stood a bust of another woman.

Puul recognised it as Shalisshakin – The Goddess of the Ephemeral. Worshipped by the Green Robes, and guardian of the Invisible Realm.

All around them were the sounds of a gentle melody that emanated from phantom instruments. It actually sounded quite upbeat and cheerful, in a certain way.

Panin gripped Kwenn and his brother tightly on their shoulders. "*Look!*" he whispered.

On the ground sat a small figure. It was clad in robes, and its face could not be seen.

"H, hello?" Puul ventured.

The figure moved its head.

"Do you know how long I've been waiting for this day?" Its voice dripped with ancient wisdom, and held a tinge of loneliness. It stood upward, revealing its tiny stature.

"Shalisshakin bless me! Someone's actually got one of the keys! A good thing too, because I'm sick of talking to crabs." It looked at a group of the scuttling creatures. "No offence, fellas."

In the aqua light, the three men could see that this being held a large staff, and that its visage was completely obscured by a mottle of hair.

It hobbled forward, and Kwenn caught a glimpse of a green, clawed hand that held the wooden club.

"What are your names?" It asked.

"My name is Puul" the Numanta introduced. "This is my brother, Panin. And this is Kwenn."

The creature clomped forward even closer. "*Kwenn*? You, you're the possessor of the water key? Well I'll be!"

It laughed, sounding like a cheeky old man.

Kwenn unsheathed his sword. "What? *This*?"

"Of course, *that*" the creature said indignantly. "What, you mean to tell me you found your way here, and you don't even know what the elemental keys are? Preposterous!"

Its hair shot outward in a huff.

Kwenn wasn't sure what he was hearing. *Elemental key?*

Puul stepped forward and bowed. "We're sorry for intruding in your home, but we would like to know who *you* are..."

"Me?" It paused, as if taken aback. "Me? I erm... well... what was it again... oh!"

It thumped its staff on the ground. "My name is *Master Lojón*! Pleased to make your acquaintance! I am the caretaker to the Four Sister Isles, and custodian of the bridge between this world, and that of the fay."

The small being known as Lojón suddenly tilted and twisted its mottled head, much like that of an owl.

"Now!" he croaked, pounding his gnarled stick again, "Have the Wizards returned? Are they trying to mess with the natural order once more, hnn?"

The trio looked at each other with uncertainty.

"The Wizards?" Puul echoed with a wary timbre. "You mean... the rulers of Gamsay-Rumm? The ones that died?"

Kwenn recalled intently what Jugo and Ilod told him about the Wizards. An ancient sect that essentially ruled Tarinn for eons; once wise and benevolent, they slowly became corrupted due to their desire to unite their world with that of the invisible realm – essentially remaking reality itself… or so he gathered. Apparently Joner was the key to their plans; an unnatural spawn of human and faerie, his life was seemingly sacrificed by his own father in order to save the world.

Now that he reflected further, he remembered Jugo mentioning some sort of device the last Wizard possessed… a device that used keys to function.

Lojón hobbled a little closer to the Numanta. "So, they're still gone hm? Good, very good… so, in that case, why are you folks here? I'm curious to know."

Now that he was closer, Lojón's appearance was a little clearer. Though his face was still utterly obscured by a mess of dirty, straw coloured hair, the trio could see that he wore faded violet rags, and one of his arms was significantly larger than the other, and looked as though it was encased in some sort of armour.

"It's a long story" Kwenn began.

For a long while – much longer than they expected, the three men told Lojón everything. From Kwenn's mysterious appearance in Gen, all the way to their accidental discovery which brought them to their present situation. It wouldn't be until a long time after, that the men looked back at their time with Lojón with curiosity. Just what prompted them to tell this enigmatic figure their entire story? What made them trust him so utterly?

For what seemed like hours, they felt completely at home in his watery domain. Somehow, their hospitable little friend even made them tea, and offered them exotic snacks that made delectable use of seaweed. They lost all sense of time and urgency, but never felt like they were deceived in any way.

Slumped on the smooth floor, Lojón bowed. They could immediately tell he was troubled.

"Hur hm. I thank you lads, for telling me so much. So much has happened… so much…" He muttered something unintelligible, and looked at Kwenn. "I suppose it is only fair that I tell my own side of this worrisome tale. For you see, you and I are intertwined, my friends."

Kwenn guessed he should have been surprised, but the fact that they managed to find this place in such an elaborate fashion quashed such naivety. He knew the twins felt the same way, judging by their expressionless faces.

What *did* surprise him, however, was the small green fire that erupted at their feet. They all jumped out of their skin, but were quickly calmed by Lojón's soft, amused laughter.

"As you well know, friends, I am Master Lojón. I am the guardian that stands between Tarinn, and that of the Invisible…"

To their utter wonderment, images sprang from the ghostly blaze. They were like pictures come to life; stars and constellations emanated from flower buds, as a lone knight walked amidst the nine moons.

"For as long as the Four Sister Isles have been here, so too, have I."

"Fire. Earth. Wind. Water. Each of these elements weave the very fabric of our existence; a very real, and tangible way of life that cannot be undone, nor denied. The Four Sister Isles are the physical embodiment of this fundamental way… of *your* way."

Within the emerald hearth, there were now people; four angelic beings that swirled around each other, as they moulded land like clay.

"Shali. The realm of water, created by Lamun. The Goddess of Reincarnation, and caretaker of Sollus."

"Arlmai. The realm of fire, created by Qual-nu. The God of Misfortune, and protector of Sollik."

"Miiri. The realm of earth, created by Tson. The Goddess of Emotion, and mother of Solenir."

"Liniii. The realm of wind, created by Shalisshakin. The Goddess of the Ephemeral."

Lojón sighed. "That last one's my favourite. Ahem."

Clearing his hidden throat, he continued. "They created the Four Sisters to serve as a barrier between the two universes. Here, on this plane of existence, the four elements represent the absolute. They are the integrity of this world; of which all life springs forth, and all death sinks into. The Four Sister Isles are the gateway... and I am it's gatekeeper, so to speak."

The small figure shuddered, and the fantastical scenes fizzled out.

"Some of this you may know. Some, you may not. Indeed, history has a way of being lost to time."

Puul and Panin looked at each other incredulously.

"You're right" the latter said. "We... I think so much has been lost. We really don't know our own history."

"We don't even know our parents" Puul added mournfully. It was an unexpected statement, and the magi seemed to surprise even himself.

"None of us do" Kwenn added. Part of it was some meek attempt at reassurance.

"Orphans, eh..." Lojón said quietly. "I am truly sorry to hear that... but if what you say is true, then many more will follow. Unless we stop this atrocity from happening."

Kwenn almost resisted the urge to toss his tea mug across the grotto. "What *is* happening, then? What do we need to do to *stop* it?"

Even though he couldn't see it, he felt Lojón look at him from the corner of his eye.

"The world. Tarinn. It is a big place. Filled with wonder and countless discoveries. Not even *I* know of it all. But I do know that there are realms beyond. So many. Infinite, some would say. The faerie realm is just one of these. It exists just beyond the periphery, and its laws of nature are unlike our own. Like Tarinn, it is neither good nor evil – it just is."

Again, the fire stirred, as the face of Joner appeared.

Kwenn gasped. He knew it was him. Somehow, he just *knew*.

The twins also recoiled in shock.

"That... that's..." Panin stammered.

"Yes" Lojón whispered. "Joner Ironmonger."

Kwenn couldn't find the words. Though the visage was obscured by the wobbling of heat waves, it nevertheless terrified him.

"How… how…" he tried to speak, but his mouth was completely dry. His guts felt like they had disappeared into a pitch black void.

"The Wizards" Lojón said, before coughing. "They were an ancient and powerful race. Some say they were descended from the gods themselves. I don't know how, or why… but they grew to hate their masters. They hated Tarinn. They hated existence itself. They became fuelled by a nihilistic desire to wipe away everything. Jugo… tried to stop that. He did, in fact. If only for a little while."

The scene of Joner shifted, to a man and a woman, who danced underneath a pale moon.

"I'm one of the privileged few to have been allowed into both Tarinn and the Faerie realm" Lojón continued. "It is… hard to put into words. It is a world beyond human comprehension… but, if there was ever one whom the humans could fall in love with, that was Queen Bean Si."

"Indeed, one human did. And she him. That human was Jugo, and their son was Joner."

Lojón's head lowered in sadness.

Kwenn couldn't utter a single word. He felt nothing now, and it was a curious sensation.

Panin squinted, almost as if he suffered a severe headache. "Jeleenn… her brother… he wasn't *human*?"

Puul looked similarly distraught. "I… don't know what to make of this. We never knew Joner. Panin and I were only very young… but he died over ten years ago. Master Ilod never said much, just that he got sick during a trip, and that they couldn't help him."

"Jugo's wife… Jeleenn's mum, Mrs. Ironmonger, died a few years later" Panin whispered.

"Truly, you are all inexplicably bound by fate" Lojón declared. "Your little hamlet has suffered so much tragedy. Gen, was it? Hmmm, yes, one of the walls to the Sacred Sites."

The tiny being continued. "Born from an illicit tryst, Queen Bean Si knew that Joner could not stay within her realm. Shortly after his birth,

Jugo spirited him away to Tarinn, and all was eventually forgotten. At least… for a little while."

Lojón gestured with his metallic fist, and the fire crackled with the scene of the same tall woman, as she embraced a similar-looking man.

"Queen Bean Si eventually recovered from her tumultuous past, and finally found the arms of her true beloved, *King* Álfhildur. Together, they ruled their fair kingdom… and all was well."

Abruptly, Lojón reduced the hearth to a mere spark. His wizened voice seemed to become quieter.

"They were so happy" he whispered.

Kwenn began to wonder if the small creature's mind trailed off to a different world. He looked to his friends, and they too looked like they were completely lost in their own thoughts.

"I can't believe this" the Numanta said, shaking with a sudden chill. "How… how do you know all of this? How do you know Jugo?"

Lojón's scraggly hair flopped about, and the small being was jovial once more. "Oh! Yes, I was very good friends with Jugo. Your master Ilod, too. An incredibly talented *moon cloth*, perhaps the greatest I've ever seen! Quite!"

"They never mentioned you" Panin replied, perhaps a little more curtly than he intended.

"Alas" Lojón sighed, "my existence must be kept a secret… the fewer who know, the better it is for everyone. Though, I must say I'm not doing a very good job at squirreling myself away, since you three found me… but hey, fate, and all that, eh?"

He cackled cheekily. "I shouldn't laugh" he grumbled shortly after." Ahem, no. No, not with what you're telling me about this Hekor fellow."

He tapped the end of his gnarled staff on Kwenn's blade. "Now, in regards to *that.*"

And then thudded it against his chest. "And *you.*"

It was a playful gesture, and somewhere in the back of his mind, Kwenn appreciated Lojón attempts to make him feel warm and welcome… because he knew. *He knew.*

That emptiness just would not go away. He knew something was wrong. Something was very, very wrong. He didn't belong. He knew it now. He wanted to crumble, and sob until everything would go black, and he would feel no more pain.

He saw Queen Bean Si, and in his heart, he knew it was her. The one who fragmented his memories, and created this entire damned situation in the first place.

She was his mother.

Yet, he wasn't her son. Nor was that other abomination – that living doll they flushed out of the sea.

"Do you…" Kwenn rasped ever so silently, "do you know…"

"Who you are?" Lojón finished with a tenderness in his voice. "No. I do not, lad." He shuffled over, and put his steel palm over Kwenn's scar. It was so warm, he could only close his eyes, as a tear ran down his cheek.

"The pain that vibrates off of you is great indeed…" he turned to the twins, "…*all* of you. You've been through a lot. Don't be sad, my new friends… we've talked enough for one day, I believe. Yes."

Embarrassed with himself, Kwenn wiped his face and sniffed. "We need to head to Camo Temple. It's been too long."

Lojón waved his hand dismissively. "Nonsense. You were all brought here for a reason. *This* is where you need to be, fellows. That sword of yours told you so! Don't tell me you haven't been listening to it!"

Kwenn looked down, and stared at the bright blue jewel with his blade's golden finger guard. It was only then he realised just how tired he was.

"You mentioned this being a key?" he asked. "How?"

"My lad, it's not *a* key. It's *the* key!" Lojón crowed, "I should know! I made it!"

* * *

WARNING: SENTIENCE LIKELY A BY-PRODUCT////:

////:

PHKN

////:

SYNCING VIBRATIONS////:

////:

////:

* * *

Wrapped-up tightly in his sleeping bag, Kwenn slept soundly.

Convinced that they were finally – *finally* – on the right path in their journey, the three friends decided to take Master Lojón up on his offer, and spend the night in the Antechamber of Water.

Lugging their supplies from their dinghy, they wondered if they would be spotted by passers-by. After all, a massive door appearing on the side of a cliff-face was bound to attract *some* attention.

Yet, no-one came. Their area of the Great River was completely devoid of maritime activity. Whether by some divine design on Lojón's part, they couldn't say – but regardless, they felt a sense of warm protection in the late afternoon glow, as great big rainbow birds sat perched in their nests, and amphibious lizards skittered between bobbing turtle shells. The waters gushed melodically, creating a sense of serenity that dare not be broken.

For the first time in a long while, Puul, Panin and Kwenn felt relaxed.

They knew it wouldn't last forever. Of course it wouldn't. After all, being on the right track meant the greater likelihood of meeting danger head-on.

"That sword of yours is the Water Key" Lojón had revealed to Kwenn. "I crafted it, along with the other elemental keys, to act as a way to open the door between Tarinn and the Invisible Realm."

He couldn't quite believe it. All of this time, he carried such an important artefact!

For some reason, he recalled the first day he ever spent with Ilod...

Ilod slid his bowl to one side and eyed Kwenn. "That sword of yours is certainly unique." Kwenn was almost caught off guard by the statement.

"It is? How come?"

"Well..." Ilod seemed to think for a moment before answering, "It is, well... it is a make and shape I have seldom seen before."

Kwenn thought Ilod was making little sense. "'Seldom'?" He echoed.

"Well..." Ilod repeated. "When I was studying it yesterday, I couldn't make out the type of sword you had. It seemed two-handed, but even then it doesn't actually seem like it was made for fighting."

Kwenn could only raise his eyebrows in interest.

Ilod thought for a minute. He then started again. "Your blade is most definitely real. It is sharp and could pierce a dragon's underbelly. It is, however, seemingly unsuitable for combat." The mage wrinkled his brow in thought before continuing, "The shape is very bulky and unwieldy. There is no elegance to it."

Kwenn shook his head. "How can you say it's 'unwieldy' when I'm the only one who can actually wield it?" He thought back to when Lumiin the guard tried – unsuccessfully – to lift it.

Ilod was about to explain in further detail when Jugo spoke in his stead. "The mage is basically saying" the innkeeper stated roughly, "that, even though your little blade looks to be worth a million coins – it's still nothin' but brightly coloured hunk of junk."

Ilod adamantly waved his hand. "I never said it was a piece of junk Jugo. I simply said that it does not seem to be an obvious battle weapon. One that is carried by brigands and guards alike."

Kwenn shook his head in disbelief. For some reason, a hot rage welled up inside him. Despite this, he remained calm and swallowed his anger. "I'm sorry Ilod" he said, "but I don't agree with you." That was all he could say.

Ilod smiled in understanding. He seemed almost happy. "That is fine, Kwenn! I was just making my opinion heard, that is all. Whether it is unwieldy or not, that blade of yours is certainly one I have never seen the likes of. It fascinates me now all the more, to be honest." He pointed to the blue gem that was embedded into the golden finger guard. "That stone" he exclaimed, "is also one that I have been unable to identify."

Now that Kwenn saw *who* it was that made such a blade in the first place, its unusual quality was now much more appropriate.

It was a revelation, and explained why Kwenn was the only one who could carry it. It explained why it filled him with warmth and why it was able to fell the deranged form of Sergeant Wilko.

It was a sword of two worlds.

"Let me guess, there are also fire, earth and wind keys?" Panin asked in between swallowing mouthfulls of tea.

They all sat on their swags, sipping beverages and making themselves comfortable. The Gen guardsman pointed out that they looked like kids on a camping trip, and now the funny image couldn't escape Kwenn's mind.

Not the fact he was wielding a fairy sword all this time.

"You are correct, my astute friend!" Lojón chuckled, as he stirred a large cauldron with an big, redwood spoon. He stood on a stepladder in order to achieve his task, and Kwenn worried he might fall in the fishy stew.

Inhaling the aroma deeply through his mottled hair, the small creature paused for a moment, before resuming his duties. "Yes, there is a key for every element. The Water Sword, the Fire Helm, the Earth Armour, and the Wind Shield... goodness, it took me a long time to create the blighters, let me tell you! More soup?"

All three of Lojón's guests helped themselves, scooping their bowls with reckless abandon.

"... but, they're called keys?" Kwenn asked. "That's how Jugo described them, when the Wizards tried to use them to bridge the two worlds."

He thought back to the harrowing tale told by the innkeeper...

Instead of seven ancient deities that sat on their thrones with unrivalled poise and grace, there was instead a lone, stooping figure. Wearing flowing garments of ruby, blood orange and pearl – as well as the pointed hat that was the hallmark of his society – the old man held an ornate blade of unconventional design. With its orange pommel, lime-green grip, and golden finger-guard that was adorned with a sapphire, it was clearly the final key required to unlock the door to the other side. With the three other keys already in place, Jugo and his friends were now on the edge of the knife.

"You are too late" the frail man announced as he waved the faux-sword in a swooping arc. "The time has come. You may have ended the lives of my brothers... but their sacrifices will not be in vain!"

"Stop!" Jugo shouted with an outstretched hand.

Ilod stood forward. "My lord… it is over! There is nothing left!"

A leery grin emerged from the old man's extravagantly braided beard. "Maybe it is... maybe it is... you people have ruined everything. We sacrificed so much to end all suffering and sadness within this world. We were finally going to bless humanity with paradise!!! Don't you understand what you have done?! Because of your selfishness, people will be doomed to endure purgatory forever! Because of you, there will always be death and destruction! You will go down as history's greatest villains!!!"

Suddenly, everything began to shake violently. Jugo's legs buckled from underneath, but he was caught by Trebor. Clouds of birds dispersed in a squawking cacophony.

A massive column of pulsing metal rose from the ground.

It was the trigger mechanism to the invisible realm. The ancient Pheekonshenee machine built ages ago in their unrelenting desire for knowledge about the secrets of the universe.

Already, there were three keys locked into place; earth, wind, and fire. All that was left was water.

If that last key was inserted, everything would be lost.

Something never made sense to Kwenn. Jugo had seen the Water Key once before… why didn't he recognise it? Why didn't he tell Kwenn what he was carrying all of this time?

Maybe he was so overcome with grief after losing Joner, he simply blocked it from his mind. He willingly forgot everything that happened, and that seeing the sword again created a tempest of emotion – emotion that Jugo just did not want to deal with.

It was only then that Kwenn realised that Ilod *knew* what he saw when he first laid eyes on that blade, during that long conversation they had in Gen all those weeks ago.

Sterlio would have known too, along with Trebor.

Why? Why didn't they say anything?!

Lojón read his thoughts. "The keys" he muttered, as he lovingly patted a hermit crab that crawled up his arm, "are very powerful things. Depending on the state of the world around them, they can change before the mind's eye. They reflect the heart and intent of the bearer…"

"So. They change shape, basically" Panin surmised.

Lojón stopped, frozen mid-stroke. "Yes. Smart guy." He slumped, and shuffled toward Kwenn's sword, which lay beside its master. He hovered his palms inches above the scabbard, and hummed lowly. "The Water Key… it is sad. It has regressed into a pitiful shape. It has absorbed so much negative emotion."

He cocked his shaggy head toward Kwenn. "No offence lad, but you haven't helped matters all that much."

Kwenn wasn't offended by that statement. Nor was he even surprised. He totally understood, from the very instant those words left Lojón's mouth.

He slowly looked toward the blade. A slow broiling of self-pity broiled from his stomach, but he immediately quashed it. For what seemed like an inordinate amount of time, he didn't even comprehend the fact that Lojón just told him that his sword was literally capable of transforming. An internal curiosity now replaced his woe, and he had to wonder why he was absorbing so much revelatory information in stride.

Again, maybe it was the strange calming effect this hidden grotto had on his mind… but a part of him was just done-in. Tired, and too weather-beaten. It was a world away from the jittery, emotional amnesiac he was just a few weeks ago. In a strange way… was he maturing? For goodness-knew how long, he was deprived of his past life, and was basically forced to become a new man. As things swirled in turmoil all around him, he ironically grew stronger foundations within his sense of self.

Now, with friends by his side, and the fate of the very world seemingly in balance… he was… stronger?

"I know" he finally said. "I know, and we need to fix that. Lojón, we need to find the other keys."

Lojón sighed. "And what do you intend to do?"

"What *should* we do?"

"I'm guessing we can't just destroy them" Panin assumed.

"No" Lojón grunted. "They cannot be. If Hekor has centred his wrath on the Four Sister Islands, then it's safe to assume the realm of the invisible is at risk. He has been using dark beings of the fay to capture children, specifically targeting the townships that guard the sacred sites. I do not know what his ultimate goal is… but Kwenn, you are right. You *need* to find the other keys."

"Do you know where they are?" Puul whispered.

Lojón fell to the ground, and sat cross-legged. "I do not… for their safety, and that of the people. I wonder how Master Kwenn here managed to get a hold on one of them…

Kwenn closed his eyes. He lay on his back, and clasped his hands over his belly.

"I think my mother gave it to me" he said after breathing deeply. "She split my memories… scattered them around the sacred sites. I don't know how I know, but I just… do. I don't know if she's dead or alive…"

Puul nodded to Lojón. The girl we told you about. Oviinia. She's on her way to the Magick Shrine to retrieve the last memory shard. At least we hope it's the last."

"Ah, the strange woman who can gather energy. Yes, I recall you telling me about her. You said she was some sort of fish monger?"

"Marine biologist" Kwenn corrected, his eyes still closed.

"Yes, whatever. She certainly sounds most fascinating. Why her, I wonder? I'm assuming your mother, Master Kwenn, was the one who gave her such an ability, hmm?"

"I don't know how. She's spent most of her life in a small village in Arlmai. She survived the attack on Gimlum, because she was saved by Rayn."

"One of the kids who was kidnapped" Panin clarified. "Another one with strange abilities. He could talk to animals with his mind, and somehow was able to spiritually escape Hekor. That's what Oviinia told us. He helped her make her way to us, before disappearing."

The small creature hopped back on his feet, and paced back toward his cauldron. Apparently satisfied with the soup, he went back to his guests, and sat back down.

"Blimey, you lot have been through a thing and a half, huh? It's hard keeping everything straight in my poor old head! Then again, these islands have always produced the weird and wonderful... and sometimes, not so wonderful."

That was the last thing Kwenn could remember, as he had fallen asleep.

* * *

For an eternity, it was all light. Or was it a single second? She couldn't tell.

Either way, it was blissful in its ignorance. There was no sense of self. At least, for a little while.

When she finally became aware, it was like a jolt in her brain. She could never go back, and she was both happy and sad.

She had awoken, and her first memories were of her parents... and the water.

It was the water – and all that dwelt within it, that gave her a sense of living.

Crystalline. Azure. Silver.

Calm. Fierce. Indifferent.

Cold. Hot. Soothing.

To her, it was everything. There was nothing else. There didn't *need* to be anything else.

* * *

Kwenn woke up with a start.

As became usual with his gallivanting ways, he tried to remember where he was. This time however, there was no time to collect his scrambled thoughts.

Within the Antechamber of Water, a bright blood-red light now shot forth between the smooth rock and the watery 'ceiling'. Standing before the alarming pillar was Master Lojón.

"Wha… what's going on?" Kwenn slurred.

Already up, Puul nudged him with his foot. "Hey, rise and shine. We need to go."

"What? Why? How? Huh?"

Waddling over, Lojón looked into Kwenn's crusty eyes. "We are going to Arlmai, my lad! To my Antechamber of Fire, to be precise."

He spun on his heel, and thumped his staff. "I probably should have urged you boys to go sooner, but I didn't want to overwhelm you with so much all at once. Also, I had to know you were genuine, and not evil-doers that somehow infiltrated my lovely little abode. I'd say you passed the test."

Kwenn awkwardly pounced to his feet, and saw that Panin was already raring to go. He had packed everything, and was carrying the loads on his back.

"Arlmai? The island? How? I'm not dressed! Give me a second!"

As his slipped his gear on and rolled his bed, Lojón explained. "I am alarmed. I cannot access the Antechambers of Wind nor Earth. They are closed off. This should not be. It's been such a long time, I never bothered to check. Yes, you can judge me later. All that is open is Fire, and I need to get there and look. I fear the worst..."

Kwenn started to panic. He didn't like being rushed, and he could just *feel* Panin and Puul's eyes silently judging him.

I'm going as fast as I can, damn it!

He paused. "Wait… we're going to Arlmai… how, exactly?"

He knew Lojón smiled. "Those fancy-shmancy purple robes weren't the *only* ones able to bend time and space to their will..."

* * *

The Wy'rm River always beckoned.

For so long, her home of Buj was a paradise. Everyone loved her, and she loved them. Always, strange and exotic travellers would pass through, and the land around her teemed with wildlife.

As she grew, she spent days on end on the Wy'rm's banks, looking for tiny aquatic creatures and riding on top of the giant newts that prowled the rocky cropping.

True, she gave her folks an endless amount of coniptions by doing so – but she was never afraid of the big-mouthed children eaters. She could talk to them, and they her. They had a mutual understanding.

But nevertheless, the Wy'rm River always beckoned.

Then one day, she decided to leave. It was time. She had always heard breathtaking tales of the endless seas of Tarinn, and the countless lands that held innumerable lakes and rivers. She wanted to explore it all, and her parents did all they could to help her achieve her dreams.

Instead of spending her remaining days as a fishmonger, she would journey to the city of Ceev, and learn.

Learn about everything she needed. Everything she wanted. Nothing could hold her back from the water, and all of its mysteries and wonders.

Because the Wy'rm River always beckoned.

* * *

Kwenn gasped, as his knees buckled underneath him.

I hate this. I hate it. I hate it. I hate it. I hate it.

Was this what it was like teleporting? *Every single time?* Because if so, then no wonder the purple mages died out – they were probably too busy choking for air!

Puul and Panin were more stoic, and Lojón seemed completely unfazed, as if he merely walked through a doorway.

"You okay mate?" Panin muttered, as he made no effort in lifting his friend off his feet.

"Yeah… just swell" Kwenn whispered.

He was not.

He craned his head, and absorbed his new surroundings. The Antechamber of Fire was very much like that of its watery counterpart; at least upon first glance. Instead of coral and quartz, there were glowing veins of lava that ran along black, glassy walls. Another statue of Shalisshakin stood, her childlike features illuminated by the flames that danced up above in the dark, like stars. Bright, ruby-red reptiles skittered away from Lojón's hobbling stride, as whistling steam wafted from cracks.

Also, it was very, very warm.

Once their dizziness subsided, the chamber's guests marvelled at their surroundings. None of them had ever seen anything like this.

"This must be what a volcano's like" Panin wondered aloud, as beads of sweat began to form on his head. "Perfect, armour-wearing weather" he added sardonically.

Worried mumbles from Lojón could be heard amidst the white vapours. "No… no, no, no… this isn't right… this isn't right at all…"

Pressing his water-enchanted staff to his forehead in order to cool himself, Puul followed the small creature. He tried to tuck his loose clothing, evidently wary of it setting alight. "What's wrong Master Lojón?"

He nearly tripped, but caught himself. Kwenn and Panin followed, and they all saw that Lojón stopped at what looked like the entrance to the chamber.

It was open.

"How... how did this happen? Why didn't I know about this? This is *not* good!" He smacked his stick on the ground in frustration, causing small shards of rock to go flying. Kwenn wasn't sure if it was the wavy air that played with his eyes, but he could have sworn that Lojón flickered briefly out of existence.

Warily, the Numanta placed a calming hand on the ancient being. "Lojón... does this mean someone has the Fire Key? The *Fire Helm*?"

"It does" he huffed. "*Darn, drat* and *damn*. I certainly do hope it isn't in the hands of anyone untoward... they managed to find their way in here, but it doesn't look like anything is damaged. Not that they *could*... but still, they better bloody not have messed with my Earth and Wind Antechambers!"

"Hekor?" Panin asked. No-one wanted to say it, but someone had to.

"I certainly hope not" Puul shook, as the sweat running down his neck became cold.

Annoyed that a pebble found its way to the sole of his foot, Kwenn slipped off his boot and shook it vigorously. He then stopped.

Someone's here.

He could *feel* them. Deep in his bones. Watching from the shadows of the entrance. His heart began to beat faster and faster, as he spent an inordinate amount of time trying to decide whether to drop his boot, or to try and slip it back on, before unsheathing his blade. His voice caught in his throat, but Master Lojón was quick to the draw.

"Hmph! In case you didn't realise from that spectacular entrance, this is *my* domain! You think I can't see you skulking about out there like a ne'er-do-well? Step forward!"

Swearing, Panin pointed his spear toward the opening, as a clearly-flustered Puul – not refined by years of drills like his brother – was slower to the draw.

After a moment of tense silence, broken only by the hissing of fissures, a voice called out.

"We don't mean any harm. Please. We're showing ourselves."

In the wavy atmosphere, Kwenn finally put his infernal footwear back on, before pouncing and drawing his blade. With a slinky weariness, he saw two shadowy figures enter the Antechamber of Fire.

Two men.

Both held their arms up. One of them, the shorter and pudgier one, was dark-skinned, with long ginger hair reaching down his backside like a horse's tail. He was quite young in the face, which was wet with sweat that wasn't helped by his thick, furry outfit that was ill-fitting for the heat.

The taller of the duo was similar-looking in his attire; all leathers and fuzz. However, his face was hidden by a helm that was even richer in its bloody colour.

The Fire Helm.

Croaking at the sight of his long lost creation, Lojón instructed his retinue to lay down their arms.

"I sense no ill-will from our guests. Please, be at ease."

Everyone did as he instructed, and the two strangers looked momentarily as the small creature in wonder.

"Are you… Lojón?" The short one asked.

"I am, my fellow."

Excitedly, he shot a glance at his partner. "*See?* I told you this was the right place."

The other man did not respond. He stared straight at Kwenn.

What's his problem?

The ginger's brow wrinkled in befuddlement. Shaking his head, he too looked at Kwenn.

He covered his mouth, and gasped.

The reaction almost made him do the exact same thing. Looking around as if there was a goblin about to pounce on him, Kwenn scrunched his face in sudden annoyance.

"*What?*"

Staring for a few moments more, the taller man then clasped his helm, and slowly lifted it off of his head.

"Yeah" he replied quietly, as Kwenn suddenly found himself looking directly at *himself*.

"This is the right place."

CHAPTER IX

Oviinia gasped desperately for air, but none came. The whole episode was made even worse by the fact she had no idea where she was – or, even *who* she was.

Tears dripped down her cheeks like waterfalls, as she became hopelessly caught in a hellish purgatory of lung-busting agony; a shapeless, incomprehensible nightmare of nothingness.

After an eternity, her senses slowly came back into the light, and she could once again fill her body with life. It was a tremendous effort, but it slowly became easier and easier. With a hint of self-assuredness, she remembered valuable breathing exercises that were once taught to her by her father.

Breath in the diaphragm... like a balloon...

Her crying finally stopped, as she recalled her last memories.

Sterlio... I was with Sterlio... we were travelling... and... and...

That was all she could muster in her frazzled brain.

As her stomach and chest became more rhythmic in their motions, she closed her eyes and tried to centre herself. Wiggling her fingers at her side, she felt the grit of dirt or sand – and this spurred her to try to focus her blurry gaze.

She couldn't see much, no matter how hard she tried. Whether that was due to her own poor eyesight, or the pea soup fog that rolled all around her, she couldn't say. Regardless, she could only make out a few details, like the solid black masses of what looked like pillars, and distant *sloshing* of waves.

Biting her lip in determination, Oviinia lifted herself off the ground. Groaning with a sudden pain in her left hip, she patted herself down and tried to find her spectacles.

They were nowhere to be found.

Resisting the urge to screech like a banshee right there and then, she took another deep breath, and shook dirt and grime out of her hair. Exploring the innards of her stained coat, she was thankful to find that her knife was still present, as was a small pouch of nuts and dried fruit she always kept on hand.

Coughing, she tried to call for Sterlio. After a couple of whispers, she finally managed to eke out something resembling a voice.

There was no answer.

No matter how hard she tried to yell, the straining of her throat was lost in the thick atmosphere. The noises from her mouth dropped away right in front of her, as if sound itself was forbidden by the laws of nature.

A chill ran down her spine, making the hairs on the back of her neck stand up. She sauntered cautiously toward the nearest point of interest, and came into view of a dilapidated fountain.

It clearly hadn't seen any use for a long time. Overgrown with weeds, the structure bore the ugly visages of gargoyles. The way their lips were pursed unnerved her, and she directed her leer toward a plaque that jutted out from the scraggly ground.

Cursing her lame eyes, she ran a hand over the faded epitaph and tried to read it.

'Oh life-giving blight that paseth through black lips of beast'
'Ever _ _ battle the the thirst _ so _ _ _ forme'
'_ it sinks toward the nether; _ realising that it e'er ascend _ souls'
'The trickster, he eternal of our damnation, _ yet solitude of our being'

'The dew it e'er sprinkles. It e'er drips. Through the lips _ _ _'

The rest was too ineligible for her to read.

Shaking again briskly, she flexed her legs in an attempt to push blood through her limbs, whilst woefully contemplating her next move.

After an unnecessarily long internal debate, she finally decided that fire and a shelter were the most immediate concerns.

Since there was a fountain, she reasoned that there must have been a structure nearby. Waving the fog away with futility, Oviinia tried to follow anything that resembled a path, and was relieved to see a large mass in the ominous distance.

Wherever she was, there was no doubt that this was a foreboding place. The sounds of lapping waves became inexplicably silent, and the were no signs of wildlife. The calls of birds nor insects pierced the thick atmosphere… but despite this, she couldn't help but feel smothered by the countless gazes of invisible people.

Her heart beating ever quicker, she approached an old building.

Surrounded by a decaying fence, she nervously gripped the handle of the rusted gate. At first, it wouldn't move, but after a couple of forceful tugs, it opened with a horrible squeal that wasn't unlike a scream from a slaughtered pig.

Gritting her teeth at the noise, Oviinia entered the overgrown yard.

Everything was dead.

Swallowing with fear, she lightly stepped her way over the cracked stepping stones, and climbed the terrace.

Again wincing at the creaking of weakened supports, she raised a trembling fist, and knocked on the weathered door.

There was no answer.

Pounding with a bit more zeal, she was still met with silence.

Looks like no-one's home…

Feeling more and more uneasy about being outside, she twisted the knob, and found it to be unlocked.

A sudden bout of terror overcame her. She wasn't sure what would be waiting on the other side, and her overactive imagination only made things worse for her poor constitution. Her mind became filled with images of horrid beasts and wicked old crones thrusting their gnarled hands toward her, and if she dared enter, they would drag her soul to the depths of hell.

Shaking her head free of such lunacy, she took a deep breath, and remembered everything she had been through in recent weeks.

No, I'm not letting this scare me… no way in hell!

She pushed the door, and stepped inside with as much confidence as she could muster.

It was pitch black, and the very air seemed to be made of dirt.

"Hello? Anyone here?" she called, knowing full-well the entire place was abandoned. Either that, or there really *was* some monster living within its abyssal bowels.

Taking mental note of that horrifying possibility, she briefly considered retreating, but held firm in the belief that she was making the best move. She needed immediate shelter, and the alternative was to wander the outside, only to possibly be forever lost in the whiteness.

No, this was the only thing she could do.

Her vision slowly adjusted to the inky interior, and she could see that the house held a standard living area. There were some wooden chairs, a couch, bookshelves, tables, and other odds and ends.

Nervously aware of the halls that branched from her sides, she loudly announced her arrival a few more times, just to be sure. Again, it felt like her words refused to carry in the air, and she cursed with both frustration and worry.

The whole situation made her feel like she was dreaming.

Where are you, Sterlio…

The dust began to make her cough, and she sorely wished she had a flask of water on hand. As she inhaled, she could also taste the mustiness in the back of her throat, which forced her to cover her face with her forearm.

Stomping toward the desks, she noticed some used candles. She said a silent prayer, and searched the drawers for matches.

She found some.

Yes! Thank god!!!

They looked like *very* old sulphur heads, but were still dry. Beside them was a strange contraption that looked a lot like scissors. She assumed they were used for cutting the sticks, but as curiosity overcame her, Oviinia tried operating the tool, but had a strange amount of friction between both 'blades'. Taking a whiff, she thought she smelled flint. Using it more vigorously, she witnessed sparks emerge.

Mentally crossing her fingers, Oviinia struck one of the long matches near the ignition tool, and hissed in satisfaction when it started to blaze.

Frantically lighting anything she could find, she wound up with three working candles. They provided enough illumination for now – and as much as she hated herself for it, she decided she would smash up one of the small desks to use as a hearth. Finding the fireplace, she proceeded to use all the strength she could harvest, and hurled one of the tea tables onto the floor.

Possibly due to its age, it shattered relatively easily. She jammed a couple of pieces into the ashy space, and used one of the candles to light it.

The fire was smaller than expected, but it was enough. Embracing the warmth was the single greatest feeling she ever had.

Allowing herself to rest for a moment, she took a better look around the living room.

There were a litany of strange instruments – both musical and scientific – that surrounded her. On the walls were strange pictures; some were clearly artistic in nature, whilst others were more abstract. She couldn't make head nor tail of them, nor some of the documents that were left laying around.

Was this place abandoned?

Groaning, she lifted herself off the mouldy lounge chair, and perused the bookshelf. Many were too faded and falling apart, but a few were still readable. Carefully, holding one in her hands, she wasn't surprised to see the pages become dislodged from the spine. She slowly browsed the contents, but was disappointed to see it was written in a foreign language. Still, there were some curious illustrations, and she guessed it was related to magic or science.

Whoever lived here seemed quite learned. I wonder if they were a mage?

She plucked up the courage to scour the rest of the home.

The kitchen had nothing. She was fearful of finding something old and foul, but the worst was long gone. Dishes, cups and cutlery were still present, and she hoped that there would be a well somewhere.

They had to have gotten water somewhere!

Worried that she might find a mummified corpse around every corner, she found a couple of bedrooms. There was very little in them, aside from old beds and a few books here and there.

She had no desire to explore further. Feeling sick in her stomach, Oviinia wondered just where on earth she was, and just what had *happened* to these people. She didn't know what the time was, or even if it was night or day. Everything was so shrouded in an oppressive twilight… no, she couldn't even call it that. It was more like a perpetual *unlight* – that was the only way she could describe it in her head.

"What the hell do I do now?" she said loudly to herself. She needed to hear *something*.

Footsteps.

Pausing in her despair, sheer fear gripped the woman's heart.

Footsteps could be heard in the house.

Scrabbling for her knife, Oviinia broke out in a cold sweat. Grabbing a broken leg of the wrecked table, she lit the end on fire – and with weapons in hand, she dived for cover behind the aged sofa.

Again, the boots could be heard. She couldn't tell if they were *above* or *below* her, but either way, her head was on a swivel.

They stopped, and she refused to breathe.

Again, they started up. *Boom. Boom. Boom.*

Are they looking for me? They must know I'm here!

Swearing, she impulsively shouted. "Hey! I can hear you! Why don't you come down and face me?!"

Why. Did. I. Just. Do. That.

The steps now became more erratic, and her chest seemed to match each one in its rhythm.

"*Oviinia.*"

She screamed, and ran straight towards the door, as *something* whispered in her ear.

With other plans in mind, the door slammed shut before she could make it outside. She madly tried to rip the knob off its hinges, but it wouldn't budge.

The footsteps got louder and more violent, and they ran straight toward Oviinia.

Although she was unable to see anything, she felt a black, evil energy shoot straight through her body, as *something* pushed its face toward her own.

Gasping in shock, she tumbled and fell out of the doorway as it suddenly swung open with a violent *crack*.

Crashing onto the splintery surface of the veranda, Oviinia tried to inhale as, once more, she no longer knew where she was.

She watched as a black shadow glowered downward at her, before it shot back into the house. Even within the darkness, she could see its human-like shape. It was a void, completely bereft of light.

Wheezing for breath, she scrambled to her feet, and bolted for the front gate.

She skidded to a halt, and her legs became jelly. Collapsing again, she was utterly petrified.

Gathered around her were people. Except, they did not look like any ordinary people.

Wearing garbs of pure light, they all stood like giants; their willowy forms completely and utterly unmoving.

Their faces. Their faces too, were still. Their stony gazes were made all the more crippling by their identical, chiselled features and bald heads.

They were all the same, and like an encroaching forest of humanity that gathered around her, they only moved outside her periphery. Like trees, any signs of life they had were far beyond her pathetically small perception.

Within each one of their foreheads were gems. They all glowed with colours that she simply could not comprehend.

Insanity crept up on her, yet Oviinia somehow found the strength to balance herself on her feet. The strange symbol on her arm – the one she received that day when she met Rayn – began to glow white hot.

Now they were mere inches from her wide-eyed, tear-smudged face.

"*GET AWAY FROM ME!!!*"

Running as fast as her inattentive legs could take her, she threw herself over the rickety wood fence, and blindly headed for the nearest point of safety.

She saw other structures now; other houses. With no concern for her guest manners, she climbed the steps of the closest refuge, and found that the door was already open.

Looking back over her shoulder, she saw that the men were not following her. Again, they did not seem to visibly move, nor did they appear to have any legs.

Cursing violently again, she jumped into the home, and slammed the door.

Fortuitously, her glowing arm helped illuminate the small interior. Grabbing the biggest chest of drawers she could see, she strained with all her might, and threw it against the door.

Looking for her blade in desperation, her snivelling was made even worse by the fact that she fell on it during her fall, and it was now sticking out of her side.

"God *damn* it…" she whispered in disbelief. Pulling it out, she was utterly relieved to see that it was only a minor wound – she had had worse fish hook incidents in the past.

Wincing at the stinging pain and the sight of blood, she came close to hyperventilating.

Forcing herself to calm, she began cutting a piece of her shirt off. Before she could even finish, an explosive thud hammered the door.

Screaming again, Oviinia backed away to the far end of the room.

Bang. Bang. Bang. The very floor underneath her shook, as ferocious blows surrounded her.

What do I do? What do I do? Oh god oh god I'm trapped oh god!!!

Covering her ears with her claret-soaked hands, she cried without abandon. Thoughts of Kwenn suddenly flooded her mind. Thoughts of her family. She desperately wanted them with her right now. To feel their touch. To hear their voices.

The thunderous cacophony was unceasing. It would never end. She would never know peace ever more. They *owned* her. She was *theirs.* She wasn't a person. She was... she was...

Louder than anything she had ever produced, she bellowed a primal roar of pure hatred.

Everything stopped.

The malicious wind that smothered the building with its overbearing heat zipped away within an instant, and the sudden stillness jolted her organs, like jumping into a freezing pool.

Oblivious to the pain that should have been racking her throat, Oviinia slid slowly onto the rotten wooden floor, as her back wiped away a large swath of cobwebs on the ancient wall.

Unsure of how long she sat there in utter mindlessness, she blinked, and began staunching her wound. Grabbing a clump of webbing, she rolled it into a fine ball, and gently pressed it into the opening.

Finishing her amateur attempt at first aid, she fought all desire to lie down and sleep, and got up onto her wobbly feet.

She knew Sterlio was somewhere nearby. She did not accept any other alternative. She would find him, and he would explain just *what in the hell* was going on here.

A part of her wanted to blame him. At the back of her frayed mind, she wondered if this was somehow his fault. That all of... *this*, was somehow related to him. As horrible as it made her feel, the merchant still frightened her... yes, he was a friend to everyone, and yes, he had proven to be of great help... but, that didn't change the fact that she barely knew him.

She had to admit it. He was deranged. Maybe it was her personal biases getting in the way of her logic, but that's how she saw him. His unstable mentality was only exacerbated by his wicked magics and otherworldliness – not to mention his *awful* dress sense.

She laughed. Because at the same time, she so desperately wanted to find him. Not only to escape wherever she was, but because... she couldn't help but *like* him. He was utterly magnetic, in his own, inexplicable way.

Balking at the idea that she was a damsel in distress to be saved by a gaudy, money hungry necromancer, Oviinia calmed herself, and tried to look for any clues.

She wasn't worried about staying hidden. She figured whatever ghastly denizens this place held already knew where she was. She resigned herself to accepting that she could be attacked by anything, at any time, in any place. She had to show a brazen bullheadedness that proved she wasn't afraid, and that these... *things* had no power over her.

Easier said than done.

She heard other laughter outside, and immediately collapsed to the floor like she had lost all of her bones.

Her heart pounded with the sound of a thousand drums in her ears. She could hear voices engaged in a conversation, but couldn't make out the words.

Crawling with a burst of vigour that hid her paralysing fear, she pressed herself onto the chest that blocked the door, and craned her head. She was damned if she was going to peek out the window – she *knew* there would be a face staring straight back at her. She read *enough* spooky stories as a kid.

It was two men. Two men who sounded perfectly... normal. They chatted in a surprisingly friendly manner, but she still couldn't make out the language.

"To hell with this."

Gritting her teeth, and mustering every ounce of courage she had, she flipped the wooden shelves aside, and kicked the door open.

There was no-one there.

Suddenly enraged, she stormed out onto the decayed lawn, and waved her knife around in the air. "I don't know where I am, or you the hell you are" she screamed, "but I want answers! *NOW DAMN IT!!!*"

Panting with fury, her arm began to glow once more. A warmth shot through her limb, as people suddenly sprang into existence.

Glowing green, and looking corpse-like, they all surrounded her. They seemed utterly oblivious to her existence, as they paced to and fro. They talked. They drove carts. Little skeleton children danced and giggled, as robed figures wowed onlookers with wondrous feats of magic.

In unmitigated disbelief, Oviinia didn't even have the sense to wail and run for the hills. Mouth opened in a permanent gape, and with stickiness in the corners of her red eyes, she slowly wandered with no direction, as she found herself in the middle of a necropolis.

* * *

Remana tol Dwen was in utter darkness.

Mad with both fear and confusion, she stumbled through the labyrinth, as unknown horrors crept and clawed around her; gnawing at her ankles. She could feel their cold, grey lips. Their diseased teeth.

Their smiles.

She had to find Qual-nu. That was the way. He told her himself.

Captain Archie Shorn was dead. She wrung his neck. She did not even see it. Only felt the deed.

How long was she running now? Hours? Days?

Surely not weeks?

This place did something to her. Was it the drink she partook in, presented as it was in a crystal goblet atop a glass alter that ran red with veins.

Veins that looked like blood.

Bones cracked under her boots. She knew they were bones.

The Tower of the Gods was closing in.

* * *

With garbled, watery language they spoke – but try as she did, Oviinia couldn't understand a single word.

She was caught between a dream and a nightmare. Like the ones she occasionally had when she slept; full of bizarre and sometimes horrible imagery that nevertheless unfazed her. The type of dreams where her jaws could not close because of innumerable, oversized teeth. Or how one time she kept pulling her nose off, only for it to regrow.

Strange, illogical, skin-crawling experiences that went away when the suns rose in the sky.

But now, she was *living* it. Her emotions felt like an unstoppable force meeting an immovable object; an immense battle that left her utterly devoid of sense.

She tried to cry. To do *something*. *Anything* to prove to herself that she was still in *her* reality, and that... *events* like this still required *appropriate reactions.*

She needed to ground herself, lest she go completely batty.

She ran, and her arm pulsed with white light. Slamming her back against a stone wall, she pressed her glowing appendage to her cheek, and was suddenly soothed by its warmth. Sliding to the ground, she curled into a ball. And watched.

Watched, as these... *ghosts* went about their business.

She was a scientist. She wasn't supposed to believe in ghosts. But even before meeting Rayn, she always thought they existed. She liked the idea of the so-called 'paranormal' being completely normal, and she was always fascinated by the work of the Numanta and the black-robed Titanicae, and their more logical, hard-nosed views on magic and the fantastical.

None of this felt logical.

What has happened to my life?

She wept now, as thoughts of her childhood came flooding back...

* * *

"Oviinia! Don't go too far, you hear me?!"

Nodding her head so vigorously that her pigtails took on a life of their own, Oviinia waved at her mother's bellowing form, before skipping along the Wy'rm River in her new, slightly-oversized gumboots.

As always, her best friend was at her side – Hoppo, the big fat golden frog.

She had human friends, of course, but sometimes she just liked being alone. This concerned her stuffy parents, but both calmed slightly when Hoppo was nearby. Despite being a monstrous, dog-sized amphibian, he loved Oviinia just as much as man's best friend. His breed was incredibly rare because of poaching, with the Trundle family finding him as a tadpole being illegally smuggled on a fishing boat.

Harrumphing as if to say 'stop worrying so much mum', he bounced alongside the little girl, as they ventured into the scrub.

Of course, Hoppo's main motivation was some delicious fish, but Oviinia was after something slightly more exciting. Early that morning, when it was still dark out, she overheard her father and a couple of his fishing buddies talking outside her bedroom window. Apparently, during their previous day's trawl, they had spotted a beam of light shooting from somewhere in the north, near the entrance to the *Merca Lal Mountains*. It was said to be bright red, and high enough that it illuminated the clouds.

They had debated about investigating, and their harsh whispers served only to excite the eavesdropping Oviinia, rather than scare her.

Before the men could decide what to do, she would beat them to the punch.

Obviously, she didn't tell her parents about her little quest. As far as they were concerned, she was only going to play in puddles and climb a few trees.

She told herself she wasn't going to go too far. As much as Buj bored her to death, she disliked the idea of getting lost; or even worse, the idea of her folks finding her, before imprisoning her in her room for the rest of eternity.

Still, Hoppo knew the way home. She could ride on his back. He wasn't as fast as the giant salamanders on land, but he sure knew how to jump like a demon.

Oviinia wasn't exactly sure where she was going, but didn't pay too much heed. She simply headed north, whilst coming up with some new tunes to whistle.

There was no path, but the thicket wasn't too demanding for her small form. She knew the area well, and would often play with the other children in the hollowed tree trunks, and leap between the bulbous mushrooms as they played knights and goblins.

She wanted to bring them along, but a part of her didn't want them to get in trouble too. Another part of her simply enjoyed the quiet, and vastly preferred the company of wet, slippery creatures.

Normally girls liked her squealed and squirmed at the sight of such things, but Oviinia Trundle has always been different in that way. She was more comfortable with frogs and fish than she was with cats and dogs, and this sometimes made her parents stressed, though she could never understand why.

Maybe she embarrassed them?

That couldn't be it. Buj was all about the water! Her dad was a great fisherman, like all the other dads! Why was it that the boys were the only ones who were allowed to like these things?

Sometimes she was teased for it by her pals, but after a scuffle or two, they would usually shut up about it. She giggled, thinking about the one time Hoppo trapped one boy inside his gigantic mouth, before spitting him out in a wave of gooey drool.

His parents were *mad* that day.

The girl looked toward the sky, and noted the clouds. It could rain today, but the birds were still singing, so she decided to press on. There were still patches of pale blue here and there, and the air was very crisp and cool.

After a little while, Oviinia decided she would walk for a few minutes more, before turning back. It was starting to get darker and darker, and she had grown increasingly bored of her plan. She wondered if this light was worth checking out after all, and that whatever it was may have actually vanished by now.

I should've bought snacks...

Sighing, she was about to loudly complain, before she noticed that Hoppo had stopped. He growled, as she crinkled her brow toward him.

"What's the matter? Are you hungry? So am I..."

She continued on, before the amphibian lashed its tongue out, and held her foot in place.

"Hey! What are you doing?! Wha–

Then she saw them. Two people, standing in the greenery. A small girl, with brown skin and shockingly-bright red hair. And a man; the tallest man she had ever seen. He was as tall as the trees, and wore clothing that covered his entire body, except for his bald head. She struggled to look at him directly, such was the prism of colours that she could not understand. They held hands, and stared right at her.

She could not move. Her heart came to a standstill, as Hoppo tried desperately to pull her away. She was like stone.

Her friend's distressed croaks flooded her ears, as the man was suddenly nose-to-nose with her.

There was a voice in her head.

Take care of your sister, young one. When the time comes, you will need each other. She did well in taking care of you. The humans, too.

Oviinia tried to scream. Scream for Hoppo. Scream for her mother. Scream for her father. But there was nothing.

Dribbles of rain pattered on her face, and encircled her round glasses. Her vision became a watery blur, and the man's form slowly vanished away.

Do not be afraid, Vatn. That light was merely a sign. You did well to respond, as you were supposed too. Now, go back home young one. And speak of this to no-one.

WARNING: SENTIENCE LIKELY A BY-PRODUCT////:
////:
PHKN
////:
SYNCING VIBRATIONS////:
////:
////:

* * *

Snapping herself out of her haze, Oviinia yelled.

She called out for Hoppo, but then she remembered.

Hoppo died years ago.

"Where? How?!"

She trembled with agony, and tried to come to terms with what she had just witnessed.

Was that a real memory?

Everyone was gone. No more spectres. No more children. No more singing. Only silence. Only the quiet side of death.

She breathed in, and dust coated her cracked lips. She embraced the nothingness that permeated the stillborn air, as her glazed vision was drawn toward a lone figure that again stared at her from the shadows.

It was the same man from her vision.

Quivering from rage and fatigue, she tried to unleash obscenities, but could only make a sound not too dissimilar to her long-gone amphibious friend.

The voiceless-voice. It pierced her mind, like a metal spike through her brain.

Moaning in blinding, unimaginable pain, Oviinia doubled-over, and resisted the urge to bash her skull against the nearest stone surface.

Vatn. You need to keep moving. Your charge is waiting for you. Obtain his fragments.

"*Shut up!*"

Scrambling along the ground like a wounded animal, the woman grabbed the nearest hunk of stone, and hurled it at the terrible figure. Her aim wasn't true, and her strength was totally gone, leading the projectile to clatter pathetically along the ground.

The man was gone. As if insulted by her lacklustre assault, he was now one with the stale wind.

It took her a moment to comprehend what had just happened. At her wit's end, she tried to fight against the raw, unrelenting insanity that crept around the blurred edges of her mind. With every ounce of will, she resisted, and focused her mental faculties toward the words that the wraith burrowed in her brain.

Her pounding heart rattled her bones, and with a sliver of defiance, she ascended with her burning legs. Her face strained with a conflict between contorted fear and steadfast bravery, and right on cue, the dead village was once again awash with undead activity.

She was positive that this place was mocking her. Whatever dread power smothered this land was feeding off her soul, and no matter what she did to try and counter it, it was always a step ahead like some perverse board game.

She was a plaything for them. Whomever 'they' *were*.

The rotting folk resumed their activities. Caught in the nether between life and death, they now cast furtive glances toward Oviinia, with whatever remained in their eye sockets.

Rigid with agony, she quelled the bile in her throat and refused to let her ghastly foes get the better of her.

Like the ebb and flow of the salty tides, her vulnerability was once again replaced with hot-faced fury. Grinding her teeth with every defiant nerve in her body, her arm became completely engulfed in white hot fire; a fire that ran through her veins and licked its way up her spine. It drowned her.

WARNING: SENTIENCE LIKELY A BY-PRODUCT////:

////:

PHKN

////:

SYNCING VIBRATIONS////:

////:

////:

////:

ABSORPTION RATE 100%

////:

////:

ABSORBING////:////:KWENNSEFULASS

* * *

WARNING: SENTIENCE LIKELY A BY-PRODUCT////:

////:

PHKN

////:

SYNCING VIBRATIONS////:

////:

////:

////:

ABSORPTION RATE 66.66666%

////:

////:

ABSORBING*////:////:*NUVUMMBURTEE

* * *

The frozen wind slashed her face.

Life surged through her writhing body, and she gargled with an inhuman voice. Her head was filled with light, and it shot forth like a beacon.

"Hey! Hey!!! Calm down! The hell!"

She felt hands clasping her shoulders. Pinning her on the frigid, solid floor. Her eyesight slowly resumed, and she saw the haggard, stubbled face of Captain Archie Shorn.

After a long, long time of laboured breathing, she whispered.

"Where... how..."

"Where at the top of the tower... the summit. Holy hell, what a scene. What a bloody scene..."

Reassured that she would no longer spasm violently, he released her and slumped.

Stars were incredibly clear in the dark above, with not a cloud to be seen. Her head thumped, and she was instantly reminded of the same thing happening in the mountains – the same thing that left her with a permanent mark on her forehead.

It was so distinct. She remembered it all too well, even if everything else that happened after her father's death was so clouded.

"What... what happened..." Remana demanded hoarsely. She slowly sat up and coughed violently.

Archie looked like hell. His clothes were grimy and tattered, and he looked as if he hadn't slept in a week.

"I don't know" he mumbled, curling into himself and shaking. "We entered this... this godless tower. The hall stretched on for miles and miles... it was the most amazing thing I'd ever seen. So many crystals and glass and jewels... But it was a front."

He spat. "A front for a filthy, disgusting, horrifying maze built by a perverse madman. We drank that damned goblet... and... and..."

The look in his eyes was that of someone reliving a past that he long thought dead.

"It was a test. A test of faith from times yore. A truly sacred site."

They both scrambled like dogs on a slippery floor, as they tried to pinpoint the direction of the new voice that suddenly spoke.

"The hell!" Remana shouted. She slid next to the captain, and they both looked at the figure which stood amidst the night, staring at them.

He was tall, and seemed to glow with an ethereal aura. Her throat closed upon witnessing his beautiful terror, as his armour was akin to a mirror as it bounced back the images of the luminary heavens in uncountable ways. A cape woven from flowers flapped like silk in the gale, interweaving with long, rose-pink and white hair, which framed a pale mask that resembled a death mould of an infant, which seemed to float like an apparition.

"Mr. Telos!" Archie croaked.

She shot him a look of disbelief.

Him?! That's him?!

"Ancient Sollikane and followers of Qual-nu" he continued, seemingly unaware of their state, "built this place. As a trial for the truly devout and brave. One simply had to drink a hallucinogenic concoction and immerse themselves in utter sensory deprivation for days. All that is evil – all that is horrible and truly woeful – it all comes from the mind. And if one can successfully navigate the many floors all the way to the top, the God of Misfortune deems you a true chosen one."

He took off his mask. Behind it, was a face of porcelain. The most beautiful man Remana had ever laid eyes on, with emerald eyes that were brighter than any star.

He smiled, and looked in her eyes. "You made it. I knew you would.

This old structure served a secondary purpose, too. For you, Remana tol Dwen. Or, should I say, Aodh."

"*You*" she hissed, practically dripping venom from her chattering teeth, "you are the one. Behind *all of this*?!"

Telos' smile vanished, replaced by that of concern and sadness.

"I… am" he admitted. "I know, I know you hate me at this moment. You want answers. I will give them to you."

An odour of something sickly-sweet, like that of rotting meat, filled her nostrils. She gasped, as a beam of light ripped through the very air in front of them, forming a door. On the other side were verdant grasslands.

"What… how" she uttered, before shrinking away from his outstretched hand.

"Wait!" Archie wheezed, indignant at Telos' seeming ignorance of his presence. "You no-good bastard!" He leapt lamely forward, stumbling in front of Remana. Standing between them, he slapped away the man's hand. "Most of my men are at the bottom of the sea because of you! Those that remain are on the verge of death, and my ship – *my ship* – is no more! All because of your goddamn 'foolproof' instructions!!!"

"Captain Shorn" Telos began, rubbing his palm. "You made it here too. I'm impressed. I actually, genuinely am! For someone as cowardly and evil as you, I didn't think you'd survive. But you did. And I can tell you, right here and right now, that this was no simple job. You *knew* that."

"Damn right I survived" he acknowledged. "I walked through hell and back, and so did my men! My *family*! All for this woman!"

He was practically screaming now, his chest heaving. "Pay me. Now. Use whatever sorcery you can muster to whip up the money. I don't care. I don't want to see your pretty-boy face ever again, you hear me?"

The wind howled, as both of them stared at each other for eons. Remana feared that she was about to witness a duel to the death.

"Very well" Telos finally relented. "A promise is a promise. Even to a pirate."

Clicking his fingers, treasure chests began to fall from the sky. One after the other, they smashed to the earth like meteors, as their riches burst forth.

Archie yelped, as he dived for cover.

It was complete bedlam, and in the cacophony, Telos again beckoned Remana to follow him through the portal.

Her head seared, and she saw no alternative. She followed him, leaving Captain Archie Shorn with the thing he desired most.

CHAPTER X

It was forever and a day.

Morning and night. New year and year's end. The Blinking of the Eyes.

It didn't matter. It stopped mattering a long time ago... how long? Who cares?

Time wasn't even a *thing* any more.

Yet, when Syyd dwelt on it, he became painfully aware that time was indeed a *thing* in his old life – and he so *desperately* wanted his old life back.

They all did. Every single child that now trailed behind him; their wispy footfalls tapping along the cold, stony ground.

There was an alarming awareness in the back of Syyd's lethargic state of mind – that, no matter what, he should *never forget*. Because if he did, he knew he would be lost forever.

But... he *hated* remembering. The more he did, the more he wanted to burst into tears...

Everything was quiet. Everything was so, so quiet. Syyd tried to whisper, but no noise could be produced. He could not breathe, he could not cry. He tried... he tried so very hard... but... nothing.

He tried to remember... that's right. He was outside -- in the rain.

Yes, now he could feel it -- the water pattering on his eyes and running down his cheeks... he was... lying down? Why was this? Where is Rayn? What happened?!

Panic surged through the boy. Blood began to pound in his ears; so painful and so loud. Where is Rayn?

He was finally able to see again. He was finally able to see... fire?

No... no! This was not right!

In a horrible rush to find his brother, Syyd turned his head... no! There was fire! Flames! It was everywhere! There was nothing left! The houses, the road! They were all gone!

"Rayn!" Syyd managed a hoarse whisper. "Rayn!" he choked. "Help!"

Smoke began to make his eyes sting. Salty tears mixed with bitter rain. He tried to get up, but found that he was unable to. He was paralysed. Even more panic overwhelmed the boy. He began to choke and cry. "Rayn!!!" he managed to scream.

Then, he heard it. Screams. Screams of the dying. Screams of the hysterical. Screams of the animals... screams of the children.

A cold, debilitating chill ran through the boy's veins and gripped his heart, squeezing it. He could not breathe.

"Stop it!" he cried, though he did not know why. "Please! Stop!!!"

Amid his cries, he saw Rayn, lying face first in the mud. He was not moving.

"Rayn!"

Nothing. No response.

"Rayn! Answer me!!!"

Nothing.

Syyd began to cry. He urged his limbs to move, yet they refused to obey. Even his fingers and toes ceased to function.

"Help!!!"

He cried and cried until his throat was hoarse. Yet no-one arrived. There was no one left...

No, wait! There was someone!

A man, or that's what Syyd thought, appeared out of nowhere. The boy could not see his face, nor could he see any distinguishing features. He was all black, like a shadow. He walked, slowly and methodically, without any urge to help the boys. Syyd once again sobbed for help, yet, the man just ignored him. He slowly – ever so slowly – walked... toward Rayn.

Suddenly, Syyd knew. This was no man he was familiar with. This was a bad man... a man who seemed to walk over to Rayn as if to claim his prize.

"NO!" *he shrieked.* "DON'T TOUCH HIM!!!"

The man bent down and brushed his fingertips over Rayn's dirty, tangled mass of hair. Suddenly, he was gone.

Rayn was gone.

Syyd screamed for his brother as the man slowly turned his head towards him. Horrible, flashing red eyes materialised on the man's face. A grin. An evil, unnatural grin appeared, full of rotting teeth. The man walked gracefully towards his second victim. He stood at Syyd's feet, and silently stared down at the boy. The sinister mouth parted and gave off a laugh. Except it was not the laugh of a man.

It was the happy giggle of a child.

He was dead. Syyd was dead. A hand closed over his face, a hand that was thin, gnarled and charred...

Everything ceased to exist.

And now... they were all here. Wherever *here* was.

Sydd, Mina, Mokee, Juun, Eyuil... plus so many other kids they had never met, but were now bonded through this trauma.

Everyone... except for Rayn. His best friend... his brother...

Where are you...

It could not have been coincidence – that of *all* of the kids that were taken, the one who could talk to animals was the one that wound up missing.

He was not dead. Syyd refused to accept that.

Again, his concentration started to waver, and he knew it wasn't entirely his fault.

This place is trying to defeat me.

Wiping the silvery hair from his face, he paced toward Eyuil, who was his (and everyone else's) light in this darkness. She was their leader. She was a Numanta… she *had* to be.

Of course, that wasn't entirely fair to her, so Syyd made it clear that she could lean on him for support. He needed to be strong; an unmoving rock, because there was no way she *wasn't* terrified in her own right.

It seemed like only seconds ago that they came across that strange parchment…

Slowly, words began to form on the blank sheet. They were written by an invisible hand, as burning ink solidified into rose-pink characters that eventually revealed their meaning.

The children around Syyd gasped in wonder as a manifesto of descriptive words were accompanied by crude drawings of...

Wait, it can't be!

It was Jeleenn!

"I can't believe it!" *Mina squealed with delight and wonderment.* "Why is Jeleenn showing up?!"

Syyd looked at the words intently. They actually talked about Jeleenn; as if it was scrawled by some sort of stalker.

One line read: Jeleenn walked very long and hard to Henra on this day. She was so exhausted? But not as exhausted as when she was arrested on suspicions of murder! Oh my!

This was accompanied by a simple drawing of a sad-looking girl in a cage.

Another entry claimed: Jeleenn fought a fierce and mighty battle! Against a fearsome foe many times her size, she valiantly protected her friends with gusto. Unfortunately, she was overpowered and taken hostage! Oh no!

This too, was illustrated with a scene of a girl being carried over the shoulder of a scary looking man.

"What *is this?"* *Syyd asked loudly, as if he was hoping for an answer.*

"*This is* nothing *like Master Ilod has shown me*" Eyuil stated as she marvelled at this freaky story.

Syyd gasped. "Look! Look at this part!"

He read it aloud, just to make sure he wasn't imagining things. He cleared his throat, "When Jeleenn awoke... she found herself in another jail. But this was no ordinary jail! This was a scary and strange gaol... which was in a scary and strange world! Yes! She met others that were being held... and it turned out to be the very children she was looking for! So!"

It wasn't a trick. Something in his gut told him that this was *different* from the other insane things they've come across in this nightmare of a place. That – yes, there *was* hope. They still had *some* control; like when they escaped the cell by running past that toad monster thing.

Ugh, I hope it isn't still chasing us...

Eyuil stopped, and Syyd skidded to a halt. The other children behind them began stumbling and hurling complaints. He didn't count, but there had to be at least thirty of them that were now a part of their crew. It was a lot, and in a brave move, Mina volunteered to watch them all from the back, knowing fully that she could easily be snared from behind by any manner of creature or predator. Such a selfless act gave Syyd a boost in morale, no matter how small.

"What's going on Eyuil?" Syyd puffed. He was looking down on the crumbly stairs, and briefly lost attention.

The young girl pointed, her white robes dangling off her small arm.

A door. They had finally reached the top of the spiral tower.

Flanked by braziers of rosy fire, the entrance was covered in vines, and dotted with large flowers. Smack bang in the middle, was a scowling form of a gigantic crow with eyes that now gazed straight at the kids.

"What is *that*?" Eyuil whispered, though she could plainly be heard by everyone.

The bird's head twitched, before clucking in curiosity.

"AAARRRRRK!!! Girl-thing, I am what lies between you and

certain death! Turn back! WAAAAARRRRK!!!"

In any other time in his life, Syyd would have fallen backwards in terror, before fleeing for his life. Yet... this place had a dulled effect on his mind, and he suspected the other children suffered as well. It really did feel like he was in the middle of a fever dream, as a sweet perfume wafted into his nostrils.

Resisting the urge to collapse into a slumber, the boy tensed his legs and stood his ground, as Eyuil let out a quick, high-pitched gasp.

"What... what *are* you?" the girl demanded, as she twisted her fingers into an unusual sign. She thrust her palms out toward the creature, as if to ward it away.

The bird-head cackled. "WARK! You children have been very naughty! WAK! Leaving your cells like that! The boss won't be happy! I'll guess I'll have to reign you in! WAKAKAKAK!!!"

Hearing a muffled commotion behind them, Eyuil and Syyd turned, and found that their friends were dropping like rag dolls. One by one.

Cries and whimpers began to echo throughout the spiral staircase, as everyone tried to hold each other up, whilst attempting to stay awake by slapping and yelling at each others' faces.

The bird laughed again, making Syyd round on it in fury. He clenched his little fists, and marched towards his foe.

"Stop! Right now! You can't do this!"

He put two and two together, and figured that the scent of the flowers that surrounded the ghastly guardian was knocking everyone out. He looked desperately toward Eyuil, silently begging the Numanta to do *something*.

Paralysed with indecisiveness, the girl did the first thing that sprang into her mind. She had no idea what she was doing, but it was better than *nothing*.

Pulling out the parchment they had found earlier, she unfurled it, and thrust it toward the beaked-face.

"Wait!" she yelled with as much authority as her throat could muster. "Before you do anything else, can you at least read this thing we found? Please, we don't know what to make of it!"

The crow's eyes shimmered with kaleidoscopic colours, before snapping its jaws shut and twitching with curiosity. "Wark? What's this? You brats have something interesting?"

"Y… yes!" Eyuil stuttered. "We found it on the steps here! Could you look at it for us?"

The crow's beady eyes were unblinking, as they became a black void. Sydd hoped for a moment that it had died or fallen asleep itself, before its gaze pulsed with light once again.

He got the distinct impression that Eyuil had thrown the bird for a loop. It very briefly seemed as though it was conflicted with itself.

Regaining its composure, it warbled once again. "Fine! Fine, I shall look at your pathetic little paper! WARK! Being stuck here for eternity, I welcome the reading material! WARK! So I still win in the end!"

It squinted, before demanding that Eyuil hold the paper open.

Realising that she had bought them precious time, Syyd frantically tried to come up with a plan. Something the bird had said couldn't escape his brain; *'being stuck here for eternity, I welcome the reading material'.*

Stuck.

I wonder…

As the girl inched forward nervously, Syyd cleared his throat. "So… what's your name? Do you have a name?"

Emitting a throaty rumble, the bird blinked very slowly, letting its irritation be apparent. "WAK! Silence child! Let me read!"

The crowd of children behind him began to stir, as a small girl with pigtails came bounding through. She clutched a round silver object, and waved it about.

What's she doing?

"Crow! You're a crow!I love crows!"

Confused, Syyd tried to stop her from getting any closer. Indignant, she clicked her possession open, and he saw that it was an antique mechanical watch.

Wow, fancy.

"Crows love shiny things!" she continued unabated. "Would you like this, Mr. Crow? It's a gift!"

"Wait, what are you doing?!" Syyd demanded, more harshly than he anticipated. "That thing looks expensive!"

She stuck a tongue out at him. "I know that! It was my momma's! But I wanna give it to Mr. Crow!"

'Mr. Crow' widened his eyes as they flickered in emerald hues. "W... wark? You want to give that... to me? WAK?"

"Sure!" She beamed. "I know crows like gifts. I hate the idea of you being just a head... and not being able to fly and collect things... and stuff..."

Warbling in obvious pleasure, the bird tried its best to retain its composure. "I mean... sure! Fine! WAK! I'll allow it! Just put it on the floor! Now, where was I?"

The girl did as instructed. She then walked back, a faint smile crossing her lips. Syyd stopped her, and whispered. "*Why did you do that?*"

The girl looked into his eyes, almost as if she didn't understand what he was saying. "I thought... if we could make him happy, he would let us pass..."

Syyd *did* notice that the bird creature seemed to be slightly flustered. He had to try.

"Everyone!" he shouted. "Let's all chip in! If anyone has anything they can give to our friend, then do it! Let's show him how nice us humans can be!"

Mr. Crow clucked loudly. "Wait, what? WAAAARK!!! Stop that! I... I don't need anything! Nobody cares about me, WAK! I... I..."

Diverting his gaze from Eyuil, he then slowly picked up the girl's silver watch with his mouth, and swallowed it.

"Well... if... if you insist..."

The children murmured amongst themselves, confused, but willing to go along with Syyd's request. He only collected a few things from them, but he hoped it was enough to grease the bird's wheels. A few bracelets and necklaces, and even a snow globe.

He felt horrible asking them to part with their treasured possessions, but he couldn't think of anything else. Most of them seemed to cotton-on to his plan, whilst a few of the groggier kids simply ignored him. He definitely wasn't going to steal from them, so he let them be.

Eyuil's arms ached slightly from holding the sheet outward. "Wait!" she stalled again. "Can we get your name? Please?"

"Wak... I don't have a name, child."

"But... you have friends, right?"

"I am a guardian. Please, let me read."

"Of... of course."

Syyd had a collection of trinkets now. As he passed Eyuil, both children shared furtive glances. They both shared the same goal; to butter-up this creature, and hope that it would be dumb enough to let them pass.

It now mumbled quietly to itself, as it's now-blood red gaze scanned the paper.

"I... this... WAK..."

It now stared directly at Eyuil and Syyd, before looking down at the offering it received.

"Nobody has ever given me this much attention..."

To the children's shock, globules of tears began to fall from its big black eyes.

Cawing in both happiness and despair, it scooped up its remaining gifts, and swallowed them too.

The choking noises the creature made was enough to make Syyd, Eyuil, and everyone else cry with it.

It was a moment that none of them would ever forget for the rest of their lives. To feel the void of despair that this thing had lived in for so long, without even realising it. To feel a semblance of love and compassion – sensations that simply did not exist in its tiny world; was something that completely and utterly destroyed it. By this simple act of kindness, the guardian of the spiral staircase briefly knew everything of existence outside of its own bubble. It both hated and coveted these small humans for making it feel this way – and every wave of its new-found awareness of its self-worth was also experienced by his audience.

It all only lasted mere seconds, but it was enough to frazzle the thing's mind.

"WAAAAAAAAAAAAAAAARRRRRRRKKK... Why are you scoundrels doing this to me?! You... you make me aware of... *me*!!! WAAAAAAAARRRRRKKK!!! And you show me... me... *that!!!*"

Its eyes rolled into the back of its head, as the parchment in Eyuil's grip burst into flames.

The magi jumped backward, and was caught by Syyd and the pigtailed girl.

The three of them watched in terror, as the crow shrivelled, and turned into petrified wood.

All of the other children were wide awake now, and all rushed upward, compelled to finally escape this accursed stairwell.

A sliver of light split the gnarled bird in half, as it opened outward. *A door. The way out.*

Their cramped surroundings brightened, as the braziers fizzled out. Wiping their smudged faces, everyone poured out of the tower in haste. As they did, they could hear a voice in the tingly air...

WAAAAARRRKKK. Save them Jeleenn...

* * *

"I did *not* expect that to happen" Syyd panted.

The children were now outside. One by one, in a single file, as soon as they crossed that disturbing avian threshold, everything in their world suddenly became sharper and clearer. The lull that smothered their senses lifted like a starry curtain, and they experienced a new-found clarity that was akin to *remembering* for the first time in their small lives.

Drowsiness and apathy faded from their personalities, as anxiety and uncertainty began to bubble in their heads.

Gasps and sobs popped through the small crowd, as friends comforted friends, and siblings tried their best not to lament their mothers and fathers.

"Gee, you *think*?" Mina scolded him, in the unique way that only she could. "What *was* that thing? What happened back there?!"

She then twisted her neck, almost like an owl. "And *now* where are we?!"

They were indeed outside now – but not in any familiar way. The escapees now stood on a massive, clear walkway; almost as if it was made of glass. It stretched on forever, as all around them was nothing but green. Trees, trees, and even more trees; an undulating forest that was dotted with towers and lights of every possible colour – all connected by hundreds of the same crystalline paths, and the biggest roots that any of them had ever seen. Stretching out over them was a night sky; albeit a night sky that was blacker than black. No moons. No stars. Not even a hint of the Great Ring.

Trying his best to not be overwhelmed, Syyd turned to Eyuil. "That was quick thinking, distracting that bird like that."

Her mouth gaping at the land that surrounded them, she snapped her jaws shut and turned her dirty face to him. "Yeah... I just did the first thing that came into my head. I didn't really have a plan. You seemed to catch on too. Asking for his name and trying to befriend him."

"That monster was putting us to sleep... if it hadn't been for that girl..."

The Numanta wiped her eyes, and echoed Mina's distressed words. "What *did* happen back there? I... that thing... I felt so sorry for it..."

"I know... did it die? Did we... make it happy? Or did we ruin its life?"

Both of them stood, awkwardly reflecting inward at what they just went through. It really did seem like they were just becoming conscious of this new world, and everything that they had been through was slowly vanishing into the abyss.

In a way, that realisation made them even more sad.

Is any of this even really happening?

There was chatter now, as kids excitedly peered over the side of the pathway, pointing out the spiralling towers, and the strange, amorphous creatures that flew through the blackness. They trailed a strange red vapour, the smell of which bought feelings of dread to the adolescent retinue.

"We need to move, quickly!" Eyuil shouted.

"To where?" Mokee jumped from the perilous edge, before landing like a legless cat.

Picking the boy up by the scruff of his neck, Mina shoved him forward. "The only way we *can* go."

Above them now, the airborne sentinels began calling to each other in an unreal melody. Their evil, hooting and honking cries smothered the darkness, and pressed oppressively down on the children.

"Mina's right" Syyd shouted, as he broke out into a sweat, "there's no other way! All we can do is keep going!"

Everyone babbled, as panic began to rise within the group. The older children began to round up their smaller kin, as Eyuil and Syyd did their best to urge everyone along the causeway.

They all jogged with urgency; which became more and more intense as the shapeless predators inched closer and closer to their quarry. The stench became overbearing, as an eggy stench filled their noses, making them gag and cry.

The dreaming numbness of the tower was completely gone now; overtaken by otherworldly fear that could only be truly felt in nightmares.

Syyd felt his vision get duller and duller, as his legs began to turn into clay. His head pounded feverishly, as the glassy path before him was without end.

"Keep… moving…" he choked, as he looked toward Eyuil, who was now on her hands and knees.

He heard Mina scream from behind. Halting in a way that made his entire body flop to the cold ground, he twisted his silvery mopped head, only to see that one of the monsters now landed between him and the rest of the group.

It looked unlike anything he had ever seen – even in *this* place.

It had no shape… but at the same time, it did. He struggled to look at it, as it bellowed a stomach-churning call that made Syyd's insides turn sickly hot. Amidst the foul crimson smoke that slowly obscured everyone and everything, it spread its massive, deformed wings, and flapped a tornado of paralysing wind that muffled the wails of its victims.

With a pain that brought a white-hot clarity back to his fuzzy world, Syyd crawled, as every joint in his small frame ground together like a mortar and pestle.

The memories came back to him. Of that day, when his home was on fire, and he couldn't do *anything* to stop it.

He lost his mother and father. He lost his brother.

He would *not* lose his friends. Not now. Not *ever*.

He tried to do anything, He tried to *shriek*. No matter how undignified his actions were, he was desperate for his body to respond – to do *something*. *Anything*. Just as long that he knew – that he was *not* trapped.

Seeing that smile… and all of those rotten teeth. Bearing down on him, as he lay there, whimpering and worthless… flames everywhere. Stinging smoke in his eyes and tearing his throat apart…

He scrunched his face as tight as possible, as his balled fists pounded the sides of his head. Gritting his teeth in agony, despair and madness, Syyd had to *fight*. He *wanted* to fight. And he had enough of being so *useless*.

There was another smile now… but… this one was different. It was good. It was love. It made him cry… It made *her* cry.

She was there, standing before him. A maiden of beauty, unlike anyone or anything he had ever seen in his tiny, tiny life. She was as tall as the clouds themselves, and her dress was the sunshine. Her wavy hair was like the stars beyond the deep blue sky, and her eyes... her eyes were everything. Times of the past. Times of yet-to-be. They were waterfalls of life and death; cascading through the endless universe of Syyd's mind.

Who... who are you?

I am... part of you. Please, save them... save all... our kingdom... our people...

Syyd's blood was crystal. It gushed through his veins, and chilled the diseased inferno that suffocated his young soul.

With a golden power that lit him from within his pounding heart, he gasped inward; and tasted an air that was fresher than any he had ever known...

... no. He *had* known it. It was the salty air of the sea. It was the air of Gen.

Rising to his knees, he punched the ground in fury. Blood flowed from his knuckles, and it glittered as it splattered all around him. He felt no pain – but rather, a rage that was both his own – and someone else's.

Rayn? Mum? Dad?

The formless winged being turned its approximation of a head towards the boy. The long, blurred face was punctured with two, deep black pits which emitted the red smoke, like hissing steam. It cocked its visage and rumbled so low, Syyd could feel it vibrate in his ribcage.

"Syyd..." Eyuil mumbled, her eyes glazed.

Feeling the oppression lifting from him, the boy slowly got back up on his own feet, and pointed a trembling finger at his adversary.

"Let. Us. Go."

He could not explain it. Yet, he *knew* that he held a mastery over this thing. He was lighter than air – and nothing lower could touch him, or his friends.

His digit glowed, and the monster shirked underneath its piercing clarity. Its brethren amidst the deep dark sky circled in confusion, as their gassy emissions slowly metamorphosed into beautiful, starry trails.

Just like Syyd's own droplets of claret; the vapours twinkled, and fell like snow. As the jewels touched the glassy ground, turquoise grass bloomed all around the children.

The seizing creature seemed to shrink within itself, before attempting to take off. It failed, however, and fell head-over-heels over the edge of the glassy pathway. It was dead silent as it disappeared into the inky abyss. Following its dramatic display, the others in the flock followed suit, as they formed into things resembling bubbles – but plummeted like boulders.

Again, Eyuil gasped Syyd's name in unbelievingness, as their mates were reinvigorated by the fantastical display. Like a mouldy piece of bread, blue fuzz spread around their feet – and the foul, fleshy smell became sweet like cinnamon.

They all turned toward their silver-haired savour with both fear and admiration.

He had fallen unconscious.

* * *

Jeleenn walked the grounds of the *Great Castle of the Leaf*.

Her bare feet pressed into the soft lawn of the main atrium, and she really couldn't tell the difference between this and the smoothest of velvet carpets. She would have been certain that every individual blade was a facsimile of the real thing, if not for the little pink moles that would sometimes pop out. They were possibly the cutest things she had ever seen… but then again, that was a recurring theme in this place. For every beautiful thing that filled her mind with an elixir of bliss, and made her blood turn into honey – there was an equally unnerving, disturbing image that her brain tried its best to filter away.

She was in a realm that was not meant for beings like herself; a world that could only be interpreted by her limited human sense.

In another life, this realm of the invisible was beauty incarnate. If you belonged here – or were invited by its residents, then you would undoubtedly live in a dimension of incomparable joy.

It may have been heaven itself, as many scholars over the eons have endlessly speculated, much to the agreement of the Eidian Mages – and the chagrin of the other robes.

But… from what she has learned since her stay… is that things have changed. For the better? Or worse? She still couldn't decide, but either way, Joner was determined to fulfil the old Wizards' final goal – to unify this realm, and her own… the world of Tarinn.

He had help, of course. There was the terrifying man. Hekor. And that old crone… but Jeleenn had still yet to learn her name.

And there was everyone who followed them; beings and creatures from a vast array of places. All of whom – for some reason – were tired of the status-quo. They wanted what her brother wanted.

But really, what exactly did he *truly want*?

Peace? To end all suffering? No more war, no famine, nor hatred? Admirable goals, she had to admit – but she read so many stories where the main villain of the piece always thought they were right, that their goals were for the betterment of mankind.

Was… was Joner truly the villain here? Of course, this was no story – regardless of how dreamlike she felt in this hazy fairyland. Everything he had said… everything he had endured… he was perfectly justified in everything he had done…

"NO!!!" *She screamed as loud as she could.* "*Joner's dead!!!*"

She fought as hard as she could, but really, she didn't have much strength.

"*It's me, sis!*" *Joner hissed.* "*I'm here! This is* real!"

She spat. "*No! You… you…*"

She didn't know what to say. She knew it was him. Even though he was all grown-up, she still knew.

But then... who in the hell was Kwenn?

"It's me!" Joner continued, "Please! I'm begging you to believe me!"

There were tears running down his face. Real tears.

She relaxed slightly, but her face still writhed with horror.

"You're dead" was all she could say.

He chewed his lip as his wide eyes looked into her own.

Slowly, he released her.

She didn't move.

"I was" Joner whispered. "I died... but I was given a second chance. No... I was given the chance I deserved in the first place. I..." he then looked to Hekor, who remained emotionless.

"I was chosen" he finished, as his eyes then veered towards the crone.

"Yes, you were" the old woman confirmed.

Jeleenn was rendered speechless. She collapsed to her knees and wept. For joy? Or for grief? She didn't know. Perhaps both.

A look of concern passed over Joner's face. "Don't cry Jeleenn! Please!"

But she couldn't stop crying. Never will she stop.

"Dad..." she finally murmured, "Dad... buried you."

Joner stood straight.

"Dad..." he said quietly. "Jeleenn... I don't know how to tell you this... but this is all father's fault."

"What?" she hissed in disbelief.

She looked at him through blurry eyes, and saw that her brother was no longer a sympathetic young man, but an enraged anomaly.

He crushed his hand into a tight fist, which shook with this new fury. "Jeleenn. Dad is responsible... for all of this!!!"

Suddenly, the room began to tremble. The golden pillars now took on a sickly, corpse-like hue, and the lush leaves withered and crumbled.

Joner pointed a finger to the void above.

"That loathsome son of a bitch killed me!!! His own flesh and blood!!!" His voice morphed into that of a mighty demigod, as thunder boomed above.

Terror overcame Jeleenn's body like a black wave, and her skin *crawled. What had her brother become?!*

He then pointed to her. "He has been lying to you! For all these years!" he roared,. "That scum!!! He has lied to everyone!!!"

Jeleenn tried to stand now, but her legs failed here. She leaned forward with her hands.

"What are you talking about?! Dad was a hero! He saved so many people! He tried to save you!!!" She cried.

Joner chuckled bitterly. "You think that's what happened? Then you have a lot to learn, sis."

He clicked his fingers, and everything was quiet once more.

Just like that.

How? What has he become?!

"Joner..." she quavered. "You... what have they done to you! You're so old!"

He laughed, before quickly covering his face with his hands.

"I was hoping you didn't notice," he mumbled between his fingers, "but... well, that's the price I paid. It was no big deal... after all; the benefits far outweigh such meagre side-effects."

He scooped up his mask, and put it back on.

"Now you've embarrassed me! Just like the old days."

Jeleenn's heart raced as many thoughts crossed her mind. Anxiety threatened to overwhelm her, but she tried to keep hold of her logical senses.

She rose to her feet.

"Joner..." she said, desperation in her worn voice, "let's leave this place! You and me! I don't care what you've done! We can fix this!" she reached out her hand.

She can have her older brother back.

"I don't know what they've told you," she continued, as she stared venomously at Hekor, "but it's all lies. Come on! We can end this!" Tears streamed down her face. "Let's go home!"

Behind that hideously-beautiful disguise, Joner's green eyes gleamed with intent.

"*We* are *home now, sis.*"

Home…

They say home is where the heart is… and as each immeasurable day passed on this fertile plane, Jeleenn wondered if that was the true reason people fought. It wasn't about who was right and who was wrong – but for the love of their home.

Joner truly never had a home though. She now knew this more than ever.

"I *was born from a tryst between a mortal man and the 'divine'* Queen Bean Si!!! *I was an abomination! A creature that was feared by all those that learned of my diabolic existence! My power is unequal! With my loyal allies… my* true *family, I will send the gods themselves to the very depths of hell!!!*"

She now knew the truth, and even after everything she had been through – everything she had seen… she still couldn't quite believe it. Not only was her long-dead brother alive… but he wasn't even fully human.

As a child, she had always known that he had a different mother. Her father had always refused to divulge any more information, and she never blamed him for that.

Now that she was enlightened, she almost wished she could wipe away her memories.

Joner was the son of 'Queen Bean Si'. What exactly she *was*, Jeleenn didn't have the foggiest idea – but she knew that Joner was a prince.

Royalty. A bastard. A royal bastard.

Apparently, their father and this queen somehow got together once upon a time… and when Joner was born, he was banished from the royal kingdom – and was raised by Jugo.

Again, whatever sense of 'home' Joner ever had was with his father on the road. They adventured together, survived together… until that day… when Jugo was forced to…

Oh god… dad…

She should have hated him for it… yet, she did not. She could only feel her heart being torn asunder for him, for the choice that no parent should have ever had to make.

Upon revealing this horrific truth, Joner's face twisted into that of an ugly old man – and that visage became even more disgusting when Jeleenn wept endlessly – not because she shed tears for her brother, but because she *also* shed them for their father.

For that, she was locked in her exquisite chambers. She spent what seemed like days with her face buried in her silken pillows, as her eyes gushed with salty diamonds that turned her dwelling into a light show of despair, as they floated like snowflakes.

Once it was all over, she was a wraith. Pale, and devoid of anything resembling human emotions.

She felt hollow, and her eyes were blinded by the sharp intensity of every single tear.

She had lost all sense of herself; and before she could fully embrace the white light of inward oblivion, there was Joner… smiling happily, and reaching out a gorgeous hand, his skin filtering and reflecting every type of colour that could ever exist.

The hues of existence itself.

Now she walked the grounds. Garbed in a nightdress of air, she glided along the bountiful, sea-green grass. Her brother appeared at her side, hands clasped behind his back.

"I may have overreacted. You had every right to weep for father" he spoke, his blank white face resembling a marble statue, with emeralds for eyes.

"I… didn't know how else to react" she answered. "It's like… how else is one supposed to react to something like that? Not only to have their own life upended, but to also be burdened with the knowledge of something like… like what dad…"

She trailed off, as she noticed one of the black knights stood at guard. She got goosebumps, because she knew it was staring directly at her.

Joner smirked. "Hm, yes. Though that empathy is somewhat

lessened when one knows that such a tragedy was only born of their own negligence in the first place."

"You seriously can't believe that" Jeleenn shook her head in denial. "Hate him all you want, but to say he somehow *asked* for it to happen…"

"The Wizards of Chanthalaroos," Joner began, ignoring the last part of his sister's reply. "You know about them, right? Was that something you read about, growing up?"

"Yes."

"According to history, they were the founders and original rulers of the empire of Gamsay-Rumm, and the head of their political power was in the great city of Chanthalaroos. No-one can definitively say who they truly were, or where they came from. Were they gods? Visitors from the stars? The remnants of the Pheekonshenee? Either way, they ruled old Tarinn, and gave birth to the Magi as we know them. Though some still say a royal family preceded even them… but let's not dwell too much on legends."

"Sure."

Joner pursed his lips again. "Eventually, the Wizards vanished from the record books, and Gamsay-Rumm's leadership was placed into the hands of the common folk; elected officials. The worst of the worst. Under their centuries of corruption, the land became a bloated, power-hungry force – and this trickled down throughout the political world of Tarinn at large. This, as I'm sure you know, led to the *Battle of the Mind*. A war between persecuted mages, and the regular, ignorant masses. All of it started by the ominous foretelling by a grey mage… pathetic. This led to the extinction of the *Arche* violet robes, and the obliteration of the continent of Amurnymm. At the end of it all, the Magi won, and became the new rulers of Gamsay-Rumm, under the so-called 'House of Free Leaders.'"

"And so it has remained, to this very day" Jeleenn finished. "I learned this in my schooling. Did you ever go to school, Joner? Or did *Hekor* teach you all of this? Or god forbid, *father*."

Joner was completely unmoved by his sister's barbed comment.

Slowly blinking once, he continued.

"My earliest memories... they were of being on the road with father. All I ever knew was learning to fight. To hunt. He instilled in me a sense of righteousness and honour that only came with..."

"... being a hero?" Jeleenn finished.

That word seemed to have more of an effect on him than her snarky comments. He visibly cringed.

"If you say so. Our lives were entirely centred around helping the unfortunate. If we got paid, then that was a bonus. We were never in one place for too long... until, father met his new wife, your mother."

"*Your* mother too" Jeleenn corrected, with a surprising amount of anger. "Don't you *dare* start blaming her too."

"I don't. I really don't. I miss her so much..." Joner bowed his head, as his wan hair fell over his face. Regaining his composure just as quickly, he continued. "I don't know if he ever told you, but they met in Qualm, in a little treetop village. They got married on a giant mushroom platform, and you were born there too."

Jeleenn's chest was hit with a brick from the inside. "What?! Are you serious? You're lying!"

Joner laughed. "Wow, they never did say anything, huh? I guess they wanted to escape their past, and start new lives, after what happened..."

"I wasn't... born in Gen?" Jeleenn repeated, just to make sure she wasn't hearing things. It was funny, that in the type of place she was in, it was something so relatively mundane that she couldn't quite cope with.

She looked back at him, noticing that she became lost in her internal revelation. The sky became dark, as storm clouds now pressed upon them. They were the blackest clouds she had even seen, and the flashes within them were blood red.

Joner was leaning against a wall, and rubbing his temples. In no time at all, he was across the garden. She didn't even see him move.

"Joner" she called softly.

"... after what happened," he repeated. "I suppose you deserve an answer. I just… I'll try to keep things calm. As much as I enjoy reverting things back to zero, I try not to do it here. I know it scares you."

She had no idea what he meant, but was thankful that he wouldn't let his trauma get the best of him. A chill ran through her, as hooting and blood-curdling screaming could be heard in the distance.

"When you were born, we were all so happy" he began wistfully. "I finally had a family, and a home. For a couple of years, I was a normal boy. I went to school. I had friends. I hadn't even turned ten yet, and yet I felt like I was ready to retire from travelling. I guess, due to my lineage, I was a little more developed than other kids my age. Heh, mother said I often unnerved the other adults. I guess that was my first clue…"

The clouds above her now receded slowly, as the pink moles swam around her feet whilst chirping in relief.

"It was around that time when it all began. Father's past caught up with him. You can't be a hero all over the lands of Tarinn, without making a few enemies, after all."

"What do you mean? What happened?" She walked closer to him, as the black knight's helmet tracked her. Like clockwork.

Like clockwork…

"To put simply, rifts began opening up. All over the world."

"'Rifts?'"

"Even in our little hamlet, reports came to father. They were desperate for someone to investigate strange occurrences that dotted the lands. Monsters and creatures, unlike any ever seen, began popping up all over the place. People were vanishing, and the very forces of nature were beginning to become unpredictable. It was when, that year, the Blinking of the Eyes happened, that all hell really broke loose. The world itself was changing before our very eyes."

Again, Jeleenn could not process what he was saying. "*What?* How come I've never heard of this?"

Joner giggled strangely, before stopping himself, clearly

embarrassed. It was so unexpected, and freaked his sister out. "I'll get to that" he assured, composing himself. "One night, people came for me. They slipped into the town, and killed a lot of folk. They were accompanied by these new fiends that were not of this world, and they completely ransacked our home… you, father and mother managed to escape, along with a few others. It was the most terrifying night of my life… we were split up at one point, and I had to carry you through miles of wilderness…"

His voice shook, but he quickly cleared his throat and remained stoic.

"Anyway, father and mother learned that all of this was happening… because of me. Because of my blood, which somehow acted as a doorway between Tarinn and… well, this very realm. The world was collapsing upon itself, basically."

"However, my existence was only one factor. Over the coming months, we found out that the wizards were still alive. Even after all of these years, they were still pulling the strings behind the scenes. There was a civil war amongst themselves… and, what were once benevolent and wise beings of pure light were now twisted, gnarled old men that stewed in their own machinations for far, far too long."

Joner grimaced. "At least, that's what I was told."

"What do you mean? That the very men that tried to kill you were right?!"

"Yes. And no. Father left mother and you at a safe place… Gen. He took myself, and met with Ilod, Sterlio and Trebor. We all searched for a woman named Dian. An Eidian magi who was seen as the reincarnation of Goddess *Shalisshakin* herself."

"Dian?"

"Yes. The Invisible Realm… was the domain of the Eidian green robes. They knew what was happening, and their province was the Four Sister Isles – the area in Tarinn which was supposedly the gateway to this world."

Once again, Joner laughed – this time, much more mean spirited.

"The Four Sister Isles. Those damned islands… everything always leads back to those islands. Father was born there. Ilod was born there. Mother died there. I hate those damn islands so much…"

Again, the storm clouds swelled above them, and the screaming picked up.

"Joner…" Jeleenn whispered in desperation.

He growled, and his face once more aged before her very eyes. "Dian was excommunicated from her order. Imagine that! The very goddess herself, punished for not extolling the yellowed virtues of an order that was under the thumb of crazy old men. She wanted the gateway between the two worlds to shut, yet, this was seemingly at odds with everything the Eidian stood for."

"Eventually, we met the keeper of the gateway. A being called Master Lojón. He was there from the inception of the islands, and he crafted four items that acted as keys between Tarinn and the Invisible; the Water Sword, the Fire Helm, the Earth Armour, and the Wind Shield. According to Lojón, 'on this plane of existence, the four elements represent the absolute. They are the integrity of this world; of which all life springs forth, and all death sinks into.'"

"The Four Sister Islands… you… is that why you attacked? Killed so many people?!" The clarity of hatred broiled from within the girl's chest, but she tried her best to control its hot flow.

"Ultimately, yes, I suppose. You see, Lojón had hidden the four keys within the islands themselves. They could take any shape… yet, were in the form of battle gear, as they were adorned by a great hero in ancient times, or so he told us. Of course, father volunteered to don the attire himself. He hoped it was enough to stop the Wizards, and close the rifts… we all did. Eventually, the old men found us, and they launched a mighty assault. It was in the midst of this battle that we learned a few things… a few unpleasant truths. I got sick, sis."

"Sick?"

"Mhm. Yes. It was only a small thing at first. Perhaps a flu or sniffles. But over the next few weeks, I got worse and worse – and it would come and go. One day, I'd be perfectly fine – and the next, I couldn't even get out of bed. I was living in some sort of netherworld, like Tarinn itself. Dian tried her best to heal me... but, I began to hate life. It was hell, like giving a steed an apple, only to whip it mercilessly. Over and over and over again."

"I was being torn apart... and to make matters worse, our foes had obtained three of the elemental keys. We only had one; the Water Sword, and we were pursued relentlessly. You think I killed a lot of people, sis? What I did was a mere pittance compared to what happened then."

Jeleenn's entire body trembled, and she resisted the urge to strike him. "You... you... how could you *say* that."

He stared blankly at her, and images of Kwenn flashed in her mind. He had that same vacant stare.

"It's the truth. They laid complete and utter waste to the islands. Only a handful of people survived."

"That's... impossible!" She recoiled; not because of the horror of such a revelation – but because she was fearful of what she just might do to him. How *dare* he say such an absurd, vile thing. "*You* were the one that caused the death and mayhem!!! You were the one that left a permanent stain of blood on *my home!!!*"

She couldn't help it. She screamed at him, causing him to wince like a scolded dog. The moles that burrowed happily through the lush greenery all squeaked in distress; their panic reverberating under her feet. She jumped, feeling like she stood on glass, and planted her entire body on a bench.

Joner waved his hand, and the chirping ceased.

"Jeleenn" he sighed, "... just... let me finish, okay? Let me finish, and if you still hate me, then we can cross that bridge when we come to it."

Frowning, she again looked at the black guard. It did not make a move. "Fine, whatever."

Nodding in satisfaction, he continued. "As all of this was happening, Ilod learned that his Numanta had an ancient Pheekonshenee artefact stolen from the wizards. A monolithic device, dredged up from the ocean ages prior, it could allegedly achieve what the old men had been seeking for so long. To make the world 'whole'. It was a missing piece of their great big jigsaw puzzle, and they figured that if they inserted the four keys, the doorway to all of their desires would finally make itself known. Except, there was one last piece that they hadn't accounted for – me."

"You" Jeleenn affirmed, too afraid to move from her position. "Because of your blood, right?"

"Right. The more I kept fighting, the more I just wanted to give in. It felt right. I never told father, but I began to… sympathise with the wizards. I thought there was something wrong with me. I hated myself… but I just wanted the pain to stop. I was only a child, yet I had already seen so much death and chaos in the world. I saw the worst of humanity, and knowing that there was another place – a *better* place – that I belonged to, made it so much more unbearable. I'd cry long into the night… and the only one who knew was Dian. She and I bonded. She was basically the goddess of my birth realm, after all. Yet, like me, she was also at odds with herself, as she desperately tried to find her place in such an increasingly cruel world. We both became tired of father's dogmatic views – both he and his friends simply saw Tarinn as something that needed to be fixed. Yet still, we remained loyal. We hoped that by sticking it out until the end, we would finally see light at the end of the tunnel. That this all really was just a bad dream."

"Against our better judgement, we contacted Uilosees. He was the last of the Wizards. The other six had perished, and he was driven mad by his obsession. I guess that's where I had doubts about the veracity of their mission. Dian and I briefly flirted with the idea of joining him; I was desperate for the agony to end, and as such, I revealed to him my lineage. I suppose that *was* the beginning of the end. Uilosees told me that I was the chosen one, that I was the one to bring the two words together as one, and to start it anew. The way it was meant to be… we… we loved his honeyed words, because we knew, deep down, he was right… yet… yet…"

"You loved dad" Jeleenn finished. "That was more powerful than anything else. Wasn't it?"

She couldn't tell if there was a smugness to her words. She almost regretted saying them, but it was the truth. She knew it, and he knew it too.

"Yes."

His emerald gaze flickered, and he crossed his arms casually. He leaned against the polished stone wall, and bowed his head.

"Yes" he said again. "Against my better judgement. Dian too, she wished only to keep me safe. 'Whatever you choose, I'll be right there with you. That is my purpose.' Those were her words to me. And just like that, we made our decision. Wrong or not."

"And you think it was wrong?"

Joner smiled. "I guess it depends on one's outlook on life. Are mistakes to be regretted? Or are they needed in life, so that we may eventually find our true path? I guess, you could say I chose the path of brambles, so that I may eventually toughen my skin."

"What are you *talking* about?"

"I'm saying, everything in life happens for a reason, sis. There's always something to everything, no matter how grim."

Jeleenn scoffed, and jumped to her feet. "Crap. That's crap. You yourself hate dad for everything. You killed people. Wiped out entire villages, and kidnapped all those kids… you, you bastard!"

Joner's eyes widened slightly.

"You're saying that – *all of that* – was just some destiny fulfillment?!" She was screaming once more, and she couldn't tell if it was real or not. She hated him. *Hated* him.

"I don't give a shit *what* you went through. You blame everyone and everything. Fine, go ahead. Do it. But when you start *killing*. When you start *burning*. You… you…"

Her eyes were on fire; her tears were like blood.

"Say it" Joner smirked.

"BASTARD!"

She knew this was the end. She didn't care. He could unleash the fury of hell itself upon her. Scatter her ashes to the wind. But it would change nothing. It would not erase the memories of Gen.

With its inhuman gait, the black knight marched towards her; halberd clutched tightly in its metal grip.

Again, Joner thrust his svelte palm forward, and the figure stopped.

The silence surrounding her was utterly deafening. It pressed against the sides of her head like a vice, and wrapped around her heart. She couldn't breathe.

"I think that's enough storytelling for today" he whispered. "I'm going to be patient with you, sis. I have to be. Even if it takes a thousand years, I suppose you still won't be able to fully comprehend everything. That's not your fault. I can't really convey everything in such a simple tongue."

Her knees buckled, and she crumpled onto the silken grass. Her vision became muted, and he loomed over her, bathed in an amber glow of an invisible sun.

His palm covered her sight, and everything reverted to blackness… to zero.

"You're going to like it here, sis."

CHAPTER XI

Oviinia opened her sodden eyes.

She felt no pain. No breathlessness. No fear.

Even though she knew everything now, she felt tremendous sadness… yet, a strange sense of happiness.

Her mother and father were not her real mother and father. She was not even human, like they were.

But… she was okay with it?

Because she knew. She had gained the knowledge.

The Tilth. Ras Temple. The Magick Shrine.

In just a few short weeks, her entire existence had been utterly upended. She marvelled at how quickly such an event could occur – almost laughably short, like losing a loved one in a split-second accident that rips apart one's life in an instant.

She wasn't the only one. So many had been affected by the machinations of forces far more powerful than they. Their agony permeated throughout her arm, which felt like a rushing torrent that would tear apart her flesh.

Yet still, she felt no pain.

What did I get myself into? Bloody hell…

"You are whole once more."

The stench of mouldy leaves and dirt wafted across her face. Opening her eyes, she reflexively tried to adjust her glasses, only to find a naked bridge of her nose.

A pale sky – almost like one filtered by ash – flickered in between trees that waved in a wary welcome. Soft singing could be heard on the barest of frequencies, to the point where she wondered if she was imagining it. She wiped her face, and sat up.

She noticed that her wounds were gone, with only the cracked, dry blood on her clothing serving as proof of their existence.

She was in some sort of grove. Silk worms dangled from the branches; their bright excrements making joyful tunes in the breeze. All around her, the ground was charred and blackened, as small rodents and mammals lay in their death poses.

Completely cooked.

"Now where the hell am I?" she asked aloud to the heavens.

"You are on Liniii, Vatn. At least, that's what it used to be."

Even without her spectacles, she could see her clearly.

A woman. Pale and thin, with her seaweed-green hair worn upward and her almond-eyes looking so white – their soft violet irises almost non-existent.

She wore almost nothing, save for a thin gown made of brambles and leaves that seemed scrounged from the forest itself.

Her skin flitted in and out of reality at seemingly its own volition, exposing patches of skeleton beneath.

This time, Oviinia did not blanch. Though she wondered if she was still in the village of the corpses, an overwhelming sense of joy nevertheless overcame her.

"Vayu!"

"I'm glad you know who I am!" the woman exclaimed joyfully. "Even in this... form."

Oviinia's arm was shining, and Vayu nodded towards it. "You found all the sacred sights, I see. Now you just need to find... what was the name of yours?"

"Kwennsefulass."

I know who you are now, Kwenn… I will find you.

"So" Vayu laughed in response, "You know everything now."

Oviinia wiped her eyes with grimy hands.

"Y, yes… I do. It's so strange… Vayu… sister. What happened? What *is* happening?"

The transiently translucent lady grabbed Oviinia's hand, and with strength that did not match her frail body, lifted her up onto her boots.

"Joner. He may have taken over this land, but *I* am still its rightful guardian. He has been with me since our awakening. He interrupted my gestation process… damaged me in the process. I… he tried to recover the memories of my charge, and was partially successful. I suppose."

Oviinia wanted to cradle her in her arms. "He did *what*? So… you never even got to grow up? Have a childhood?! How? How did that bastard do it?!"

Vayu linked arms with her sister, and ushered her along.

"We must hurry. He will be here soon. Or one of his goons. Don't you recall? You were in southern Shali. I brought you all the way here… I used a stolen Pheekonshenee device. A teleporter. It triangulated onto your position once you were fully activated, and brought you to my coordinates."

The Magick Shrine… dammit, I hope Sterlio is okay.

"Joner… how can he do so much? How is he so powerful?" Oviinia hissed.

"A perfect broth" Vayu lamented, as she guided her along a road through the trees. "The progeny of human and elder, which gives him power. The access to both Pheekonshenee technologies and Arche magics. A guiding hand of a ruthless being. And most importantly of all… pure hatred."

"It almost seems like he himself is a tool. An experiment… just like us."

Vayu laughed again, as her skull showed itself underneath her clear flesh. Embarrassed, she tried to cover it up. "Who knows how far the machinations go? Either way, he went through time and retrieved me. My embryo. He tried to take all of us, but since my mother seems to be working with him, I was easy prey."

"I'm so sorry" Oviinia sniffed, not even feeling her feet move. "You mean, all of this time, you have been hiding? From the very one who was supposed to protect you? To love you?"

The thin lady scoffed. "Protect. Hah. I've been doing a fine job of protecting myself. I *have* a family. Believe it or not, but not everyone from the invisible realm is on Joner's side. Nor even Dian herself. They want this to end, just as much as Tarinn does. The two worlds aren't meant to merge. I have a family. A rebellion. And now, I have you, sister!"

It was so much to process. Even knowing everything, Oviinia realised that there was still *more* to learn. There always was, it seemed.

Like an air current through a flourishing valley, they floated through a world of tree trunks and glowing eyes of all shapes. Of bouncing fungi and gushing streams.

It was a long road. "What happened to Linii?" Oviinia asked. She was concerned for Jugo and Ilod, who were supposed to be travelling to this very island.

"Merged with the invisible realm" Vayu said quietly, as she waved to something in the pitch black, before continuing. "I don't know how long it has been like this. Especially in Tarinn's linear timeline. But I can hazard a guess."

"How long?"

"Everything, Vatn. Everything that has happened. Everything that Joner... that Hekor.... that Dian have been plotting and scheming. *Everything* is because of a small boy, whom the hopes and dreams of the Kingdom of the Fay lay upon. A small boy who represents the last of their bloodline. Their *pure* bloodline."

Oviinia and Vayu entered a small village. Or more like an encampment.

People moved about, along with beings who were decidedly *inhuman*. She could barely grasp the forms and languages of those that trotted and garbled with the more familiar normalcy of regular humans. As she entered this hub of activity, she suddenly felt much more lucid, and no longer in a dream.

This was real.

A lot of them looked at her, but most continued with their tasks. Weapon crafting. Cooking. Spell-making.

A veritable what's what of a fighting force.

"This" Vayu heralded, releasing Oviinia's glowing forearm, "is Liniii. At least, what remains. The last of its people, and those of the invisible that want their home back. We are the rebellion."

Rebellion...

She was still uncertain on her feet, and collapsed on top of a crate.

My head...

"Vatn?" Vayu expressed with concern, immediately kneeling to her sister's side.

"I'm... fine" Oviinia assured. "It's so strange. I still remember my life in Buj. With my family. And my career... and everything. Yet, now these new memories are sharing space within my soul. Almost like I've lived two times over."

It was as best as she could explain it, especially considering the organised chaos that surrounded her. She was caught in a swarm of almost unfathomable sights, like being in the centre of one of the troll markets that she had often loved reading about as a child.

She craned her head, and could not see the sky, as they were completely encased in a ceiling of branches, brambles and writing vines that stretched endlessly in every direction. Encased within a tomb of green, hundreds of folk worked busily and without concern for sunlight, seeing as torches, braziers and other strange fuel sources lit everything like a miniature city, with crystals, luminescent plants and more silkworms creating a natural glow amidst the impenetrable thicket above.

The more she absorbed it all, the more speechless she became, as her terrified 'Oviinia' personality clashed with the clarity and resolve of her true 'Vatn' self. The centre of her forehead felt like it was a whirlpool, as the liberation of finally shedding her mental chains gave way to a minor identity crisis. Her chest heaving, she unexpectedly barked out a laugh, as the brand on her arm pulsed.

"Calm" Vayu said softly, "calm, dear. All is well. You're just suffering from some post-awakening jitters, I'd hazard a guess. You are still you!"

Wordlessly, she held out a slender arm that almost seemed to billow in the breeze. A small creature emerged – a man with hooves for feet.

A faun.

His long, brown hair was braided in an uneven way by an array of different coloured threads, and all parted by gnarled, yellowed horns. His large nose gave a friendly frame to his face, as did his large, doe eyes. Otherwise shirtless, he wore a sash which was stuffed with all kinds of papers – some of which would fall out and be carried by the wind.

"Lady, you're back!" he exclaimed excitedly, wagging his little tail. "Are you alright? Did anyone follow you?"

With a wide expression akin to a child seeing a shop full of confectionery, he gasped breathlessly at Oviinia.

"Is this... really her?"

"I'm fine, Gnoat" Vayu smiled. "I believe we got away safe and sound. Yes, this is her. I told you the device would work!"

She spread her arms, both now waving like noodles. "Gnoat, this is my sister Vatn. Also known as Oviinia Trundle. Daughter of Lamun and Sapphire of Shali."

Gnoat jumped excitedly, and placed his small hands within Oviinia's.

"I can't believe it!" he bleated "We've finally found one! One of the four sisters! I mean, three... I mean..."

He stepped back, and stood at full attention.

"Ahem. Nice to meet you, Vatn... AKA Oviinia. I am Gnoat. Vayu's right hand and… I guess you could say, second in command around here?"

Before she even had a chance to offer a genuinely happy reply, a gruff voice cut her off. "That's to be debated, mate!"

All three of them looked to the chariot that now pulled up in front of them. Shaped like a gigantic set of teeth, the carrier's pearly whites sparkled as they were pulled along by a couple of the few remaining horses that could be found within the camp – and most probably the entire island.

Snorting, they stomped onto the soft, leafy ground, heralding the arrival of two faces that Oviinia couldn't be happier to see.

Jugo and Ilod exited, the nimble jumps obfuscating their creaky ages.

* * *

"The Four Sister Isles" Joner explained, as he sipped his brandy, "were created by four gods. Shali, the realm of water, created by Lamun, the Goddess of Reincarnation, and caretaker of Sollus."

Wary, Remana tol Dwen sipped her own. It was the most wonderful brandy she ever tasted. It took genuine effort to hide her pleasure.

"Mirii " Joner continued, "the realm of earth, created by Tson, the Goddess of Emotion, and mother of Solenir. Liniii, the realm of wind, created by Shalisshakin, the Goddess of the Ephemeral… and Arlmai. the realm of fire, created by Qual-nu. The God of Misfortune, and protector of Sollik."

"Okay" she replied, annoyed. "Everyone knows that. Is that supposed to be revelatory?"

They sat in a small study, on luxurious silken chairs that felt like water. Water that did not yield to the roaring hearth which filled the white marbled room with a warmth that was far, far preferable to the desolation of the western seas.

She still habitually checked her ribs, and looked into the mirror in the corner of the room. Her headstrong refusal to buy into the fact that she was no longer hurt kept interrupting her focus.

And she *should* be focused. She was conversing with a man who scoured the world for her.

"They don't teach you *everything* in schools" Joner chuckled. "I would know."

He waited for her to reply. She stared at him however, not playing his game.

"The islands" he continued, lowering his eyes almost shyly, "were in fact created by the gods. Not natural volcanic eruptions or some other nonsense. Unless you equate nature with the divine. Either way, despite their blessed creations, the lands were in fact a representation of all that is natural in the world. Namely, fire, wind, water and earth."

Crossing his legs in an oddly feminine way, he gestured around the room. "I mean, you can see it here, yourself. The fireplace. The natural stone. The water used to make this beverage… everything we have is thanks to these gifts of Tarinn."

Remana drank deeply, and dropped the glass on the ground, shattering it.

"Best water I've ever tasted."

Joner laughed. Almost like a silly child, and her power-play was rendered moot by her visible shirking.

Collecting himself, he licked his lips and resumed his story. "The Four Sister Isles were created as the gateway… or, rather, the threshold that marked the dividing line between the faerie realm and Tarinn. A very visible… border, you could say. The line that is not be crossed."

"However, the Pheekonshenee did. The old folk, with their endless pursuit of knowledge, basically took the islands, and made them into giant experimentation zones. Research stations. Nothing as crude as if something like that were to happen today, you see. The flora and fauna were very well taken care of."

"Okay…"

"Eventually – and in a way I still cannot comprehend – they learned of the existence of another world."

Remana scoffed. "Another world? A world of fairies?"

"Yes. That's right. And this world was created by Shalisshakin, who assisted the other gods in keeping the balance of nature. It was said that she entrusted one of her devotees, a legendary sage and smithy known as Lojón, to create four artefacts that act as keys, so that she may travel between the two realms. These keys were based on the elements, and contained the very essence... the *consciousness* of the islands themselves."

She was getting angry, and it surprised her. Remana found herself becoming afraid, and it was as Archie told; for some inexplicable reason, she believed what this man was saying. Her belly was sick with a foreboding that came with an impending, life-altering event. These *things* he was telling her. This *place* she now sat in. It turned her into a meek mouse, and that went against everything she was as a person. It almost felt like she was being violated in a cunning, indirect way.

The man finished his brandy. "Not only did they find proof of the existence of these legends, but they found Lojón himself. Alive and well, and living within the islands. He, it was said, explained to the Pheekons that he was the caretaker of the Four Sister Isles, and was vehemently against the work that was being done to them. They didn't care. They enslaved him and forced him to give up the locations of the keys. By systematically wiping out the previously-protected flora and fauna."

"That's garbage. The Pheekonshenee were a people that valued life above all else."

Joner scrunched his face into an ugly mess, and she almost wanted to flee in terror. "Perhaps" he conceded, settling down. "Their exact methods were unknown. Perhaps I should ask a white robe." He stifled another laugh. "Either way, Shalisshakin's little pet eventually broke, and provided the locations of the keys. The Pheekonshenee were surprised to find that these 'keys' were in fact weapons and armour. A sword, a helm, a shield and armour... all of which could change shape depending on the heart of the wielder. A far cry from the old 'sword in the stone'!"

Raising from his chair, he swiftly plunged his arm into the fireplace.

Remana jumped from her own seat in alarm, before he held two fingers up with his other hand, indicating that there was no need to panic.

With sounds of clinking and clacking, he pulled out a shield.

It was very basic in appearance. Almost shabby, with its basic iron design otherwise given character by a large green jewel that glittered with a small spark of life.

"This" Joner announced, unaffected by the blaze and smoke that drifted lazily into the ceiling, "Is the Wind Shield. One of the four elemental keys. The others are the Water Sword, the Fire Helm and the Earth Armour. Speaking of blacksmiths, I'm sure you would like to take a look?"

She couldn't deny that she was curious, and that feeling was clearly plastered all over her dark, exotic face.

Joner grinned, expressing a handsomeness that really *did* give Captain Archie a run for his ill-gotten money.

As much as she hated to even *think* about it.

Tapping her impatient digits on her armrest, she cautiously arose and stepped toward her host, who gladly handed her the armament.

It really felt little more than a buckler; almost as if it was forged by cast-off, before slapping a pretty emerald in it – which went against all logic.

It really perplexed her... yet, there was something about it. Something that spoke to her heart, a silent voice that cried for help, and before she even realised, she began to bawl.

"How..." she choked, before collapsing back onto the chair.

Gently removing the object from her shaking grasp, Joner placed a soothing palm on her heaving back, and offered her a silk handkerchief, to which she accepted without protest.

"What" she lamented as soon as she was able to reform her words, "*was* that? What did you *do* to me?!"

"I did nothing" Joner replied softly, still sitting by her side. He nodded to the Wind Shield, as it seemed to sit in a shadowy corner like a neglected child. "It was that. It belonged to a woman named Vayu... your sister."

Vayu... that name... he mentioned it...

Wiping her eyes, she fumed. Somehow, he'd known she would react the way she did. Was it a spell? A simple trick? Either way, his attempt at humiliating her *would* backfire.

"You bastard" she hissed, tossing the cloth back at him. "Why did you *do* that? What was the point?!"

"Don't be mad at *me*" Joner replied with a strangely earnest impatience. "I'm trying to *show* you, Remana. And I think I did. You felt it, didn't you? The very *soul* of that shield. It spoke to you, because *you* are its family."

She was assuredly angered now. Making fists, she jumped to her feet.

"*Vatn, Acasta, Vayu* and *Aodh*" Joner continued defiantly, squaring up to her, face to face. "Those are the four names. The four names of the beings created by the Pheekonshenee."

All those names... he... Archie mentioned them all...

Aodh...

"Created. By the Pheekonshenee" she replied, in an attempt at sarcasm that didn't fully convince.

"Yes" the man nodded emphatically. "Yes, yes they were. Trust me, I couldn't believe it myself when I first discovered it. But... I was shown it to be true. Everything in my damn life that I fought for... and it turned out the ones I was defending were *just* as reprehensible."

"What do you mean?"

Joner's face seemed to darken, as he looked back at the shield. "The Pheekons, in their endless pursuit of knowledge and transcendence, sought to discover the secrets of other worlds. Other dimensions. The Four Sister Isles were unlike anything they had ever seen; gateways that represented their ultimate emancipation from Tarinn and that of the material. Not only that, but it seemed as though they could unlock the very secrets of the gods themselves – who and *what* they truly were. Here it was, actual, tangible proof of their existence… hell, could *anyone* pass up that opportunity?"

Again, she sat. He mimicked her, and looked her square in the eyes with his own.

"Using every single bit of knowledge they possessed, they worked with Lojón in crafting a device that would use the keys as… well, keys, in order to reopen the gateway to the invisible realm. The ultimate ingredient in all of this… was *you*."

Remana did not answer.

"Myself, Dian and Hekor… we discovered the truth during our journey. The concept of elementals had always been of fascination to the Pheekonshenee, as well as anything else that could be considered 'othernatural' in their world. Very little is still known about how they viewed the very concept of existence, with blatherings about 'philosophy', 'analogy' and 'wit' often masking a lack of true knowledge, which is met with ire by the Numanta when you point that out to them. Nevertheless, they sought to 'give life', as it were, to the Four Sisters. To create an amalgamation of 'our side' and 'the other side' to act as bridges. Holy or unholy? I'll let you be the judge of that."

Her heart seemed to slow to a snail's pace.

How… how can this be? These rantings of a lunatic… they are… speaking to me…

Aodh… Aodh… Aodh…

"'Amalgamation?'"

"A hybrid. A chimera. However you want to call it."

Remana could've sworn she heard him mutter 'bastard' under his breath. He was quiet for a long time, as if daydreaming.

"Are you well?" she asked, before he almost jumped.

"Yeah… yes" he replied almost timidly. "Fine. Just fine."

Now, it was his turn to grip the armrests; so tightly that his waif-like hands throbbed with purple veins. Completing the mimicry, tears of his own started to flood his jade sight.

"Remana tol Dwen" he said, completely changing his tone. "I need your help. I *need* your help to save this world."

It was a curse. The incomprehensible weeping curse. Her nose ran once more, and her throat constricted.

This man sent villains to my home. Kidnapped me. Left those villains to die on a desolate rock. Why? Why do I believe him?!

Because he is telling the truth. Merca Lal tried to tell her. Saumen tried to tell her. Her *entire life* tried to tell her.

And now, *he* was telling her.

"Okay, Mr. Telos. Tell me everything."

* * *

Kwenn was lucky that he was wearing a bandanna. If not for the modest, wine-coloured cloth, the salty sweat of his brow would have intermingled with the steaming-hot fervour that welled within his stinging eyeballs.

His doppelganger slowly lifted the Fire Helm from his head, revealing the same scraggly dark hair that Kwenn himself possessed.

"Bloody hell" the man said.

"Bloody hell" Kwenn parroted.

"Now there's *two* of the buggers!" Lojón jumped with a vigorous, furious energy. "*And* they both have my elemental keys! What a day!"

The shorter, dumpier one was stunned – and he did not bother to hide that fact. He put his hands over his mouth, and then elbowed his compatriot. "It's him, isn't it?" he whispered excitedly.

The man's gaze refused to leave Kwenn, and Kwenn returned the favour. He was utterly slack-jawed.

Sheathing his sword, he shuffled lifelessly toward them – completely uncaring to the potential danger they posed, and blind to frenzied orders of Panin and Puul.

The man likewise met Kwenn halfway, and the two of them stood eye-to-eye.

There was no fear. No trepidation. They both knew they had just found each other – that they had finally, *finally* had found their past.

"Kwennsefulass, right?" the man asked, an expectant smile crossing his face. He was a mirror image – with the only difference being his blue eyes, beard and lack of a scar.

Kwenn felt his lip quiver, and tried to hide it in embarrassment. "Yes… that's… that's what…"

He pulled out his emerald necklace, and showed the fine engraving of the word.

"Holy crap" the man said ineloquently. He in turn produced a necklace of his own; a chestnut piece with the same design. He flipped it, and showed the word that was emblazoned on his:

Nuvummburtee.

"The name's *Nuv.* Looks like we got a lot to catch up on, eh?"

* * *

They all sat around a tree stump, drinking hot fungi soup dipped with buttered bread. After cleaning herself up and eating her fill, Oviinia wanted nothing more than to sleep. But try as she might, she couldn't. She had so much going through her mind, and the constant worriment about being attacked put her on the edge.

She was still numb from what happened at the Magick Shrine. She refused to talk about it, save only that she confirmed that she had no idea what happened to Sterlio.

The orchestra of clacking, banging and yelling surrounded them as they ate as peacefully as they could.

"I hope he made it out in one piece" Jugo muttered, sitting with his massive arms crossed. "He's resilient, but not unkillable."

Though he tried to put on a stoic front, it was clear that he was deeply concerned for his old friend.

"Neither are we, Mr. Ironmonger" Gnoat huffed, tying a new braid in his hair. "I have just gotten word that the enemy was spotted closer that any time previously, just around the remnants of the *Fountainscape Balustrade*, merely only a kilometre away. They are getting closer."

"I know" the innkeeper grunted. "Within a day's end… it'll be time to move."

"Move?" Oviinia asked. "What is happening here?"

His eyes closed, Ilod took another sip from his bowl. "Jugo and I… when we took off from Gen, we sailed straight towards Liniii. As swift as possible, with nary a stop on the way. After only the second day at sea, they found us."

"'They?'"

"Joner" Jugo said outright, refusing to tiptoe around his son's name. "We attempted to take the inner lane between the islands, in a brazen move to counter his expectations of us sneaking around the east. Also, we figured the heightened security of the communities would give us an opportunity to blend in, with cooperation from the naval authorities. Things went smoothly at first…"

"…then, they did not" the Numanta finished, sensing his mate's loss of words. "We were roughly west of *Qsem*, when we were bombarded by creatures… things that I had never seen before. They were like witches on broomsticks, but even more misshapen and abominable, and utterly unlike the skinwalkers that are said to stalk the *Rraldole Rock*. It was then that we realised that those heinous buzzards were not of Tarinn, as they swarmed out of a tear in the sky above, just as the suns had congregated behind the horizon."

"Who knows *what's* natural to this bloody world any more" Jugo muttered in a stony observation.

Ilod gave his friend an almost puzzled look, and then continued. "We did our best to bat them off and sail like mako sharks from hell, but it was useless. Their cackles were distorted by vile orifices that… *resembled* mouths, I suppose. We could *feel* and *smell* the sound waves as they blasted us, causing the water to turn into glass and explode, the salt piercing our hull and cutting us up…"

Jugo slumped, before lifting his sleeve, revealing a massive, deep scar.

"I had an artery cut" the grizzled man said quietly. "I was… dying.

Oviinia was stunned, and more than a little bamboozled. She looked at the wound with a strained effort that enabled the innkeeper to read her thoughts.

"I know, it was only a few days ago. It's healed pretty good, huh?" he laughed, in his own poorly-disguised attempt at hiding his own mind troubles.

Noticing the subconscious chess game, as only a wisened Numanta could, Ilod cleared his throat. "As you can probably guess, we did not die."

He lowered his bright blue eyes, before catching a quick glance at his friend.

"After fighting tooth and nail, we lay in a pool of our blood. On a sinking boat. It… was the end. We had resigned ourselves. We were ready to die."

Again, silence.

"It would've been a good way to go, mate" Jugo finally said, slapping his pal on his thin shoulder.

"Would it have been?" the magi suddenly asked, his all-knowing mask slipping.

Jugo crossed his arms again, and gave him a disapproving look.

"Yes" he said, with no hint of uncertainty.

The hustle surrounding them seemed to vanish from the periphery of Oviinia's world. She had only known these two men for such a short time, but felt like she could trust them with her life. Seeing the remains of Gen, and the twisted situation that they had to endure – their friendship was clearly their bedrock, and it almost made her sad that she didn't really have anyone like that in her own life. She was always dedicated to her studies and her research… always travelling. Not even a brother or sister to call her own. And she wouldn't even dare *think* about her love life.

Until now, she was an outsider. She really *was* like Kwenn in that way, and her heart ached for him. To give him what he thought he had lost.

His life.

Her 'Vatn' thoughts were still a little hazy. Her 'life before her life' was clearly *there*, a shining beacon in her remembrance, but she still struggled to consolidate the two threads that now entwined around her cognisance.

Taking a deep, exaggerated whiff of her steaming food was surprisingly helpful.

"It was not your time" Vayu interjected, placing her hands on Ilod's other shoulder. "And I am eternally grateful for that."

"How did you survive?" the biologist asked, again trying to adjust her phantom spectacles.

"Jugo" the magi grinned, noticing her silly gesture. "His connection to the fay. It is what started all of this, and ironically, it is what saved us. It was… her. She heard his soul departing, thanks to the aforementioned tear. Some how, some way, she brought us here, to Liniii."

"The… Queen?" Oviinia asked pensively.

"Yeah" Jugo smiled, surprising himself. "Bean's still alive. I knew it. She still thinks I can save him…"

She was stunned. She was all but certain that Queen Bean Si was gone. She wept for joy; her tears spattering in her broth.

"Why… Liniii?" Oviinia asked after she had recovered.

"Of course, the island of wind created by Shalisshakin" Ilod said, as Oviinia loudly blew her nose on a hanky, "is the one place in the entire planet that is closest to the invisible realm. The Great Castle of the Leaf is the epicentre of the Eidian Mages, and as such it was the thinnest barrier that Joner could break through. He is here. In the castle that is now his domain, a twisted continuation of the Wizards' will."

The Wizards of Chanthalaroos. This is what they wanted.

Oviinia's eyes widened once she realised. "Wait… we are right under his nose?"

They all nodded.

"During his attack on the other side" Vayu whispered, "Hekor claimed me. And before he could claim the others, he was pushed back by the Queen. My charge… was destroyed."

Her voice quavered.

"I failed before I was even born."

"*Don't* start that shit again" Jugo suddenly growled, rising from his seat. It made Oviinia flinch.

"It *wasn't* your fault" he continued. "You are *not* a failure, Vayu. You are *not* worthless. To hell with the Pheekons. I don't give a damn about their 'plans'."

He gave a side-look to Ilod, as if to say 'no offence buddy', to which the old man tiredly shrugged.

"You are your *own* person" he finished. "You did all of this. You saved us and bought us *all* together. *Don't* forget that."

Like a reassured little girl, Vayu nodded. "Your daughter is lucky to have a father like you."

Jugo scoffed.

"I didn't yell, I guess that's an improvement."

A small knight in golden armour walked up to Gnoat, who then knelt and whispered something in the faun's ear. He then straightened and bowed to all, before trudging off again.

"Excuse me, business calls" the small being said. "We *need* to make final preparations, my lady."

Vayu glided over to her assistant, and held his hand. "We need to go" she said, regaining her composure. "I fear we have very little time left… Jugo and Ilod, please tell my sister everything else you need to impart."

Without waiting for an answer, they left, vanishing within the crowd.

Oviinia didn't need to ask. Yet, she did.

"It's going to get horrific very soon, isn't it?"

The men cast their eyes toward the earth.

"From Liniii, they spread" Ilod rasped. "The power of the fay alone isn't enough. Inexplicably, Joner also obtained the time and space powers of the Arche, and used them to attack each of the towns in Shali. Each town that was linked to a sacred site, because he knew he had narrowed down his search. Whatever he was looking for, it was in our home."

"The *children?*" Oviinia bristled with rage and disgust, as thoughts of poor Rayn came back. "*Why?*"

"We still do not know. But we *do* know he has them. Along with Jeleenn. And we'd wager that the castle is the best way to find them."

So many needless deaths. Gimlum, gone. Henra, gone. Gen, gone. She bubbled with fury, as the mordant wounds reopened.

Ilod waved a dark, bony hand around him. "As you can see, Liniii is not entirely gone. People managed to survive, including Eidian that rebelled. Make no mistake, the green robes do not deserve any blame for this, nor do the denizens of the invisible realm. Like us, their lives have been caught in this turmoil, and wish nothing more than to restore order."

She looked around, and goggled at the array of beings in the camp. Humans – regular, unremarkable humans – co-existed with fairies, sprites, trolls, pixies, goblins… and those were just the ones she could *label*. Some were so strange, she was almost scared to look at them.

The Numanta followed her gaze. "Of course, it was out-and-out bedlam when the island was converted. You know how humans work. They seek to eliminate anything that is different. Still, whatever few remained survived thanks to Vayu. She escaped her captors, and despite her… state, she too, survived. And created hope."

Oviinia was in disbelief. She took the last mouthful of mushroom, and pondered.

"How long *has* this been going on? This… this war? How long *has* Joner been preparing?"

The two Genites cast glances at each other, as if ready to spill a big secret.

"Time" Jugo elaborated, "is different here. Oviinia, what seems like days ago... has been weeks here. Perhaps even months."

The look on her face must have spoken louder than any words she could muster.

"Your cut..."

He exposed his arm once more, and felt his wound. "Yeah. When me and Ilod washed up here, we were saved by Vayu, and helped her build her army. We've been here for far longer than the mere days that have passed in Tarinn. Fancy that, huh?"

She shouldn't have been surprised, but it occurred to her that she had only been here a little while. How long had it been on the outside? Her parents must have been worried sick... or were they even aware? Had her entire campaign been nought but a few seconds to them?

She couldn't help but ponder Jugo's remarks about what *was* and what *wasn't* 'natural'. Who knew any more? Everything had been twisted and turned and pulled inside out; the very fabric of reality seemed like it no longer had a foundation. Time meant nothing. Space meant nothing.

Was Tarinn even real?

Her stomach knotted, and her pride and joy in being able to scientifically quantify her world was withered to a husk. There *was* no science.

Her whole outlook on life was a lie.

She was ready to sob again. She may as well have been still stranded in the Magick Shrine, a prisoner of her own insanity.

She swallowed it all, however. She was stronger than that, and she knew it for damn sure. She would *not* be a victim of her own cursed thoughts. She would use them as a weapon – the way she always knew how.

All of this, she reasoned, was because of the damaging effects Joner has caused. His dimensional interference causing ripples through *everything*; creating a mishmash of anomalies and aberrations that has even influenced our own perceptions. Maybe what we thought *was* natural in Tarinn was in fact *not*? Maybe the 'true' Tarinn was completely different to how we *thought* we knew it?

Dizzying theories that were way beyond her fishy field of expertise, sure, but one thing she *knew* for absolute certain – Joner *had* to be stopped, and the worlds *cannot* merge.

She wanted to live in *her* Tarinn. The pure, beautiful blue Tarinn.

A horn blared, rattling her chest and causing her to drop her spoon with a clatter and splatter. Her fuzzy blanket of musings ripped away by the cold, critical urgency of the here and the now.

"What's that?" she bellowed, her ears ringing.

The two gentlemen looked at each other, weariness plain to see within the crags that lined their aged faces.

"We're in the middle of a warzone" Jugo reiterated, clenching his jaw. "Oviinia… thing's are gonna get ugly, real quickly. Turns out not even the realm of sparkly pixies is immune from the realities of bloodshed. At least, not any more."

She knew all too well. She found herself trembling, and it caught her by surprise. Considering who she was, and what she was capable of… why was she so afraid?

Because, in the end, she really was still just a child.

Ilod cupped her small hands, and the venerable Numanta filled her with a healing warmth that made the soup positively pale in comparison.

"Professor Trundle" he said softly, "… or should I say, Vatn? Which do you prefer, my lady?"

She laughed, the corners of her bright eyes twinkling.

"Things have been… complicated, recently" the magi declared. "To put it mildly. But the one constant. The one thing that will *never* be corrupted or twisted, is our faith and friendship in each other. Even the Pheekonshenee recognised that. Even the gods and goddesses recognise this. Is that safe to say, oh daughter of Lamun?"

He said it so matter-of-factly. She didn't really think about it, but she must've been like a living deity to him. Indeed, her (and her sisters') very existence could even cause a *boatload* of political unrest amongst the magi.

She shuddered, and banished *that* particular realisation in the back of her mind, locked it up, and threw away the key.

"If there are truer words, I'd like to hear them" she concurred. Gently withdrawing from Ilod's grasp, she dug her fingertips into the surface of the table, and clenched tightly. Looking around, that unmistakable air of impending doom nevertheless remained tangible – even in these far-fetched surroundings.

The horn sounded again, and voices began to get louder and louder. The forest ceiling undulated with a howling wind, creating a light show much like a thunderstorm.

"We have to go, Ilod" Jugo urged, rising to his feet.

"What is happening, exactly?" Oviinia canvassed, suddenly done with platitudes.

The elderly mage followed suit. "We are assaulting the Great Castle of the Leaf. We are taking the fight to them, before more lives are needlessly lost."

CHAPTER XII

A dewy breeze passed through her hair, and moistened her lips. It was enough to jolt her into life with a start.

Something is happening.

With clarity, Jeleenn looked stealthily at the woman who stood in front of her. Her peek was noticed however, and she couldn't help but shrink because of that.

She was certainly intimidating. Tall, muscular, with dark skin and an alluring face that reminded her of the sketches of the people that were said to inhabit the land of *Culken*. Her red hair was streaked with coal blackness, as it swirled into a large plait that framed her head, which looked to bear some sort of mark or brand.

That forbearing wind brought clarity to her, and she knew that she had been staying in this place for too long already. Languishing like a damsel, she cursed herself for being helpless, and wanted to scream until her throat imploded.

"He's certainly convincing" the woman – known as Remana tol Dwen – mused, as she leaned casually against a tree. "Not a liar in the least. I really don't think so."

That simple deduction caused Jeleenn great despair. She could not refute it.

Still, she had to admit that it bought her some semblance of comfort to meet another outsider. Another victim whisked away from their home, and planted like a root in this blurred realm. Joner seemed quite happy to introduce the two; undoubtedly glad that he had bought his sister a friend to play with.

It was cynical of her to think of him in such a way, but regardless, his enthusiasm… warmed her? She was still his brother after all. Even though she told herself that he was in control of his own actions, she still found herself occasionally weeping for him and everything that he had to endure. A literal child, going through hell and back… there was no way he would have emerged from that unscathed.

Does that mean Hekor is the devil?

She was truly thankful for not seeing that beast again, and she hoped that she could avoid doing so. He scared her witless, but upon seeing Remana and the strength she exuded, she became a little less afraid.

"We need to get out of here" Jeleenn pleaded in response. She clasped Remana's iron forearm. "People have died. Friends and family. And the few that remain… I need to know they're alright! I have to find them!"

The tall woman smiled, and placed her hand on top of the girl's. "Look, you're not the only one who's lost it all. I'm still trying to unwrap all of this nonsense… and diving head-first into even more trouble will only cause more insanity and confusion."

"What did Joner tell you?"

She shook her head. There was quiet for a while, as Remana inhaled deeply. They stood in a grove of flowers, inside one of the inner courts of the castle. Honeycombs sagged the trees which stood here, and singing bees were busily pollinating as they were herded by squat creatures that grunted, spat and swore. They hopped on three legs, and were completely covered in fur, whilst wearing vests stuffed with bells, whistles and bottles. They seemed to mostly ignore the women; their round, bulging eyes moving independently of one another.

Remana lit a large pipe, and began to puff with fervour. "He said that I'm some sort of ancient being" she replied, black smoke pouring from every orifice. "An experiment of the... Pheekonshenee. A fire elemental born from the spirit of Arlmai, and given human form."

She laughed at the words coming from her own mouth.

"I wouldn't believe it" she continued, "were it not for... y'know, my entire life. It explains so much. My birth family, to which my adopted parents refused to ever talk about. My abilities. My visions..."

"Visions?" Jeleenn probed.

"It really only started when I almost died in the mountains" she began, offering the girl a puff of the intimidating-looking apparatus. Jeleenn shrugged and partook, and was surprisingly proficient. "When I was rescued by an old man... somewhat of an ancient being himself. I can't remember most of it, and I sometimes wondered if it was a dream. That's when I got this symbol on my head, and when the 'Aodh' name was seared into my head. When he said it... Joner, I mean..."

She swore softly, and turned her back. Jeleenn guessed that the woman didn't want to show any weakness, especially to someone she undoubtedly viewed as weaker and more innocent.

"I'm supposed to be a weapon. A tool" Remana said. "My whole life, I was sheltered from this... and when it all went to the dogs, this 'task' has now suddenly made itself known. It was as if I was being punished for daring to live my own life. That fate decided to kick my house of cards down, and spur me into action, like a good little soldier."

Hate seared her throaty voice now. She turned, her eyes reddening. "What am I supposed to be, some sort of prophet or something? Like in the old tales? A religious icon? A plebeian designated a divine task? To spread the good word? Pah!"

She nearly tossed the pipe to the ground, but thought better of it. Still smouldering with embers, she put it back in her mouth like a pacifier.

Jeleenn did not know what to say.

"You don't strike me as a plebeian" was all she could scrounge.

Remana smiled. "I appreciate it, girly."

They talked for a long while, and if there were any suns in their world, then they surely would have set. They shared their life stories, their fears, and their dreams; whilst feasting on honeycomb, smoking what seemed like lead shavings, and laughing at anything and everything in between coughs. It was the happiest the both of them felt for a long time, in this world of absurdity. Even if it was just for a little while, they shed their guilt and simply lived in the moment.

Looking from the shadows, Joner beamed. He too, finally felt gladness. Of course, it would only be fleeting.

Something is happening.

* * *

A tidal wave of life, in all its forms, spread through the green of Liniii like frothing seawater.

Only, this seawater did not recede. It moved ever onward, passing through the black forests unchallenged; with not even the mightiest tree trunk nor the thickest of scrub halting its march.

They were few; but nothing would deter them. Any resistance they faced, they immediately cut down with precision and intent.

The turmoil. The arduous survival. The endless nights of hiding in fear. The anger. The violence. The hopelessness.

That vile seed cracked open – and from it, sprouted hope.

Vayu's cloudy eyes became that little bit clearer. Pride warmed her cold body, as she led her squadron of fay.

Once, during a particularly awful night of self-loathing, she referred to herself as the 'eternal tadpole'. A slimy, incomplete creature that would never become the frog.

Gnoat – after surprising himself and her by slapping her across the face – eventually told her to embrace it. To become a symbol for her people, because her destiny now took a different path. The Pheekonshenee's plans for her were now moot, and the sooner she accepted that, the stronger she would get.

That moment surely was a turning point, and Vayu had the faun's small, stinging palm to thank for that. Of course, he had never stopped apologising. Grovelling incessantly, even after inadvertently giving birth to a coat of arms that achieved the impossible.

And so, bearing a banner that defied the looming spectre of the Great Castle of the Leaf, was the *Eternal Tadpole*. Vayu, daughter of Shalisshakin and the Pheekonshenee. Guardian of Liniii, and – most importantly – friend and leader to all who now trailed behind her.

Her unit numbered some six hundred, and was composed of different races of the various invisible kingdoms. Wielding various gizmos and gadgets, Gnomes formed one of the core infantry groups, as did their Leprechaun cousins. Normally, they did not get along, but (like everyone else) they were all caught in these stranger tides, and were willing to fight tooth and nail to get their homes back.

Flanking them were trolls, large brutes that were greatly angered by being uprooted from their holes. Neither knowing nor caring which world they belonged in, they desired only to smash and maim; which caused no end of grief to their companions and Vayu, who had an insurmountable time in taming them. Their spiked clubs bashed aside thicket with a cacophony of throaty bellows, and in turn, the altered forest fought back with whipping thorns and gnashing, toothy fly traps.

The remainder of the ground troops acted as splinters, with Abatwa mini-humans and Mikolasak imps riding Kitsune foxes, as they bounded from branch to branch, cackling with glee. The mounts would often whisper evil words, which echoed ominously through the meadows. It was in their nature, so Vayu could not reprimand them too much. She only asked that they try not to sway nor influence any of her soldiers toward undesired actions, to which the gold creatures grudgingly agreed.

A Jabberwocky tended to the skies, along with a giant bat known as Blayang; who often complained loudly about his 'brother' (much to the annoyance of everyone else). Fairies provided much-needed light in the gloom; their ethereal forms bringing warmth and comfort to the stillness that stagnated the air.

For indeed, there was no wind.

From the western side of the small island, they advanced northeast, toward the edge of the outermost wall of the castle.

In truth, the Great Castle of the Leaf took up the majority of the land of Liniii. The former epicentre of the Edian order, it was a gigantic acropolis more akin to a small city. Rising in layers, the very tip was the *High Priest's Abode* – home to the leader of the Green Robes, who was always said to be the reincarnation of the goddess herself, and always named Dian.

That's where Joner undoubtedly made his lair, Vayu figured.

She wasn't sure if Dian chose to betray her order, or if she was ultimately corrupted by her conspirators. It no longer mattered. The fact was that she took the sacred teachings of the Eidian, and twisted them into something else entirely. Perhaps it all started with the Wizards; that the conflict against them utterly broke her. Maybe it was her bond with Joner, and her decision that his well-being meant more than the fate of the world itself.

Regardless, that fact that she was supposed to be the embodiment of Shalisshakin meant that the Eidian order was utterly decimated, and that turmoil no doubt raged within the *House of Free Leaders* within this very moment, as they wondered just what was happening in their 'holy land'.

Just like the invisible realm it was supposed to protect, a civil war broke out amongst the emerald magi – with those still loyal to their teaching scattered into the four winds.

It wasn't just the mages either, but everyone else who lived on Liniii. The caretakers, farmers, cooks, fishermen, workers, guardsmen… all were forced to pick a side. The only ones spared from the agony of choice were the children and novices, who were immediately swept up by Dian, to be locked up and never be seen since.

This saddened and infuriated Vayu the most.

It would be weeks or even months before Chanthalaroos could act. Though she herself was utterly unfamiliar with Tarinn and its governments, she was assured by Jugo that immediate help was simply too far away. As for the merchants, navy and other seafarers that may have been nearby? Not a word. As expected, the land was impenetrable from the outside – and that was assuming the outside even knew of what was happening. Of course, word spread quickly after the attacks in Shali... but this far north? She was doubtful.

Those Edian – the ones that dared stand up to their matriarch – were out for justice.

Like Vayu, the very idea of shedding blood was utterly inconceivable to them... but also like Vayu, they soon learned that their morals and teachings simply did not matter.

They were the first she had found, once she herself slipped from her captors' grasp. The first victims. Emaciated and utterly shattered, they sobbed and wailed for their faith, and their mother who had forsaken them. They wanted nothing more than to disappear from this world; to become one with the dark green. Only with the arrival of Vayu did hope shine forth, along with the creatures of the fay, who were even more lost and frightened than they.

All of them. They all became family. Her family. And now she was possibly going to die alongside them.

Jugo's voice rang in her hollow bones.

It would've been a good way to go, mate.

Yes, yes it will.

* * *

The Blemmyes wretched and gasped, as Jugo's blade ran straight through its head.

Though 'head' would've been a misnomer, as the naked, man-like creature's face was in fact located on its torso. Its large mouth gaped like a fish, spurting black blood all over the innkeeper.

Before he could swear, more of them congregated. Bouncing and skipping like children playing hopscotch, their ludicrous movements masked their murderous intentions.

The Fountainscape Balustrade was overrun, and they were taking it back. Mounting a surprise, diversionary assault on the mangrove, Jugo and Ilod led every able-bodied man and woman on a daring strike, as they hoped to soften the main force's target.

The two were well aware they were not leading trained soldiers. Still, *nothing* compared to the fury and determination of one who was fuelled on both revenge *and* love.

Nonetheless, the two organised and led them with aplomb, as their crude weapons tore through their foes, aided by the magics and knowledge of the Eidian who commanded them.

Trying vainly to remove his blade from the still-writing corpse, two of the victim's brethren shoulder barged Jugo like a bull, sending him flying.

Gasping as he hit the hard and crooked roots of the everglade, they were on him before he could swat the stars from his vision, wrapping their gigantic hands around his neck.

Something suddenly broke the atmosphere with its loudness, as a vine whipped like a blur, smacking the foes with an impact that replaced their gunning visages with a dark mist.

"Get up, old man!" someone shouted amid the chaos, as he was pulled up.

It was a man. A green robe. Karnon... something, or other. A tall fellow with brown, curly hair.

"I ain't that old yet" Jugo panted. Rolling with a deftness that surprised the magi, he yanked his sword from its fleshy home, and flicked the gore off.

Hundreds of the same creatures poured from the chasm – the chasm where deep blue waters once flowed. They were aided by large, beetle-like beings that glistened like opals, in addition to centipede/snake things that looked like they came straight from a fevered nightmare.

The humans fought tooth and nail, and were making steady headway. Thankfully, they had managed to do some reconnaissance on their enemies before their first retreat, and had at least *some* idea on how to repel them.

What made these beings so dangerous was that so many of them were utterly alien – even to the Eidian. They emerged from the deepest and most hidden of worlds, so that it was like filling a completely new bestiary.

In any other time, that would have been a joyous experience for *any* egghead.

This was not that time. A time of death. A time of hatred. A time of maddening fear.

This? *This* is what Joner wanted?

Rancid mud exploded, as bombs were thrown in a desperate push to stymie the Blemmyeses, who moaned dully as they fell, only to be used as stepping stones by their brethren.

"Little monkeys are playing with fire!" screeched one of the beetle commanders, who was the size of a carriage, and dual wielded immense hatchets. His tiny wings buzzed, before slamming the filthy sludge below and causing a shock wave.

Even from his distance, the impact was just as potent as the explosions that knocked around Jugo's thumping heart.

"I don't think these bugs will be easily squashed!" the young mage shouted in the innkeeper's ear.

Jugo uttered a vile curse. The boy was right. There were a good view dozen of them; all of them armed to the teeth, airborne and harder than a iron-clad coconut. Worst of all, they were smart.

Never mind the serpentine monsters that now writhed; like worms, they dug through the earth, consuming the bodies of the fallen and making themselves stronger.

It looked like an insurmountable situation.

"Remember the plan" Jugo spat. "Keep them busy. Keep yourselves planted. And let Ilod flank them."

Screams echoed now, down the embankment. Sounds of metal ripped the treeline.

The Eidian could not keep up their protective barriers forever. Using their arcane arts, they erected gargantuan cocoons that smashed anything that ventured underneath, bungeed by elastic slime that did not snap. They also conjured glowing spider webs that entrapped and blocked all; funnelling the opposing forces into choke points.

If there was *some* good to come out of this situation, it was that the intersections of Tarinn and the invisible realm helped to amplify the magic of the green robes. If only just enough so that they can withstand the battering that they now endured.

A horrid smell choked the two men, making them gag.

"Happy holidays!" another beetle wailed, as his reflective, viridian carapace opened up, exposing a fleshy white hide that seeped gaseous fumes. With pinpoint gusts, he fired clouds of stink that ate away at the fortifications like acid, whilst sizzling the throats of anything doomed enough to be in the way.

"Evil, hideous swine!" the magi cursed, desperately covering his mouth. Behind him, a party of eight brave souls coughed. Even at their height and distance, the stench was almost unbearable.

With Jugo at their head, they scouted the upper ridges of the Balustrade. Meeting resistance along the narrow road, they forged ahead, as they aimed to waylay their enemy with a pincer attack.

The other side would fall to the Numanta.

As the main force would be preoccupied in the valley below, it would be up to them to strike quickly and decisively.

Truth was, they didn't have much information to go on. The ultimate goal was to buy Vayu some precious time in storming the castle; their dual brazen assaults hopefully creating some chaos within the enemy.

The problem was, thinking and planning on straight military terms was hard when dealing with such formidable and alien interlopers. What were their supply lines? How much of them were there overall?

What were their weaknesses? What was their hierarchy?

Thank god for Vayu and the Eidian then, who really achieved the impossible, and somehow managed to build up *some* pretense of a fighting force.

How long had she been here? Jugo mused, as he slew another foe with a savage hack. *To begin life like a weak, premature babe – only to somehow defy her fate, and carve out a new path... how long? Ilod and me... it feels like we've been here for months. It could've been years for her.*

He swore. He swore, as the inky claret mixed with the squelching mud. He swore that once all this was over, he would give her a home. He would adopt her, and take her on adventures. Let her see the world.

Just like I should've done with Jeleenn... or, was I right to always keep her within reach? Did I do the wrong thing with Joner? Did I raise him too fast?

He bellowed, his grief and anger coating his blade and giving it an extra bite. It howled as it danced in the dried air, lamenting the corpses of its allies which sunk into the bog, never to be seen again.

* * *

"Lord Numanta! Are you hurt?"

The Golden Knight lifted up Ilod with a single, effortless tug. Despite his diminutive stature, he was as strong as an ox.

"I am fine" he replied, ashamed of himself.

What kind of master mage trips over from nothing?

His wounded ego was quickly forgotten, as the serpent could be heard again.

"Let's move!" the knight hollered.

Their plan was working so far; as much as he hated to admit it. One of the snake-centipede creatures had grown to an enormous, gigantic size. Easily one hundred meters or so now, it caused the very trees to sway and creak with its crawling. Dubbed 'Jethro', its hissing and wheezing echoed through the ground, scaring the squad out of its skin. Its uncountable legs created a rhythmic song of impending annihilation, which was given bass by the clacks of its jaws.

It was a plan both desperate and foolhardy. After observing its habits and abilities during dangerous excursions, they had captured one of the monsters. Keeping it in the remains of Mehn Station in the south, they then proceeded to feed it the bodies of enemies assassinated in the field, taking meticulous notes of its growth depending on its food.

It was long, dirty and sinister work; but it had to be done. Thankfully, Ilod had nothing to do with the 'project', so his hands were clean from this particular instance. Nevertheless, he provided counselling and healing sessions to those that suffered a crisis in morality – mostly from the Edian.

Some creatures simply disappeared when killed, but those that left discernible remains were absorbed by Jethro. It made him bigger.

Much bigger.

When the day of the assault arrived, it was time to test their latest weapon. They would lure a very hungry, very cranky Jethro to the heart of the Fountainscape Balustrade.

He had morphed considerably, his varied diet sprouting extra eyes on his long body, and thick hairs that dragged along the ground, absorbing all moisture and leaving a cracked and parched trail in his wake.

They had created a leviathan.

Ever noble, and a glutton for punishment, Ilod offered to lead the deadly mission. The Numanta's magics and technology worked in tandem with two Edian who accompanied him, as they kept Jethro in a relatively calm state.

Well, they *tried*, at least.

The Golden Knight would defend them from any enemies that they may encounter, though Ilod himself wielded a Pheekon device which emitted a blast of supersonic waves.

The Numanta were very adept in combining spells with technology, and few could do it as well as Ilod. They used all tools in their disposal for healing – that's what the white robes did. However, they could prove to be wily in battle in dismantling their foes – usually with non-lethal means.

Though Numanta took a vow to never kill, Ilod had broken that promise years ago.

Refusing to lose himself in his past, he followed his stumpy protector.

He was certain the Golden Knight wasn't human, as he had come from the invisible realm. The warrior never removed his helm, and was inseparable from Vayu. He shared a close relationship with Gnoat, and greatly protested in leaving their side for this dangerous mission. Either way, an order was an order (especially one from the Eternal Tadpole), and he reluctantly embraced his new-found duty.

It didn't take him long to become Ilod's new best friend. He greatly respected both the mage and the innkeeper, as they had told him tales of their old exploits. In a way, Ilod found him charming in his almost childlike-naivety. He was a simple being, with a one track mind.

The four of them moved as fast as they could. Panting and sweating, they clambered through the ravine as the distant clamor of battle reverberated over them. Thunderous cracks rippled the landscape, and the stench of decay assailed them even at their advanced distance.

The hollow Fountainscape gaped out before them; an endless maw that seemed to get bigger and bigger, as it portended the swallowing of the entire island.

The river would have been a marvel to see in its lively state, as rainbows were said to be everywhere one looked, as a veritable paradise of wildlife lived underneath their prisms.

Now, it was all gone. Beyond life and death, it was a chaotic shadow of nature. A meandering mash of dimensions and elements that have lost their place.

To think, is this what will become of the entire world?

To their left, trunks smashed and toppled, with the high pitches of death wails breaking through the harsh discord.

"Jethro's causing a bigger ruckus than before" one of the drenched Eidian pointed out. "It's getting harder to keep him under control! How much longer do we have to go?"

"We meet Jugo at the other side of the chasm" Ilod huffed.. "We will release the monster before then, after they set off the fireworks. The enemy is coming from below... that is where we need to strike."

"And if the beast isn't enough?"

"It won't be" Ilod answered gravely. "It won't be. But hopefully it will be enough to sow havoc. So that we may meet with Vayu, and go on to the castle. Either way, it ends when Jethro gives up the ghost."

He shuddered. As horrible as the beast was, Ilod felt that they weren't much better.

That's what war does. Human or not, it is all the same.

Am I even worthy of wearing these robes any more?

"Good lord" the Golden Knight exclaimed, as he hopped onto a crumbly hillock and surveyed their destination. "It is positively *teeming* with the enemy! Like an overflowing ants nest, I dare say!"

Jethro screeched again, and the very ground rumbled.

The knight almost lost his footing, but quickly regained solid ground as he jumped deftly in front of the group. Using his comically oversized lance, he impaled the dirt like some sort of surveyor.

"Onward! We do not have much time, dear magi!"

* * *

Death was altering the very air itself.

Screams and wails punctured the land; the trauma manifesting itself in the grinding, coagulated atmosphere of conflicting energies.

The battle of the Fountainscape Balustrade dragged on, with no time seemingly passing. The agony of the fallen wafted above and through them like a soup, and their feet and minds became heavier and heavier.

Senses dimmed, and life and death became indistinguishable. Soon, both armies were of one entity.

A tar of absence. A sludgy mass of regret, hatred, rage and an infinite loop of sheer torture. A collision of the very worst of both worlds, resulting in a void of incomprehension.

Oviinia saw it all. She felt it all.

She was no fighter. Even as Vatn, she abhorred violence.

But life would always challenge her. To dip her hands in blood.

She travelled with corsairs and navy, as she journeyed the eastern seas in her endless studies of ocean life. Always writing papers. Always under the thumb of the university.

She loved every second of it. That was meant to be her life. Even as she was invited to Shali to study the Tilth, she never felt trapped. Gimlum became her home, and she was content.

What were my plans for the future? I never really thought that far...

She was called back, of course. She was the guardian of Shali. An entity created from experiments of the Pheekonshenee; to harness the element of water within an artificial life form, so that she may act as a key to the other realm...

How did I forget all of this?

She was an amalgamation of worlds. Along with her sisters. They should not have existed. They were unnatural; an affront to the gods of Tarinn, and reviled by Queen Bean Si and King Álfhildur.

It didn't matter. They had served their purpose. The Pheekonshenee managed to achieve their goal. They gained access to the realm of the fay; a realm that literally provided a whole new world of discoveries.

That is where it all started.

She had to find Kwenn. She had to find Aodh and Acasta. She had to protect Vayu. And she had to find the prince...

I can do this. I am not *an abomination. We* are *not* abominations.

She yelled. Screamed. Bellowed. Her arm lit up like a sun, its cerulean beams cutting through the mire like a knife.

They all surrounded her. Their gaunt, grey faces doing their damnedest to protect her. They swung their swords, chopped their axes and bashed their shields for *her* sake. They barely knew her – yet, they *died* for her.

A short-sighted marine biologist. From Buj.

They died. And died. And died.

This was *not* Joner's land. This was *Vayu's* land. This was *their* land. *Tarinn.*

Water. From the sky, it fell. Thunder cracked overhead, and as the liquid splashed their faces, their eyes brightened and colour flushed their cheeks. They remembered. The taste. The feel. The purity.

They cried from joy. From the realisation that they were still alive. That they could still fight. That they were *not* trapped in purgatory.

Oviinia broke out from her protective guard. Clad in a simple leather tunic, she pushed back the blackness. The rain swirled and battered the filth that encrusted the air, and it recoiled with a roar. Jagged teeth behind grey, cracked lips clattered at her, only to spit and sputter once they got a mouthful of nectar.

Horses neighed around her, their hooves dancing in the fresh mud. They too recalled their lives before the chaos. The smell of the grass. The freedom of the roads. Even the swatting of flies. They squealed in their desire to go home, to be free from the binds that tethered them to the supply carts.

"What in the…" one of the insects garbled, as his retinue of Khepri shrieked. The beings had bodies of men and scarabs for heads, and used weapons made from hardened dung. They began to kneel and bow nonsensically.

"Sun comes after rain!" they chanted. "Sun comes after rain!"

All over the frontline, they fell and mimicked each other, causing a great deal of confusion amongst the beetle commandos.

Lightning shot down from the broiling sky, exploding great trunks and causing them to topple onto the enemy. The sharp, rich colour of the embers were almost too painful to look upon, as they erupted like clouds of fiery pollen before being extinguished by the ambrosial shower.

It was rain. Just rain. And it was the most empowering thing these people had felt in a long, long time.

"It's a miracle!!!" they cried, before charging with a replenished hardiness that caused their foes to recoil.

"What did you do?!" a young woman gripped Oviinia by her shoulder. They were both shaking like leaves.

She was unable to answer. The light still pulsating from her arm, she looked at the girl in front of her. She couldn't be older than her late teens, and she wielded a sickle that was dulled with use. Her freckles gave her an innocent look that contrasted with the blood and cuts that covered her.

"I'll tell you what she did" an Eidian yelled, as he pulled the girl away and pointed her toward their adversary. "She just gave us a fighting chance! My god, Vayu was right! You *are* a special kind of something, Miss Trundle!"

Happy with her answer, the girl ran head-first into battle again.

"CHAAAAAAAAAARRRRRRRGGGGEEEE!!!"

One by one, like a blaze spreading through a dry brush, barberry trees began to illuminate with a greenish-blue, apple fervour. Life began to remember itself, as the faded spectre of the Fountainscape sparked under the taste of water that splashed under the boots of the brave; the leaves and branches twinkling and trickling,

Oviinia howled, her voice melding with the thunderous sky. She saw death. It stalked her. It put its clammy hands around her and tried to whisper with a tongueless, lipless mouth. That she wasn't *really* alive. That she was just a quivering, quavering mass of Pheekonshenee jelly. An affront to nature – and one that should have been smothered by her divine 'mother', so that she be spared from knowing the misery of it all.

The misery of life.

They kept calling her. The Magick Shrine. Their faces; joyful in their lethe and oblivious of their oblivion.

But life jabbed her with its thumb. Painfully. It poked her in her eyes, and pulled her hair. It slapped her, and pointed impatiently.

Hello?! Remember me?!

She *did* remember, and her neck pulsated from a second scream, as she thrust a knife straight into the oversized eye of *something* that stood in her way, before it fell noiselessly and evaporated under her sanctity.

I remember alright. I remember me. I am the daughter. My parents love me. My goddess loves me. My sisters love me, and I love them.

Love. That was it. That was the answer.

It was love that made her keep going. Made her fight.

She saw the bulging, black eyes of the draft horses as they whinnied and neighed, and she saw something worth fighting for.

She saw the young man who fell face first in the mud, before being lifted by a wounded comrade, and saw something worth fighting for.

She saw the world spring to life around them as they advanced, inch by inch, and saw something worth fighting for.

In the corner of her eye, she could've sworn she saw Hoppo. Sitting happily on a stone, and letting her know that he was still watching over her.

* * *

Jugo swore.

The sky – which had been void of light for as long as he could remember – now suddenly pulsed.

A torrent washed over them, and far down in the swampy valley below, a curtain of rain paradoxically made things clearer to his eyes. It was like he was now fully awake.

For better and worse, as a gigantic bug was heading straight toward him in all of its horrible glory.

Fear pumped through his heart, as his squad behind him took position.

They had made it to the canyon, and were inside the belly of the best.

Hurry the hell up Ilod!

"So, this is the mighty Jugo Ironmonger!" the bug cackled. Its voice truly was hair-raising, as if it tried to speak human with parts that weren't *built* for speaking human. It was huge, like the others, and clattered on jagged legs that looked as though they could cut steel. The carapace was caked with skulls from other conquests, and its hideous head was enclosed in a cage that had a large bell dangling underneath it.

"Thought you could sneak in here, eh, you old rat?" it continued, stomping menacingly toward the group. With long, chitinous arms it held the biggest morning star the innkeeper had ever seen.

The bell was tolled for the humans.

Jugo waved his blade skilfully and defiantly. A hot swell of fear rolled along his back, and he wasn't sure if it came from himself, or his friends that were now undoubtedly soiling themselves.

"Lookit the size of 'im…" one of them groaned in an utterly petrified voice.

"Behind me" Jugo ordered, refusing to look away at his new opponent. "Spread out. Now."

The rain intensified, and the cold drops felt almost like shards of glass on his skin. The sensation took him by surprise somewhat, as it made him realise just how long he had been stuck in this place with the Numanta.

Certainly not like the old times, eh Queen?

He had no time to reminisce. The monster was already halfway toward him, his massive weapon knocking aside any minion that didn't get out of his way fast enough.

"Juuuuuggggoooooo" it bellowed, almost like a theatrical ghost-in-chains. "Juuuuuuuuugggggooooooooo!!! JUUUUUUUUUUGGGGGGGOOOOOOOOOOOO!!!"

He heard feet squelching at his flank, and was relieved that they weren't squelching in retreat.

"Don't rush in!" he shouted. "Stay defensive! Keep an eye out for reinforcements! You know what you need to do!"

Will any of these kids die today, I wonder?

The bug suddenly became *a lot* bigger than Jugo had expected, and the reach of the morning star felt like a kilometre, as it bared down on him with the force of a toppling tree, before exploding the ground in a mushroom of brown water.

The innkeeper dived to the side, but a little too late to avoid the aftershock of the blow. His ribcage felt like it turned upside down, and he instinctively swiped his blade, which bounced off a deformed leg that immediately tried to pin him down.

Rolling like a log, Jugo pulled out the only thing he could think that would make a dent in such a beast.

"Jugo, no!"

The young Eidian leaped to his superior's aid, as the club was once again tearing through the air. He threw a pouch at the creature, as it clunked against the morbid shell and unfurled, releasing four large seeds that cracked open and released a sticky, woolly substance that tangled the legs of the giant.

He collapsed, swearing and clicking in another language. The bell banged with a discordant bellow, matched in tone by Jugo as he homed in on a vulnerable joint area of its arm, ripping its sinew with quick and powerful chops.

Steaming red blood sprayed like a geyser, before thickening like syrup in the rain and making him recoil from the overwhelming metallic funk. His disappointment at his failure to fully decapitate was softened by the screeches that whistled from the caged mandibles.

Knowing better than to relish in his brief victory, Jugo moved as quick as he could, but again he was totally unprepared for the speed and ferocity of the other arm of the wounded adversary, which shot forth like a piston and smashed him square in the chest.

He flew bodily like a child, crashing into the thicket that now began to light up, spotlighting the arch of claret that streamed from his mouth and nose.

"Jugo!"

The innkeeper coughed violently, as he rocked helplessly in the beryl brilliance which cradled him like a wounded animal, as his sword bounced, clanged and vanished in the brush, whilst his other weapon still hung in mid-air, before falling back to the earth in what seemed like slow motion.

Karnon cursed.

Bombs did *not* like sudden impacts.

He ran as fast as his thin legs could muster, but the gummy mud and blood stuck to his soles and sucked him down. Discerning that he couldn't reach Jugo in time, his fledgling mind tried to manifest something – *anything* – to save himself.

He was too inexperienced, however. No spell immediately came to his mind. All his body could do was awkwardly jerk in the opposite direction, and dive downward toward the putrid safety of the sludge.

They all carried one; the secret armament that each of them were entrusted with. To carry through the black cavity of enemy territory, and to pierce their heart with a white-hot blade.

Nine explosives, constructed carefully by the Eidian from ingredients scrounged from what little remained of Liniii's natural form. They were one tip of the 'trident' that was wielded by the defenders; with the other two points being the hideous, slithering monstrosity led by the Numanta, and the main assault force that bravely battled the enemy head-on.

Jugo led what was essentially a death squad; eight of the hardest, most suicidal men that took these highly volatile equalisers on their persons, knowing that they could utterly obliterate them at any time.

The young Eidian mage only managed to join them, because the bombs were *his* invention. Weapons that were specifically designed to work in this oppressive environment, after months of research.

An idea he cursed himself for ever having, as the coconut-sized sphere of incredibly condensed power plummeted; the continuous, airborne kinetic energy triggering its 'faux-gale' reaction, as its acidic concoction of gaseous berry juices, venom, sulphur and runic magic interacted with its crowning ingredient; a hyper-compressed core of ball lightning harvested from the corrupted faerie 'weather' (if one could call it that).

It hissed and emitted noxious fumes, and he screamed and covered his head with his heavy, soaked sleeves.

Still struggling to rise, the monster looked quizzically at the globe that whistled and cracked apart like a superheated walnut, as it spattered right in front of its bulbous, pale eyes.

"The hell is this?" it wheezed, before it created the most horrible sound that ever assaulted the man's ears, as a flash like a Sollik itself blinded him and cooked him alive.

* * *

The Fountaincape Balustrade came alive in a daisy chain of brilliance, and the entire marshland joined in, as the black sky was pushed back by the ether of life.

Thunder crashed from above and below, as war melded with the heavens in its trumpets of glory, before being underscored by flares of ruination that lit the horizon like the rising suns.

It was unbearable. The noise was simply too much for Ilod's old body, which felt like it was about to collapse in a pile of bones.

He had to keep moving.

To him, the unendurable, world-shifting events that now happened all around them was a reaction. A recoiling by their foe, who could not believe that it had finally been struck a blow.

The rain. The thunder. The light. It was both cathartic and painful, like gulping air after almost drowning, and the fact that people were still dying down below sobered him quick-smart.

They had successfully detonated the bombs. Jugo's squad of madmen actually did it, as the canyon belched fire like the gates of the underworld itself.

"That is our cue!" he shouted with the strongest voice he could produce.

They were close. Close enough to feel the heat, and see the frenzied chaos that ensued, as insect-like figures scattered from their burning colony. The Golden Knight's metaphor was apt.

"Release Jethro! Now!!!"

The Eidian both nodded to each other, as they proceeded to gasp and fall in complete exhaustion, releasing their hold over the abhorrent thing.

Even in the lashing rain, he could see how flushed they really were.

A warble could be seen in the air, much like a heatwave, and millions of symbols floated like jellyfish in a brief instant, before vanishing with a pop. Curiously, the fingernails of the mages grew a few inches – a side effect of their spell.

Ilod immediately tended to them, proud of their work. The Golden Knight watched over them silently.

They would not have much time. Jethro would wake from his stupor, and then go on a rampage that made the death and destruction seen so far seem like mere child's play.

A chill suddenly washed over them all, spurring them to avoid lingering for too long.

"It is time to move!" the knight proclaimed in his echoed, velvet voice. "We shall regret staying for too long! Lady Vayu and Lord Jugo await!"

* * *

He was awake. For quite a while, he suspected.

It was only now that he became cognisant of that fact, and he tried to move.

He couldn't.

His breath was rattly, and flames licked his sides, as the rain attempted to quell their spread.

Damn it... what happened?

Acrid, tawny smoke drifted, dulling the brightness of the grove that swayed as if it tried to fan the fire away from him.

Blinking harsh, metallic water away, Jugo was relieved to see his fingers move, and his feet sway from side to side.

Damn it!

Finally recalling his gigantic, cockroach problem, he desperately tried to raise, but it was even more of a battle than the one he had just prior.

He heard breathing. Inhuman gasping that instilled both terror and pity within his heart. He had no idea what he was hearing, but he wanted it to stop.

Moaning in agony, he felt his chest pull apart as he rolled over, before rising to his knees like a belligerent drunkard.

Somehow, against all odds, he stood; albeit hunched in a crooked way. Feeling blood slowly ooze from his lips, he limped in the muck and mire of carnage. Biting his lips, he spat, and saw the source of the haunting rasping that cut through the roiling vapour.

It was his foe. The beetle. Or what was left of it.

Only a portion of it remained, and yet, it still clung on. A gaping cavern where its body used to be, it dripped with orange and pink innards, which was slowly being eroded by the cleansing water. It clutched its morning star, and the cage that enclosed its head was now twisted and fused to it.

Jugo also saw the young Edian man; Karnon. He was on the ground, still and practically invisible, as his body was the same colour as his surroundings.

The bomb.... that damned bomb.

He was too reckless. He tried to use it against the monster. He knew he stood no chance of defeating it one-on-one.

I guess it worked, he thought grimly.

He stood over the dying monster.

"Y... you..." it whispered with what little strength it had left.

"Me" Jugo replied, not sounding too dissimilar.

"You..." it said again, its voice already sounding weaker. "Yoooouuuu.... Humans. S... such a blight... such a blight..."

He felt pity. As he always did when confronted with a dying foe. No matter how many fires he endured, nor how tough his skin became from years of hardship, Jugo was still that young, idealistic young man at heart. The one that took any challenge and helped any in need, regardless how obfuscated he was by his naivety. Even as a father that fought tooth and nail to protect his child from the evils of the world... he was still truly a soft, loving man.

Deep, deep down.

"I'm beginning to think we are" he conceded in a hoarse voice.

A grating, bubbly noise agreed in its last breath. "For... for... R... R... Restrentuliousolou'sdent-shaneekaladai!!!"

Its head lulled, the deformed clapper clanking its last.

Jugo clenched his entire body in both pain and shock, as he looked blankly at the beast's body. For too long, he suspected, but he had to stop himself from thinking – even just for a few moments.

Growling, he gave the corpse a wide berth, and approached the green robe Karnon, fearing and expecting an identical fate for the young boy. Falling to his knees, he grabbed the befouled and seared form, and turned him with great effort.

He was alive, and awake.

Jugo thanked whatever god was watching over them, and breathed loudly in deliverance.

"Kid" he said, cupping Karnon's crusty face. "Kid, you still in there? Answer me!"

"I... I'm here..." he said without a trace of emotion. "I'm... I'm here, Jugo. I'm here."

Another explosion punched both of them, as another bomb went off some distance away.

It was enough to shoot Karnon's body upward with a scream, like a vampire roused from its coffin.

"Another one!"

Darting his head around on a rubber neck, he absorbed the destructive surroundings, before screaming again at the sight of the monster's decimation.

Jugo slapped him sharply, whilst imagining Ilod lecturing him about the danger of concussions.

You ain't here, old man.

"Hey! Hey! Kid! Kid, calm down! I'm here! Calm down!"

Relenting under the innkeeper's grip, Karnon did as he was told. After collecting himself, he showed the inner strength his elder knew to be there, and promptly renewed his focus on their mission.

"We must move, Jugo."

As if in agreement, another explosion clapped.

"The men, they're doing their job" Jugo confirmed in pride. They did what he could not; they managed to infiltrate the enemy's stronghold, and hit them where it hurt.

Godspeed, you hard buggers.

They had no problem dying for their cause, and made it very known back at the base. In fact, Jugo tried to lecture them about what he perceived was their misplaced fealty, and that they should've valued their lives a lot more than they did. That they merely used death as an excuse to finally escape.

He wondered if he was right to do so?

Supporting each other, the two of them made way alongside the canyon, in the hopes of meeting up with Vayu and the other men toward the east.

* * *

Sound became prosperous once more.

The longer they fought, the more they advanced inch by inch, their ears opened to the thundercracks of the realness and perceptibility that had almost become lost to them forever.

It was not all beauty. There was also horror.

But that horror, in some malign way, fuelled them even more. It was corporeal.

It was human.

Their world. The world of Tarinn. The history of humanity. Love it, or loathe, but it was built upon war.

It was primal, and Oviinia had no time to philosophise nor ruminate. She was with them all now, and it didn't matter if she wanted it or not.

None of them wanted this. But they had to press on, because it was their only way to freedom.

For themselves, and Tarinn, whose foundations were soaked in blood.

* * *

Prince Elytrasio cursed in the language of his people, as he pummelled one of his Khepri honour guards in the head with the pommel of his sword.

Boulders and filthy liquid continued to rain down on them from above, as everyone around him were either crushed to death or drowned by their gawking stupidity.

It did not stop. Not for one second, and he began to panic

They had painstakingly created this base from the ground up, and now it was coming apart. *All* that time driving out those filthy *matters*, only for them to come back like a plague.

This? They were somehow supposed to co-exist with *this*?

His father and that Joner... both of them, mad as hatters.

He should have committed regicide when he had the chance. One of his brothers would've done it eventually.

And now, he would never know the taste of kingship. His entire campaign was literally falling to pieces, as saboteurs managed to sow destruction right at his front doorstep.

He crowed again in rage and despair, his diminutive, topaz-like body dulled with dirt and dust, as his wings desperately tried to repel the filth that dared soil his personal substratosphere.

One of his aids – at least, one of them that still lived – crawled on broken limbs, before pathetically handing him his face. It too was cracked and sullied, and Elytrasio snatched it from his servant's shaky grasp, and planted it on his head.

"We are not retreating!!!" crackled the shrill mask, as it observed its war council with one functioning eye. The fat old fools were going around in circles, bellowing in unison whilst shoulder-barging each other like needy larvae.

"We must go!"

"All is lost!"

"I told you this was a bad idea from the start!"

It was a sad, undignified scene, and it enraged the prince enough to behead one of them on the spot.

That put the others to a stop, as the body of their confidante lumbered about a bit, before slipping on another corpse and tumbling its last tumble.

As if giving him his cue to rant, blood spurted like a fountain.

"We still outnumber them!" he began, his shoddy half-face disfiguring his words. "Retreat is not an option, you hear?! We're not letting a bunch of *matters* scare us, just because they finally decided to strike back… after, what, how long?"

They stood in silence, still in shock over the fuzzy head that still rolled.

"I SAID HOW LONG?!"

"A… as long as we wanted!" one of them finally cried out. "As long as we wanted!"

"As long as we wanted!" the others echoed – unconvincingly.

"That's right, you nincompoops! And just because they decided to whip out… what… what is it? Some sort of weapon? Some sort of weather machine? What, that's going to make us fly away like locusts?"

"The bombs too, m'lord" one of the advisors added, as a portion of earth fell behind them, crushing countless more reserve troops.

"The bombs too" the prince added scathingly. "We *can't* forget that, *can* we, Strepsilva? And how, pray tell, did *bombs* get into our stronghold, in the first place?"

The pandemonium surrounding them did not lend itself as a suitable background for an impromptu scolding, and when Strepsilva didn't answer quickly enough, he too was beheaded.

"Gather the troops!" Elytrasio wheezed, waving his sword and flicking blood all over his charges. "Find General Scleritoux, round up the rabble, and prepare a counter-strike!!! NOW!!!"

They all dispersed, too slowly for his liking. The face fell to the sodden ground and splintered like glass, leaving the prince a chittering mess that flew around the dead and dying. He navigated the catacombs of his blemished base, as the black fires from their war machine foundries mixed with the descending, ruddy sparkles from the enemy's bedevilled weapons, creating volatile vacuums which ate away at any living thing that got near them.

Damn it all!

Momentarily preoccupied by the sight of a Blemmyes carrying what he *thought* was his royal coffer of gems, Elytrasio collided with another of the creatures.

He screeched ugly profanities, before being hit by another. Then another. And then one more.

Before he knew it, there was a countless amount; a tide of pale, naked bodies frantically fleeing, their dullard faces displaying a rare sign of genuine distress.

They engorged the canyon, running and tripping over each other in a senseless, savage act of self-preservation, and the prince barely escaped with his carapace intact.

What are they doing?!

Futilely waving his little arms with royal wrath, he finally saw it.

A creature. It was one of theirs… wasn't it? It looked different though.

And massive. Very, very massive.

Its writhing silhouette eclipsed the light show in the sky, with the arcs of lightning giving the barest glimpse of its shadowy form.

It was a *giant*. A beast from the furthest reaches of the prince's nightmares, and it navigated itself downward, straight towards them. He saw eyes glint all around it... no, *on* it, and it seemed to swell up *even more* as it sloshed in the filth of the liquid refuse, inflating like a perverse, degenerate sponge.

Everything in its way evaporated, and though it briefly screeched when passing the pockets of vacuity that littered its slapdash route, it jiggled in annoyance and continued to wreak destruction.

It was a god of chaos, and its voice impressed his soul with unquestionable hopelessness.

What did those wicked, foul, miscreants create?! Or... was it one of theirs? Mutated and gone feral, thanks to the changes these filthy humans brought upon the climate?

His trembling claw dropped his sword, and it vanished from both his sight and mind. He found himself not caring in the slightest – only the fact that he literally just shat himself.

*　*　*

Against a stone wall, they pushed.

They pushed. And pushed. And pushed even more.

Somehow, some way, the stone wall moved. Inch by inch, it relented in the hopes that it would satisfy them.

It didn't. So they kept pushing. It would never be enough. Not until that stone wall was gone.

Not until they had won.

Was it happening? Was it actually happening? Were they moving forward? The blood that drowned all of them... was it actually going to be worth it?

Would they emerge, finally gasping that sweet, sweet air?

They could see again. They could hear again… and now, they could smell. Smell the copper which coated their throats… and the gooey, spoiled decomposure of life, as it lay rotting around them.

They all cried. Cried and wailed as they made it to the edge of the battle.

Oviinia wondered how she got here. She stood side-by-side with the commandants whose names she barely knew, and it was only now that she realised that she never recalled volunteering for this fight in the first place.

Did something take her over? Was it Vatn?

It mattered little, either way. Her face unrecognisable, she was covered in layers of the swill and sediment of evil; an indubitable golem created as a tribute to one thing, and one thing only:

War.

I… am a fighter, after all.

CHAPTER XIII

Joner inhaled deeply.

The rains swept the horizon, as Tarinn's thunder shattered the glass that separated itself from Liniii.

Hekor approached from behind; his harsh, heavy footfalls echoing off the old stone pillars which formed the foundation of the castle.

"They've finally decided to strike back" he rumbled, standing beside him.

He was truly a giant; dwarfing Joner in both height and mass. His bone-white skin bloomed like moonlight, and as usual, he wore very little clothing, save for the furs which protected his modesty and the large boots enveloped in leather. The yellow eyes which shifted in his skull-like face would have terrified anyone else – but to Joner, he was his comrade and brother.

"Yep" he confirmed cooly. "This is Vayu's doing, no doubt…"

"She obviously has the means to take us head-on" the giant observed, clenching his fists. "What do you think? Mages? Her sisters? Maybe even--

"Dad and his crew?" Joner spat. "Anyone and everyone. Bring them all on… I've had enough. As soon as we find that brat, I'm headed home."

There was a silence between the two for the longest time, and Joner could have sworn he heard Hekor's throat constrict.

"About that..."

"Yeah?"

"There's been... a snag."

"What do you mean?"

"They escaped."

Joner erupted, suddenly and fiercely like a snake. His face snarled with many teeth, yet Hekor did not move. He had long grown accustomed to these outbursts.

"*WHAT?!*"

"I'll get them back."

"*HOW?!*"

"It doesn't matter."

He punched the thick balcony, obliterating a large chunk. Dust clouded them, and he breathed it all in, before exhaling it all skyward like a tornado.

"You done?" Hekor chided, after a moment or two of heavy, laboured breathing.

"How... did it *happen*, Hekor" Joner asked again, his fangs now dispersing.

"I think they had help."

"From *who*?"

"I'm still trying to work that out. Look, calm down. They won't have gotten far... and besides, only one of them matters. The rest are expendable."

"Don't hurt them."

The big man scoffed. "What does it matter? We're all going to the same place anyway."

Joner pointed a finger at him. "You were too reckless. Killing all those people. Damn it..."

Hekor slapped the dainty hand away. "Don't try that with *me*, son. Remember who you're talking to. Again, like I said, *it doesn't matter.*

Don't let your sister get into your head."

They stared into one another's eyes, each silently daring the other to try something foolish. They both did this frequently, and it almost became a twisted display of affection.

"Just get ready" Hekor finally grunted, losing this particular round and averting his reptilian gaze. "They're advancing."

Before he could acidly counter, Joner dropped to the ground with a pained gasp.

* * *

Vayu stopped. Her legs gave way, and she stifled a sob of both happiness and despair.

From the Great Castle of the Leaf, a light shone forth.

It blessed the good, and punished the wicked.

She knew. She knew where it was, and who it belonged to.

I'm coming. Just hold on.

* * *

The light was like a beacon. A lighthouse amidst a craggy, grey shore, and Jugo wept. It reminded him of her. Reminded him of Joner. Reminded him of Jeleenn. Reminded him of the goodness he once fought for, and the love which once guided his life.

Karnon caught the older man in his arms, and he too, felt it. The entire reason for his existence; of the Eidian order, and his devotion to his faith.

* * *

To her, it was a star. A crystal of beauty that supercharged the rain and thunder, and washed away all the evil in the world.

Oviinia laughed. She couldn't help it. Happiness overcame her, even for just a brief moment.

Behind her, a voice echoed in her ear. "Oviinia? Is that really you?"

"Rayn?"

* * *

"What... what *is* that?" Jeleenn sighed with veneration, as Remana clutched her chest and looked out toward the dark distance, which seemed to lift like a veil – even for just a moment. A pulsating energy washed over them, and their bodies and souls felt crystalline, sparkling and pure.

Joner appeared. In a wreck, he approached Remana tol Dwen.

"I... need your help. Please..."

"What is happening? What... what was that light?" Jeleenn buzzed, breathless and staggered. "Joner? What's wrong?!"

"It's him. Or her. I don't know..." Joner said, wiping his eyes. To her, he looked more innocent and human than she had seen him so far.

"Who?"

Like a creaky old toy, he slowly turned his head to face her.

"You want the truth, sis? Okay, here it is."

He looked back at Remana. "You both deserve to know. Everything."

They both didn't know what to make of this sudden development.

"You mean you still haven't told me... *us*, everything?" Remana flinched, not keen on getting a face-full of man-tears. She still couldn't tear her gaze from the ray of splendour, which now began to taper. "What was that?" she urged, repeating the younger girl.

"That" Joner said, following Remana's starry-eyed stare, "is the one."

Booming resounded from below. It sounded like an army was marching.

"The one who can end all of this."

Suddenly, he cupped Remana's hands in his own, and to Jeleenn's surprise, she did not relent or struggle.

"Remana. I want to show you. Show who you really are. I've realised that simply trying to explain it to you is useless. I need to take you on a journey. Beyond time and space." Her face crinkled in bemusement, yet, there was curiosity behind her coal eyes.

Again, Joner looked at his sister, and nodded. "Don't worry sis. We'll be back before you know it."

Jeleenn fell to her backside, as the two suddenly vanished from her eyes. She yelled, and then cried. For a long time.

Silent and completely forgotten, the black knights looked on.

* * *

How long did she sit there on the grass, mewling and blubbering like a baby?

She had lost it all. Her own sense of self was gone, as was her brief friendship with the only other person she could relate to.

Joner said they'd be back… yet, something told her she wouldn't ever see them again.

"Pathetic."

Jeleenn looked up, and saw an old woman. A very old woman, much like a witch from the children's tales. On her head was a dead bird, held together by tangles of white hair, and she wore dirty green robes that covered her stooped body. Her large, hooked nose held tiny little ruby glasses aloft, magnifying two pale, crossed eyes.

Jeleenn yelped mid-sob. "Who… who are you?" she choked.

The crone shuffled over, taking her own sweet time. Standing above the dewy-eyed, snuffling girl, she grinned hideously.

"Not like your father at all."

"Excuse me?"

"Your father. Jugo" she drawled. "You deaf, missy?"

Jeleenn stood slowly. "I… I know you from somewhere… the banquets, right? You were there?"

She huffed and raised her lip in a sneer. "I'm *always* there. Why wouldn't I be? Joner's gone again, hasn't he?"

Jeleenn nodded.

"That'd be bloody right" the crone cussed. "Little bugger is always doing those trips… it'll be the death of him, mark my words!"

She screeched, and began waving at the corpse which hung inert on top of her.

"Piss off!"

Jeleenn took a furtive step back. Who *was* this crazy old bat? The maid? Some sort of nanny?

She then took a closer look at the robes.

A magi… an Eidian?

"Are… are you Dian?"

There was no way…

"Yes!" she snapped, evidently done with her manic episode. "Who do you think I am? Besides, that's not the point, deary."

This… this was one of dad's friends?

Dian sidled up to her now, and placed a clawed, thin hand on her shoulder. Jeleenn shuddered, as the green robe pulled her closer.

"I… am *sick* of your crying" she whispered maliciously, her breath smelling of strong tobacco. "You keep sitting on my bloody lawn, and you cry. You little… look you need to get out there! Get some fresh air! It'll be good for you!"

Jeleenn tried to pull away, but the old woman's grip was unnatural. She whimpered, and then fought for her breath, as she was suddenly looking upon a young, beautiful lady adorned with a majestic falcon which looked curiously down upon her.

"Oh, I'm so sorry!" Dian said, still holding the young girl tightly. Her newly-youthful face radiated with kindness, yet there was still something strange that hid just behind her gaze. The falcon picked at Jeleenn's chestnut hair. "What I meant was, you need to go out and investigate the source of that wonderful light. Can you do that for me?"

She gulped painfully. "Why… why are you doing this? What's

happened to you?"

"Yes, why don't you answer her, Dian?"

Hekor was now in front of them, standing with his massive arms crossed.

Jeleenn tried to scream, but her mouth was smothered in a flash.

"Go kick rocks Hekor, I'm trying to have a conversation with the girl!" Dian grimaced, as she steadfastly held her without effort. "What are you doing here?"

The giant stomped toward them, a sour expression on his hideous face.

"Dian" he grumbled, "we are preparing for battle. The enemy is knocking at our door, and we need you more than ever. *I* should be the one asking what you're doing here!"

She couldn't tell if she held her breath, or if she was simply being smothered; but Jeleenn was without air. Her wide, green eyes looked upon the ashen titan with both fear and slight tinge of reverence.

Enemy?

The Eidian matriarch relaxed her grip on Jeleenn, allowing her to pull away.

"The light. It is the child" she explained, squaring herself up to Hekor and caressing his immense forearm. "I know it!"

He looked down at her, and then directed his gaze to Jeleenn, who looked like a stunned foal.

"Where is Joner?"

"He went on one of his trips. Took the other girl with him. The fire one."

His chest heaved with a frustrated sigh. "Now? Of all times? Damn it all!"

The falcon screeched.

"Yes!" Dian jumped "I agree! See? She can help us, Hekor! This has to be fate!"

"Fate!" A high-pitched voice echoed from under the soft ground. "Fate! Fate!"

Hekor stomped, not in the mood to hear nonsense. "Shut up".

"The light? The child?" Jeleenn ventured to interrupt. "Does this have something to do with... them? The kids you took?"

"Yes" Hekor replied coldly. "They're out there, and running amok. I don't know if you had anything to do with it or not, but..."

He slowly twisted his head to look at Dian, who gave him a knowing nod.

"... but you, girl, are going to fix this. You're sick of being holed up here like a prisoner right? Well, now here's your chance. Get out there, and bring those children back."

Jeleenn blanched. "Back?! BACK?! I will never do that! You'll have to kill me first!"

Taking on the visage of a crone once more, Dian toddled up to her, and slapped her across the face.

It was like being struck with a hammer, and trying as she might to hide it, Jeleenn cried from both shock and pain.

Surprisingly, Hekor barked at the crazy witch, before kneeling down over the girl's sobbing mass.

"Stop crying" he ordered, "and find those kids. If it helps you, perhaps there'll be a possibility of escape later. Who knows what'll happen? A great battle is about to commence. Perhaps daddy dearest will swoop in and save the day?"

It was her turn. Balling her fist, she rocketed her arm out and smacked him in the mouth.

The only effect it had was to make him smile.

She screamed, and began to scratch at him like a cat. She hated that smile so much.

Grabbing her by the arms, he lifted her up, and pushed her lightly against the stone wall. She ran at him again, and this time he shunted her downwards with his boot.

"She still has fight, little imp!" Dian cackled, as the dead falcon's head lolled to the side.

"Get dressed" Hekor ordered. "Go and find them. You think you're a fighter? A hero? Here's your chance to prove it!"

* * *

Hand in hand, they walked. Slowly. Steadily.

Like a music box, infinity's tinkly tune ran through Remana's soul, and exposed it to a nirvana of which she would never escape, ever again.

This was what beyond time was really like. At that moment, she understood Joner. Understood why he did what he did. Why he was the way he was.

His knees buckled, and she had to help him up. She liked it. She liked helping the man who showed her the truth.

Her life was always one of two things; questions and pain.

Questions and pain.

Questions and pain.

She now knew. She now knew that she was born to experience these things.

She saw her own birth, and that of her sisters. Those questions. That pain. Both came full circle, as she gave in to despair and rage.

She really *was* a monster. A freak. A science experiment that was anything but natural.

She saw them. The Pheekonshenee. Their majesty and magnificence moulding a world that was completely different to her own. It was an unrecognisable Tarinn; and from it was born four little girls that would change everything.

"We need to go back" she heard in her head. Over and over.

"We have lost touch with the world."

"We *can* go back."

"Why not further? Even beyond matter…"

More worlds. More realities.

Fire. Earth. Wind. Water.

From which everything was born.

Thus, is what shall be shattered.

Elements… no more

Vayu. Vatn. Acasta. Aodh. In the cold, they were created. Joner pointed, and there was Lojón, who knelt before the four keys.

"I'm so lonely" he lamented. "I just wanted to see you again… forgive me… please…"

He was only a small thing; a shivering pup that became lost in his own home.

Remana cried for him. She then cried for herself, as four foetuses floated, like idols of worship.

But nobody bowed. They showed neither love nor adoration.

Project QCA is ready.

Computation genomic structure is optimal.

Babylon shall be activated as per the Primordia Initiative.

Entanglement countdown to begin.

Three… two… one…

A monolith loomed above her, and it swallowed both her and Joner in its void.

His grip tightened intensely within her own, and she heard a soft snivel.

"Please Remana" he rasped, "don't let go."

Sunshine blinded her, and she felt her skull tearing apart.

Crack. Crack. Crack.

Bone split, and reformed itself until she felt the weight of a helmet. It sunk her downward, such was its burden, and she descended deeply into the lava which bubbled at her feet.

She's not ready for it. None of them are ready.

Give it to him? No! That's impossible! No… we cannot…

The Pheekonshenee arrived. A new world. The *Aos Si Kingdom*.

They were not welcome. Like gods, two beings stood before them, showing great wrath at the blasphemy which now polluted their land.

This was not supposed to happen… wasn't it? How did she get here?

How did *he* get here?

I am *the anomaly after all, aren't I?*

Seething rage, unlike anything she had ever experienced, coursed its white-hot metal shards through her veins.

We were nothing *to them.* All *of them.*

Remana tol Dwen now felt everything Joner Ironmonger felt. There were one being; of the same thoughts and emotions, as they watched the events play out before them.

The Four Sister Isles were never meant to be used like this.

The Pheekonshenee – at least, *these* Pheekonshenee – they did not care. Subject to the anger of *Queen Bean Si* and *King* Álfhildur, diplomacy was short-lived.

Who struck first? It was impossible to tell.

But Joner made sure he'd be the one to finish it.

A great war began, and its ripples were felt throughout the ages.

Utterly incomprehensible, the same Pheekon – who were supposedly above physical squabbles – devolved as time went on, such was their madness.

Matter and anti-matter. Smashing together. Over and over and over...

What was the end? How did this story originally go? It was no longer relevant, because Joner was going to change everything.

From beyond the chronology, he appeared. Hekor on one side, Dian on the other. Fighters for freedom.

Freedom from fate.

Freedom from gods.

Freedom from despair.

In the end, none of this will matter.

With an army of obsidian, they struck.

Black is the spectrum of everything, don't you know?

This army was not of flesh and blood; but of machinery. Gravestones of the wickedness of their ancestors. Of the 'abominations' that were created over the history of time. The bastards. The stillborns. The deformed. The ones shunned from life and made to suffer in perpetuity. The ones that died in complete loneliness.

The forgotten.

The Black Knights. All with the face of one man. All of them, emotionless robots, made to move with the souls of the shunned, given a second chance to usher in a new existence and a brand new start.

Joner... you are insane...

Am I?

"I'm not being rhetorical" he said, from somewhere inside of her, "but I've long since given up entertaining such quandaries... because I know who I am. And I know what I've seen. And now you see it, too."

The Black Knights were always being chewed up and swallowed. Chewed up and swallowed... by the 'heroes' of ages. The faceless deaths of those who dared to stand in the way of the 'stories' of those deemed cosmically more important than them.

The nobodies. The don't-matters.

"You're still sending them to their doom..." Remana howled, as an entire kingdom crumbled before her in an eye blink.

"And they are reborn within me" he declared tenderly. "We are all the same soul now. We are one, beyond ego... because when you no longer have an ego to attack, that is when you can truly be emancipated."

Underscoring his testament, was the final, quiet scene of a single acropolis.

Now devoid of life, it stood crumbling, surrounded by the decimation of battle. The land was now sullied, scarred, and irreversibly changed.

At the foot of the ramparts, a man stood over a woman, his blade to her heaving chest.

"This is it" whispered Joner, a single tear leaving a clear trail on his cheek.

The woman, incredibly tall and clad in what used to be a divine dress (but now looked closer to rags), was respiring dryly, as she clearly had no more tears to give. She choked, and her long, pointed ears dribbled with blood.

"I'm sorry… for everything…" she wretched.

"You don't even know me" Joner snarled, another droplet escaping his green eye. "You abandoned me! Even father! This ends *now*!!!"

The woman shrieked, and it didn't sound quite human. "I don't know what you mean!!!"

In a flash that blasted Remana with a frigid gust, another man appeared, and was on top of Joner. Like the woman, he was similarly statuesque, and possessed pointed ears that were lined with starry jewellery.

They clashed with a fury which uprooted dead trees and tilled the grounds in a wash of earth and stone.

"*Alf!*" the woman moaned, her once-majestic face now contorted beyond recognition.

"Get back to the boy!" the man cried back, his raven hair flapping like a ship mast from underneath a helm of fire. He bled profusely from his forehead, and swirled a fearsome sword made of water. "NOW!!!"

"Boy?! So it *is* true!" Joner thundered, running his own throat hoarse. "I really *was* a mistake, wasn't I?!"

"You *made* the biggest mistake of your life!" Álfhildur shouted through an engorged, broken mouth. "You and those *humans*! I will not stop, do you hear me?! Never!!!"

Despite his wounds, he danced as if he was in a ballet, his amorphous blade splattering amongst his own bloody droplets. His movements were at once graceful and fitful, as he thrust and sliced with no visible beginning nor end.

Using the wind shield, Joner knocked back his assailant with a zephyr, and followed it up with a destructive blow of his own crystalline glaive – its blurred edge grinding along the earth armour that both protected and drained the king's life-force.

He brayed in a deep, animalistic way, as his innards contracted and made him buckle to his knees.

"Alf!" Bean Si screamed. "Take those things off! Please! They're killing you!!!"

He could not. This protection – crafted by Lojón – was the only thing that could help him make his last stand.

For his land, and for his family.

The Pheekonshenee were long gone now; their part in this war drawn to a close. By him… the man from beyond, flanked by a woman once thought loyal to the Invisible Realm, and a giant of a fiend, who cut down all in his path…

Shalisshakin… why?

He looked up at him. Joner.

The Wind Shield in one hand… and on his back, strapped tightly, was one of those evil things… an embryo inside a container. Formed just enough to look like a babe, it drifted and twitched, as if it was aware of the hell its non-birth created.

With all four of them no longer in their possession, the Pheekons could not last long in this world.

Evil. Pure evil.

"No…." Remana trembled. "No… no we're not…"

"Live, my wife" he whispered back with a smile. "Live, and keep the verdant light of Aos Si close to you…"

Rising to his feet one final time, he charged.

Bean Si convulsed and reached her hand out to her husband, before being grabbed and pulled away by Lojón.

"Please, my lady!" he sang out, stifling his own emotion from behind his filthy, burned mop of hair. "We must go! We must go!!!" His other arm was burned to a crisp, yet within its twiggy grasp, it held steadfastly onto another container.

Vatn.

"They had them" Joner said to Remana. "Yourself, and your sisters. "They had you, and I tried to get you all back. I failed… I could only save Vayu."

Álfhildur leaped like a cat and struck downward on his foe, and the collision affected everything around them with calamitous energy.

Caught in a tornado of desperate struggle, the land swirled around them; its own attempt to quell the last moment of savagery that would forever blight it.

Remana tol Dwen saw Joner once more with her own two eyes. He stood beside her, drenched from head to toe like a slaughtered beast. Clasping his hands behind his back in silence, he bowed his gummy head.

"I don't know what happened after this" he clarified with a low murmur. "Lost in a haze of rage and shock, I had awoken in a forest…"

They stood now, in a quiet, beautiful grove. The sunshine was high in the sky, and birds sang their trill melodies amidst the wet canopy; lush and alive with scurrying creatures that snacked on the nuts and berries which hung plentiful.

Curled in a ball, he rocked back and forth, the leaves crunching under his swaying. He mumbled and blubbered, as the child he tried to emancipate lay still in a puddle of fluid, its tiny lungs gasping for air.

Night came, and Dian now stood over him. Crying in relief and sadness, she scooped the little one into a bundle, and knelt down. She looked at Joner in his wide, sightless gaze.

"It's not your fault…"

Strips of moonlight shrouded the three of them like a stain-glass mural, which would forever take a spot in Remana's memory. Such a beautiful, tragic scene was one deserving of legend; to be told and passed on from generation to generation. Embalmed for all time, it spoke to her more than any words could.

Mimicking the Ediain's own display of affection, Hekor lifted Joner in his arms, and like a big brother, he assured him that everything was going to be okay.

Joner blubbered in his shoulder, as the three of them walked away, and vanished into the dark of night.

"They are my real family" he affirmed. "Together, we went through hell and back, and saw how sick this world really was. How the evil energy it created from eons of suffering have forever tainted it, like a tumour."

He closed his eyes. "You've seen it, Remana. You've lived it. Over and over again."

I am, aren't I? I am talking to a man who can do it. Who can actually destroy the world.

"And you… what? Want to right all wrongs? Remake Tarinn as you see fit?"

He shrugged. "Kind of. I don't want to rule… I … I just want to be free and happy, and for everyone to be the same. Sadness and despair? Why have we come to accept these things? Since when did the gods have full control over us, and treat us like playthings? Tearing our hearts and minds asunder whenever they see fit?"

"So… this is about the gods? About fighting *the gods*?"

All was black. Slowly, one by one, stars came into focus. The nine moons hovered around them like spectres, and like a seam, the Great Ring split the sky in two.

"I don't even know if the gods truly exist" Joner admitted. "Try as I might, I could never meet one in person. Even Dian, who is supposed to be the embodiment of one, really didn't convince me."

"But I do know one thing" he continued, "I have the power. Whether through some divine purpose or not, I have it. The Pheekonshenee. The Arche. The Invisible Realm. It all existed for my benefit. As absurd and egotistical as it sounds, it's the truth. My purpose is to lead all life to the next stage… a new world. A wonderful, wonderful new world."

She had no time to repartee, or pronounce him deluded. For before her, stood his entire life. No time. No place. Yet all at once. It was all so amazing, and she became utterly absorbed by it. The terrified little boy, lost within nothingness… only to be found by Hekor, and bought back. The journeys they went on together. The training. The learning. It wasn't all bleakness and despair. There was laughter. And joy. And thrills. They sat around the table and made merry. They battled eldritch foes. They took a reluctant Vayu and brought her out of her shell, and made her live life again. They befriended the souls of the abandoned and hopeless, and made them see the light of hope once more.

But… the disease was always there. Always within reach. Always one step behind them. They *had* to find a way. They *had* to fight it.

The Sadness. That's what he called it.

She saw a man, and knew it to be his father. The Sadness was in his eyes, even as he tussled Joner's locks, and played hide-and-go-seek in a golden wheat field. As he taught him to swing a sword at dummies stuffed with straw, and to properly skin a carcass with speed and precision.

It was at its strongest, when a little Joner asked about his mother.

He leaned over them. His own child self, and Jugo, who knelt down to meet his gaze. "Of course, he led me to believe that she was dead. It was easier that way, and truthfully, when Jeleenn was born, I finally got a real family that would make things better. It really was then, that I realised that I had people that cared for me all along… dad's friends, and all the allies he made."

Another baby now nestled itself in his arms, as big brother formed a shell around little sister; a shell that would *never* be broken, even by death.

"That's what made it all the worse… all the worse."

Remana tol Dwen didn't want to see any more. But she couldn't tear her igneous leer from the boy, who now began to decay before her; his sunken face desperately trying to hide the terror, as he balled his little fists, and his healthy brown hair aged into a wolfen grey.

He fell into dust, and she begged him to take her back. She could take it no longer.

She felt like she was losing her mind, and feared that she too was truly dead; that she was caught in a purgatory of no reprieve.

Why? Why am I caught in a never-ending loop of suffering?! My home being attacked… my father… my brother… those pirates and that tower… and now this… is this me? Is this my fault for existing? I never asked to be born!!!

She erupted; her face melting like slag, and her hair becoming a trail of flame. She became a living flow of lava, and swallowed Joner in her madness and raw pain.

I am Qual-nu's essence. The Cerberus Girl, right? That's what they all call me. I don't want it to be true, but it is. This is what I've spent my entire life searching for... here. Right here. And I do have a family. I do, and I can't let them down. I can't let them be used as playthings any longer... we deserve better!!!

She thought of Nūk, and of her own childhood. How her parents made her work hard, and how proud they were of her for being so strong in times of great sadness. Hunger, cold and the evils of men wore them to the bone. It claimed so many... but it didn't claim her. She was the one who wouldn't *die* – no matter how much the world seemingly wanted her gone.

"Tarinn isn't right. It hasn't been for a long time. The Wizards wanted to fix it... somewhere along the way, the world began to fall apart, and its inhabitants have been struggling to exist ever since. Lands are vanishing. Societies are collapsing. Water is getting blacker... sooner or later, it will all end."

Joner rose from the depths of Remana's turmoil, and helped her find herself once more. His cool skin soothed her, as he brushed her cheek and reassured her that all was well. That all *will* be well.

"The true sign of the end... is the Sadness. The pain of those forgotten and left to rot. I... *we* can't let this go on. Help us, Remana! Help us save the world! Let's show them! Let's show them that they can't get *away* with this!"

Her scalding body shivered, and black smoke surrounded all.

All... except them. The two of them; face-to-face. Fire and ice, staring into each others' abyss.

"'They?'" she echoed, steam drifting from her cracked, blackened lips.

"They" Joner reiterated, inhaling her essence. "*Those* that have taken advantage of an old and decaying world, and have used it to rule with evil. *Those* that have enabled this, with their deceptive intent – intentional or otherwise. The Gods... or whoever they are... I'm certain… I'm certain they're *part* of this. Somehow. Some way. And I *know*… the Pheekonshenee *knew* this."

He smiled, expressing a tenderness that caused her to mirror him. "I'm not perfect, Remana. I'm going to make mistakes. I'm just a wild child caught up in an adventure that's just gotten a *little* too big for me. Okay, it's gotten *really* big, and it's left me with *more* than a few lingering issues. But that's what I have my family for. To keep me straight, and tell me when I screw up. And I need you to do that, because I have a feeling you'll pull no punches with a spoiled, angsty brat like me."

This is what she had been searching her entire life for. Her purpose. She had only one question left.

"Do you know where the Fire Helm is?"

* * *

Joner stared at his mask. The face of the faceless, it probed his mind with that thing Hekor had conveyed to him. He couldn't stop thinking about it.

The man that supposedly looked exactly like him. The one with the scar on his cheek.

Someone out there is running around pretending to be me.

He was with Jeleenn.

Was he some sort of side-effect? A soul, taken and manipulated, and given free will?

He often struggled with the creation of his Black Knights. To the casual observer, he really did seem like a tyrant; creating an unfeeling army and powering them with the soul energy of the forgotten.

But those souls were not slaves. They fought – to escape their low frequency, and to ascend to a higher plane upon destruction. He gave them bodies, because they deserved them. They deserved to escape the endless loop of suffering and rebirth, and they freely joined his cause.

He wanted nothing more than to usher them into the new world.

Matter or don't matter, it'll all be the same.

He needed answers. He needed to find out the identity of this doppelganger. The idea of someone out there manipulating some poor soul made his guts turn.

* * *

"Jugo!"

Ilod slid down a runny hill, his once-white robes now dark with grime.

Karnon, with his hair stubbornly clinging to his eyes, breathed in relief, and set the older man down onto a relatively dry spot of ground. The Eidian followed suit, falling into an exhausted pile.

Only two of the sappers returned from their explosive mission. Likewise blackened, they found the duo by sheer chance in the endless forest, and clearly suffered from shock.

Now that a Numanta was here, they found the inner joy to wave and call out.

The rain still poured, but thankfully now not as hard. The lashing gales receded, though thunder still provided a show above, and it slowly eroded the darkness like smoke. It was like they were finally opening their eyes after a hundred year slumber, and the brink between worlds was ever shifting, as the surreal and incongruous of the invisible clashed with the returning natural.

A flock of rosellas sang overhead; the first birds any of them had seen in a long time, and it was enough to make them embrace each other and cheer.

"I say, what unusual little creatures!" the Golden Knight observed, as he helped the other green robes down the precarious hillock.

"'bout time" Jugo remarked, before letting loose a rattly cough. "Here I was thinkin' I was finally going to die peacefully, surrounded by twittering birds and doe-eyed bunnies."

Ilod pressed his hands over his friend's sternum. "Not if I can help it... bloody hell Jugo, what were you doing?"

"He was fighting a beast" Karnon answered, as his fellow Eidian gathered around them and offered their own methods of care. "We slew it, but it dealt him a blow."

"We saw, heard and felt the eruptions" the Golden Knight interrupted, his armour somehow remaining spotless. "I felt like I was back home, amidst the screaming demons of the hell pits!"

Jugo seethed and clenched his jaw, as Ilod examined his torso which looked as if it was rubbed all over with charcoal. "Speaking of screaming" he grunted, "we could hear *your* handiwork from half a world away. Nearly made me fill my britches... ouch! Crap, I still might..."

"Looks like a collapsed lung, and a couple of broken ribs" Ilod disclosed gravely. "Damn it all Jugo, you're lucky to still be breathing. I don't have anything with me that can fix this... all I can do is try and stabilise, until we reach Vayu's regiment."

"We should hunker down for now" one of the Edian suggested. "Moving in this condition will surely get us killed if we rush. We need to heal, and keep an ear out for any other surviving bombers."

Ilod knew that Jugo was about to sputter and argue, and he quickly silenced him.

"I agree. This is your domain, dear Eidian. You know this place far better than I." He cast a sideways look at Jugo, and wordlessly dared him to put up a fight.

The innkeeper capitulated.

"But... Vayu..." Karnon began, not willing to give up.

"Even if we *could* make it, we're no good to her like this" the Numanta advised. "Let's lick our wounds, while we still can."

Looking down, the rosellas bobbed their heads in approval. The Golden Knight craned his head upward, the edges of his honey helm sharp enough to cut the droplets in two.

He was entranced.

CHAPTER XIV

Hot springs broiled, as unusual, blue-faced monkeys looked out at them from heavy brows which were partially submerged in the bubbling pools.

The Antechamber of Fire, as Kwenn and the twins were told, was located deep within *The Jagged Form of Deshalmanik*.

Located deep within the Merca Lal Mountains on the isle of Arlmai, the honeycombed landscape of poisonous sulphuric caves and glassy cliffs protected a secret paradise. A secret paradise guarded by primates that seemed only all too disinterested in seeing their first humans for generations.

Rather than fiercely protect their home, the round, waddling creatures were happy to sit back and observe their strange new guests. Once in a while, they would swing from vines that webbed the fertile canyon in complete silence, acting like ginger wrecking balls that would smack against certain spots in order to release a cavalcade of nuts that scattered to the ground; before plopping into the volcanic pools and inflating to ten times their size.

"This… this is incredible" Puul breathed, moved almost to dullness by his wonder. He looked to the sky – its baby blue face leaking from in between incomprehensibly large arches of land that criss-crossed above like strands of a ball of yarn; their reflective surfaces creating the illusion of undulating waves.

Kwenn looked to Master Lojón, and almost wished that the diminutive being would come clean – that this was all a big, elaborate prank. "We're… really in another land? Just like that? Somewhere completely new?"

"That's all correct, my good man" Lojón puffed his chest out, clearly chuffed. "My goodness, this place hasn't changed one bit! Still untouched by time, just the way I like it."

He twisted his hairy head slowly to Nuvummburtee and Ya'k-lum, and Kwenn could tell that he was both impressed and perturbed.

"How did you two make it here?" he demanded, cracking his staff onto the ground and sending bits of rock flying.

Ya'k winced, and Nuv hurriedly pointed. "We were guided here! By a… man named Saumen. He said you'd know the name?"

"Aye" Lojón murmured, "I do. That pickled bastard sent you here? He was supposed to lead you to the other Sacred Sites! At the very least, lead you to your charge…"

"Charge…" Nuv repeated. "You mean the woman. Remana. That's what he told us."

"So, that's her name, huh…"

Kwenn had no clue what they were talking about. It was only to be expected; they both had a lot of stories to tell.

Is it 'catching up', when neither of us remembers the other? Or does he remember me?"

"So… you know her?" the man known as Nuvummburtee asked.

Kwenn was irked. *Do I really sound like that? Does* Joner *sound like that?*

He couldn't help it. He kept staring as his 'brother' talked, and his awkward gaze was met with the one called Ya'k-lum.

They both looked away in embarrassment.

"I suspect I know *of* her. And of Kwenn's own charge. There were two others, as well."

Two... more?

"Are you serious?" Kwenn stepped forward, now completely oblivious to this exotic new world he found himself in. "You mean… there are two more of us, too?"

He still hadn't told Lojón about his strange clone that was found in the sea. Neither did Panin nor Puul, and he wondered if they judged him for it. At the very least, they respected him enough to feel that it wasn't up to *them* to disclose that information.

Maybe he should.

Lojón shook his head, looking like as if someone twirled the head of a mop.

"I don't know."

Panin walked up to the group, confident that the surrounding environ was secure. He was sweating profusely, and began to unbuckle his leather grieves. "Fellas, you sure those monkeys won't attack us? They won't go feral at night, or something?"

"He's right" Ya'k-lum nodded respectfully to what he perceived was some sort of soldier. "We have more immediate worries. We went through unending turmoil trying to get here, and as inviting as this place seems, I don't want to make it my grave!"

"Relax, boys" Lojón inhaled deeply. "This is a sanctuary. Just leave them be, and you'll be fine."

He looked to a steaming pool, which was unoccupied. "In fact…"

The first to note his implication, Puul rubbed the back of his head. "Really Master? Here and now?"

The ancient's slight form shuffled eagerly to the wafting waters, his hidden feet making him look like some sort of moving doll.

"It's been so long…"

Without disrobing a single item, he fell into the spa face first.

All the men just looked, unsure of what they were witnessing.

A tiny, darkened lump of stringy hair appeared above the surface like some sort of pond devil, before a stream of liquid whizzed from it.

"Minerals are feeling *good* today! Come on crew, we all have *a lot* of stories to tell each other! So, we may as well make ourselves comfortable!"

A nearby ape huffed in disapproval.

* * *

Sliding the blade into its scabbard with a gratifying clack, Jeleenn's life somehow became clearer.

She was herself again; albeit under less-than-ideal circumstances.

Something horrible was about to happen. Her bones screamed it, and the air was befouled with tension that almost constricted her throat.

She knew killing was going to occur, and everything from this moment on would change forever. No matter what would happen – even if she had found the children all safe and sound, there was no coming back to this life of misty captivity.

It would occur either through her own will, or that of Joner's death.

She frantically did not want the latter to happen. Not again.

But she had a duty. She could not take on the entire world by herself, so she would instead make it a little better by doing what she first set out to do since she left Gen.

To save them. All of them.

How would she get out? She had no idea.

Who would be storming the gates of the Great Castle of the Leaf? Again, no clue.

Fear was like a little parasite that wormed in her chest and stomach, and she breathed as deep and as loud as possible.

Maybe the fighting will provide a way to escape. It has *to.*

"Nerves, little miss hero?" Hekor jeered, as he handed her her hat.

She hadn't seen it since Henra. Had he kept it all this time?

She snatched it from his bear-like paw, and fitted over her topknot.

"So, who's keeping me under check?" she sneered. "You're not letting me go out there alone, obviously."

"For your safety, as much as it is for ours, believe it or not" Hekor imparted, as he beckoned her to follow him through the outer gardens that bordered the dark wilds.

She wondered if she was lying to herself. This was no ordinary backwoods. Even under the normalcy of Tarinn's heavens, the territory of Liniii would have been both foreign and impenetrable to someone like her. It would have been a tremendous feat to dive into an unfamiliar place like this for someone like her *father*, let alone a girl barely out of her teens.

But to look for a small group of younglings in *this*? What was she thinking?

She had *one* thing to guide her, and that was the light.

Even completely gone, its energy could still be felt. Her eyes were constantly drawn to a particular spot in the far distance, under the clashing lightning storms of both realms. It was uncanny, almost like it was watching *her* as much as she was watching *it*; an invisible signal that reminded her of the lighthouses that dotted Shali's coasts.

The blackness almost seemed to be traversable. Almost.

They must *still be alive out there, somewhere.*

"I believe it" she answered acidly to his muscular back. "I'm sure you can't *wait* to lock me back up again, with my ducklings in tow."

He turned and laughed. "Don't blame me. You're a Joner problem. A problem that can finally begin to earn her keep, as far as I'm concerned. Maybe, if you're successful in finding the kids, he'll let you in on our inner circle, hm? Finally become one of us?"

She blanched at that, and tried not to give him the satisfaction of falling for his words. Clenching her jaw, she looked at the two Black Knights that marched silently behind her.

They would be accompanying her.

She wasn't sure how she was going to shake them, when the time would come. She tried to formulate strategies, but her thoughts were already overwhelmed enough as it was. She could not bear to think about them, knowing what hid under those helmets... would they listen to her? Are they even aware? Of their own existence?

She learned that there were countless more, and that they made up the majority of Joner's fighting forces.

Emotionless killing machines. Souls without souls.

She tried not to cry. Not here. Not now. She had to focus.

"Where did he take Remana?" she asked, trying to glean any bit of intelligence she possibly could.

"To open her eyes" Hekor replied cryptically, as the duelling storms flashed and truly gave him the appearance of a horrifying wraith. He stopped and knelt to the ground, and ran his hand across the dirt.

The action actually reminded her of her father, and it literally made her feel ill.

He sniffed (from *what*, she had no idea), and pointed. She could vaguely see it; the cobwebs of ancient bridges and walkways that surrounded the inner structure; the same ones she walked when she was ushered from those cells.

How long ago was that?

"There" he divulged. "That's where they are, somewhere in the north. You feel it too, don't you?"

She confirmed she did.

"Then get to work."

* * *

Kwenn seriously considered never moving again.

The warm afternoon sunlight lingered on his dripping forehead, as beads of sweat tinkled on his necklace.

His body sorely, *desperately* needed this.

Aside from Lojón (who remained fully-clothed) all five of the fellows were stripped down to nothing, and submerged within a soup that reminded them all of the colour of tomato. In a circle they lounged, with plenty of space for all, and the bliss that Kwenn felt was one that he wanted to last forever.

As his muscles fell off his bones, he assumed that – like himself – each of them felt a little guilty for enjoying themselves so much in this natural spa. However, common sense dictated that Lojón was right; it was better to heal themselves and get acquainted with one another… because they likely would never get a chance like this ever again.

Nuv and Ya'k-lum were not particularly hard to convince. For intents and purposes, the two had been through a tough journey, and had no compunctions about getting naked and enjoying their first semblance of luxury in a long time.

Kwenn didn't really blame them. Just by looking at them, they were hardened and weatherbeaten men, and as they eventually told, lived in a harsh region.

Still, Panin, Puul and himself were a bit more reluctant. Not used to seeing each *other* in skivvies – let alone complete strangers – their urgent desire to leave this place was slowly placated by Lojón's pleas.

So, in they went.

And now, if they had their way, none of them would ever leave.

Bliss was plastered inelegantly all over their faces, as Kwenn couldn't help but observe the scars that dotted both Nuvummburtee and Ya'k-lum's bodies.

What kind of lives did they lead, exactly?

And so, he listened and learned. And in turn, he told of his own tale to their eager ears.

It was both illuminating and shocking for both parties, to hear just how unbelievable things had become in the Four Sister Isles, and how Nuvummburtee and Kwennsefulass were intertwined by fate.

Were they truly brothers? How else could they explain it?

How was Joner linked to all of this?

Why were their memories gone, only to have them linked with mysterious women?

Did they really have a 'mother' who orchestrated all of this?

For each of them individually, their questions lead to so many strange answers. Now they they had found each other, their confusions were now doppelgangers that butted their heads together painfully.

Having learned of all of this whilst nude just added to the exasperation.

They sat now in silence, each of them absorbing the other's words. A couple of hours had passed, and Kwenn was hypnotised by the drips that rhythmically chipped away at his emerald.

"This… Joner" Nuvummburtee said, rubbing his beard slowly "he was supposed to have died, right?"

"Yeah" Panin answered, the mood amongst them all now having become sombre. "Yeah. I… we, still remember the day. Kinda. When Jugo and Ilod returned… the very air around them, it was like they had no colour. Like they were shells of humans…we didn't see them nor Jeleenn for a couple of days. That's how I recall it… Puul and I, we eventually figured it out, because it was the same as when our own folks died. When she emerged outside, we didn't ask any questions… we knew, and she knew. We just started playing, and that was that."

Puul whispered "'That was that.'"

"So… do you know? How he died?" Nuv inquired.

The three of them looked at each other, now very uncomfortable.

Eventually, Kwenn decided to just say it. "Jugo… his father. He sacrificed him, apparently. To save the world from tearing itself apart."

They both shook their heads in utter misery.

"Poor guy…" Ya'k said, looking at his own murky reflection. "Poor bloody… guy."

Nuv sharply glanced at Kwenn, his blue eyes sharply contrasting with his own dark, hazel ones. "So… what are *we* supposed to be then?" he asked with a higher urgency than before. "We're the spitting image of this kid, right? How's that? Why do we each have these 'elemental keys'?"

"You're guess is as good as mine."

They all shifted their dull attention to Lojón, who floated on his back with his hands behind his head.

Somehow, his face was still well hidden amidst the impassable jungle of hair, and his inflated plum robes gave him the buoyancy to bob on the water like an anchor float

"I know nothing about that" he restated with slight annoyance. "I left the Invisible Realm... a long time ago."

"But you knew Queen Bean Si, Joner's mother" Puul reminded him. He then nodded to Kwenn. "and from what you remember, yours too, Kwenn."

"What are you suggesting, moon cloth?" Lojón splashed around as he flipped to his belly, before paddling to the Numanta like an excitable puppy.

Puul shrugged his slim shoulders, as he gently pushed Lojón away with a finger. "I know I'm one for conjecture" he said, "so let me conject. What if Kwenn and Nuv have somehow inherited Joner's memories? That... maybe... somehow, in some way, his very being was split up into multiple copies of himself?"

Nuv laughed.

"I'm still having a hard time believing that there is another damned *world* that exists, master Numanta" he said, now almost angry. "I can't... this is ridiculous!"

With a deluge of mineral-rich waves, he got up to his feet. "I'm taking a piss."

He stomped away; the cold air creating steam that misted off his pruned body.

"Jeez, sorry if I touched a nerve..." the mage muttered.

Ya'k waved dismissively. "Bah, don't mind him. He gets like that, sometimes. It's a lot to take in, right? I'm still trying to unwrap all of this myself... I guess my imagination makes me better at processing the absurd. Poor Nuv can't compare... honestly, he was happy living in our village. He never wanted to leave."

"I imagine *none* of us did" Panin mulled, as he jutted a thumb over to Kwenn. "Even mister scratch-face over here."

Kwenn frowned at Panin's name-calling. "I don't know *what* I wanted, actually. Even if I were to live in Gen for the rest of my life, what would I do? Fish? I don't know how to do anything... at least Nuv managed to become useful. He seems to have made a life for himself, from what you've told us."

In a way, he actually was a little jealous. Nuvummburtee almost seemed like a superior version of him in every way; a stranger who made the most of his time learning, earning and *not* yearning.

What did *Kwenn* do to earn his keep? Maybe they gave out awards for self-loathing...

"Yeah" Ya'k replied. "He was lucky to have a close community that had his back. I mean, it was tough for him. They made sure he wasn't a burden, even if he *may* have come from divinity. They made him work."

"And you befriended him?" Kwenn inquired.

"We were both... different, in our own ways" Ya'k explained, trying not to fumble his words. "I guess that's what got us off on the right foot. I'm what is sometimes called the 'black sheep' of my family."

"I saw your papers" Puul said, noting the rucksack. "Are you an artist?"

"A writer and poet, mostly" Ya'k said, his face reddening. "You can imagine how well *that* hobby is viewed in the Merca Lal Mountains. I always wanted to go to the university in the south... sell my works, travel abroad. Heh, I guess I'm getting one of those wishes granted."

"Ceev? That institution?" Puul interpreted. "I believe that was the same one Oviinia went to, right?"

Kwenn acknowledged Puul's guess.

Oviinia... I hope you're well. I hope you're somewhere right now, relaxing just as I am.

"Someone built a university on one of my islands?" Lojón cut-off. "When did *this* happen?"

"About a hundred and fifty years ago?" Ya'k answered with slight nervousness, as he too rebuked the drifting figure with his own finger once he got a little too close for comfort. "You don't know, sir? It was established by the *Guild of Worldly Purpose*, in cooperation with the magi, who wished to further research into the west."

Puul finished off the young man's explanation, impressed with his knowledge. "The humanities were eventually implemented, thanks to pre-eminent scholars like *Sarmo Seep* and *Crying Horse Anauelle*, who really made waves in academia with their philosophies and treatises formulated by the beliefs buffered by this part of Tarinn and the rest. Am I right?"

Ya'k-lum likewise nodded in deference to the white mage. "Yeah, that's right. I remember when a traveller came by to Jhasé, when I was little. He had a cart full of books, and said he was from Ceev. He was what was called a 'missionary'... I still remember that. He wanted to help bring literacy and joy to the villages of the mountains, and to show us that there was more to life than what was simply in front of us."

He pooled some of the tinny liquid in his hands, and splashed it on his face. "Not surprisingly, many in the communities didn't appreciate his remarks, and some even accused him of leading youngsters astray from the teachings of Sollikane, as well as belittling our own myths and stories. My father was one of them, but my mother, bless her, she smuggled a couple of works for me... and that's what started it all, more or less. My infatuation with the quill."

Nuvummburtee emerged once more, and began to put on his pants, clearly done with his cleansing treatment.

"Is it okay if we sleep here tonight, Master Lojón?" he asked.

"You are more than welcome" he replied, waving his metallic hand like that of a master dismissing his servant. "It gets a bit cooler at night, so you shouldn't be too uncomfortable .Just stay away from the amaranth-coloured pools. Those ones are hot enough to cook meat."

"Good to know."

He picked up the Fire Helm, and caught Kwenn's eye.

"Is it– Kwenn began

"Enchanted? Yeah. It weighs a million tonnes to all besides me. That's what you were gonna ask, right?"

"Among the countless other things." He leaned around, and pointed a wrinkly finger at his blade. "That thing is the same. It doesn't look like much, but it's saved my life before. I'm not much good with it, though... I only had a few lessons. From Joner's sister, of all people."

"And her name is Jeleenn?"

"Yes."

"And she was captured."

"Right in front of our eyes" Panin interjected, who now also decided he had enough of a soak. "I'll help you set up camp, if that's alright?"

Nuv smiled, and Kwenn couldn't help but think it was a concerted effort to appear a little less hostile.

"Sure thing."

Panin's sloshing disrupted his brother's calm state, who got a face-full of more than he ever wanted to see.

"Your twin brother's a doctor mage, huh?" Nuv started, as he two walked off together in nothing but their bare essentials, surrounded by ogling simians "What's *that* like?"

"Well, let me *tell* you..."

Their chatter receded as they got to work, leaving Puul to mope.

* * *

She was the little girl lost in the woods.

Surrounded by tall, greying trees with crooked fingers reaching out to swallow her in their gaping maws, she looked pensively around with every step, with the only light provided by a lantern in one hand – and the tempest above.

Flashes created new shadows. New figures. They made the unseen laid bare, and the more she saw, the more she preferred to be draped in darkness instead.

But this little girl didn't carry a picnic basket, nor treats for her grandmother. She carried a blade. She carried a crossbow. She was weighed down by the weight of not one, but two worlds.

It was because of this, she kept going. She turned this back-breaking albatross into her power; an obscene gesture to the higher powers seemingly determined to to straddle her with pain and tragedy.

She spat in their face.

She would save them, and get the hell out of here.

Droplets fell from the sky, and she laughed to herself, imagining the gods returning their own spittle as revenge.

Rain. It's been a while.

Contrary to the trouble it would normally cause in a seek-and-rescue, Jeleenn found herself welcoming the showers with joy. It was real, and somehow, she felt as though it was here to help, rather than hinder.

How? She couldn't really tell… but there was one thing. One tiny, incremental thing that she noticed.

The Black Nights paused momentarily, and looked up.

Why did they do this? It was a quick gesture, and before she could dwell on it, they urged her forward with their marching gait.

She spoke to them. Of course, she didn't get any replies,or even a courteous nod… but she continued to talk as they trekked the twisted land, just as she did countless times when she was in the castle.

She talked… and talked. And as usual, she tried to believe that they at least listened.

Did… did she become *friends* with them? No… no that wasn't it.

It was pity. Pity and sadness she felt for them.

It was hard to be heard above the cracks in the sky and the barbarous howls that sometimes permeated the lightlessness, but she couldn't stop. She had to let them know.

Let them know how sorry she was.

The rain hid her tears.

* * *

Just as Master Lojón had said, it did in fact get nice and breezy by the time nightfall arrived. Now, it was the moons that scattered their light across the glassy upper regions of Deshalmanik, creating a show of celestial flames that made them all stare in complete reverence.

It was hard to believe that such a dangerous land could be so beautiful, and Nuv aptly made the comparison to a colourful, poisonous plant.

After all, there *was* a reason why this place was so well hidden.

They broke bread together and talked a little more, before going to bed once their hoarse throats could not hold out any more. They still had ample food and drink to share, and they even tried the sponge-like nuts dropped into the pools (which unfortunately tasted vile, despite Lojón's assurances of their health benefits). Tellingly, they did not bother to make plans for their next move, nor what was in store for their immediate futures.

That would have to be a whole separate discussion.

Despite the wonders the hot spring did for his aching joints, Kwenn could not sleep. He suspected the others couldn't either, with each quietly dealing with their own inner turmoil. He was undoubtedly tired, but it was more of a fatigue of life in general. He even briefly toyed with the idea of simply fleeing – of hiding himself away so he may live in peace and quiet. Damn his past life, and damn the fate of Tarinn.

Of course, that wasn't an option.

He was in it for the long haul, and for the first time in a little while, felt fear grip his heart. It was undoubtedly due to meeting Nuvummburtee.

He still didn't know what to make of him, and their meeting only served to make things even more complicated and tumultuous.

He felt a sense of guilt. He *should* have been happy, and a part of him was. But this was so far beyond a normal family reunion… if they even *were* family.

As he lay there thinking, he felt a slight kick at his feet.

It was Nuv.

"Can we talk?" he said quietly.

They both each held a cup of broth, and made themselves comfortable under the stars.

There were no apes in sight. They had all vanished, leaving only the sounds of bubbling.

Nuv began, sipping. "Sorry to wake you. It's just... uh, you know, we never talked. Alone. I felt like this is something we should do."

As Kwenn suspected. "I know. I guessed we'd both be going crazy right now. Too crazy to sleep. What a day, eh?"

Nuv laughed, and Kwenn noticed it sounded a bit gruffer than his own. "I'll bloody say. More life, what a life... our lives, they really haven't been all that long, when you really think about it."

"Mine's been shorter than yours" Kwenn corrected. "From what you've told me, you awoke nearly a year ago. I woke only a few weeks... right before the Blinking of the Eyes, where the suns change. Apparently Tarinn goes through natural and magical shifts, and it happens every year. Coincidence?"

"Probably not" Nuv shrugged. "I think that's what's pissing me off the most... that everything is all 'connected' and is all a part of some 'plan'. I hate the idea of it... I just... why can't anything be the way just as nature intended?"

Kwenn drank, and burnt the tip of his tongue. He silently cursed. "I can't tell you..."

He thought.

"No. There's something I *haven't* told you" he began. "Not even Lojón knows. I suppose I should have... but, well, damn it there's just so much happening already."

"What is it?"

Kwenn breathed. Loudly. "There's another one. Of us. We... we found him. His body. In the ocean near Shali."

Nuv looked. His blue eyes seemed like they could pierce metal. "What?"

"It was after the second Sacred Site, on Sechon. After we fought Wilko, that crazed man we told you about. We... we were sailing back to Gen, before we found him floating..."

Damn.

He knew this was going to happen. As he recalled the memory, his nose began to well. He sniffed.

Nuv bit his lip, and looked down. He didn't raise his head. "You serious? Why? How? Who was he?"

"We don't know. We tried finding answers, but nothing. His remains are with a friend. That Lord Sterlio man, the merchant."

Kwenn looked down. The broth provided little comfort, and he felt safer dunking his head into one of the amaranth pools Lojón warned them about.

Nuvummburtee was unreadable.

Jeez, is this how I come across? Kwenn thought.

Silence had never been louder. After a time, he seriously wondered if Nuv had fallen asleep. His face was dark; obfuscated by both the shade of his brow and his long hair and beard.

He shifted though, and finally looked skyward. "I guess that's what we were told, right? That there could be more of us? These girls... these elementals or whatever... there were supposed to be four of them. We know of two. Stands to reason there'd be four of us, too."

Kwenn nodded, and they both drank at the same time.

"That's not all."

"Huh?"

"He... he wasn't like us, Nuv."

He was terrified. Even after everything, he knew Nuv wouldn't believe what he was about to say. It was ridiculous. Absurd. Insulting.

He said as much, but Nuvummburtee urged him to spill it.

"He wasn't made of flesh and blood. He was... what was the word... artificial. He was like some sort of doll. Made from parts. Not human."

There, I said it.

Again, like a moment stuck in time, destined to replay over and over, Nuv bowed his head and hid within his shell. Kwenn didn't dare move.

"Good night Kwenn."

Nuvummburtee got up, tossed his remaining beverage on to the ground, and walked away.

Kwenn sat alone, and remained until dawn.

* * *

Pale faces often peeked out from the shrubbery, before quickly withdrawing in a giggle and a wink.

Jeleenn tried as best as she could to ignore them, but they made the skin on her back crawl.

There was more than one battle raging, she felt. All around her, there was a subtle pressure in the air; a perpetual pushing and pulling that made her feel wobbly at the knees and her head thrum steadily.

For no reason, she kept wiping her nose in irritation, making it all the harder to focus.

Despite this, she knew she was making progress. Against all odds, her heart showed her the way, and her eyes pierced the mire of deception that was so abundant and stifling.

As much as she hated to admit it, she *was* thankful for the backup she received from the two knights, who trudged in the wet path behind her.

She looked up, and still saw the great causeways in the sky above the forest awning. They were so imposing, and made her feel like an ant. The spider web thoroughfares seemed to stretch on even beyond the roiling pea soup that crashed against them, and she became genuinely worried that they may break and collapse, causing an utter calamity.

The deepness of the abnormal wildwood worked to her advantage in one way; and that was the relative shelter it provided from the rain, such as it was that it writhed and squirmed in its temporal unpredictability.

She wondered yet again. *Is something happening?*

They had been moving for a couple of hours, by her reckoning. Progress was lethargic, but that ethereal signal was still guiding her; gently pulling her by the hand.

Like a child would.

The mud sucked at her boots, and she yelped at the sight of hands emerging from the sludge before making a beeline straight to her. Their long, broken nails clutched at her legs, but she was quick with her blade, and she hacked at them with a relative calm that surprised even herself.

The Black Knights appeared right by her side, and they thrust with their halberds, causing the evil things to scatter back into wherever they came from.

Jeleenn's chest raced, and she looked to her backup in both confusion and gratitude.

She thanked them.

They did not reply nor acknowledge her.

She expected that.

Wary that they may return with backup of their own, she continued on, fighting back against the shock and fear.

As the storm raged on, her lantern began to flicker and waver, so she decided to take a brief respite underneath massive leaves that reminded her of the elephant ears that grew abundant in the Forbidden Forest.

As best as she could muster, she lit a tiny blaze, and tried to dry her soaked feet.

She was unsafe here, and she knew it. Nowhere was safe.

Chewing on some tack, she quickly refilled her lamp with the remainder of her spare oil, and scanned her sword for any blood to be cleaned.

There was none.

She had to speculate what those things were. Ghosts? Illusions? What was *anything* here?

There was zero point in thinking about it. Because, in a way, they were just as lost as she was – transient beings that were swept up from their worlds in a terrifying event that was caused by Joner.

Who was *also* a victim in this, ultimately.

Who isn't a victim here? Who is to blame for all of this? Hekor? Bean Si? All of this... it has to be someone's fault. There has to be someone or something in which we can all point the finger at.

Still feeling beat, she continued on. She had to find them, before she and they would be totally engulfed in darkness.

What would happen then? Would Hekor come to the rescue? Would he mock her for her failure, before tossing her into a cell like the worthless thing she was?

I would rather die.

Gritting her teeth at the explosive shafts of red-hot and ashen light that lanced its way through the trees, it became harder and harder to knuckle down and focus. The deafening sounds and the blinding visuals dizzied her, and she almost welcomed the darker areas of traversal that gave her brain a chance to reconstitute itself.

She could not maintain this pace forever. She was being assaulted from every angle; the flashing bolts created welcome brightness, but bedazzled her senses and made it hard to see small details; whether they'd be footprints, or small creatures ready to jump at her throat.

She admitted it. She was glad that the knights had her back.

They trudged loudly, and with no fear nor wariness. They were always alert, and she hoped that their racket did enough to deter any wild thing that lurked around them. For approximately another half-hour, they weaved their way through a green world which seemed to slowly change with every step.

She wasn't sure if it was her eyes merely adjusting to the gloom, but she began to see... brightness? Life?

She couldn't quite put her finger on it, but the faint whiff of sap and grass passed by her nostrils, and a nutty tang persisted in her throat.

It became much more of a slog to move now, as weeds caught on her legs, and rotting logs collapsed under her weight.

The Black Knights were having even more trouble than she was, as they began to falter and waver, and it seemed like that was the first glint of genuine humanity she saw from them.

A scream echoed. A person's scream.

A *child's* scream.

The petrifying sound was very close; close enough for Jeleenn to almost lose all control of bodily functions in terror.

The jitters quickly passed her by. She wouldn't let it catch her again, and boldly, she immediately gave orders to her knights, telling them to head towards the sound.

To her surprise, they obliged.

She followed close behind, nipping at their heels as they crashed through the thicket.

There was a commotion. It was getting clearer and clearer. Voices. Many voices. Even the rain and thunder couldn't quash it, and it seemed like a battle was raging.

All three of them burst into a clearing; onto a terrible scene.

She had found them. *They* had found them.

The children of Henra, Gimlum and Gen.

A couple dozen or so, all gathered tightly together in a little camp, wielding anything they could to fend off a monster.

Syyd was at their head, and light emanated from his palms.

"Stay back!" he yelled, as the thing hobbled toward them.

With a slight jolt, Jeleenn realised that her emotions were gone. Whatever elation she would have felt upon seeing the kids again was entirely replaced with a battle-minded state that hardened her to the immediate task at hand. She did not even pay heed to Syyd's state; everything was fixated on the slimy devil that moved in on them.

Is… is that a toad?

It was massive; a human-like reptile or amphibian that jiggled and jowled with its deceptively smooth mobility. Its gigantic maw drooled and spluttered with endless rows of yellowed mannish teeth, and its glowing eyes bulged like balloons. Bizarrely, a monocle was stuck on the end of one of them, and its ensemble consisted of a ritzy robe of a clear material that reminded her of a fly's wings.

Wait... he actually looks familiar... did I not see him once with Joner?!

There was movement. Something slick and wet.

Damn!

There were two more of them. Smaller, but still big enough to easily take down a full-grown adult, and they grinned with those awful, square-toothed smiles. They each wielded their long tongues like lassos, as they twirled them about as sparks shot from their wriggling tips.

What in the...

"REMEMBER!" The big one boomed with a voice so deep, she could feel it through the dirt. "Don't kill the glowy one! We need it alive! We'll eat the rest!"

The children yelled, and threw stones at them, which was met with uproarious laughter.

It sucked on its fingers, almost as if it was imagining the taste. "You little brats thought you could put a spell on me? ME?! Try and impose your will on ME?! THE ARROGANCE! RIBBIT."

He then opened his mouth toward the sky, and Jeleenn took this opportunity to strike.

A lance of electricity arced downward, and he consumed it with a gurgling bleat that created a seismic wave of energy which blew everyone off their feet.

Lit up with what seemed like a miniature sun, the toad-man's bones and organs could be seen plainly, before the energy moved to his back and shot outward in flames.

Horns exploded from his engorged head in a fountain of blood, and he screamed again; only this time it sounded even more evil and demonic.

Shit.

She regained her composure, and pulled out her crossbow. She then looked to the Black Knights, who got to their feet in a way that gave away their true nature. Their limbs flailed briefly, before their legs planted firmly into the ground, and lifted their entire torsos upright.

"You guys" she ordered without a second thought, "as soon as I fire, each of you take one of the smaller ones! Understand?"

They nodded stiffly, and widened their stances. They froze, and did not move an inch.

The billowing blaze that spewed from her target now provided plenty of visibility.

She fired.

The bolt thudded, and that warm, pleasing feeling struck her back.

"RIBBIT!"

With a voiceless cry, the Black Knights charged, their halberds the glimmering death which sliced water, thunder and fire.

The toad monster bellowed, and ripped out the bolt from its arm. Lava glooped from the wound and extinguished into a hissing black liquid as it hit its feet.

"What the god-damned he--

Another shot, straight into its cheek.

As it wailed, Jeleenn was already reloading. She tried to draw it away from the children as fast as she could.

"Get away from them, you disgusting bastard!" she yelled, releasing another bolt that hit its fat belly.

Its minions grunted in shock, as they realised they were being accosted by two of its supposed allies.

"The hell are *they* doin' here?!" One of them slobbered. "Why're you fightin' us?! CROAK!!!"

The only answers they received cut them to the bone.

The Black Knights slashed and thrust with both speed and power, and the toad-minions leapt backward, whilst cracking their whip-like appendages with an extraordinary speed of their own.

Flashes cracked between the opposing blows, and almost burst the eardrums of Jeleenn and the kids.

"Jeleenn!" a voice shrieked over the clamour. She didn't know who it was, but the pain behind the voice made her roar until her own throat scratched. Again and again, she shot at the colossus that lumbered toward her.

She was fighting a demon from hell, and she couldn't care less.

She saw the children scatter, and the likenesses of Syyd and Eyuil shouting desperately.

She hoped to god that they wouldn't run away. She somehow had to round them all up, and make sure none of them fled in fear.

One thing at a time... one thing at a time!

"YOU!" Toad slobbered, his punctured body dripping. "You're Joner's kin! Trying to steal my glory, huh?! RIBBIT, trying to deprive me of my retribution?! I AM A KING!!! *YOU WILL DIE!!!*"

A squirming, tentacle-like thing shot from his jaws. Pulsating with muscle and various mummified corpses that stuck to it, Jeleenn yelled and withdrew her sword as fast as she could.

She struck air, as the thing changed direction and arched over her. It seemed to play with her, as it darted constantly out of her reach.

She cursed. She had no time to switch back to her crossbow, so she ran back toward the brush in the hopes of creating space and overextending the thing's reach.

"RUN GIRL!" he laughed in a gush of drool. "RUN!"

The rain did nothing to smother the urgency which hammered her temples and took her air away. She panted and gasped as she desperately dived back into the darkness, rolling and stumbling back through the path which she came from. It was both vaguely familiar, and well-trodden thanks to the knights, so it was the best option she had.

Damn it... damn it... oh god what do I do?

Without thinking, she turned. The tongue was stretched now, and she saw that its master had turned around, and was face to face with Syyd.

With his belching back turned toward her, she looked on in horror as the dried bodies fell from the toad's tongue like newborn foal, before they began to race towards her on bony legs.

"You have *got* to be kidding me" she yelled. She continued to slice at the tip of the disgusting feeler, which kept her at bay whilst its army of carrion lumbered toward her.

She began to panic now, and she had no clue what to do. She wasn't experienced enough to think on her feet; not like her father.

She saw Syyd. His entire body glowed now.

* * *

Syyd's entire personage vibrated with an energy that called to the world around him.

What remained of it. *His* world. Which one was it? He wasn't so sure... couldn't it be both?

The monster loomed over him; its teeth spread far and apart in a truly repulsive grimace.

The hot rain of Gen washed through his head again, and the rocky ground stabbed at his back.

It was the same thing. It was happening once more.

That putrid grin. The void that swallowed him, his brother and all of his friends.

The one that slaughtered his parents.

The fire. It burned everything down. Its acrid presence was like needles in his eyes, and a pine cone shoved down his throat.

He couldn't breathe.

Fire.

Fire.

Fire.

* * *

"Syyd!"

Eyuil dropped to her knees; her greying robes providing scant cushioning.

The boy levitated off the ground; and he reminded her of a pale reaper.

His eyes grew wider and wider, as his ears lengthened into sharp points. His white hair shone with an exuberance that eroded all evil around them; replacing it with a magnificent melody that made the forest around them sing.

They could all hear it. Birds. Insects. Squirrels chittering and streams bubbling. Blowing winds.

The children were no longer afraid. As if by some omnipresent urging, they all gathered and cheered at the sight of the black knights that fought for them, and the woman who cut a swathe through gnashing revenants; the flickering life of Liniii reignited within her green gaze.

"Jeleenn?!" Mina cried

It all happened so swiftly, but it was enough to stun her foe, who bellowed in terror and shrunk away from the boy, his own fire momentarily extinguished.

His tongue reflexively receded, and Jeleenn plunged her blade down onto it as it rushed by her boots, as hard as she humanly could.

It wasn't enough to go all the way through, but it made him squeal in pain.

"M'lord!" one of the toadies garbled, taking his attention off his foe.

This proved a fatal error, as one of the knights, battered and sizzling, chopped downward and planted its halberd clean through the creature's cranium. Gargling and croaking, it jumped backward from sheer instinct, as sparkles rocketed from its mortal wound. Its body shot into the chaotic sky, disappearing forever.

Many of the kids moaned in wonder at the fantastic death.

Black blood sputtered on Jeleenn, but she strained with all her might to lodge her short sword as deep as possible, and not let the force of her quarry wrench it from her slippery grasp.

The monster king's panic in withdrawing his organ further opened the laceration, and a veritable deluge of foul, oily mucus showered forth like a fountain.

Jeleenn screamed again in rage and bloodlust, but finally yanked herself free as the remains of the decrepit undead hobbled back toward her as they slipped and slid in the dense ooze.

"You li'le bathtardth!"

Swallowing both his pride and his damaged goods, the aberrant amphibian choked as his cavernous mouth became flooded with his own essence. Like a waterfall, he hawked liquid and spat as if he was eating a particularly seedy fruit.

"Syyd!" Jeleenn wheezed, suddenly feeling the breathlessness of fatigue. "Move! Get away!!! Syyd, can you hear me?!"

The boy looked at her briefly with a confused look on his face, before nodding.

"I can do one more thing" he said.

Balling his fist, he threw himself downward, slamming the ground.

Like the breaking of glass, cracks of light jolted from his fingertips, before hurtling toward – and past – Jeleenn, zapping her pursuers and turning them into dust.

She could not comprehend what she was witnessing.

Syyd... who... what are you? Is it you who Joner's after? The reason for all of this?!

She knew the kid since he was a babe; both him and his brother.

I know Rayn was supposed to have abilities... but this? What the hell?

She could find answers later. Right now, she had to *keep fighting*.

As she ran up to them all, Syyd began to falter.

Eyuil caught him in her arms, as a dazed look overcame him. His facial features returned to their normal state, before his eyes fluttered.

"Move, now!" she ordered them – with more ferocity than she

meant. "Eyuil! Mina! Whoever's oldest! Just keep to the treeline! Don't worry about the knights, just keep together!"

She had nothing left to say. Time was up. She had to kill – or be killed.

Without a cry or whimper, the kids promptly did as they were told. They were soaked to the bone, and she hoped that they would find somewhere relatively dry.

And somewhere to run, if the worst should happen.

Without another thought, she charged at her retching prey.

She jumped onto his back, and it burned her fingers. Craggy and pulsating, she gagged from the stench and texture, and despite it feeling like a pile of razors, as she easily got a hold with one hand, and began to slash like a woman possessed with the other.

Whatever looked soft, she ripped open like a wildcat. Again, unholy, caustic goo splashed on her face. This time it got in her eyes, and she wailed in agony before halting her attack, and desperately giving her enemy a wide berth.

She couldn't see. Her vision became blurred, before the awful flash of fire lit up her world.

He had reignited, and he was coming for her.

Agonising, heart-stopping fear overcame her. She began to cry in intense horror; a true, existential despair that she had endured only once before in her life. Memories of Gen came back, and she was in her father's inn once more, stuck in a perpetual hell of demonic assault and mental torture that almost made her take her own life.

Blind, she crawled on all fours. She had lost her blade. She could not breathe. She was not even allowed the privilege of sobbing, as she felt a gigantic weight press down on her back. It slowly pushed her down into the grime, relishing the fact that it was taking away her dignity.

A young scream emanated from somewhere far away, and it was met with a gurgling, hissing chuckle.

Suddenly, the weight was gone.

Her face caked in sludge, Jeleenn raised sharply and gasped for air. Regurgitating her tack, she scrambled in an unhallowed pool of every bodily liquid imaginable, as sounds of combat shadowed her.

The rain flushed out the toxins from her eyes, and she began to see once more.

No... no... it can't be.

The Black Knights. They had come to her rescue.

She hadn't noticed that the other toadie had been dispatched, and now they both came to her aid. Both were battered and scarred; their armour melting in various places as they moved like... like...

Broken toys.

Yet, they still fought. One had lost its arm, and it swung its halberd like an axe. The other seemed to have its sense of balance damaged, as it listed heavily to one side.

They both circled their last adversary, as he swiped at them with his webbed hands. The flames rolling off his corpulent frame made the duo sizzle and pop as they got close, but they were immune to the torture.

They were immune to their own sense of self.

"Joooonnneeerrr... sendths hith kin to off me? *Me*?! He. Will. PAAAAAAAAAYYYYY!!!"

She could run. Right now.

She *had* to. If she didn't, they would *all* die. Even if they *somehow* managed to prevail against this monstrosity, they would only waste precious time in trying to make their escape.

She *had to go.*

Yet... she couldn't. She could not just withdraw, and leave her allies to their fate.

Allies...

She knew who they were. She knew *what* they were.

Even if I do run now... we may never be safe. This thing could pursue all of us without end; until we perish from exhaustion... or worse...

Agonising thoughts went by in the space between her breaths. Time crawled like a wounded animal, just as she herself did. Her inflamed and raw gaze looked to the huddled mass of children, as they called and desperately beckoned to her.

She shook her head.

Stay right there.

She had a job to finish.

Swallowing a choked sob, she spun on her heels to face her fate.

One of the knights was ensnared, and was lifted like a doll. It kicked its legs, and its one arm had sent its weapon plummeting.

Jeleenn dived, and despite her tangled mass of hair doing its best to hamper her vision, she caught it.

With another scream, she awkwardly sent it downward, onto the King's exposed toes, severing two and leaving one hanging by a thread.

Not waiting for the ear-splitting reaction and eruption of fire that would boil her alive, she thrust the pointed end of the obsidian pole weapon upward, piercing his goitre as it jiggled in its disgustingly slimy way.

It was like trying to cut into a coconut. It didn't seem to do much, but it was enough for him to release his prey, as the other knight followed her lead, also jabbing upward in an attempt to get under the thick, green-brown blubber.

Like oil and water; so much fluid surged, and again the blood ignited, searing both the recipients as well as its owner.

Jeleenn gasped, barely escaping the cascade as it hit her arm and immediately set her sleeve alight. She jumped back and rolled in the mud, thanking the gods for the rain, which pounded down and eliminated the worst of the heat.

Smoke hissed, and in the fog, a looming figure stood over her.

She moaned.

It was Joner. Or was it Kwenn? It didn't matter.

Because *they* didn't matter.

They were the 'don't matters'. She heard them referred to as such.

Sorrowfully, she tried to crawl backward. Her arm felt as though wasps had their way with it, and the man continued to lurch forward.

The Black Knight held out an armoured hand.

Its face... *his* face. It had no expression. It was not flesh. Its doll hair was mostly singed, and one of its eyes was completely gone.

Curled like a scolded, abused puppy, Jeleenn blinked away her pain.

Trembling, she held out her hand.

The Black Knight's gauntlets wrapped around her svelte forearm, and it pulled her to her feet.

The thunder. The smoke. The water. The fire. The earth. It raged all around them like a whirlwind; the essence of the world. Of Tarinn. It tore a hole into this realm of the invisible, desperate to reclaim what was lost.

They stood together. Face to face. Staring into each other. Their own essences laid bare.

Nothing needed to be said. Jeleenn now knew she was all cried-out. That was the last gasp, and she had nothing left.

The knight let her go, and they resumed the battle.

Their ally was still standing. Just barely.

It was on its knees now, its legs mangled. It shuffled without pause, and its helmet was almost completely caved in.

The loud whirring and grinding of gears could be heard.

"YOOOOUUUUU... will never... WIN."

The monster grabbed its head within its own grasp. Even mortally wounded, it grinned.

And squeezed.

A pop. So loud, not even the storm could dull it.

Jeleenn moaned again, as if she was stabbed in the heart.

The Black Night fell into a limp heap. It no longer moved.

It was gone.

Jeleenn no longer had the strength to shriek nor even utter profanities. Still, she would not fall. She would not lament. Not now.

She would die with dignity.

Spitting out the last shred of terminal despair that poisoned her, she became strangely calm.

This *is what it feels like… to accept the end.*

Alongside her faux-brother, she marched toward the target of her unbridled hate.

Quivering and wheezing, the toad was *still* smiling, even as his life-force dwindled. His bodily flames now dulled to a bluish flicker, and he was positively saturated with his own oily blood.

"Come…" he warbled, "meet. Your. END!"

Snarling, Jeleenn sped up to a jog.

Opening wide, an explosion of sooty swill shot out from his mouth, as he attempted to ensnare her within his maw once again.

She was ready. The tongue was slower this time, giving her the chance to roll forward as it shot above her.

Without a single order, the Black Knight wrapped its arm around the revolting muscle. Once more, the toad-man instinctively withdrew, bringing his new passenger with him.

Whether it was from a dulled mind, she wasn't sure, but Jeleenn saw the look of surprise on his face, and she sprang forward.

She saw her sword. Glinting as it lay partially submerged, she made a run for it.

The Black Knight slammed into the mouth of the monster, and a croaking bellow burped in reply, as the force of the armoured figure shattered some of its pearly whites. He clawed desperately at the foreign invader that blocked his air, and he began to asphyxiate.

The gurgling gave Jeleenn the power she needed. Hearing him suffocate, the harrowing pain in her calves dulled, and she swept the blade up in one smooth motion.

"*DIE!!!*"

It was at this exact moment when she changed. Much later, Mina would tell her that – for the first time in her life – she was scared of her sister. Jeleenn transformed from a hero, to something less-than human.

"It was your eyes" Mina would say. "Your eyes and your face."

And when Jeleenn looked back, she was not at all surprised. She did not *feel* human.

She did not feel human, as her insane thirst for victory did not slow her, even at the sight of her foe bent over and gagging. She did not feel human, as she went straight for his eyes and head.

She did not feel human when she stabbed. Stabbed. Stabbed. Stabbed. Stabbed. Stabbed. Stabbed. Stabbed.

Until finally, she stopped, upon realising that the terrible, child-eating villain no longer moved.

CHAPTER XV

"**S**o, what happens now?"

Ya'k-lum sat crossed legged; quill in one hand and a tatty journal in the other. He spent most of the early morning scribbling down thoughts and sketches of the hot-spring haven, almost convinced that he would forget it all once they had finally resumed their long journey.

The question now lingered off his lips, and hung in the heavy air.

They were all packed, and it was time to say goodbye to Master Lojón. Kwenn, Panin and Puul had decided that they were not going back to Shali, and would instead accompany Nuv and Ya'k.

It was without a doubt that they all shared the same destiny.

Kwenn had finally spilled the beans to Lojón regarding the body they had found by Shali's coast, and the old man had been quiet all throughout the dawn.

Now though, was no longer the time for rumination.

"Your charge, Nuvummburtee, is one Remana tol Dwen. You need to find her. If she has already visited Saumen, then she has already begun the process of data transfer... I think you should head to the southernmost sacred site, and ask around there. Heh, funnily enough, that site just so happens to be one Ceev University."

Ya'k and Puul both looked at each other excitedly.

"Before you two squeal like children" Lojón hastily continued, "let me add this is not going to be a walk in the park. However, it *will* be easier to get to Nūk from there, rather than directly taking the mountain passes. Saumen... he said this Remana came from Nūk, right?"

"He did" Nuvummburtee nodded from under his shining helm.

"That makes sense... what *doesn't* make sense is why he would send you two directly here, rather than the sacred sites... hmmm, I've got a bad feeling..."

Lojón then swivelled like a top, and looked up at Kwenn. The man was visibly lost, and didn't notice he was being addressed until he was tapped on his shin.

"You there, son?"

Kwenn didn't seem to react. "Yeah" he said.

"Good. *Your* charge is Oviinia Trundle. She was headed to the last sacred site, right? The Magick Shrine? Then what? What was the goal from there?"

Kwenn shrugged. "Like we said, Panin, Puul and I were going to Camo Temple. From there... well, we really didn't have a clear plan. We're kinda flying blind here... we *were*. But now..."

Kwenn looked at the sky, and the faint trails of sulphur that stretched like elongated fingers in the far horizon. The aquamarine clouds were probably a result of light and gas distortion (according to Puul), but he nevertheless found it beautiful and divine.

He then nodded to Nuv. "I think it's better if we stick together from here on out. Oviinia... if we really are so intertwined, then no doubt she will eventually find me. Find *all* of us."

Nuv returned the gesture.

Kwenn put his hand on Master Lojón. He was genuinely sad to go, and even felt the sniffles coming on.

"I think I can learn to trust the power of destiny a bit more."

* * *

They truly had a trek ahead of them.

They simply could not go straight south to Ceev. Even to the relatively experienced Nuv and Ya'k, carving their own path through the lower ranges would be all but suicide. Not only would they have no roads, they would also have to face the frequent storms that batter the lowlands, and the avalanches that helped feed the Wy'rm River and its offshoots; and of course, they also just happened to be travelling in flood season.

Instead, they were to travel a fair bit north, to the holy city of *Keráan*.

The Capital of Arlmai, and the home of the leaders of the Sollikane, it was truly a daunting prospect, particularly for Ya'k-lum, who spent his entire life hearing about the gloriousness of the place, and how he would never be worthy to set foot in its hallowed ground.

Never. Ever.

Funny how things go, huh?

On the path to the far eastern city of Nūk, this Remana tol Dwen would have passed through on her way; at least, they had hoped.

Potentially, they could kill two birds with one stone. One, they could ask around for information regarding the elusive woman.

Two, they could potentially make a fast trek to Ceev.

Kwenn, Panin and Puul were surprised to learn that Keráan and Ceev were actually linked.

Despite being at almost opposite ends of the island, the two settlements were connected by an ancient underground road; one that ferried both people and supplies between the north and south via an automated rail-car system that was constructed by the Pheekonshenee.

This absolutely stunned the Numanta Puul, who almost fainted at the revelation.

"So, the red mages use Pheekon tech to their advantage? I thought all the robes considered them unholy, or something?" Panin quizzed, fanning his brother.

"I'm not sure, but I don't think it's that simple" Nuv pondered.

Nonetheless, that was their ticket, so to speak. The main problem was that not just anyone could use it; to get the privilege, you had to have special permission, or pay an immense contribution to the Sollikane.

Acutely aware of their lacking financial situation, the men shook their heads in dismay.

"Actually, there may be a chance" Nuvummburtee offered. "Remember Ya'k? When I first arrived at Jhasé? A few of the Angakkuq from the villages wanted to take me to Keráan, to test my legitimacy as a... divine figure."

They could all feel him wince as he said those last words. He quickly clarified that the idea of a divine figure wasn't absurd – just the idea that he *himself* was one.

Indeed, Nuv was quite devoted to his faith, they had realised. Despite spending a little under a year with the people of Jhasé, he truly felt that he was one of them. They were his family, and he theirs.

"Maybe the idea isn't so absurd, then?" Puul remarked.

Nuv conceded that maybe the Numanta was right. Legitimate or not, they could use his questionable status to get into Keráan, and maybe even a meeting with the high council itself.

"Maybe we should go back to Jhasé first?" Ya'k-lum considered to the group. "Maybe it'll be easier if we get Angakkuq Trafr'ad's permission? Set up something official?"

Nuv paused mid-walk to think hard about his friend's input. He then continued on, shaking his head. "It'll take too long. There's a war going on. A war that is unseen... but a war nonetheless. We don't have time."

War.

For all of them, it still truly hadn't sunk in. They really *were* at war, weren't they?

None of them really spoke about it. They spoke of everything *but* it. That is; the ultimate price of war.

Death.

Would they be all dead when this was over? Would the world as they knew it change forever? Would they all somehow live, only to see Tarinn writhe in agony as it endured an unimaginable fate?

Ultimately, that's what terrified them the most. The unknown. The concept of fighting something that was simply beyond their comprehension.

It was one thing to shed blood for a piece of land or a sovereign nation. That *at least* made some semblance of macabre sense.

But a spiritual conflict? One that challenged their very ideas of existence? One that defied all rationale and made every attempt to fight back feel utterly impotent and blind?

It was paralysing.

Yet, they were in this together.

At the very least, it was *real*. People died. Towns burned. They *weren't* combating phantoms of the mind. As Henra proved, they *could* strike back. They *did* expose a weakness.

They just had to do it again, and it began with the steps they took together as new friends.

And soon, as brothers-in-arms.

* * *

Master Lojón still stood. It was hard to dam the incoming caterwauling.

He had thought his capacity to feel sadness had long been eroded by time... but here he was, snuffling like a truffle pig.

Even his long hair did little to hide the droplets. He had been alone for so long, that having this brief interaction with other beings – kind beings – was almost enough for his little heart.

Still, those boys have a job to do. I don't envy 'em... not one bit.

Noises began to sound around him, and it bought him out of his blubbers.

The apes began to speak. One by one, they huffed and hooted.

Something is here.

He looked upward, and it was very easy to see.

A massive beast looked down upon him; its huge hands gripping the vines, as it visibly heaved from its breathing.

The suns obscured his vision, leaving Lojón with only a shadowy reference to what it was.

But he already knew.

Almost embarrassed to be caught in his moment of weakness, he cleared his throat, and pointed a green, clawed finger at his silent observer.

"Really? After all these years, you're deciding to come out and play? Well, it's your choice, I guess…. keep those boys out of trouble, ya hear?"

Fog jettisoned from the beast's mouth, before jumping away into the steamy cavity of the mountains.

Briefly, Lojón was knocked for six. He then chuckled, before toddling off back to the Antechamber of Fire.

"What an interesting couple of days… reunions all *over* the bloody place! Time for tea, I think."

* * *

Oviinia was led by Rayn.

The shadow-boy floated in front of her, his ethereal form visible not just to her, but to everyone in the platoon.

They had won the battle. Those with the strength to cheer did so, and their joy almost made up for the pain felt for their fallen comrades.

The Eidian led the clean-up in the enemy's devastated base. Jethro was nowhere to be seen, and the hope was that he was either slain, or decided to direct his rampage straight to Joner's main force.

The cold rain began to settle, with the storm now headed towards the Great Castle of the Leaf.

Someone had asked Oviinia if she did this intentionally. She couldn't answer. Nor could she go on. She had to rest. She was anything but a soldier of war, but nevertheless all of her fear and energy had been sapped. She was too tired to even feel the effects of post-war trauma, though she expected that it would come soon enough.

She had seen some cruelty by both brigadiers and privateers during her wilder days as a swashbuckling scientist, but was always thankful that she never had to witness any death during her short time on the grey side of oceanic law.

Of course, those days were long gone now, and sometimes they felt even more distant than her life as Vatn. Brief skirmishes echoed from the valley, as many of the survivors from the opposing force clearly refused to surrender.

It was an utter catastrophe, and the realisation that she had not only *fought*, but *survived* a violent, bloody battle was enough to send her knees buckling.

An Eidian and a young boy cleaned her up, and ordered her to rest.

She tried to protest, especially at the idea of a *kid* telling her what to do, but Rayn shushed her, and thanked the boy, who was called Juun.

Juun looked only a little older than Rayn, who said he was ten. He remarked that one of his younger friends from Gen shared the same name as the grubby lad.

He's so small... I can't even imagine... him going through this too.

She guessed that the platoon leaders were huddled together and were planning their next move, completely leaving her in the dark.

Honestly, she didn't mind. Not one bit.

Underneath what barely could be considered a tent, she was huddled in a bundle. Suddenly, she was very aware of the chill in her bones, and not even a hot porridge could smother it.

She shook like a leaf.

"You need to sleep" Rayn said, as he flitted about as if he was paper in the wind. "I'll keep watch over you. Trust me, I won't go anywhere... you'll need all the energy you can get."

"Rayn..." Oviinia mumbled through cracked lips. "Where were

you? Were you stuck… here? Have you found your brother? And your other friends?"

He was quiet. Finally, he spoke, and like their first meeting, it sounded as though his words came from the ground. "Yeah. Well, I managed to squeeze between this world and ours… and yeah, I found them. I actually managed to possess one of the monsters, and tried to let them out of their cells… I… it was too hard, and they ran away before I could explain that it was me."

Oviinia looked around. Her neck ached, and she wondered if she obtained any long-term injuries. Torn muscles? Slipped discs? Rayn's words went through one ear and out of the other, and she was transfixed on the others around her. Crying and rocking from the shellshock that was now spreading, and further off, she saw rows of cots that were filled with bloody bodies. Some moved. Some did not.

What little stoic Eidian remained worked with a fortitude that Oviinia revered.

She wanted to help.

But she couldn't move.

At least she bought some water. It would help with cleaning wounds.

Do infections exist in this place?

"Oviinia?"

"Yeah?" Her mind was wandering all over. "I'm sorry…"

She wiped her eyes. "Rayn… you and I, we've been through the ringer, huh?"

That was the last thing she remembered saying, as she somehow drifted away to the land of dreams.

* * *

Flower flapped, her wings blowing away the dark matter that desperately clung onto each and every droplet that showered from above.

It fought to remain. To exist outside its own reality. But it was a losing battle.

Balance was being restored.

It would not last, though. Not if the enemy had their way.

The bird was like a ruby refracted by sunlight. Her blood-orange body was much like the mythical phoenix, heralding a rebirth that would burn all with its divine fire.

Really though, Flower wasn't *that* grand. She was but a parrot; a loyal compatriot of a young man who was on a quest to find his brother, and make everything right once more.

Her feathers ruffled at the audacity. Her masters had gotten themselves into a *world* of trouble, and they thought they would leave her behind?

She wasn't so easily abandoned.

After the horrors of seeing everything she loved burn, it was her love for her humans that kept her going. The fire of that day... it was anything but divine. It was not a blaze of cleansing, but one of boundless cruelty that took joy in the lingering torment of its victims.

Flower was one of those victims. Her passion for the world had died; her black, intelligent eyes cloudy with defeat. She mourned as she flew across the land northward; the skies weighing her down and tearing at her heart, with only the prospect of seeing her boys once more keeping her going.

Above the hills. Under the suns and moons. Against the gales. She kept going.

Until... until she met *her* phoenix.

The pretty blonde lady. The water nymph. Looking into her glasses... oily like an iridescent bubble... the coolness of her essence doused the demons from Flower's soul – the breath of life blowing away the smoke, and leaving a seed within her little breast.

A seed that bloomed into a bud.

She was alive once more. And Rayn caressed her and gave her kisses.

Sure, he looked a little... odd. He was all shadowy and clammy, but he was still her human. And she would go to the ends of the earth to find Syyd, her *other* human.

So now, here she was. At earth's end, and looking down at the strange land below.

For a long while , it really did scare her. It was so dark and mystifying, and her animal senses did nothing to help. Her sense of direction and place was all wrong, and even her smells were nothing but gibberish.

Finally though, she was getting used to it. It was starting to make sense again.

Bolts crackled in the horizon, and she again felt a deep gratitude for the blonde water lady. No wonder Rayn liked her so much!

Others of her kind met her now. Smaller, but of similar colours and looks. They called frantically and gaily, as if they had just awoken from a long stupor.

She answered, her deeper voice resonating across the luminous canopy.

The dark matter shirked back. She was unaware of the fact that humans could not see such a thing; the oily, spidery mass that clung to their skin and entered their eyes and mouths. She hated seeing it, and ruffled her mane at their seeming ambivalence toward the parasitic invader.

Rayn saw it, though. He was different from the others, even to Syyd. He could examine the world in a different way; talk to Flower and her other feather, furry and scaly friends with an easy eloquence. All creatures, great and small, were drawn to him.

It was bestial.

Her new pals chittered excitedly. They told her that there was something interesting, off in the distance.

I know, Flower drawled back, *the light! I see it!*

Not that! Down there! Look!

The world was both light and dark, so Flower had a hard time focusing. After squinting long enough, she knew what they were referring to.

Humans?

Sequestered under a mighty tree unlike any she had ever seen, with its grey-gold appearance dotted with bluish pine cones, was a group.

They were hurt. And they were fighting.

Wait a minute…

She knew them! They were from Gen! The old fellows! The one from the building of nice smells! The other one, from the holy place! They were two of the town's wise men!

She cawed. She wanted to get to the light, before anyone else could. That was her mission. But she couldn't leave these folk to die…

* * *

Jugo hawked up blood again, and fell.

This isn't good.

He couldn't even lift an arm to defend himself. He had only the power to crawl closer to the tree's milky-dull trunk; to clutch at it pathetically and hope it would provide adequate protection.

He endured *a lot* of self-hatred over his life, and this moment had to be near the top of his list.

He watched helplessly, as Ilod, Karnon, the Golden Knight, the remaining sappers and Eidian fought tooth and nail against the ambush. They had only been resting for what felt like minutes, before they were assaulted by a revenge squad of those beetle bastards.

Sending the rosellas screaming, they fell from above like boulders; crashing into the sodden ground before unfurling like blossoms of razor metal.

With what little vigour that remained, the men created a circle of arms. Brandishing their worn weapons, they spat and dared their foes to make the first move.

There were five of them in total, ranging from the size of a large dog to a draft horse. Each carried instruments that clearly meant to torture as well as kill; uneven, serrated blades that wrapped into vague forms which could never be used by someone with only two hands.

Their telescopic squints reminded Jugo of one of those steam machines, as disgusting, worm-like feelers drooped from their heads and snuffled along the ground.

One of them hoovered up a large cone that fell along with him, before spitting it out toward the sky, and laughing as the distressed calls of birds echoed back down.

"Reckon I got one!"

The Golden Knight stepped forward, ushering everyone else behind him. He readied his mighty spear.

"Back, knaves!" he bellowed, his voice matching the thunder's tempo. "I'll not let you defile this land any longer!"

The biggest of the assassins hovered forward, pie-facing one of his subordinates in an act of dominance. His visage was different from the others, with tusks that dripped with maggots which fell into his palm, before he sucked them up. His face almost seemed to be in an enduring state of rot, with wounds pocketing his soft, fleshy areas.

"Ya think's that easy?" he guffawed. "None's you leaving here alive!"

"Tell 'em!" one of the others buzzed. "TELL 'EM!"

They all laughed; their devilish ballad creating an air of repugnance which twisted the bellies of the men. Their legs shook, as they watched the guerrilla force spread out and surround them.

The smallest one struck; far too quickly. Unbeknownst to one of the Edian, its weapon extended like a whip, covering the distance between them both in an instant. The mage's hand slid from his arm in an explosion of claret and stored magic, and he fell back with a scream.

The other four moved simultaneously, taking advantage of that precious second of distraction. Fortunately, both Ilod and the knight were well aware of this common tactic, and they had no time to run to the man's aid.

"KILLEMKILEMKILLLEMKILLEMKILLEMNOWNOWNOW!"

The wild verbosity was rattling, and both Ilod and the magi knew that power was being used with these words.

"Damn it all, they're casting a spell!" Karnon wailed, his voice now warble from the terror that only comes with inexperience.

"Then don't allow them the pleasure of completing it!" the Golden Knight boomed, before jumping into the air like a grasshopper, leaving a thin stream of water akin to an umbilical cord.

This caught *everyone* by surprise.

With a potent holler, he showed the enemy his *own* ability to plummet like a comet. Tearing the air with a shredded whistle, he rode his spear downward – onto the head of one of the bugs.

Spiny limbs, intestines, shell shards and goop sprayed like a melon flattened by a hammer. The shock erupted in the minds of all, signalling the breaking of the curse – and the beginning of the chaotic fight.

Both sides rushed each other; neither giving itself time to absorb the savage scene that just played out in front of them.

Except Jugo, of course, whose eyes goggled almost like that of the buzzing executioners. He gripped the tree so hard, his muscles cramped, and his throat constricted.

He watched with both dread and vigilance, as the Golden Knight evaporated in a swirling, sandy mist.

He's gone.

Could that awesome dive have drained the being's energy? He couldn't begin to speculate, never mind mourn the fact that they were now down two men.

Crap.

Like drones, the dingy, wicked pests scampered unfeelingly *through* their buddy's corpse; kicking entrails and inhaling the bodily gasses before it could escape in the air. They barked and yapped, clearly hyped from its effects, as they swung their tools of destruction without grace.

Not to be browbeaten from the wickedly primal display, the Eidian gathered together. Limbs quickly entwined, they erected a thin shield of roots that slithered around them.

Noting the small timeframe he had, Ilod sprang to the injured mage, and dragged him alongside Jugo. Like a tap, blood poured from his stump, but somehow, he was conscious enough to utter a hymn which caused pine cones above to pelt themselves at the small creature which snapped at their heels.

It was a minor annoyance at best, but it was enough for one of the sappers to make a move. Disregarding his own safety, he tossed a knife at the thing, which bounced off its carapace. Undeterred, he charged with his shield, battering it and stabbing away with his sword.

Screaming and cursing unintelligibly, he tangled with his foe, before the side of his torso ripped open. Still, this did not seem to slow him, and Ilod (already exhausted), tried to run to him to provide aid.

Jugo clutched his robe, and thrust his head downward at the rocking Eidian. "Help him first! You know that! We need you *here*, not *dead*!"

He coughed, and the Numanta growled and snapped a dirty look at him.

You know I'm right, you old fool.

The sapper fell, but took his opponent down with him in his final struggle. He had managed to cut into the beast's 'neck' so deep, its head almost fell off. Despite this, it managed to return the favour, and Jugo closed his eyes in distress. It stumbled around a few moments more, before succumbing to the fatal blow.

Rage watered his eyes.

Thanks... you won't be forgotten mate.

The three remaining beetles hacked through the wall of roots in what only seemed like seconds, and one of them managed to push through and slay another Eidian.

"What... what do we do?" the injured man under Ilod's hasty care groaned. The elder man tried to stifle the bleeding, his dark face a cragged contrast to his pale blue eyes.

Jugo knew. Jugo knew the Numanta wanted to give-in and keel over... but he was always far stronger than that. He was always the professional, even in the middle of a maelstrom of death.

"If you can, run" Ilod ordered, as he cast a quick glance at the other magi who just died in front of him. "Run to Vayu."

"Wh... what about--

"I ain't goin' anywhere" Jugo croaked. "I *can't* go anywhere. Ilod's right, you need to go. Now. Call the others... *now!*"

* * *

The ear-splitting, squawking cloud spiralled like a waterspout. More species began to emerge from the nothing – as owls, gulls, and even flamingos bubbled forth from the unseen crack that connected the realms.

Her world was pushing back, but Flower was more concerned with the massacre that was about to happen below.

That's Mister Jugo and Ilod... Rayn said, as he looked through her enhanced vision.

Braving the avian blitz, the parrot descended toward the battle; an ugly blotch in an otherwise mesmerising, endless undulation of leafy jade and beryl. The land seemed to roil before her, and it unbalanced her steadiness.

Easy there, her human advised.

He was right. She had to be careful. Who knew *what* kind of unpleasantness this commotion would draw in. This land was still in a battle of its own; and fell things roamed the churning skies.

With her large claws bared, Flower tried to land as close as possible. Her rippling wings stiffened, and the rain misted lightly around her.

Sodden, she planted herself onto a branch, and hastily groomed and puffed herself.

Bobbing her head, she inched sideways to get a clear view.

It was not good.

She could feel Rayn's heart plummet within her own.

Jugo and Ilod were surrounded. Three large, bulbous monsters shuffled toward them with a jarring, graceless gait; and their 'arms' looked indistinguishable from their 'legs'. They wielded gnarled, bladed *things* that reminded Rayn of the hot pretzels that travelling merchants would often sell in Gen – only here the salt resembled shards of murky glass.

Dead bodies were strewn about; two people and two more of the monsters. Blood was *everywhere*, even as it was slowly being absorbed by the rainfall.

Both men were messy and hurting. Rayn had never seen either of them like this before, and he had to know.

How? Why are they here?!

Thanks to his friends, he had heard the stories. Jeleenn had sometimes told them that her dad and the town's mage were once heroes a long time ago, but he had honestly never believed it. Syyd was always more interested about that, but Rayn had always mocked his brother for being so gullible.

I never even had to say a thing... just roll my eyes and scoff... maybe I was wrong after all.

Yet here they were, and before his and Flower's eyes, they were about to be slaughtered.

He tried hard to gulp in fear, but his spirit form wouldn't permit it. He urged Flower to fly. Fly away, as fast as she could, so that he did not have to see what happened next.

But what happened next... was not what he expected. At all.

A dizzying sensation popped both he and his feathery avatar, and it looked as though the space between Ilod and Jugo folded in on itself; warping and smudging Rayn's perception of the scene.

Within a blink, everything was normal again, only now this time, another being now stood in the middle of the fray.

It was him. Rayn knew it. Deep within his essence, he knew it.

Flower shivered and shook, and she began gnawing at her wings in distress.

They had to move. Now.

* * *

Jugo's eyes were red.

Gasping and retching, he slithered through the slime like a worm, and reached out a pale, faltering hand.

Ilod wrapped his arms around his brother. They both breathed and felt each other's pained gasps. The mage planted his head into Jugo's heaving shoulders, and silently begged him to calm.

But no serenity could possibly come. Not when Joner was standing in front of them.

"It's... it's him!" one of the creatures screeched. "The boss! BIG BOSS!!!"

They all lowered their arms, and respectfully made space for their dear leader.

"Good work. All of you" he began, not taking his emerald gaze off his father. "You did a great deed. I'll be sure to give *all* of you commendations. You bravely defended the honour of the fallen prince..."

He turned to the three monsters, who now blubbered and wailed like babes. "We may have lost the Fountainscape, but all of Restrentuliousolou'sdent-shaneekaladai will hear of your noble quest. You, and your fallen brothers!"

He waved his bejewelled hand. "Head back to the main force, and to your king. Rest, and await further orders! We will have time to mourn later!"

They happily obliged, as they now both laughed and cried as they vanished through the impenetrable forest.

Watching them go, Joner smiled. He was still for a long time, frozen in place like a painting.

"I remember when I first came across them" he finally said, not turning his head. "These bizarre, insect-like creatures from a land far away within the fairy realms. Though unseelie, they were oddly endearing to Hekor and I. They were enemies at first, but we eventually won over the friendship and loyalty of the king after helping them rid their city of the Blemmyeses that spread a great plague that they brought from them from Arika..."

He turned, his eyes now pale like a dead man's "... from Tarinn."

Jugo was gasping. His breathing was now shallow and agonising, and Ilod had withdrawn into himself, as he used every mental technique possible to stave off his distress.

"Joner..." his father rattled, blood bubbling from his lips.

"Dad. Good to see you again. How's it been?"

CHAPTER XVI

It had the face of Kwenn. Of Joner.

It was the same thing, either way.

Its one eye saw nothing now.

In the cold rain, it finally rested. The honour of being a true corpse; deformed and crushed from a battle well-fought, its hands clasped over its breast.

It was the least they could do. Give it some semblance of a dignified death.

"They… they're the bad guys…" Eyuil had observed like a mouse, as Jeleenn softly stroked the Black Knight's remaining mangle of dark hair. "Right?"

No, she realised, *they weren't.*

* * *

The children were all safe, and gathered together under the thickest, leafiest ceiling they could find.

Many of them shivered, and the paltry blaze Jeleenn stoked did nothing to warm their chattering bones.

She was truly being tested today. There were a lot of them to keep an eye on. She doubted that these were the accumulation of all adolescents from Gen, Gimlum and Henra – just the ones unlucky enough to get snagged.

She created a buddy system for them, and matched the youngest with the oldest when possible, and made it abundantly clear that her word – along with Syyd's, Eyuil's and Mina's – was law.

There was no grumbling and pushback; and rather than relieve her, it only made Jeleenn all the more concerned and saddened for them.

They had been through too much. Their spirits were gone. They were starving, freezing and traumatised.

Eyuil offered what little healing her Numanta training had allowed, and Syyd's miraculous gifts had somewhat of a soothing effect.

Still, there were plenty of tears, once things quieted down a bit.

Jeleenn could barely move. Her legs had given up the ghost, and she was marred by cuts, burns and bruises. She didn't think anything was broken, but she was still in a lot of pain.

How am I going to do this...

She had to learn to trust the kids. They were smart and capable.

She instructed two pairs to try and spread the flames into as many hearths as possible, whilst another three would gather leaves and twigs for bedding. The rest would try as best as they could to use the tree trunks as privacy walls, so that they can take off their clothes and shoes and dry them.

They had to avoid any illnesses. In a place like this, she wouldn't take any chances.

She then asked Mina and Syyd to keep an eye on both groups, and Eyuil to gather drinking water.

It was a start.

Food was the major concern. She didn't know how they managed for this long, but she knew that kids could do some amazing things when put in a survival situation.

She closed her eyes, and reminisced deeply about the journeymen who would visit the Queezy Fennick, as they shared their wild tales of the wilderness with her and the staff.

She recalled a couple of stories of children who managed the impossible, from escaping their captors, to being raised by wolves.

Only legends, to be sure...

She snorted, and realised that she was slumbering where she sat. She would not be any use lounging like an invalid. She had to scrounge up *something*, even if it killed her.

But she didn't know where to begin. Again, she cursed her lack of familiarity with this land, and resolved to remedy that.

Even if it was as simple as finding an edible fruit.

"Jeleenn, no!" Eyuil started toward her, and pushed her back to the spongy ground with a gentle hand. "You can't! You need to rest! I'm serious!"

She was both impressed and annoyed with the girl's bedside manner.

She's Ilod all over...

"You guys need food" she groaned. "I need to grin and bear it. For your sake and mine. We won't last very long out here at this rate."

Eyuil puffed her cheeks out. "No. No! I can't let you. I won't. I know you're the boss, and I'm just a kid, but I *do* know a lot about health, y'know. I've learned *some* things. And when it comes to medicine... well, then *I'm* in charge. I'm sorry... but I'm putting my foot down on this one."

She stomped to emphasise her point.

Jeleenn grinned, and winced when she tried to shrug.

Eyuil gave her a smug look.

"Fine" she relented. "I'll listen, you brat. I'll stay and watch. Just keep collecting the water, and we'll figure something out."

Now that she thought about it, she *did* start to feel her jaw swell. "Can I at least wash myself? While it's still wet."

The young mage relaxed. "Yeah. We'll try and make a bed for you. Just... just take it easy, okay? Don't stress, we'll get there, one step at a time."

Jeleenn looked into the small fire. It had a slight fuchsia base, and the smoke it emitted smelled of freshly-cut grass. "How did *you* get so cool-headed, huh?"

Eyuil bowed, and she recognised it as the Numanata greeting that Ilod often did with other magi.

"I have good teachers. That, and I'm already freezing cold."

* * *

Most were asleep now.

Only he was left awake.

Did he do this intentionally? He didn't know.

But... they were definitely safe. He was sure.

Syyd sat alone.

Alone, but not quiet.

The world was speaking to him. It didn't stop. Not since the escape from the tower.

Not since...

What is happening to me? How...

Those words. They went over and over in his head. They would not leave.

I am... part of you. Please, save your brother... save all... our kingdom... our people...

His eyes stung, and his heart ached. It became a habit lately; to sit all through the night when everyone else was slumbering.

His mum and dad were dead. He would never see them again.

He wished they were here, with him. They *had* to have known.

Why he was like this.

Did this have something to do with Rayn also? Did they *both* have abilities? Powers?

As usual, after the sadness, came the anger. Anger at his parents for hiding the truth. Anger at the ones who decimated Gen.

Anger at the voice. Anger at his brother for leaving.

The ground around him vibrated. Puddles rippled and weeds swayed, as he tried to bottle his fury.

It stopped. He was getting better.

His silver hair hung lank and went over his face, and his simple tunic was soaked and coming apart at the seams. The soles of his shoes were coming loose.

Yet... he was comfortable, in a way. This world... whatever it was, it sang to his spirit. It was a sense of coming home; of returning after a long, long time away.

He was sitting in the rain, overlooking the small encampment of his friends. On top of a fallen log, he sat in the dark.

Except, to him, it was no longer darkness. It was light; as bright as gemstone, and twice as beautiful.

He was starting to see. How things truly were.

He didn't want to tell anyone. He didn't understand what was happening, and he was loath to burden Jeleenn with more concerns. All he knew for certain, is that something within him was changing... or awakening? Come what may, he decided to try and focus on getting everyone home safely.

What then? Do I go back? Or do I try to find answers?

He saw the lightning, and the rumble of thunder followed. It wasn't letting up, and he guessed it wouldn't stop until the war was over.

What that war *was*, he obviously had no idea. But the tension was there – the sky was thick with dread, and as his perceptions changed, so did his awareness of the pushing and pulling all around him. The never-ending conflict that made the back of his head buzz with disquiet, which replaced the *things* that lurked in the forests as his main fear.

Jeleenn had not said much to them after her rescue. Her first concern was to find shelter and make sure everyone was safe. She had promised to explain, but had passed out from her battle.

Syyd had never seen anything like that, and he would ever forget it. Even his own small part in the fight was nothing compared to what he witnessed from Jeleenn Ironmonger, the girl from the inn he always had a crush on.

She was no longer a girl to him.

He watched her. She dozed on a pile of leaves, her bare feet drying by a pile of blackened, crackling wood. The wounds were showing up clearly now, with her swollen lip, blackened cheek and cut forehead discolouring her comely face. She breathed quickly, clearly not sleeping well at all.

I have to do something... but what?

He sunk deeper into his grief. He looked at his palms, and found nothing but trailing droplets. He wasn't sure what he was expecting, but there *had* to be an answer *somewhere*!

"Syyd!!!"

Syyd yelped – a lot more higher pitched than he would ever willingly admit. He fell backward, and landed on the ground, his thin legs kicking the air.

"What?! Who was that?!" he blustered, feeling both daft and irate that something managed to sneak up on him.

He scrabbled upward, and his hands began to throb with that increasingly-familiar power. "I said who's there?! Show yourself!"

"Syyd! Up here!"

He directed his head up, and felt water run down his throat, drowning him like a turkey. He sputtered, unable to see the source of the noise. He truly felt like a dunce, now that he was caught unaware. The concept almost frightened him more than the actual threat, and he got scared knowing that he was still just a stupid kid that could be killed in an instant.

His world was suddenly overtaken by a great form, with wings that flapped loudly at him.

Bright wings.

Familiar wings.

Really familiar wings.

Wait... no way...

Instinctively, he presented his forearm. Catching himself with his odd response, he began to laugh as Flower hopped on, before jumping on his shoulder and rubbing herself fretfully and happily on his face.

* * *

Jeleenn smiled, and her face berated her for it.

Everything hurt, but she couldn't help it. Things just got weirder and weirder by the day, but for once, this weirdness was a good thing.

So, her face just had to put up with it.

But, there was a subtext for her crooked grin. It was also a surrender; a white flag – as alabaster as her teeth – that simply said 'I give up'.

She gave up trying to make sense and order from this chaos. She apologised to the gods, and vowed that from now on, she would just go with the flow.

She accepted the weirdness.

Fate just wanted to beat her down, pick her up, and then beat her down again. All the while, it made a mockery of her limp-wristed attempts to strike back.

This is what I wanted, right? To be a hero like dad?

Perhaps she was being a tad nihilistic.

It could've been the pain talking.

Either way, she smiled.

The kids before her laughed. The first genuine happiness she had heard in a long, long time. It was a small thing, but it was enough for them. They desperately needed this, to take their minds off things – even if it was just for a few minutes.

They patted and stroked the red bird, and the animal was clearly relishing every moment of it. This, for some reason, attracted even more flocks, which seemed to sense that this was a safe haven.

What had happened after was somehow even more of a miracle, as the birds began to drop fruits, nuts and berries for them all. Whatever they could scavenge, they deposited in piles for the hungry youngsters. Much of the edibles were strange and foreign to them, but when one was starving, one tended to be anything but picky.

It was a magical sight, and Jeleenn truly would've loved to see Liniii at its full glory as a nature reserve for the Eidian.

They needed this. They needed this win.

Maybe... maybe this *was* a result of her actions, her attempt to make wrongs right. Maybe... she really *could* take charge, and control their circumstances? To have a genuine effect, and not be pawns in some game?

She bit into a small, green fruit, and she welcomed the bitterness as it pulled her from her profoundly abstract dilemma. It wasn't the most edible nor ripe she had ever had, but she sure as hell was not going to voice her displeasure. It was enough to keep her going a little longer, and that's all she could ask for.

She looked to Syyd who sat next to her, and beside *him*, was Rayn.

At least, that's what she was told who it was. All *she* saw was a shadowy form that seemed to speak to her through her mind and the ground at the same time.

Of course, she had never heard his true voice. Syyd's brother had always been a mute, but could supposedly talk to animals.

Another power... just who are *these boys?*

They claimed to know nothing, and she believed them. How could they? They were only ten years old, and had grown up in the same seaside town as she. Aside from Rayn's peculiarities, she had had *no* inclination of their abilities, and neither did anyone else. Their parents? Well, they would never know now, as they had been killed in the attack. Her father, the ultimate keeper of secrets? Again, she had no clue.

Were they related to this? *All* of this?

Of *Kwenn*?

It was too much. They *had* to be.

The rain had finally begun to settle a bit, but darkness still enclosed them. The kids had done an admirable job of using large leaves, logs and strips of bark to erect a basic little shelter, and the canopy roof provided enough shelter from the elements. They avoided venturing too far into the unbroken wild, and instead straddled a relatively open area that possibly could have been a favoured road once upon a time.

They had a greater chance of being spotted once Hekor came calling, but Jeleenn reasoned that eyes were all over the place regardless, and they had a better chance of actually knowing where they were headed.

And now, she knew.

Rayn had told her that her father was here, as was Ilod. Not just that, but there was an entire fighting force that had been struggling to reclaim the land from Joner, and that they were marching onto the Great Castle of the Leaf.

How had he learned all of this? How did he escape capture back in Gen? How was he here, as a spirit? Was he dead? Did his parrot *really* fly all the way from Shali?

Syyd hammered his twin with endless questions, and received little in return. Rayn was just as lost as they all were, and simply just accepted things as they were.

Jeleenn smirked. *Just accept it. Aren't we all…*

Thunder grumbled, reiterating her misgivings.

"Rayn" she whispered through a stiff jaw, "have you seen my dad? Master Ilod? Are they well?"

The wavy apparition flickered for a second, and replied.

"Yes. I have. I was stuck here for a long while, until I caught up with Oviinia. I mean… Ms. Trundle. She told me both Mr. Ironmonger and Master Ilod are here, and that they've gone off to fight somewhere…"

He had mentioned her before, this Oviinia. Who was she? How did she know her father?

"She knows Kwenn" Rayn explained. "She's someone special, like… us. She didn't know it, either, but she does now. She's the one that caused the rainstorm, actually. Her sister is leading the army against…"

Rayn hesitated.

"It's okay" Jeleenn shrugged. "You can say it."

"Your brother."

Brothers. Sisters. Fathers. Sons. Mothers. It seemed like everyone involved was related in some form or fashion.

Syyd looked at her with a crinkled forehead. "Brother? You have a brother, Jeleenn?"

"I *had* a brother. I thought he died years ago… but he's alive… and he's the cause of all of this."

She had a *lot* of explaining to do. These children deserved it.

* * *

The battle had begun.

The army of the Eternal Tadpole clashed with an endless expanse of black.

A tidal reflection of the electrically-charged unrest of the firmament, the Black Knights spewed forth from the bowels of their maker.

In rigid formation, thousands of the cold, impassive soldiers moved as one. Their movements robotic and stiff, they offered no quarter to the offence of Vayu's front line, even as she herself hacked at their armour and synthetic joints with her light-yet-deadly feather blades.

As they pushed further north, the land began to thin out and offer new dangers to the liberators. The cover provided by the scarred and incinerated woodlands melted away in the gushing streams of fire from both worlds, as the mirror elements vaporised each other in a terrifyingly beautiful symphony of deletion.

* * *

Joner was sweating.

The travel through time took a serious toll on him, and Hekor caught him as he fell.

"Time displacement *and* teleportation? On the same day? A bit gluttonous for punishment, aren't we?"

"Oh, sod off" Joner grunted as he pushed himself away. "It had to be done. We're approaching the finish line, and we can't afford to hold back now."

He looked around and squinted. "Where are we?"

"In Dian's greenhouse. You can't tell by the smell?"

Joner rubbed his throbbing temples, and did indeed see the moving walls of flora, as they shifted and changed states in cubic chunks, before rising weightlessly upward.

Under his boots, blue-violet globules undulated like squishy beads, his weight burying them in the crunchy ground before they emitted silent, supersonic screams.

He always hated the language of the plants, but of course, Dian had always been enamoured with it. Her… *quirks* had often been the result of a botched translation or two.

The frosted ceiling wobbled like mercury, and looking at it didn't do his head any favours.

"Right" he said. "Has contact been initiated?"

"The fighting's begun, if that's what you mean" Hekor pursed his lipless mouth, as Joner turned and began to walk.

He followed, as usual. "You have your father?"

Joner didn't look back. He exited the main greenhouse hall via a spiral staircase. "Yeah. Yeah, he's here. Along with Ilod. They're both pretty banged up."

Hekor wasn't sure what to say. "You… okay? I mean, this is the first time you've seen him since…"

"I'm fine."

He didn't buy it. His large hand grabbed the smaller man's shoulder, and stopped him in his tracks.

"Hekor" Joner began, still refusing to look at his friend.

"Come on" the larger of the two growled. "Don't give me that 'impassive' act. Talk to me. It had to be a shock, seeing him. Kid, you're allowed to show some emotion."

Joner guffawed. He turned, and jerked his head up to stare him in the eyes. "Coming from you? That's funny."

"I can be emotional… when I want to."

"What do you want me to say?"

To his surprise, Hekor looked to be genuinely angry. "For you to at least *comment* on the moment we've been training for! You know, when I pulled you out of hell, and we travelled from one corner to the other, and back again? You remember that?"

"No, forgot all about it" Joner sarcastically riposte. "Nope, it's all gone. You have to remind me for the millionth time."

Hekor could have easily swatted the little whelp. He did it before, and he certainly would do it again before time.

But this was not the time.

"Fine" he brushed past him, his boulder-shoulder tapping Joner with clear purpose. "I've no time for this" Hekor rumbled.

"*We've* no time for this" Joner corrected. Now it was his turn to follow. "Vayu has come, and we need to focus. We could lose it all, right here and now. What's the situation?

"Elytrasio is dead, and we lost the Fountainscape" Hekore declared loudly, to a crowd that was not seen.

"I know" Joner returned angrily, his footsteps quickening to match the long strides that echoed through the crumbling halls. "But they thought they caused a distraction. Let them."

"They *did* cause a distraction" Hekor skidded to a halt, and smacked his fist into a palm. He twisted his neck and spat. "That storm. It devastated us. How did they do it? It wasn't regular magic. No Eidian could've done that, aside from Dian. *Certainly* no Numanta!"

"Dian betrayed us, huh?"

"No" Hekor resumed walking. "The hall needs answers. The king wants his son's killers brought to justice."

"I'll get it out of them. The Numanta first."

"No" Hekor repeated, this time with more authority. "No, Joner. Your people need you *now*. Dian will talk to your father and the mage first. Trust me on this."

Hekor could feel the bubbling emotion rise from his back, but he was done with placating his friend. He had to go to war.

"Okay" he finally heard, a hint of acceptance in the voice.

"What about *her?*" Hekor inquired, after the two entered the council hall.

There were no banquets now. No golden leaves falling amidst the sweet air of fruit and nectar. No heavenly strings of instruments filling every violet corner and crevice with mollifying luminescence. No mirth, nor joy found in the company of friends.

It was all different. The former seat of the Edian was now a blue, morose battleground of its own, as barbs were traded between the leaders of the invisible realm and their constituents, as the vile rot of politics took hold of their hearts.

"I think I finally managed to convince at least *one* of them" Joner sighed. "I finally got a win. What a day huh?"

They all looked upon them expectedly now. Races and peoples from every layer of the unseen world, all brought together through one dream – one ultimate goal.

To end suffering. To make everything as one. To right the wrongs of the gods.

"We'll need her… now more than ever."

* * *

Fixing.

That's what I do.

That's what I've always done.

I also create.

Create from nothing.

Like a god? Hah, sure, if you see it that way.

But I've destroyed so much, too.

Like fire. I can breathe life from nothing.

Like fire, I can also burn it down to ash and bone.

Am I good? Am I evil?

I would spend countless nights pondering this.

All I wanted… all I *ever* wanted to do, was to help.

I helped… by… making weapons? Tools of death?

But… I also made nails, so that Mrs. Ratang could start her soup stand after her husband died.

I also made parts for schooners, so that the fisherman could feed the entire town.

Why? Just because I had a gift? That couldn't be enough? It also had to bring with it a curse? One that ripped my family apart and almost… almost…

… burned it all down.

I'm sitting in the dark now. Thinking.

Fixing.

Fixing my mind. Rebuilding.

Joner didn't do this to me. I did.

He showed me a kindness that no-one ever had.

He didn't lie to me.

Even if it was uncomfortable. Even if it was traumatic… he showed me the truth.

I'm not angry. I'm not happy.

Just… thinking.

What do I do, from here on out?

Be my own person, and go down a road both exciting and terrifying?

Embrace my destiny? Fulfil my duty as guardian of Arlmai?

They turned me into a weapon. Or was I always meant to be one?

I am more than that. A weapon is more than what it seems.

Embrace the fire? Escape it?

…

The new world…

…

Whatever that may be…

…

Will *not* tell me who I am.

Not any more.

* * *

Liniii gagged on death.

It mattered not what form it took. The crystalline clarity of Tarinn nor the dreaminess of the invisible was enough to conceal the true nature of death.

Ironically, this is what Joner wanted to end.

Death. Suffering.

But he also wanted to destroy life.

Vayu knew that, no matter what this supposed 'new world' would've offered. From what she saw all around her; the very rejection between the two realms was enough to convince her that he wanted to mix oil and water, to force an unholy union between two unwilling beings that screamed in protest and dismay.

This is what the great and mysterious Wizards wanted?

Over her dead body.

They were vastly outnumbered. Her scouts estimated that they were fighting a foe three times the size of their own.

But they were advancing. By the gods, they were advancing.

Black helmets flew, revealing the pale facsimiles of Joner himself as he fell. Without emotion, nor an inkling of who they once were, they were souls of the damned and forgotten, given a cause.

How... how could they have agreed to *this*?

It was far beyond her realm of capacity. She couldn't understand it. Maybe she never would.

She lived in her world, and they lived in theirs. Did death bring a sense of revelatory awakening that the living simply couldn't process?

Perhaps. But she wasn't going to find out. Not when she had come so far.

She admitted it. She could not even begin to understand what Joner had seen. What he had been through. He had tried to tell her about his journey through the very fabric of reality, but she was not interested.

His trauma… it did not excuse his actions.

It actually took her a long time to come to this realisation. His words and actions always rang in her mind, and she – like many others – seriously wondered if he was actually right.

But no. No he was *not*.

Damn him. Damn the Wizards. Damn the Pheekonshenee. And damn any others who sought to manipulate and pervert for the sake of a 'better world'.

She knew it better than most. She *was* one of those perversions, after all.

Now, she did not care. It wasn't about her. It was about everyone who looked up to her. Who loved her and wanted to end this insane war.

The storm became more and more violent the further they pressed. A maelstrom swirled over the central towers of the castle; the inky clouds almost fighting amongst one another, as stars crashed and exploded.

No, not stars.

Ice.

Or, what seemed like ice. It came falling down like bolts of glass, piercing both friend and foe alike.

Vayu bellowed for all to take cover. Without thought, she slid under the body of a fallen black knight. Its eyes met her own.

Face to face, nose to nose, they stared at each other, as screams and thuds were followed by whistles and grinding that echoed throughout the land.

Whispering her apologies, she pushed her knife into its neck. Backwards and forwards. Backwards and forwards.

Until it simply stopped moving.

Its lank hair tickled her skin.

"Mum!!!"

"I'm fine" she called. A mechanical arm pushed the body off of her, and she was met with the wide-eyed gaze of a gnome who piloted one of the bipedal steam machines.

It spurted both oil and boiling water, as its overhead cover had simply vaporised into ash.

Everything the glassy spears touched had the same effect. Bone-white dust trailed all around them like sand, as fighters died with their stricken bodies evaporating into nothing.

She scrambled to her feet, but was acutely aware of her draining strength.

"Bastards!" the gnome bellowed, his powdered visage falling from his mangled vehicle, as he rushed to give her a helping hand.

"Vile bastards!"

She had to wonder if they didn't use the rains to their advantage. That somehow, they gathered enough water and used some sort of sorcery to transform it into their world's version of the element.

That's not possible.

It almost seemed like the work of Dian. She wouldn't have been surprised.

Shalisshakin. A goddess incarnated. My mother. That's who we're up against.

The Goddess of the Ephemeral was far more than one woman. Vayu never accepted that Dian represented her fully – that she in fact was merely a physical manifestation of a far greater power that resided in heaven.

Do the gods truly want this? Do they want to see a new world? Or are even they fighting amongst themselves, in this very moment?

She wrapped her thin arm around the gnome's small shoulders. Her skeletal frame had bared itself all over her body, as her skin had turned completely invisible.

There *were* no gods here. Not in this mire of hatred and violence.

"Your name…" she whispered.

"Jnkelteeny, mum" he answered. "Second Brigade… Artinfantry…"

She looked to the sky. There was no telling when another strike would occur.

Hundreds of knights still advanced ceaselessly, as they stepped over the bodies of their fallen.

"Gather every gnome from the Artinfantry and fall back!" she ordered. "Do whatever you can to create mobile cover for us. Tree trunks, boulders, whatever you can think of! Focus on construction, and we'll hold under the canopies!"

Jnkelteeny saluted and mounted his crackling armour. It moved with a great, laboured effort as he hurriedly relayed the order.

"Fall back!" Vayu shouted.

They had come achingly close to the embankment where the outlying buildings were located, which had once been the only settlement in all of Liniii, aside from Mehn Station.

She couldn't risk another push forward to capture any buildings. Stretching her assault too thin was exactly what the enemy would've wanted, especially if they were desperate to both reach their target and take shelter from a potential killing blow from up on high.

"Fall back!" echoed voices around her. "Fall back!"

A crew of five Abatwa sprouted from the ground. They were her field messengers and intelligence collectors, and she saw their black muscles glisten with strain as they muttered and mumbled in their foreign tongue.

"We need to hold the line" she answered back. "They need to work fast, because we won't be able to stand here for long... get the trolls to the front, now! And have the Mikolasak and the rest of your people continue your guerrilla manoeuvres! Understand?"

They all bowed, and pounded their fists to their hearts. They dived back into the dirt – save for one – who tugged at her leg.

She looked down in confusion, and the small man pointed toward the direction of the advancing knights.

"What is it...?"

He then immediately burrowed down, following after his company.

Vayu glanced ahead, and saw what he was pointing at.

She gasped.

It was a woman. A very tall woman, who walked through the litany of black knights. They parted for her, and a hush draped over the battlefield, which just a second earlier had been overflowing with the shrieks of the theatre of war.

Who... who is this?

She was clamped in a fearsome looking getup; a set of armour that glowed like magma cracks, but also radiated a dark aura that gave its design a fearsome life; three snarling wolf motifs. Two covered each of her arms like gauntlets, designed so that it looked as if her hands were protruding from their toothy maws. The third head wrapped around her own; the snarling mouth choking on a dark, fearsome face. Red hair with coal-black streaks was sorted in plaits, with what looked like rusty nails used as holding pins.

A symbol seemed to have been branded into her forehead.

Vayu knew instantly.

It... it can't be!

She held a huge harpoon, and its total absence of light reflecting off the metal was almost a mirror image of the gaze that rose from smouldering eyes.

Aodh...

"Commander!" someone shouted after her.

She didn't know who it was, nor did she acknowledge them. She was lost.

Lost in the gaze of her sister.

"Commander!"

"Stand back!" she yelled. "Hold the line, and don't follow me!"

She did not look back. Hobbling slightly, she strode forward. Over the bodies of the dead and dying automatons, and through the slurry of carnage, she approached her.

Aodh did the same.

It was the longest walk of her life. Even when running like a doe through the shifting forests of Liniii, half-dead and mad with fear, she felt nothing like the way she felt now.

Even in this terrain of pandemonium, Vayu was still barefoot. Cold mud and grass squeezed between her toes, and sharp rocks tried to pierce her soles.

She felt no pain. She was numb, with only her pounding heart vowing to knock down her ribcage. Her peripheral vision smudged, and she experienced a light-headedness that almost toppled her.

She did not want to be one of the fallen. Not just yet.

They both stopped, standing only a meter apart. The distance may as well have been both a hair's breadth as well as opposite sides of the world.

"Well, it's been a long time" Aodh daringly spoke first.

Vayu almost winced. Her body had a mind of its own, and she could barely keep it under control. "It really is you, isn't it? Aodh?"

"Call me Remana. I don't like formal titles" Aodh amended. She observed Vayu, looking her up and down. "I'm sorry about what happened... to you."

Vayu's face welled up, and she knew she would mourn. She didn't have to guess. She knew, somehow, that Aodh had joined the enemy.

Remana had seemed to notice. Her chiselled face softened, and she too looked almost like she would betray her impassive act.

"Vayu..." she added gently.

The pale woman tightened her jaw. "Don't... just... don't."

"I need to *explain*" Remana countered, "you owe me that. For god's sake, we're not actually going to fight each other, right here and now, are we?"

"What's there to explain?!" Vayu screamed. "*Tell me!*"

Her armoured kin looked taken aback, no doubt due to her sister's warped deformity flaring up like a ghost story come to life. Still, she regained her ground, and stood forward so that she was almost touching noses.

"We've been *lied* to, sister. All of them. Pheekons and the goddesses. The queen. They used us like tools, because that's all we *were* to them!"

"We were born to be *protectors*" Vayu spat, "the four elementals!

Both Tarinn and the other world! We have a duty--

"A duty as *what*?" Remana jabbed her finger into her sibling's chest. "To be a glorified harem to a bunch of useless men? Men who aren't even *real* men?! *We* were twisted and mangled to serve a *selfish* purpose!"

"Protecting the boy... a *child*. *That* is selfish to you? To fulfil a mother's dying wish, and to see her home flourish once more?"

Vayu couldn't help it. She pushed back, and Remana was caught by surprise by the strength hidden by the waif-like arms. She stood back.

"Aos Si is gone" she growled. "Kingdoms come and kingdoms go. That's no excuse to use us... even you, who escaped. My god, why do you defend them?! *Look at you!*"

The Eternal Tadpole struck, slapping Remana across the cheek.

It was like striking metal.

Her palm blazed with pain, but her sister did not reciprocate. She simply rubbed her face, and closed her eyes.

"Your man. Did you even *meet* him? Did guide him on his *heroic* quest?"

Vayu did not answer. She had not. Of course she hadn't.

"Neither did I" Remana continued. "Nor do I want to. I don't care. Even when he has the Fire Helm in his possession, I don't care. I don't need it. I don't need him. I am my own person. And I will create a new future – for myself, and all who were wronged in this bastard world!"

Vayu's lips quivered.

"Please... don't cry... don't, Vayu. I can't... please, just speak with them. That's all I ask. Speak with them! I'll bring you! We'll find our other sisters, and we'll do this together! *Please!*"

She shook her head. "New future... Aodh. Remana. Whatever your name is, I've *been* with them. I *was* one of them. I will *never* go back. New future, you say? Listen to yourself! A world without suffering? Suffering cannot exist without joy, and joy cannot exist without suffering. Joner just wants to collapse everything into a singularity. Into nothing. And what then? A new world? One that is completely incomprehensible from our own? He is not that powerful. He is a fool. Like the Wizards, he has become insane. And somehow believes he knows more than the divinity of the gods. This new world will be nothing but an endless void."

She would not tell her about Vatn. About Oviinia. She did not deserve to know.

Remana bowed her head. "The gods have done nothing, Vayu. They don't care. Not any more. Even Shalisshakin – your mother – wants this."

That was enough.

Vayu was quicker than Remana had expected, as she thrust a blade like a viper toward her. She barely managed to block the strike with her gauntlet, before leaping backwards.

"*She is not my mother*" Vayu bellowed, striking again and cutting the stale air as the taller woman folded her knees and went low.

"Vayu, stop!"

She was blind and deaf. A fury hotter than all three suns had engulfed her, and she attacked with every ounce of strength she could summon.

Vayu's front-line took this as the signal to advance, and the fighting resumed between both sides. Despite finding herself amidst the enemy, the black knights ignored the two women. Evidently, they were aware enough to realise that intervening in family drama was not advisable.

They stayed well clear of them, giving Remana ample space to sweep her harpoon in an attempt to trip-up her sister. She clearly did not want to kill or even harm her, but the lady of the wind did not make it easy for her.

"Vayu!"

Leaping and floating like a sugar glider, she pummelled downward, her loose tunic billowing like furious waves lapping a grey shoreline.

Despite her own brawn, Remana's weapon was simply too ungainly to quickly answer the acute offence. "Damn it! Vayu, listen to me! You're fighting the wrong war!"

Realising she couldn't separate herself quick enough, Remana suddenly advanced, and used her superior power to send her attacker flying with a push from her harpoon's handle. She then punted Vayu square in the stomach with the weapon's base, causing her to double-over.

She still did not drop her blades.

"Damn you" she hacked. "Wrong war?! You *started* this! *People are dead!*"

"It won't matter, when it's all done!" Remana bellowed as she kept herself at bay. "Alive or dead, *all* of us will be reborn! You're thinking too small, sister! You've been blinded by the rules as imposed by the gods. By this existence. You can't fathom a greater form of consciousness, so you lash out. You're scared! I understand! I was scared too!"

She offered her hand.

"We can fight later, if you so choose. At least just hear us out…"

Vayu chuckled. Her stringy hair swayed, covering her emaciated face. Droplets fell from the rolling curtain.

"No. No, I'm afraid I can't. It's not just me, Aodh. It's not just me. It's everyone that I care about. Everyone I love. Everyone who wants their homes to return. And thanks to you and your new friends, many of them will never see their loved ones again."

"Not if you work with us. For a new tomorrow."

Vayu raised her head.

"A new tomorrow is what we both want, huh? Only one of us is going to get it. You say death won't matter in the end? Prove it. Kill me. But I won't make it easy."

CHAPTER XVII

The Jagged Form Deshalmanik of lived up to its intimidating name.

For three days and three nights, they navigated the perilous hidden roads that threaded the sulphurous region, as Nuv and Ya'klum retraced the path that had been provided to them by the mystical Saumen.

Using a phosphorous concoction derived from strange ingredients that Puul remarked was akin to a witch's brew, each man handled a torch that seemed incongruous at first, but would sputter and dance when close to the right path. The flames would then reveal a cloud that signalled the clean air which cut through the thick miasma.

It was very much divine interference; much like the path to Saumen himself, it was as if nature itself was manipulated in order to accommodate Nuvummburtee's quest for truth.

But it wasn't just Nuvummburtee, wasn't it? It was also made for another.

Where was she now?

If only the answers were as clear as the sweet air that carved a lifeline for the five; as they meandered through the gassy valleys where nothing lived.

Well, almost nothing, as they would often see movement that jostled the poisonous-looking flora, as well as reptilian-like creatures that glided overhead – their thin, membranous wings flaunting spider web veins through the dimmed sunlight.

It was hard going, and Kwenn could only have guessed at what lurked within the hidden depths of the eye-watering, throat-clenching land. During the nights, they camped out in the open, unconcerned with bandits or bad weather making their awful sleep even worse. Of course, they took the time to get to know each other a lot more, and spent most of their night hours playing games and telling stories, and even 'contributing' ideas for Ya'k's writing.

It made the suffocation a little more bearable, though they eventually learned that the terrain wasn't *entirely* inhospitable for humans. There were a few small settlements that nipped the safer edges of Deshalmanik, and people would often harvest the unique plants and materials that would grow from the land.

It was a group of these foragers that would meet them at the end of the third day. To Kwenn's surprise, they had been expecting Nuv and Ya'k.

They had *not* expected, however, for them to return with friends.

They rambled excitedly, and their oxen were clearly agitated by the commotion. Rightly, they couldn't understand how three strangers emerged from the bowels of the sacred island, and demanded answers from Nuv.

Kwenn, Panin and Puul were eyed with suspicion, as things were slowly explained to them as they followed the oxen back to the small village.

It got colder and colder as they finally made it out from the noxious land. Over the next day, they bid farewell to the heat and sour air, as the ground slowly became crunchy with ice and snappy winds carved away at the canyons.

Neither Kwenn, Panin nor Puul had ever seen snow before, and in an odd way, trudging through the clumps of white had more of a profound impact on them then anything else they saw so far. It was so simple and pure, and totally unlike their lives on the seaside. The salt was gone. The fish were gone. The sounds of waves? Gone.

It had an unexpected, jarring effect on them – particularly the twins. Even seeing the fog of their breathing was more fascinating than any magical doohickey or blue-faced monkey.

They were going to a place called *Hoof's Range*, which was part of a village known as *Yui*. The Sollikane there had initially taught Nuv and Ya'k the methodology of making it through Deshalmanik, and this had caused somewhat of a fuss amidst the community, who had already heard rumours of the strange 'Ember Mind'.

That fuss returned with greater ferocity, now that the Shali men had arrived.

The village was small and simple, even for Gen standards. One of the guides explained that Yui was dedicated to the processing and export of the unique ingredients they harvested, and that they relied on the importation of food and other essentials, due to the soil of the land on which they were perched.

The view was something else, with Deshalmanik's glazed arches and soapy haze dominating the entire south-west stretch. Some strange looking observational devices were stationed along the range, and several large buildings smoked from different coloured chimneys, indicating the importance of the work that was conducted here.

To the east, just barely visible amongst the clouds, was the *Floating Castle of Eelow*, the eternal sky sentinel that had loomed for as long as anyone could remember.

"We're small, but always busy" the guide had told them, baring his bluish teeth in a friendly grin. In fact, it looked as though *everyone* in town had the same shade of ivories.

Once the shock had worn away somewhat, the workers and residents had become a lot more hospitable to their guests. Now that dusk was settling in, Kwenn, Panin and Ya'k were invited to bathe themselves and have dinner, whilst Nuv and Puul had the unenviable task of meeting with the Sollikane mage that led the village.

If Kwenn was entirely honest with himself, he didn't remember much else from the night. He had a feeling that the beverages he downed with glee were slightly more potent than he realised.

* * *

"Keráan is quite a trek" the Angakkuq of Yui observed, his eyes almost like that of a chameleon, as they seemed to examine both of his guests at the same time. "I was one of the Angakkuq that pushed Jhasé to release you to the holy city" he added, his long beard almost catching the fire of the crackling pit that separated them, "so this is good. Very good."

"Are Numanta welcome there?" Puul asked, as he warmed his palms. "I don't want to cause any unrest, Angakkuq…"

"Keráan is secular, but not unwelcoming" the red magi nodded with reassurance. "I will personally add my seal to that of Angakkuq Trafr'ad's, so that the permission you carry will be ironclad. I cannot say as to what the council will have in store for you boys, but this I can at least provide."

They both dipped their heads in gratitude.

"If what you have told me is true" the Angakkuq added, "then you will need all the help you can get. All of us will. The gods have made it so… we are now living in a time of great, impending trial. You, Nuvummburtee… and now this Kwennsefulass of the Solluskane… what is coming, it will test *all* faiths. I will pray for you. May Qual-nu forgo his misfortune on you all."

"May Qual-nu forgo his misfortune" Nuv echoed.

* * *

Panin stood guard.

This was what he was trained to do. It was his entire life.

He was a shield.

It was a simple life, sure, but it was one he loved.

He had always wanted to travel. Eventually... maybe once he had had enough of the job? Maybe he and Puul would journey somewhere? His brother, a fully-fledged Numanta, would offer his services to poor souls, whilst Panin would help... in some way. He didn't know. He didn't have all the details sorted.

Would he have a wife? Children? Would they come with him, as he satisfied his wanderlust? Or would he eventually settle back down in Gen to retire?

He had his whole life ahead of him. Maybe he would finally tell Jeleenn his true feelings.

Pah. Now that's *a fairytale.*

He was pretty sure that was all gone now.

Lumiin was dead. His best friend and mentor. His second father.

Most of his brothers. Dead.

His old life. Dead.

He didn't remember the last time he stood guard.

He looked down at Kwenn, who was sleeping soundly huddled against a dozing ox, its big bell covering his snoring face.

It was when you showed up. And everything changed.

He didn't blame Kwenn. The poor guy.

At least, he didn't any more. He didn't tell anyone, but he hated him at first. Not even Puul knew this.

But, Panin knew it wasn't his fault. Kwenn was just a physical embodiment of everything that went wrong; a visible *thing* that the guardsman could point his finger at and curse.

Enough people did that already. Panin didn't need to pile-on, to infect another man with his hatred, to spread more evil when there was already plenty of it to go around.

Henra. That was when Kwenn really showed his true colours, and when Panin could really call him a friend. The battle with Wilko, too. That was an eye-opener.

And now there was another one! Nuvummburtee. This one was a little gruffer than his brother, but seemed to be just as good of a person, thankfully.

Not like Joner.

Geez Jeleenn… and I thought my *family had issues.*

He stared at the aurora that waved in the sky. It was the first time he had ever seen one.

"You have them in Shali?"

Ya'k-lum sidled up beside him, munching a piece of dried meat.

"No, I don't think so" Panin replied. "I can't believe I'm still on the isles. It's like I'm on the other side of the world."

"I guess it'd be the same for me" Ya'k thought. "I've never seen the sea. Never been on a boat. Or even a beach."

"Boats are overrated" Panin muttered.

"Huh."

They sat, sharing a bag of jerky.

It was the little things.

* * *

As luck would have it, a shipment of goods was due to depart for Keráan within the next week. However, by the grace of Yui's Angakkuq, the caravan was ordered to leave early in order to accommodate Nuv and his friends.

"Don't the red robes celebrate chaos and misfortune?" Panin quizzed, as he helped pack a crate of god-knows-what. "They seem bloody nice to me." He cast a sideways glance at his brother, who was hunched over some documents. "Nicer than any Numanta I've ever met…"

Puul ignored him. He was too busy reading up on the properties of some of the cargo, his white boots dangling over the end of the carriage.

Kwenn and the twins were strongly advised to bundle-up. Where they were going was going to be the stark opposite of the warm climes of Shali, and he could already feel it as the dawn approached.

His soft vest and cotton trousers did an admirable job so far, but as they would go further northward, he would need a lot more.

Thankfully, his boots were already made for this terrain. To think, the black and white footwear was given to him by Jugo simply because there was nothing else available at the time. He never bothered to switch them out during his travels, and was now mighty glad he didn't.

Under watchful constellations, the five of them were joined by a group of another eight on horseback, in addition to three pack yaks and three carriages each pulled by two draft horses.

The suns were beginning to creep over the east, when final preparations were earmarked by a blessing conducted by the Angakkuq and two other Sollikane. On top of the standard fare of wishing good tidings for the travellers, the ceremony was particularly directed toward Nuv, whose face and helm was smeared by the blood of a lamb.

Kwenn quietly blanched at the idea of killing such an innocent creature, but kept his thoughts private. This was their way, after all.

The stuff was quite potent, and he wondered how Nuv stood there with barely a change to his expression.

The Angakkuq moved toward Kwenn, and he gulped.

"Kwennsefulass. Am I saying that right?" he asked, as he marvelled at the sapphire that glinted from his sword.

"Yeah. I mean, yes" he answered.

"You really are the same as Ember Mind. Two of a kind. Two for each land. And perhaps, there are two more of you as well?"

"Perhaps."

"Do you aim to find them?"

Kwenn looked to Nuv, who shrugged. "I'm not sure. I think, if it is destiny, then we will come across them eventually. Like Nuv, I can't say who we truly are, or where we came from... but maybe we really *were* sent by the gods, on some mission."

The old man smiled, clearly very happy to hear those words.

As they said their goodbyes and made for the perilous, winding road, the Angakkuq said one last thing.

"Take care of each other. That's what family does."

* * *

It would take at least five days to reach the city, good conditions permitting.

Huddled within furs and crates, Kwenn carved himself out a nice little burrow within the bouncing transport.

Space was at a premium, so he was quite cramped with Ya'k and Puul, whilst Panin and Nuv rode outside on their own steeds, no doubt breaking bread with their new pals.

As far as he knew, Kwenn had never rode a horse in his life, and wasn't in the mood to learn in this environment. No, he would stay as a lump for the next week, eking out an existence by nibbling on foodstuffs and getting himself dirty as sparsely as possible, in order to save unnecessary bathing.

God I'm pathetic.

Perhaps it was the last traces of the hangover that was talking through him.

They had been on the road for a couple of hours already, and it had now become bright and crisp outside. White trees and boulders could be seen from his point of view as they receded around rocky bends, and curiously purple dirt splotched the thin, browned path they were rattling along on.

Unfamiliar calls blurted from the rocky overhangs, and little foxes zipped between bushes like barely noticeable smudges.

Though Ya'k has never been in this particular region, he regaled them with everything he knew about the Merca Lal Mountains.

Kwenn had only been half-listening, when his ears perked up at the description of the 'Meerajaff'.

"I think I heard that name somewhere before. Or maybe I read about it. What are they?"

"Very strong, very agile and very smart creatures. Aside from religion, they're the biggest export of the Four Sister Isles... well, kinda" Ya'k explained. "They're really hard to breed, and only the very wealthy can afford them. They're not replacing horses any time soon. They're bipedal creatures, and are supposed to be a mixture of reptile and mammal, from what I learned."

"They're supposed to be able to climb anything" Puul added, "even with a rider in tow. Their powerful legs can jump great distances, and their big claws can grip like a vice. We used to see them occasionally in Gen, when merchants bought them during the festivals. They look scary, but are actually pretty timid."

Kwenn shook his head. "Seriously?"

"Yeah. Remember that horse with horns you saw on your first night in Gen?"

Kwenn did. "The Grinoaga, was it?"

"Yep. They're really rare and expensive too. I heard that there's a bitter rivalry between Grinoaga and Meerajaff enthusiasts."

"Of course!" Ya'k jeered. "What else would rich people do? Solve hunger and war? Hah, that's child's play!"

"They come from here?" Kwenn asked.

"Meerajaffs? Yeah, but they're basically extinct in the wild now. You can only get them from two ranches in all of the entire isles" Puul revealed. "One on Shali, and one here on Arlmai."

"The one here is actually near Silver Lake, where Nuv was found" Ya'k added. "I heard it's huge."

Kwenn closed his eyes and leaned back. "Hm. Tell you what, when this is all over, we should all go visit. Promise?"

"Promise" Ya'k and Puul said in unison.

* * *

Being on a rugged trip such as this, the possibilities of danger were many.

Avalanches, storms, rock-slides, animal attacks, injury and illness…
they were all very real things. Highwaymen were also known to prowl
the mountains, though they were fortunately very rare occurrences in
such a frigid scape.

Indeed, the common consensus amongst all within the mountains
was that *choosing* to become a bandit in *this* type of place was
tantamount to a death sentence.

Waking up with a pain in his neck and mouth drooling, Kwenn
saw that it had gotten darker, and that the carriage had stopped.

The smell of smoke enticed him to crawl out of his nest, and stretch
with *pops* and *cracks* sounding from every one of his joints.

"Look who's up." Nuvummburtee met him, a bag in one hand and
a pile of branches tucked under the other. His helm was sat aside, and
his long dark hair was tied in a topknot.

"Sorry, I must've crashed…" Kwenn grumbled, not appreciating
Nuv's judgemental stare. "Anything I can do to help?"

He handed him the bag. "You can feed the horses if you like."

He did so, and observed the camp. They were set up on a clearing
a little ways from the road. They were now in a wide valley, and a
river slushed nearby before vanishing into a dark wood. The suns had
already gone down, though there was still a little light leftover, as it
bounded off large grey clouds.

It had gotten *a lot* colder.

His bare arms were covered in bumps by the time he had attached
the last feeding bag, and he hurried on over to the camp fires.

"So, where are we?" he asked, rubbing his hands.

"Between places" one of the guides – a bowman – answered. His
cadence was very calm and almost meditative, as he reclined and
tinkered with his bow.

A woman came up to Kwenn. She was short, but very lithe. All
wiry muscle and ink, she gave him a long, careful look. He actually
remembered her from the night before, and he recalled that she was
also a hunter. She had become *very* friendly with him when they shared

drinks, and even invited him on a hunt.

What was her name? Waz?

"You can't hold your drink" she finally chuckled. "Kwenn, was it? You've been out all day, poor cub."

Kwenn smiled nervously.

Waz laughed again, before slapping him on the arm. "Let's hope you wield that pretty blade a little better, eh?"

He had left it somewhere with his stuff. Should he have brought it? "We're expecting trouble?"

"Hah, you never know" she answered, giving him a drink.

Oh god...

"I just wanna see how good you are with it!" another man added, clinking his cup with Kwenn's. "Cheers brother."

Kwenn drank with them, and just as he had feared, it was the same stuff as last night.

It is nice though...

"I'm afraid I'll disappoint you there" he confessed, licking his lips. "I'm not very good. I've only used it a couple of times, and I've only had a few lessons from... friends."

Should he be ashamed of being taught by a young girl like Jeleenn?

"It's yours, isn't it?" Nuv said, as he entered the conversation with a hunk of bread and cheese. "Like the helm is mine. I'm sure there's some deep memory there that's waiting to be unlocked and turn you into a killing machine."

He said that so plainly.

Kwenn rejected Nuv's theory with a distasteful grimace. "Sure. Like how you spent hours learning the art of the *helmet.*"

This brought gasps and tittering from the crowd, and Kwenn realised he may have made a *big* mistake with such a smart ass comment.

Nuv was *much* tougher than that, of course. He took the joke on the chin, and even almost seemed proud that his brother finally showed a little backbone.

"Bloody hell, you're already killing *me,* you bastard" he laughed with a mouthful of food.

Kwenn often forgot; Nuv spent his 'life' amongst a rugged community of hunters and the devout. He was a lot more calloused than he was, and he speculated just how much an environment can mould a person in such a short time. They were both almost like children; their minds were wide open to absorbing the world around them, and those first few weeks of existence were the most crucial in creating an impression.

Are we actually children, I wonder? How old are we really?

That night, mirth, food and drink brought some warmth to the snowy country.

* * *

The next day, Kwenn was a little more at ease.

His hangover wasn't *quite* as bad as the previous one, and he recovered quick enough. There was no dawn farewell ceremony to interrupt him this time, so he managed to sleep a bit more comfortably.

On day two, he wanted to absorb the sights and sounds of the trip a bit more, and even forced himself to ride a steed for the first time.

Of course, it was a graceless affair at first, but he got used to it very quickly. He even got compliments about his natural proclivity in handling the mare, boosting his confidence a bit more.

I guess I do have some latent talent.

Riding with Panin and keeping the carriage drivers company, they traversed their way through a thick pass of glacial walls, and visited their first village at midday.

With flakes falling lazily, they did not want to spend too long at the stop-over, which was basically a few skin huts, a stone chapel and a gathering stall for excursions to relax, feast and resupply.

Some trade was undertaken by the caravan, whilst Kwenn and his friends expectedly drew stares and whispers from everyone who glimpsed them. They ate at the establishment regardless, and Kwenn grinned into his hot porridge, because now Panin and Puul were *also* unusual strangers in a strange land, just like he was in Gen.

They left within an hour, and to their relief the weather didn't get any heavier for the rest of the day.

But, when night came…

* * *

The hunters had taken on Kwenn as sort of a special project. Whether it was due to boredom or kindness, he didn't care. He was just thankful that they were willing to teach him a few more fighting manoeuvres and proper blade handling.

Sure, there was only so much he could get from a few hours worth of lessons, but it sure as hell was better than nothing, especially if he ever came across something like Hekor or Wilko again.

Sweating, he forgot all about the temperature, as his legs and arms ached from repetitive swings and disciplined footwork. Strikes from wooden sticks left his body stinging, and he was sure his back would bruise heavily from being slammed to the ground.

He kept his emotions in check, even as he got battered. He hadn't had an outburst in quite a while, and he was proud of himself for not having some sort of deep subconscious meltdown resulting from his past life.

Nuv, Panin and Ya'k were all roped in, and they all sparred with each other. It was needed, they all realised. They needed to toughen up. They needed to be ready, because things could go south *very* quickly. They were fighting a war, even if they weren't in the middle of the battlefield. Things far beyond their own power would be coming for them – and if not, then they would be heading for *it*.

They could not get soft.

Puul, of course, had skills elsewhere. Even at the urging of Panin that he should at least learn to defend himself, the Numanta declined, preferring instead to not waste the short time they had on himself.

It was a reasonable conclusion. The others had no magic nor healing abilities; their training took priority. Puul could learn fisticuffs later, if the need arose.

Well into the dark, they worked themselves until exhaustion. Even Ya'k-lum showed what he was made of; his gentle, almost pacifist personality hiding a true grit that impressed all.

When it was all over, they boiled water and scrubbed themselves clean.

It felt good. *They* felt good.

Aching, they all iced their joints and shared warm, tangy beetroot stew.

No spirits. Not tonight.

* * *

"Help! Help!!!"

Kwenn heard a voice. He was dreaming, right?

It was coming down hard. A blizzard had arrived out of nowhere, and everything was white.

There was yelling. It was real, and he was definitely awake.

The hell?

He felt like he hadn't gotten any rest whatsoever, and his body was as stiff as a board. Moaning in pain, he tried to shuffle outside.

"Help!"

"It's a woman!"

There was a commotion. It definitely had to have been past midnight, maybe early morning, yet somehow, they had a visitor.

With the wisps of torches and lamps in the flurry, Kwenn wrapped himself tight and headed toward the source.

"The hell is happening?" Panin yelled as he joined him.

"I dunno, I just woke" Kwenn answered.

The horses were bucking wildly. Frantic, they had to be held down.

"Help, damn it!"

Kwenn and Panin quickly followed orders, and it was a lot more intimidating than he thought, trying to calm such a huge, muscular creature – even with another person in toe.

"Help! Can you help us?"

It indeed was a woman. *And* a man.

Two people, coming from nowhere in the middle of this whiteout. Both were not natives, with incredibly pale skin that was almost indiscernible. They were very tall, and had strange, aquamarine hair that waved almost against the wind.

The woman had a lantern of her own, though it was completely dead.

"Who goes there?" asked one of the hunters, notching an arrow.

"Please, don't shoot!" the woman pleaded. "It's just me and my husband!"

"We're… we're in trouble!" the man spoke, standing in front of his wife. "Our cart is destroyed… our horses are dead. Gone. Everything is gone…"

Puul, ever the Numanta, stood in front of everyone, offering help.

"White robe!" another hunter reprimanded. "Get back here, they could be bandits!"

"Do they *look* like bandits?" Puul fussed. Now that they came within feet of them, it was obvious they were unarmed, and they did indeed look half-starved and frantic.

The wife had a long dress that was completely unsuitable for the environment, and her boots almost seemed too large for her. The husband was barely any better, with a pale blue suit that seemed to belong to a fancy dress ball, and creamy, pointed shoes that strangely had not an ounce of dirt nor snow on them.

"Are you hurt?" Puul pressed.

"We… we're not. At least, seriously" the man replied. "It's a miracle. By god, a miracle!"

"What happened?" the female hunter demanded. "Did you have an accident?"

"No… no, worse" the woman trembled. It was clear she had been crying a lot. "We're… we're being hunted!"

* * *

Things certainly got complicated, *very* quickly.

Camp had been packed promptly, and it was decided they would travel early.

Fortunately, the valley was relatively wide, without any bottomless cliffs nor risks of landslides.

Avalanches were always a possibility, but according to the Merca Lal people, this wasn't the worst storm they had endured. Nevertheless, it was certainly a rough one – enough for a luckless person or two to get lost forever in.

But the two new arrivals were *very* lucky.

Well, depending on one's view, of course. Because from what they had imparted, 'lucky' was the *last* thing they could be described as, Kwenn decided.

The man was called Lunae, and the woman was Doer. After being looked over by Puul, they had ravenously consumed the food and drink without much in the way of etiquette, before shivering in their furs.

They did not shiver from the cold.

Because of his lack of equine expertise, the others didn't want to baby-sit Kwenn as they trudged through the ill weather, so he was shoved back into the carriage. Along with Puul and the leader of the hunters (a scarred, grim-looking man named Ruyik) they questioned the new arrivals.

They certainly looked strange, but then again, they definitely weren't the first eccentrically-attired people he had met.

Sterlio still takes the cake.

"Were there others with you?" Ruyik questioned, his frame blocking the opening of the carriage. He was squatting, with his hands gripping the roof. He was very wary, almost on a state of alert.

Kwenn couldn't help but feel the same. A sense of anxiety pattered gently against his sternum. Was it the storm? Was it this couple? Maybe it was what they would say next…

"No" Lunae replied, his pale face looking ghostly in the dim light of the lamp. "Just myself and my wife. We were going… somewhere… before it struck. It had been on top of us for days, and we just couldn't *shake it*!"

"Shake *what*?"

They both became quiet, clearly reluctant to give any more details.

"A mountain lion?" Ruyik pressed. "A boar? A man? Spill it!"

Puul lifted a hand, wordlessly asking for the hunter to be a bit more patient.

"A monster" Doer finally whispered through her thin blue lips. "A *monster*! It won't leave us be! It gutted our beautiful horses! Overturned our cart! It's been *toying* with us!!!"

She became frantic, and Lunae embraced her. He whispered something in her ear, and the words almost seemed to relax every muscle in her body as she smiled and slumped.

They're mad with fear.

Ruyik spat in anger, and Puul asked him of any animals that may fit with what the couple were describing.

"Nothing like that" the hunter mused. "Unless it was a particularly monstrous boar or lion, like I said. They're the biggest predators in these mountains… aside from, like I said, some deranged lunatic of a man."

"The animals… they were acting scared" Kwenn said, suddenly remembering the panicked horses. "You don't think…"

"I am. I'm thinking it right now" Ruyik growled. "It's definitely not the blizzard, that's for certain."

He squinted at them. "Did you see it?" he asked, clearly trying to steady his tone.

Lunae and Doer looked into each others' eyes.

They did not reply.

* * *

The suns were up, but they did little to relieve the foreboding tension.

It felt eerily quiet, even as the storm continued.

Progress had ground to a crawl, and everyone was on high alert. If what the spouses said was true, then they were in trouble.

But from what? If not for the behaviour of the beasts, Kwenn would've dismissed their mad ravings. Or, if they had in fact been attacked by something, then it would've been long gone by now.

If it was as horrifying as they had described, then how did they escape it?

Maybe it was toying with them, like a cat with a mouse?

That then circled back to his original question: *what* was *it*?

Something definitely wasn't right here, and everyone he spoke to echoed the same sentiments.

The anxiety had almost become fear. Everyone was antsy; twitching in their seats and snapping at each other, as they passed through a narrow pass.

Things only become worse when the hunters could not recognise their surroundings, despite being on this road countless times.

Once they had time to calm and readjust their minds, Lunae and Doer became a little more receptive to their hosts. They showed their gratitude by giving some details of their background; despite their clothing, they claimed to have been born and raised in Arlmai, and spent a good portion of their lives within the Merca Lal Mountains.

They had been on their way southward to visit friends and 'see some sights', but when asked about their hometown, they refused to elaborate, for fear of being 'spied' on by their stalker.

They were definitely not completely recovered. What the hell had they been through?

"The only thing we recovered was this lantern" Doer lamented, sniffing as she raised the ornate housing for Kwenn to see. It kind of looked as though it was made with horn and shell, and a black oily wick stood within.

Kwenn must have been hallucinating, because the candle looked brand new.

There was yelling outside, and he snapped out of it.

Again? Now what?

Nuv climbed into the cart. "Stuff's getting weird out here" he relayed. "We're stopping for a bit, so the guys can reorient themselves."

* * *

Nuv didn't know what to do.

He was frustrated. He couldn't take charge. This wasn't his neck of the woods, and he hated being left in the hands of people who seemed equally lost.

How? All they had to do was follow a damned road. How was that so complicated?

No, something was definitely up.

They were in some place that looked almost like an icy tunnel. The sky was covered in roiling mist, and snow still fell, but it still felt like they were *enclosed* in some way.

A 'killing corridor' as Ya'k had put it.

Lovely.

He worried. About himself and everyone.

He and the hunters agreed.

They were being followed.

But by what? Both he and Ya'k felt almost like they had back during their traversal of the mountain to Saumen, when something huge had passed right over them.

Both of them had their hairs standing upright, and the bickering amongst the camp didn't help at all.

Those two, Luanae and Doer. He didn't know what to think of

them. It was obvious that they were highly traumatised, but something didn't sit right. After notifying Kwenn about the break, he caught them staring at his helm.

They were practically drooling, and all he could think to do was quickly excuse himself.

But… they were right. Something *was* pursuing them.

He thought about this as he went to boil some water, and caught the tail-end of an argument between two of the men. He heard the mention of 'monster', and they were furiously talking in hushed tones.

"What is going on?" he asked with impatience. "Do you have an idea of where we are?"

Ruyik stood between them and shushed. "Idiots" he scolded. "Don't listen to them."

"Listen to what?"

"Mountain folklore" the grizzled man snorted.

"They're talking about beast men" Puul popped in.

"Beast… men?" Nuv had to make sure he heard right. "Wait… you mean, like the yeti?"

He had heard old tales of the creature back in Jhasé, mostly from a couple of the elders who swore up and down that it was real. It was never outright dismissed as a fantasy, but very few put serious stock within its existence.

"Yeti?" the mage queried.

"It's nothing!" Ryuik clapped.

"So, what do you suggest is following us? And *cornering* us?" one of the other men challenged. "Look where we are! An enchantment has made us lose our way!"

"It's not a god damned yeti!"

"Well, whatever it is" Nuv said sternly, "we can't lose our wits. The beasts are hungry and thirsty. Let's take care of them, and then we can figure this out."

Everyone seemed to agree, and he breathed a sigh of relief.

"All of you, just keep your eyes open" Ryuik sighed.

* * *

Kwenn was sore. His legs ached, and he made a meagre attempt at stretching them out.

Walking around with Lunae and Doer, he tried to make them feel a bit more welcome, but they were clearly not feeling it.

"They're blaming us, aren't they?" Doer asked, as she looked in concern toward the thickening blanket of snow.

"They're scared" Panin flatly stated. "We all are... I hate to say it, but whatever did this to you, isn't giving up so easily."

"You said you knew these mountains too" Kwenn remembered. "Do you recognise where we are?"

They both looked, almost as if they had to make sure that their eyes would not mistake the glittering concave walls that seemed to stretch for an eternity without bend nor break. Lunae shook. "I cannot say. *We* cannot say..."

"I reckon we should turn back" Panin voiced. "The hunter girl., Waz, she was saying it as well. Ya'k agrees."

Before Kwenn could add his own opinion, a mighty roar erupted from behind them. Somehow both human and *not*, it filled the air with a hot terror and smell of rotting meat. Kwenn's knees buckled under the terror, as did Panin, Lunae and Doer.

After seconds of paralysing quiet, screams and curses soon followed after.

Everything was in tumult, as the animals heaved and strained their harnesses in a maddened desire to flee, as both bows were notched and blades hissed from their scabbards.

Lunae and Doer wailed.

"It's here! It's found us!!!"

"Pack it all up, now!" Ryuik bellowed, almost as loud as that of the beast itself.

In an instant, the delivery retinue had become a military operation, and without a full awareness, Kwenn began to take orders from mouths that he could not hear. His body moved of its own accord, as he helped the married couple back into the carriage, vaguely aware that he had promised to protect them.

* * *

Wherever they were, they had exited the natural tunnel after what seemed like days.

It was dark when they emerged onto a flat, featureless tundra. There were no stars, and only a single, pearly white moon was visible.

Like ants crossing a lake of salt, they rode on and on and on.

Doer's lantern was alight. It swayed side-to-side; its pale flame almost draining the colour of everything it touched.

"We're somewhere where we shouldn't be."

That observation was repeated by everyone, at some point during the trek.

No-one could say where they were. No galaxies guided them. The Great Ring was invisible. And not even the identity of the moon could be guessed at.

Some said it was Lotup, the rarest of them all.

But Lotup wasn't white.

None of them were.

The swaying of her lamp… it reminded Kwenn of the ocean waves, back in Gen.

The ocean… they had to hit it sometime, right? They were on an *island* – they couldn't go on forever.

Or maybe we could…

Songs were murmured throughout the night.

Whatever the monster was, it had ample opportunity to attack.

They had nowhere to run.

Nowhere to hide.

* * *

"I was thinking" Ya'k-lum whispered. "About another legend. Of the mountains…"

He had leaned over to Nuv, as they both brought up the rear of the company.

He whipped his head around, almost afraid that the wind itself had ears.

"What?" Nuv asked, tired and miffed.

"You know the scary one? Of Moon Man and Sea Woman?"

Nuv's brain was running on empty, and he had to strain hard to think.

He remembered. "The one where those two…?"

He stopped, and darted his gaze to the cart where Luane and Doer were sleeping.

"Oh, get off it Ya'k" Nuvummburtee spat. "Those poor people have been through enough without you making up stories. In case you haven't heard, a *real* thing is hunting us. You've heard it too."

"The yeti."

"Yeah, sure, we'll call it that."

"Something's going to happen, Nuv" Ya'k said, his voice suddenly harder. "We can ride all we want but you and I both know we're wasting time. Let's not beat around the bush. It has us, and it's only a matter of time before it strikes. Either that, or we die out here in this cursed land."

Nuv didn't speak.

"I mean *literally* cursed" Ya'k emphasised.

"What do you want *me* to do?"

"We turn and we fight."

Nuv was genuinely shocked. "That's awfully brave of you. And stupid."

"What's the alternative?! Wander? Flee like rats, as it wants us to do? Until we run out of food or run out of sanity?"

Ya'k leaned away, clearly angry. "We're trapped, Nuv."

He rode off, leaving him to contemplate his friend's advice.

Nuv swore.

* * *

This night would not end.

Even Kwenn could tell it was well and truly due for sunrise.

The ocean waves pounded in his ears. He did not take his eyes off the lantern.

The candle petered out.

Lunae and Doer held hands.

* * *

Waz lay dead in her saddle.

Her horse was in a trance, before snapping out it and bucking with madness, launching her body onto the snow.

No, it was salt now.

Puul bounded over to her, and checked her vitals. The animal whinnied and squealed, nearly trampling them both.

It was calmed by the hunters, who all knew that the steeds and pack animals were close to complete mental and physical exhaustion.

"What's happened?!" Ryuik bellowed.

After a prolonged attempt at resuscitation, the Numanta shook his head and drew a short glyph in the air.

"She's... dead" he declared with a chill. "I... don't see any wounds. It almost looks like she was asphyxiated..."

"From *what*?!"

Panin rounded on the hunter, telling him to give his brother some space to work.

With clenched fists, the distressed captain didn't back away, but neither did he move another step.

Puul placed a hand over his mouth, and Panin knew that was a sign of frustration.

"I can't tell" the magi said.

Shouting vile obscenities, Ryuik sidestepped Panin, and marched to where Lunae and Doer were located.

"Hey, what're you doing?" the guardsman shouted, following him.

Before they knew it, the twins were met with arrows, all pointed at them.

"What the hell?!"

Slapping the curtains aside, Ryuik drew his sword and pointed.

"All of you! Out! NOW!!!"

Nuv and Ya'k dismounted, demanding what the man was doing.

The husband and wife emerged, terror in their eyes.

Kwenn was nowhere to be seen.

"I want answers, *now*" Ryuik hissed. "Either this is all happening because of you..." he then turned, and pointed his blade at Nuv's chest. "Or this is happening because of *you*."

"You're mad!" Lunae said. "My wife and I have been most gracious and hospitable!"

Nuv picked up on those weird words, but was nevertheless busy trying not to get him and his friends killed.

He raised his hands, determined to not to escalate things. "You seriously think we're responsible for this? For summoning a devil to come kill us all in its magical hellscape?"

"Give me one good reason to not leave you all here to rot" Ryuik snarled. "One of my best daughters has just died. We're lost, in a land where we all know like the backs of our hands. Chased by something. *After* we picked up two frilly castaways, and a group of men with strange relics and even stranger stories! *None* of this has been right from the start, no matter *what* the Angakkuq said!!!"

He pressed the tip of the weapon into Nuv. "So tell me again, how this *isn't your fault!*"

Nuvummburtee was mad now. The words meant nothing to him,

but as soon as he felt the pressure of the sword sink into him, rage thawed his soul and set it aflame.

He couldn't do anything, though. He would be dead as soon as he tried something.

"Look" he began, keeping his voice calm, "you're right, Ryuik. We're under attack. You know it and I know it. But killing each other isn't going to help… and I'm starting to think Ya'k might be right, too."

"Right about what?" Ryuik glowered.

Nuv looked to his friend, who gave a slight tilt of his chin as a wordless acceptance of an apology.

"We have to stop, Ryuik. We have to stop and fight."

The hunter lowered his blade, arm shaking from fury, grief, fear and cold.

"You can't *fight* it!" Doer laughed, her lantern's light now swaying as if caught in a storm.

"We'll… we'll sure as hell try" Ryuik communicated, both to the woman and to his crew, who all understood the order.

Nuv breathed slightly easier as they lowered their bows and got to work in making preparations.

There would be time to mourn later. Either that, or that would all join Waz in the afterlife.

"You don't know what you're getting into" Lunae advised, his sunken face looking almost as gaunt as that of the bonemeal land that stretched forever around them.

"Maybe not" Ya'k answered. "But it beats exhaustion, starvation and prolonged insanity."

The roar of the beast was cast back at them, almost in agreement.

It was coming.

"What do you know of those things?" Doer laughed again. "You know nothing, Ya'k-lum, besides your words and your little fantasies!"

"Ouch. Maybe not, but I'm always open to new experiences."

"Are you?"

"Now dear" Lunae put his hand on his wife's shoulder. "Stop this.

They want to fight. We can't stop them. They'll all stop breathing, one way or another."

* * *

The waves ate away at his stone.

He was crumbling.

Oviinia… where are you?

Lamun? *This* is what you were?

He was drowning.

If he went too low… he drowned.

If he went too high… he drowned.

The pale moon. So pretty. So sad. So lonely.

It washed the water. However it wanted. That was its only joy.

Chewing and swallowing. That's what they did. That's what they *all* did.

We were nothing. The don't matters.

He could not be an individual. He was nothing.

A toy.

Rotten. Eyeless.

The waves took him.

CHAPTER XVIII

Kwenn leaped from the carriage.

Imbued with an azure force, he swung his sword at Nuv, who barely got out of the way in time.

His eyes were not his own. Glazed like that of a dead fish, he snarled and jumped, slicing downward and hitting the sour sand with a powerful blow.

His blade was glowing. What would have otherwise been a missed strike caused a cloud of saline to shoot like a jet, blinding Nuv and creating a coughing, hacking bewilderment by Ya'k

"Kwenn!" Nuv yelled, his spitting mouth shrivelling. "What are you doing?! Stop!"

He did not answer. Did not even blink away the crystals that lodged themselves within his eyes.

He attacked again.

Nuv was ready this time. Slipping his ulus from his belt, he deflected the whistling metal, and could immediately tell that there was a far greater strength in him than when they had sparred.

This was something else. Something anomalous.

The knife flew from Nuv's pained wrist, and it twirled before landing at Panin's feet, who was the first to notice the commotion.

"What the *hell* is going on now?!" he howled.

"We can't breathe" Kwenn mumbled. "Nuv. We're not supposed to breathe."

Ya'k jumped on his back, and tried to pull him down.

Once more, the animals went wild. Much more frenetic than they had been before, they foamed at the mouth and their eyes bulged as they screamed.

Kwenn got a handful of Ya'k's ginger hair from behind, and tried to rip the smaller man off his shoulders. With his other hand, he tried to adjust his sword so that he could stab him in his side.

Nuv tackled him before he could, and all three of them fell into the sharp powder.

"Ember Mind" Lunae said, bending over casually. "Is something the matter?"

Nuv was too bewildered and laboured to answer, and as Panin quickly approached, spear in hand, Doer stood in front of him.

Her lantern's light was now dim. She smiled.

"What the? Out of the way!"

Doer shrugged. Her hair was now the same colour as Kwenn's sword.

She then kicked off her boots, sending them soaring.

Panin gasped in horror, as hooves presented themselves for his viewing pleasure instead of bare human feet.

He readied his spear toward her.

"What... what the hell are you doing? Where are your *toes*?"

Her boots landed with a boom, followed by another roar.

"He's coming" she grimaced. "We need to wrap this up."

The light went out, and a choking sound rang out from behind.

It was Puul.

Without thinking, he turned around.

"Puul!"

The Numanta was on the ground. Thrashing and gasping, he clawed at his neck and kicked up salt with his quivering boots.

"What the hell are you... *you're* doing this!!!" Nuv wheezed, trying to pin Kwenn down. He looked up at Lunae, who still looked down upon them all with delight. His hair too was also alight. It was clearly too much to be a coincidence.

"What... did you *do* to him?"

Lunae grinned.

Nuvummburtee raged at the smirk, before telling Ya'k to get off and tie Kwenn down with something.

"I've got him! Go!"

At first, Lunae didn't move nor try to stop him, but as he got to work bounding to and from the carriage amidst the rapture with a rope, the man circled around them, as Nuv held his brother in a headlock whilst Ya'k bound his feet and wrists.

"Good show!" he proclaimed, as they lay there panting, "but can you save the poor magi?"

"*What?!*"

Luane indicated to Panin, who was hunched over Puul in a panic. They were dangerously close to being trampled.

"The hell are you doing to him?!" Panin yelled to Doer, who was now mimicking the animals' stomping. "Stop this!!!"

Nuv was in disbelief. Springing to his feet, he grabbed the man by the throat, and pinned him against the carriage.

"*You*" he snarled, squeezing his grip. "*You're* doing this! Stop, now, or I'll break your damned neck!"

His own helmet now came alive too. The ruby red jewel burst with a crimson luminescence, and this made Lunae smile even wider.

"*Ember Mind*! It's true! Oh, Qual-nu!"

"Shut up!"

Nuv squeezed as hard as he could, but it didn't seem to do anything. The red light only made his emaciated face even more detestable, as his thin lips could barely contain his teeth.

"Nuv!" Ya'k called, still straddling a berserk Kwenn. "Oh hell... oh hell... oh *shit*... Nuv! *LOOK!!!*"

Nuv tossed Lunae down and pressed his boot on his neck. He looked to where Ya'k was focusing his terror.

Now he lost his breath.

Oh. God damn it.

A *massive* shadow was coming towards them.

It's the beast. It's coming for us.

Lunae screamed; a genuinely terrifying yelp that shook Nuv's legs.

He grabbed him again by the neck, and pulled him up.

"Let Puul go, and you won't get fed to our new friend!"

Lunae laughed, and Nuv struck him with a mighty fist.

"God damn lunatic!"

Some of the animals had broken free and were now fleeing.

Everything was falling apart.

Doer, realising that the monster was upon them as well as the assault on her husband, got on all fours and galloped like a gazelle.

Ryuik saw this, swore again, and fired an arrow at her, which bounced harmlessly off of her. "I knew it! I knew we shouldn't have picked them up! Moon Man and Sea Woman! *Moon Man and Sea Woman!!!*"

"*I* knew it!" Ya'k shouted.

"Not *now!*" Nuv barked back.

There was something off about the couple from the beginning. Ryuik suspected it, and Nuv should've listened. They *all* should've listened.

Did they do this? *All* of this?

The monster approached them, and Nuvummburtee at least realised *one* thing.

They were going to die.

Not like this… no, not on my knees. I'm going down with blood in my mouth and a scalp in my hand!

Nuv yelled a guttural hunting cry. With a knife in one hand and his Fire Helm blazing like Sollik itself, his blood was like a frothing torrent that pumped within him.

The monster approached, and finally – *finally* – Nuv knew what he was dealing with. What was chasing them. All this time.

It was a giant.

Standing about eight or nine feet tall, it was a hairy, man-like being.

God damn it Ya'k. I have to die knowing you were right twice in a row.

It was a yeti. *The* yeti. It *had* to be.

It was a living, breathing giant. Its smoky fur did little to obfuscate its muscles, and its face was more human than beast. Its blackened skin reminded him of frostbitten corpses, and its beard looked… looked…

Familiar?

Nuv was beyond fear. He couldn't even find the energy to fall and beg for mercy. It was a feeling that eclipsed all other emotions; a moment of transcendence that must have come for people shortly before their deaths.

Doer and Lunae huddled together; shaking like scared children.

The yeti did not move to attack Nuv. It slowly turned its head toward the couple.

"You can't do this!" Lunae whimpered. "They're *ours!*"

"We… we worked so hard!" Doer said, kicking her cloven hoofs like a child throwing a tantrum.

The yeti then looked down at Nuvummburtee, and Nuv was stunned. The intelligence behind its eyes was nothing like that of an animal. He was stupefied, and it caused him to fall to his backside.

"Nuv!" Ya'k called, his voice tight and hoarse.

It then observed the camp. The wild stock and the thrashing Numanta.

Again, it then looked to Lunae and Doer.

It began to move toward them.

"You bastard!" Doer screamed.

The yeti lunged at them, and grabbed them both in each giant hand.

"*Bastard!!!*" she shrieked again.

The yeti bit her head off.

A fountain of dull red gushed toward the moon, swirling and filling the orb like a vessel.

Nuv and Ya'k sat, their mouths hanging open as the moon became a sun. Sollik, to be exact, and the void around it lightened into a soft blue.

The yeti tossed Doer's body onto the ground, and it sank like a stone, vanishing without a trace.

Lunae chuckled.

"Until next time, then."

He was then met with the same fate, only this time *his* blood stained the salt pink. The gushing was endless, and soon the entire ground from horizon to horizon was unrecognisable. The salt vapours drifted into the air, encircling the space next to Sollik and forming the sun Solenir.

Everything was normal again.

Lunae's headless corpse ascended upward, following the vapour trails before dissolving.

A quiet came over the camp. The animals finally began to calm down, and Puul gulped in a giant amount of air. His lungs nearly popped, as whatever curse that had overcame him was now lifted.

Kwenn stopped writhing.

Everyone was in a state of stupefaction. Their minds had become an insensibleness; like a chicken placed on its back and made to stare into the clouds.

Soaked in the gizzards of its victims, the yeti's steamy breath was rank as it finally shuffled over to Doer's lamp.

It stood on it, crushing it into oblivion.

＊ ＊ ＊

Kwenn was hot.

Really, really hot.

Despite being face-down on a pillow of frost, his face was flushed and stinging, like he had been cutting himself shaving.

I can't move...

His shoulders and wrists ached, and he knew he was bound.

Again...

Nothing was wrong with his ears though. The sounds of pounding waves slowly receded, replaced with loud voices. Some of them sounded on the edge of sanity; warbling throats and cracked tones vibrated around him.

It all became much clearer when he was suddenly pulled up to his knees.

The suns blinded him, and he swallowed and groaned at once; producing a ludicrous sound.

"You okay?"

It was Ya'k-lum.

"I... I think?" Kwenn replied.

His head *really* hurt now, especially when he tried to move his eyes.

"No more insanity?"

Kwenn had no idea what he was talking about.

He tried recalling his last memory, but was completely frozen by the scene that played out in front of him.

There was Nuvummburtee, also kneeling down. Surrounding him were Panin, Ryuik and the hunters.

Were they protecting him? Their weapons were drawn, and they were all pointed toward a figure.

A beast. A massive, mannish thing covered in hair and blood.

"No more insanity?" Ya'k said again.

Kwenn was shot to pieces.

"What? Insanity? No? I guess? What is going on Ya'k?"

He felt the binds on his wrists loosen.

"Good enough" Ya'k decided. "We're gonna need your help man. Like, *a lot* of help. I hope you have some of that power left in the tank."

Kwenn couldn't tear his sight from the dramatic confrontation.

"Wh… what? *What is that thing?*"

Not answering, Ya'k's blurred form ran past Kwenn in order to stand with the others and fight.

The monster didn't seem to move.

"Stay back!" he heard Ryuik warn.

Kwenn looked for his sword, and breathed a sigh when he touched the half-buried, wet hilt.

Here we go again…

He tried rising to his feet. It was incredibly hard, and took far longer than it should have. His muscles burst, and he instantly knew that he would be utterly incapable of defending himself.

Whatever power his blade possessed, it was now running on empty.

In the end though, it was all for nought.

The beast man receded.

Literally.

Kwenn was convinced that an injury to his brain had made him hallucinate.

But no. He watched it all.

As clear as day, the hairy figure slowly shrank.

Not into the distance. Not retreating.

But rather, its body began to morph.

Its limbs became smoother and skinnier. Its mass of bulk withered and became nothing more than skin stretched over bone.

Its head, much more recognisable.

It had become a human.

Everyone gasped, as an old man now stood before them.

Slightly stooped, his black skin and bloodshot eyes made him look like something that had emerged from a cave. His massive beard was wrapped around his form, doubling as a rudimentary set of protective 'clothing'.

With blood still sodden around his mouth, he smiled and bowed humbly.

Kwenn heard Nuv wheeze a word.

"Saumen?!"

* * *

The animals were serene.

All this time, they had not been terrified of what was following them.

They had been terrified of what was already *with* them.

Moon Man and Sea Woman. Ancient beings that were a part of Merca Lal legends for generations, they were said to have lured unwitting travellers to their doom.

Depending on who told the tale, they were either an allegory for the perils of the mountains… or very real spectres that intentionally left some traumatised survivors to spread the tale of their misdeeds.

Kwenn and his friends had learned that they were very, very real, and now someone was dead because of them.

There may have been another victim, if it had not been for another mythical creature.

The yeti.

Otherwise known as Saumen.

He had saved them all from the couple's enchantment; particularly Puul, who came perilously close to being the second person to perish.

As he slowly recovered, the camp slowly regained a slim veneer of uniformity as they got their bearings, whilst mourning the loss of Waz, and a couple of the horses who vanished when they ran off.

The old man, in his cracked, wispy voice, made it clear that he had not meant any of them any harm. In fact, he *had* been chasing them all this time, but for a completely different reason.

It turned out, Saumen had been following them for quite a long while even before they had encountered Lunae and Doer; ever since Nuvummburtee and Ya'k-lum had ventured from Jhasé, in fact.

More precisely, it was when the two had entered his domain, and he had explained to them their role in the upcoming events that would unfold, as well as showing them the way through the Jagged Form of Deshalmanik.

He was protecting them.

Not just for their benefit – but for Qual-nu.

For Remana tol Dwen.

"I am sorry" he rasped, now bowed so low his face was buried within his smoky facial hair. "I couldn't be here sooner. They had kept me at bay, and I tried hard to break through… too late for the poor girl."

Ryuik had wrapped Waz's body, and now carried it to a place where it would be devoured by wolves.

As was their way.

"I think" Saumen continued, "it was when they decided to manipulate the Shali boy, that their guard was down."

His red eyes looked toward Kwenn, who still reeled from everything. The last thing he could clearly recall was being within the caravan with Lunae and Doer, talking with them and trying to stay warm.

Saumen pointed a crooked finger at Kwenn's blade. "They tried taking *that* into their own hands. Big mistake. Big mistake."

Kwenn tried not to look at the browning blood that plastered the abominable snowman's lips.

Big mistake? I'll say…

He would be told later of the bloodthirsty details, but for now, they had to figure out where they *were* exactly.

The hunters tried to ascertain their location, but there was no need, as Saumen knew exactly where they were.

"*The Mortal's Path*" he revealed. "It's where they always go, in the end, back to their own realm."

"Wait, so we're *north* of Keráan?!" Ya'k exclaimed in shock and dismay. "How did we go so *far*?"

Kwenn had seen a map of Arlmai. 'The Mortal's Path' had indeed been printed in the upper stretches of the parchment; a long strip of plain land that reached the northern reaches of the island.

Now that he was supposedly here, he could see why. They were surrounded by an utterly lifeless landscape; where swirls of dirtied snow mixed with ashen ground, and strange rock formations known as 'fulgurite' loomed like nightmarish timekeepers.

It reminded him very much of Deshalmanik; but here, he felt a tightness in his body that made him almost shake with anxiety.

Maybe it was an after-effect from his possession, but he really couldn't stand this place.

"What is the Mortal's Path?" Panin asked on behalf of his brother, who still couldn't speak.

"An evil place" Ryuik whispered, lowering Waz's shrouded form onto the flattest stone he could find. "But still a land of Qual-nu... a land where Waz's spirit will indeed become strong. Stronger than any of us will ever be..."

He turned to Saumen.

"Great yeti... please, can you bless her? It would be an honour for her and all of us. To have one of God's eldest help her through the next realm?"

The ancient one bowed, and his beard began to spark. Smoke started to puff out of his hair, and his large, fearsome eyes displayed a compassion that went beyond that of a short-lived mortal.

"It would be *my* honour."

* * *

It was their first time witnessing a Sollikane funeral.

Or did Saumen predate the Sollikane? Were his rites some sort of paganistic progenitor to what would eventually become the religion of the red robes?

Was he really *that* old? Like Master Lojón?

Either way, it was different. And powerful.

Kwenn remembered the ceremony held for Fultyne, the late mayor of Henra. How the sky rained heavily, and how sad he was, despite only knowing the man for a short time.

It was the same here. He never knew Waz too well, but she was beyond kind to him and his friends. A soul that relished the companionship of others, even if they were totally different from her in every way.

Kwenn knew she didn't deserve this… but the followers of Qual-nu begged to differ.

It was the little things. The ways their views on life and death deviated, which brought an eye-opening contrast to something like the Numanta or the Pisistrati'e.

He got a glimpse of it when they were blessed by the village elder, and he's seeing it here now.

Is this what Nuv and Ya'k lived for? Was this *their way of life?*

With the metallic stench of blood in the air, the hunters saw this event as a divine sanction for Waz's soul. By the grace of heaven, both the Ember Mind and Saumen were here for her, which could have only meant that her next life would be something incredible.

Partaking in a hallucinogenic concoction with the others, Kwenn wasn't sure what was real and what was the result of his furtive, frenzied imagination.

Did Saumen *really* dismember her body, and consume her heart?

He would never know.

* * *

He awoke in the early morning.

Beside him within the carriage was Puul, who dozed.

Saumen was huddled up near him, looking at the magi.

"Ah, you're up. Quicker than I thought. Your body isn't used to our ways."

Kwenn could tell his breath smelled bad. He scratched at his face, and flakes of dried blood fell like the snow outside.

"Do not worry. All is well, hm. You just need a clean, I reckon.

We'll be in the city by sunset, I wager."

"What happened? There was the service for Waz and—

"Best not dwell on it" Saumen smiled. "It is over now. We are moving on."

Kwenn looked at Puul. "How is he?"

"He will be fine. It may take a few days for his voice to come back properly, but he is otherwise strong. I've always found the white robes so curious... you'd think with their fascination with the old ones, they would be a little more god-fearing. Alas, curiosity and cats, you know?"

Kwenn didn't. At all. But he nodded nonetheless.

"Though I can't help being a tad curious myself" he continued, before pausing to chew on something. "About what happens next."

Kwenn looked for his skin, and was relieved to find some water still within it. Strangely, whatever he partook in the night prior left him with no splitting headache this time. Only a soft numbness that slowly vanished as he moved his arms and legs.

"What do you mean?" he asked, after consuming the last drop.

"What those two – Moon Man and Sea Woman – what they did was a lot more brazen than usual. They seemed to know who you and Nuv really were. They played with fire, and rather gleefully at that."

"Wait, you've run into them before?"

Saumen swallowed loudly. "Many times. I try to keep them in check. But I can only do so much."

"Oh. Well, you seemed to take care of them pretty definitively, from what I was told."

The old man grinned, baring his yellowed teeth that almost fell off his gums. "If only it were that simple. But... I need to know. What is bringing about these changes? First Remana... and now the Ember Mind. Not to mention you, of course. I am scared, Kwennsefulass. Scared for you, and for my home."

Kwenn scratched his face again. "You sound like Lojón, Saumen. Have you met?"

"Once or twice. And he's right, my lad. And if *he's* right about something, then it's time to worry."

"You know? About Joner?"

Saumen bowed his head. He looked to Puul once more, and almost seemed to lament the dramas of the young and reckless. "Yes, more or less. I thought staying out of sight... out of mind, would be the best thing. I thought it wasn't my place to meddle in the affairs of those greater than mine... but now, I realise different. Yes, I think I do. I wanted to guide you boys, at least until you were out of my reach, but now Qual-nu has made it very clear."

Kwenn became slightly nervous.

"What's clear?"

* * *

The city of Keráan.

The crown jewel of Arlmai, and the holy centre of the Sollikane.

Casting its shadow far and wide over the Merca lal Mountains, its stone walls of schist created mighty etchings of 'charact'ry' that were seen as the literal words of Qual-nu.

Its unique dragon blood trees created an impenetrable wall that kept out all blasphemers and the profane, whilst its citizens occupied three layers of 'plates' that were stacked in an askew way.

The lower plate housed the common artisans and workers who formed the foundation of the city. The middle plate was home to the magi schools, training grounds and temples. The highest level was reserved for the Council of the Sollikane; the elite magi who oversaw the worldly affairs of their faith.

These levels were connected by a gigantic public elevator system that ran at regular intervals, whilst geothermal energy harnessed from deep below provided power to the entire structure, and red fire lit even the darkest of streets that were permanently left in shadow, unable to catch their own sunlight.

South-west along the Mortal Path they went in silence, until the lights of the great structure finally came into view during the late afternoon.

Winding its way through narrow gorges barely lit by chasms of scoria, the caravan entered a lowland peppered with the dragon bloods; with their wide crowns that were apparently harvested for their red sap.

They became more and more plentiful as they went along the bumpy road, and soon a forest surrounded them.

Finally, as twilight dimmed the sky, they came across people.

Real, genuine people.

A patrol of city crimson guardsmen, they were taken aback by the sudden appearance of the caravan coming in from the north.

Ryuik spoke with them in quiet, and after a brief inspection (and a few raised eyebrows toward some of the travellers), they were allowed to continue on toward the checkpoint just outside the city walls.

After another twenty minutes, they arrived at the station.

They had made it.

Kwenn couldn't believe his crusty eyes. Keráan was the biggest thing he had ever seen; a man-made structure that seemed to *defy* the gods rather than *deify* them. Every time he glanced upward, he felt like the entire thing would fall and bury them all.

He got dizzy, so he stopped.

Looking down wasn't much better.

As they made their way here, Ya'k had told him about the capital. Despite this, he forgot to mention one minuscule little detail.

It was built on top of an active volcano.

So it was a choice between being crushed to death or melting in lava.

Wonderful.

Being here, though, was far more preferable than the turmoil they had endured *out there*. The natural walls surrounding the metropolis were in fact remnants of an eruption; lava frozen in time and left to solidify. Like a stone dropped into a pool, the 'splash' was forever unmoving, with Keráan cradled within.

"We're here" Ryuik announced in solemnity. "We're here…"

Nuv ventured to place a hand on the hunter's shoulder. Thankfully, there was no retaliation.

"We made it Ryuik. Thank you, for everything. I really, truly mean it."

"*We* mean it" Panin clarified, also showing his gratitude. "We wouldn't have made it without *all* of you."

* * *

That night was spent in the inn that was attached to the terminal.

After their business had been sorted and the appropriate paperwork filed, the caravan spent one last night together, drinking to the memory of Waz and a friendship that was now set in stone.

Many years later, a new legend began to pass around the mountains. A legend about a group of hunters that somehow managed to defeat the dreaded Moon Man and Sea Woman, thanks to the help of the fearsome yeti and a group of adventurers that managed to tame it, turning it into an old man who would serve them unquestioningly for the remainder of his days…

CHAPTER XIX

Nuvummburtee could see her.

Remana tol Dwen.

Beside her was Qual-nu.

His form was a blurred abstract. All Nuv could see was a pair of naked, shredded legs reaching forever into the cosmos.

What did they want from him? To unlock his memories? To complete his mission?

He didn't want that. He didn't care.

She's screaming at him now. In pain. In hate.

She's screaming at them both.

She needs help.

Ceev… go to Ceev…

* * *

The inn – called somewhat quaintly *Hot n' Cold* – really didn't give off the vibe of being on the threshold of an uptight, religious city.

Of course, it had smatterings of Sollikane imagery and household talismans, but it was very much a welcoming, family-owned establishment.

Kwenn wasn't sure what he was expecting. From what he saw from the faith of Qual-nu, he dreaded a building that was akin to a slaughterhouse, where the children laughed as they sunk their little hands within the innards of dead creatures.

It wasn't like that.

"I don't know. Is our faith so strange?" Ya'k-lum chided him, as they all sat having coffee.

They had bid their farewells to Ryuik and the hunters, who had gone off to the city to do their business. Without an explicit invitation, Saumen seemingly opted to stay with the younger men. They had asked him if he intended to accompany them to Ceev, but he instead focused on his smoking stick and his drink, stating that it was too early in the morning to make decisions.

"I guess it is, to foreigners like us" Panin admitted whilst polishing his greaves. "That can't be too surprising, right? 'God of Misfortune'? You gotta admit that's an eyebrow raiser."

Puul desperately wanted to add his thoughts, but could only croak.

Ya'k tilted his head apologetically. "We shouldn't be talking about theology in front of the mute magi."

"I don't mind this new Puul, honestly" his brother stated.

* * *

Opting to go on foot in lieu of hiring steeds, the six trekked to Keráan proper.

They youngsters were worried about Saumen at first, as the man looked not too far from death. However, they all knew his appearance was deceiving, and he was fleet-footed with nary a breath rattling from his frail form. Clad in a robe and clutching a cane, he looked nothing more than a beggar or pilgrim in search of an anointing by holy men.

The road certainly helped their sore feet. No longer at the mercy of the harsh environment, the soles of their boots were cushioned by a steady pattern of stone, which made the ascent up the side of the mountain relatively easy.

Crossing people of all trades and backgrounds, they passed under great arches of amethyst and statues depicting important figures of the Sollikane faith.

The city was structured in a way so that the three plates were each planted at a triangular point, with an overlap within the centre. The lowest level bore the brunt of the volcanic energy powering most of the city, with the deep, subterranean aqueducts used for both waste disposal and for water treatment.

Both to Kwenn's disgust and fascination, Keráan had created a way to transfer human refuse into drinkable liquid, via an alchemical process. He nearly spat up all over Puul upon learning this, which led to amused looks by the other people, who were undoubtedly used to seeing such violent reactions.

Still, it was to the mountains' benefit, as this ingenious way of keeping the populace hydrated meant that there was less strain on natural resources – namely, the ice harvesting, which was also a major industry. The coldness of Arlmai was still very much vital; both for supplementing the water usage, and for cooling the city-wide machinery when needed.

They were close to the outer gates.

Like a suspended tidal wave, the wall of Keráan was at once comforting due to its undoubted reliance, but also completely terrifying – considering that it was once an eruption that would have likely annihilated the entire island.

Stretching to the clouds, they could just barely see the top plate.

It was *loud*. It had gotten loud when they first made their way here, but now, Kwenn could barely hear himself talk.

People were everywhere. Hawking wares. Bellowing orders. Chanting. Kids were yelling and being a nuisance.

And we haven't even gone in yet!

The secondary checkpoint was far more congested. From what Saumen told them, there were only two main entrances from the capital, with the northern side being relatively more quiet.

Relatively.

"Saumen, have you been here before?" Panin asked.

"Only once" he replied, barely audible over the din of the crowd.

It *was* busy, but the people *were* well-behaved. This was a holy place, after all, even as Nuv's appearance went unnoticed.

They waited in line for an hour. As they slowly made their way forward, Kwenn craned his neck so much that it began to hurt.

He couldn't help it. The majesty of what the red robes had built was just too amazing. From within the solidified goo, they carved an immense monastery that both welcomed and bid farewell, as horned deities loomed from above and poked their long tongues into a serpentine pattern.

"Once we're in" Nuv said to the group, "we should find an inn. At least it'll be a quiet place to get our bearings. And who knows how long it'll take to get an audience with the council? We could be here for days."

"We don't have much money left, Nuv" Ya'k grumbled. "We'll need to start selling stuff shortly. We can barely afford a decent meal."

"We'll figure it out."

Puul tugged on Panin's elbow, and began gesticulating.

"Oh, I think he wants to find a Numanta consulate" Panin guessed, to which his twin impatiently nodded. "Maybe find some work?"

"*Yes*" Puul wheezed.

"You won't do good in that condition, young man" Saumen said gravely. "Don't worry boys. With Ember Mind's Angakkuq seal of approval and yours truly, we shall have no problem making our way through this swell of government and paper shuffling."

His blotted eyes followed Kwenn's own, and they rested on the wicked icons that almost seemed on the verge of coming alive.

"The Sollikane could stand to be reminded of what they truly represent."

They shuffled through a massive corridor.

Since the lowest level of Keráan was closer to the south, visitors could not simply enter immediately from the northern gate. Instead, they had to take a thoroughfare that stretched directly over the exposed caldera of the mountain.

Called *Baphomet's Bluffway*, it was viewed somewhat as a symbolic cleansing to those passing to and from the city, as their skin felt the warmth of the divine fire.

Again, the mysterious red fire was used in abundance here, as dangerous gasses were kept at bay, and miniature biomes of hearty flora and skittering skinks split the two opposing traffic paths.

It reminded Kwenn a lot of the Antechamber of Fire, though this didn't seem quite as hot, thankfully. He wasn't sure if this was due to magic or some other reason, but the flow of people they were trailing clearly had no trouble, nor did some of the horses they saw.

After passing through yet another checkpoint, they were finally in the city proper.

Keráan was without a doubt the busiest, nosiest place that any of them had ever seen.

Hundreds – if not thousands – of people undulated between the square, stone buildings; all demanding their voices be heard, as the whistling of steam dashes their vain efforts.

Kwenn and the others were all wide-eyed and helpless like newborns.

Quick on his feet, Ya'k-lum purchased a city map from an information booth, and began to study it with fervour.

"Was it *this* busy the last time you were here, Saumen?" Nuv yelled in the old man's ear.

Saumen tightened his flaky lips, obviously uncomfortable with this much activity. "No. The city was smaller back then…"

* * *

Joner had their father.

Rayn told her, and she somehow wasn't surprised.

She knew it would come down to this.

She didn't let it cloud her current goal. She finally had all the kids, and she was going to get them out of here.

They followed Flower. The bird flew westward, chirping hurriedly as she kept a vigilant eye on her herd.

They saw lights. They saw people.

They finally made it. To the place Rayn told them about.

Salvation.

A blonde woman saw them. She waved her arms, and began to call, leading others to her. Some wore green robes. Others were normal folk, decked out in shabby armour. Others still were young – even more kids, stuck in this world.

"Oviinia!" Rayn called, his nebulous shade zipping toward her.

That's her…

Jeleenn smiled, and fell.

* * *

"So, you were the one? That light?"

"I guess… yeah" Syyd confirmed.

Oviinia didn't know what to do. Or say.

She knew the boy. She knew who he *really* was.

These memories… they keep coming. Fast. Too fast.

Vayu would have known, too. That's why she fought so hard. She knew; he represented the ultimate hope that this war could be won.

But something else bothered her. Bothered her greatly.

Who is Rayn?

"If you don't mind me saying, that was pretty fantastic" she said, trying to keep things nice and friendly for the poor boy, who clearly suffered through a lot. "You kicked some major behind. You *all* did."

She got a small look of delight for her efforts. "Thanks. All that rain and stuff was awesome, too. It was hard to keep dry."

She resisted ruffling his mop of white hair. The kid was too precious. They *all* were. They were *all* heroes.

When they had arrived at the camp, nobody could believe it. Rayn and his bird had done the impossible, and brought back something that itself brought joy to the faces of all that had been scarred by battle. Children. Children who had survived. They represented the strength of humanity; their resolve to live.

They all slept soundly, now that the emotional moment had passed. The Eidian gave them what must've been their first decent meal in an age, and they were all cleaned of their filth and sores.

The one that had protected them all this time – aside from Syyd – was the girl.

Jeleenn.

She had not woken yet. She was in terrible shape.

But she would live.

"You can control water? Like a mage?" Syyd continued.

"Ehh… kind of" Oviinia stumbled, not sure what to say. "I'm not a mage. Just a scientist."

Yeah, that'll do for now.

"She's the smartest person I've ever met! " Rayn told his brother. "I know! I've seen her fish! In the big tank!"

"A… scientist? Does that have something to do with that guy who showed up in Gen? That Kwenn guy?"

She stroked her chin. "It's complicated. But in a way, I suppose so."

She thought for a moment.

"Listen. Syyd. I know it was… that the attack on your home happened when Kwenn showed up. But I can tell you right now that he had nothing to do with it."

He bowed.

"Do you know who *did* do it?" he whispered.

"Yes" she said decisively. "I want to be honest to you. To *both* of you. Yes, I do."

"It *was* him, wasn't it? Jeleenn's brother?"

She nodded.

"But why?" Rayn asked, his ghostly voice barely audible. "Why us? Why mum and dad?"

Her chest was wrenched.

"It's complicated. I want to tell you. But I want to wait until Jeleenn wakes, so everyone can hear the full story. Is that okay?"

Syyd wiped his face. "Okay."

* * *

Vayu fell.

She was done.

Her frenetic breathing reminded Remana of a newborn.

She plunged the harpoon deep within her sister's body, ending her life.

Aodh screamed.

* * *

The battle was lost.

The wind of Vayu gusted throughout her home.

Liniii.

She told them all. Told them all to live. To live for her. To live for the future.

They had to flee. They had done what they could.

They ran. The Army of the Eternal Tadpole would not die this day.

Within the wind, was fire.

An inferno of grief and rage tore the land asunder.

Everything burned.

A new world needed to be born.

One day, a sapling will rise from the ashes.

This was the cycle of life and death.

Of Tarinn.

This was Vayu's last message to her sister.

* * *

Nuvummburtee's head exploded.

In the middle of a crowd, he suddenly felt like his entire body had been thrown into a fire pit, and his helm became brighter than any of the street lighting.

Chaos flooded the scene, as panicked people began to flee, and guards rushed onto the scene with magi trailing behind.

"Nuv!" Ya'k yelled, trying to hold his friend tight.

He, too, was burned.

He jumped backward into Kwenn's arms with a start.

"Do something!" he pleaded, looking up at him.

Kwenn couldn't do anything.

Or can I?

With no thoughts clouding his mind, he drew his blade, and pointed it toward Nuvummburtee.

Vatn. Lamun. Help me now.

He saw Saumen change. He was now a beast man once more, and his massive maw snarled at the Sollikane and guardsmen who surrounded them.

A pinprick of sapphire light blasted out from the tip of Kwenn's sword, and hit Nuv's helm, directly into the blazing red jewel.

This is the cycle of life and death.

Of Tarinn.

"And it's worth fighting for!" Kwenn roared.

Smoke blasted off Nuv's kneeling form, as waves of ruby and sapphire rushed over the masonry, buildings and stalls.

Both Kwennsefulass and Nuvummburtee heard it resonate within their heads.

This is your power. Alone you are brave. Together, you are mighty.

Nuv's uncontrolled energy began to wane, and his argent form slowly returned to normal.

"I've got you" Kwenn said. "I've got you."

Fire licked the stonework of Keráan, only to slowly die out as if smothered by an invisible torrent.

"I'm hurting, Kwenn" Nuv mumbled. "Something bad's happened…"

"I know" Kwenn reassured him. "It's okay."

They were together now. In this until the bitter end.

They saw Saumen; once again a wrinkled old man. Beside him were Panin, Puul and Ya'k. They all protected them, weapons drawn, as the law looked on in terror.

"Now" Saumen growled "I think that's proof enough? Can we see the council now, please?"

* * *

Joner could feel her.

Her?

There were a lot of women in his life. Jeleenn. Dian. Remana.

His mother.

But no… it was Vayu.

The wind gushed; wafting his clothing and trying to tear the mask from his face.

No…no… not like this… not like this…

He collapsed. Fell into a darkness that mangled his very selfdom.

It happened over and over.

He came apart at the seams, begging to whatever higher power out there.

He didn't want to lose another friend.

But there *was* no higher power. Not any more.

It was him.

It was *always* him.

The wind.

The rain.

The fire.

It all tore at his skin.

And it will *never* stop.

Not until …

… not until he ends it himself.

* * *

Jeleenn had made it.

Maybe not *all* the way, but it was damn good enough.

She didn't remember arriving at the camp. Only the vague images of a red bird fluttered around in the jumble of her mind; a visual anchor that kept all other recollections from floating away in the stormy seas that caused her brain to throb.

She had been confused upon waking; a walking epitaph of her traumatic battles, she looked upon her carers with empty eyes, as they tried gently to soothe her back into their reality.

Using herbal tea and ancient massaging techniques, the Eidian eventually coaxed the girl from her shell, to which she promptly wept uncontrollably for the next couple of hours.

Afterwards, she was like a whole new person.

Sure, she still hurt; but her recovery bought a clarity in her world that she had not witnessed since before her capture in Henra.

The smothering hugs from Mina, Syyd, Mokee, Juun and Eyuil most *definitely* helped.

As did her introduction to Oviinia Trundle.

The woman looked to be in her mid-twenties or so, with long blonde hair tied up into a bun. She was comely, and somewhat unassuming, lending to her background as someone who dressed for work and never for play.

This was reflected in her mannerisms, to which Jeleenn could only describe as 'boyish'.

If her previous life as a seafaring 'biologist' (whatever that was) didn't encourage this demeanour, then her experience in war certainly did.

Jeleenn saw that everywhere she looked. People who wore faces that were clearly not their own, as they underwent tasks with a discipline that was moulded by the struggle between life and death.

And seeing friends and family succumb to that struggle.

I guess we all have something in common...

In more ways than one, as she would soon learn.

"We have *a lot* to discuss" Oviinia said with a warm smile, after introductions were made. "I can't believe I'm finally talking to you. You're just like Jugo, you know that?"

"I'll take that as a compliment" Jeleenn said. Her gaze was directed to the strange symbols on the woman's arm.

"Yeah, this is a new thing" she addressed almost timidly, resisting the urge to roll down her sleeve.

"Really? What about those blue streaks in your hair?"

"The what?"

Jeleenn handed Oviinia a small looking glass, which the Eidian provided so that she could see the extent of her injuries.

The scientist squinted, and then swore.

"I'll be damned."

* * *

The scouts arrived.

A great commotion was raised within the camp.

The battle had been lost.

Vayu was dead.

Jugo and Ilod had been captured.

What Rayn had seen was true.

Jeleenn and the children barely had any time to react to the appearance of so many strange new creatures. They flooded the grounds.

It was over.

"No!" Oviinia Trundle bellowed, her face now a rainstorm of its own. "*No it is not!!*"

She looked toward Syyd, and then toward Jeleenn.

"No… Vayu knew… she knew… hope is still alive. It stands before us, right here and right now."

Gnoat limped forward, stooped and shaking.

"Vatn" he whispered. "Will you lead us? It is what… she would've wanted."

Oviinia's lips quivered.

"I will… but on one condition."

"What?" Jeleenn asked.

The daughter of Lamun thought of Kwennsefulass. Of Queen Bean Si. Drying her eyes, she looked to the forests of Liniii, and prayed.

"That I will tell you. Tell you *all* the truth."

CHAPTER XX

Álfhildur lay dying.

Aos Si was a kingdom no more; its people now dust in the wind.

"My... my wife" he wretched, as life rapidly faded from his large eyes.

Bean Si knew nothing. She was empty.

She was one of *them*.

The empty husks of Joner's army, strewn across the desolate battlefield. Their hollow faces mocking her – yet, at once begging for her love.

She hated herself. Because she still could not hate *him*.

He was her child. And she failed him.

"The boy..." the king choked. "Our little prince... don't... don't let him..."

He closed his eyes.

* * *

She wandered.

The days and nights went by.

As her prince would cry for his mother in a lonesome castle, she walked the dust that was once pregnant with life.

The lives of the elves.

She barely heard his bawling. She paid no heed to the lamentations of Lojón, who trailed after her like a wounded dog, begging her to come home.

The Pheekonshencc wcrc gonc.

The invaders from the other world. The men of the cold.

They had razed it all.

It was all her fault.

Not Lojón's, who was tortured by them.

Not Álfhildur's, whose only sin was being a devoted husband and father.

Not Jugo's… who was just a human.

Not Joner's.

Hers.

All hers.

The flesh of her people gave way to white bones.

Fabricated forms lay with them; their black armour rusted and their gears exposed.

The dolls.

Her dolls.

* * *

Time was gone.

The prince screamed for his mother. Hungry and alone.

She spent her days locked away in her chambers, leaving Lojón to raise him.

The walls of Aos Si soon withered away. Buildings collapsed. Cities became buried in silt.

Storms pounded at the ramparts, and nature slowly erased the evidence that her people ever existed.

Yet, they did not go.

Joner's visage.

They never left her alone.

Her baby was always there.

Hers.

Her babies.

* * *

She talked to them.

Dressed in rags, she began spending her time amongst the rotting machines.

She sang songs. Told them tales about their father Jugo.

My boys.

The prince soon began to crawl, and began to follow his mother on her treks. His uncle Lojón always brought up the rear, huffing and puffing whilst trying to keep the spirited babe from getting into trouble.

She did not forget them.

She would *never* forget them.

* * *

Mired from head-to-toe in grease, cuts, bruises and powders, she worked.

Had she finally become mad with despair? Was this the workings of a white lady, a ghost who roamed the halls to be with their loved ones once again?

If she looked in a mirror, what would she see?

She did not care.

Aos Si was gone. The women, men and children – all particles within the cosmic sphere.

Only *they* remained.

This was *their* world now.

Her husband was now interred. He would watch over them all.

She took the three relics that destroyed him – the elemental keys – and kept them locked away.

The three foetuses; the shameful, detestable leftovers from the Pheekon weaponry that allowed them to penetrate the veil. She had found them; inexorably linked as they were to Lojón's creations.

It was a miracle.

But it wasn't the one she wanted.

Within their devices, they floated. Like a preserved tribute to the ugliness of humans, she raised her hands in agony and fury, wanting nothing more than to end their miserable little non-lives.

Lojón stopped her. Begged her.

Enough was enough.

No more death.

She lost it. She struck him in a wild fury, and for a second, she was a lioness once more. Her fangs dripped with hot slobber, and she loomed over her eternally suffering steward.

She had *sons*. *Not* daughters.

She looked into their little bodies.

She couldn't do it. She knew it.

They were only little girls. The three sisters.

One of them was already gone.

She hugged Lojón, and vowed she would never let go, ever again.

* * *

The Kingdom of Aos Si saw its last son take his first steps.

His little pigeon-toed legs pumped vociferously, as he desperately tried to grip his mother's gown.

He fell, but was caught by a strong hand.

He looked up, and laughed his baby laugh at the deadpan face of his brother.

Bean Si knelt down, and stroked his fluffy white hair.

"*Cundljósálfar*" she whispered, her voice barely able to contain her joy, "this is Kwennsefulass. He will always be with you."

* * *

Kwennsefulass

  Nuvummburtee

  Gemmadwyer

  Maacinertheen

"Those are their names" Bean Si declared, as she watched the re-purposed, bionic Joners look around their new home with curiosity.

"You… how did you do this?" Lojón breathed, his own artificial arm rattling in protest. "My lady… is this safe?"

"It is" she smiled, closing her eyes as if in silent prayer. "It is. We will never be alone. Never again. This is our family, my dear Lojón. Even as you eventually depart back to the other side… I want you to know. To know that we will never be for want of love and affection here…"

"My lady…"

"And that the little prince will grow. And learn. And blossom into the new future of the elves… whatever that may be."

Lojón observed them again, as they hovered over the boy. In truth, it looked as though the machines themselves were the ducklings, with their only instinct being to follow Cundljósálfar.

Their shiny, fraudulent skin and visible joints really did remind him of the Black Knights that laid waste to their lives. Audible mechanisms within whirred, and their puppet-like way of moving brought back too many awful memories.

"Do they… do they have souls?"

She was serene. She pondered the question for a time, but did not seem at all conflicted.

"In a way. Not like… the way Joner did it. No. They… they are new.

They can learn."

"*How?*"

He was afraid. Afraid that she had dabbled in something she should not have.

"Are you concerned?"

"Every day I breathe."

He looked up at her. She was not the same queen he had known. Of course she wasn't. She was shattered. And what had been put back together was not as it originally was.

She had been through countless tragedies. They *all* had.

He dared not speak it aloud, but the thought mangled his insides.

Had she gone insane with grief?

She stroked her pointed ear. It was one of her old habits, and one of the only things that reassured Lojón that she was *still* her.

That, and the love of her children.

"The girls. They helped. Their energy gave them life."

Lojón was struck with terror. "*My lady*! I... I don't know what to... the... the very thing that caused *all* of this?! What killed--

"Killed? Killed the king? Killed our people?" She cut short.

"Pheekonshenee sorcery" Lojón ventured, fearing wrathful reprisal.

She glowered at him.

"The gates to the other world are still open" he continued, emboldened by her silence. "We should... we should've."

"Killed *them*? The babies? For the greater good?"

"It was *my* sin" Lojón cried, drawing the attention of the meandering 'brothers', who all tilted their heads like distracted dogs.

Bean Si placed his hands within her own.

"Sin or not" she soothed, "it doesn't matter now... it doesn't matter, Lojón. We are here now. We can turn these weapons into something good. Something *beautiful*. New life, against all odds. Against everything that tried to tear us apart. We can heal."

He looked at her, and very briefly, she really was her old, regal self.

"We won't be the same. We will *never* be the same. But we will *go on*."

* * *

Vatn of the Water.

Aodh of the Fire.

Acasta of the Earth.

They had lost their sister, Vayu of the Wind, but they were still immensely powerful, especially when paired with their respective elemental keys.

They were the culmination of the Pheekon's efforts to cross from their world into that of the fay; little clumps of cells that were Tarinn's elements given flesh.

Elements that did not belong in this land of the invisible.

But within them, they had the key to divinity.

These elements were created by powerful gods; gods that may have very well created the Aos Si and everything beyond it.

Shalisshakin. That's what convinced Bean Si.

Shalisshakin. The Goddess of the Ephemeral. She helped in the crafting of the Four Sister Isles, which meant that she did not exist solely in this realm, but that of Tarinn too.

Were the Pheekonshenee right?

More and more, this question got stronger and stronger, as she learned everything she could from their work.

What did Joner learn from them?

Why did her goddess – in the form of a human woman called Dian, ally with him?

She became obsessed. Obsessed in unravelling a technology that was unlike anything the elves had ever seen.

She interfaced herself with the elemental keys, even after seeing what they did to Álfhildur. She communicated with the sisters, whose genetic memory showed her the building blocks of a world that was big, blue and incredible.

Was *this* the future? The future for her and her children?

A future of ascendency? Of stepping beyond the threshold?

She thought of Jugo… that amazing man…

Or could this present an opportunity?

An opportunity? Of what exactly?

Of survival?

Or of revenge?

* * *

The Great Castle of the Leaf, for what little remained of it, became a home again.

As he grew into his body, Prince Cundljósálfar ventured outside on his own.

Frequently, and with greater taste for adventure, he would run along cliff edges with nary a concern for his well-being, nor for his poor brothers that would chase after him, their joints creaking in a marching melody of vexation.

He would swim dirty ponds, swing through groves, and bound over blasted chasms in gusts of starshine and sunbeam; his headstrong spirit giving his arms and legs a royal power that would never serve its people ever again – a royal power that would now only be spent at play and satisfying a forever-youthful wanderlust.

At night, his mother taught them – taught them all – about the history of their world.

She often thought that such schooling was a lost cause, considering that their world was no-more.

But she still liked to remember.

And decreed that they do so, to.

* * *

Time was not as it was here as it was in the human realm.

From what Bean Si could learn from the sisters, the people were reliant on a universal 'rule' that made them slaves to a linear path. They were born, they grew, and they died in a very quick fashion, as they entered a cycle of reincarnation that led to a specific goal in mind.

She thought of Jugo, and the fact that such a remarkable man was simply another seed in this garden of life and death.

How the humans travelled through this multi-layered reality was heavily influenced by the way they perceived their world, and it saw the most focus via their faith, represented by religion and sociological structures that formed basic tenets of life, such as the concepts of 'right' and 'wrong'.

Right and wrong.

Did Joner see himself as right? Or wrong?

The further she dived, the harder it was to breathe. To come back to the shimmering surface of blissful innocence and simplicity.

The Pheeknonshenee, for some reason, fell victim to this flow of time.

They understood so much, and seemed like an unfathomable threat to Aos Si.

So how did she survive?

As a matter of fact, she couldn't understand why they had left. Joner had been working with them. As did Dian… but *why*? And *how*?

It couldn't have been something as simple as vengeance, could it?

For him, yes.

He hated her.

And the Pheekon?

They simply wanted power. To satiate their unending hunger for power and knowledge.

It couldn't have been anything else.

But… Shalisshakin…

If Dian was indeed her – or even simply a fragment of the goddess – then that meant everything to Bean Si.

Because that insinuated a crack in the armour of infinity. That whatever lay *beyond* – whatever inconceivable power that held together this thread of worlds – was imperfect.

It was *fallible*.

And that meant…

Joner…

Was he truly…?

* * *

"I'm right!" Cundljósálfar pouted, flicking the pieces of the board game in frustration.

Maacinertheen, otherwise known as 'Mac', wordlessly shook his head, refusing to submit.

"This sucks!" the prince grimaced. "I had eighteen traps. *Eighteen.* That doesn't count?"

Mac repeated his gesture, and then looked to the others to back him up.

Kwenn, Nuv and Gemma copied the disapproving body language.

"Are you *agreeing*? Or *disagreeing*?" Lojón sighed, as he counted his own pieces. "I sometimes can't tell with you lot."

Mac pointed at his own retinue, and then to the prince's. He then grabbed a handful of his own spare units, and poured them into the centre circle.

Five extra nullifiers and two infantry. If he could smile smugly, he would.

The boy bared his little teeth, and flopped on his back.

"Damn!"

"Language!" Lojón grumbled, suddenly wary of his own deck. "The robot doesn't lie!"

The other three all now nodded.

"You guys aren't even playing!" Cund said, looking at the clouds. "You have no say in this!"

It was a bright day. The six of them sat on the grounds of the castle, overlooking the hills and just catching a snippet of the ruins of the city districts.

Still, it looked a little cloudy off to the other side of the old battlegrounds, with a storm being teased within the rolling rouge.

It looked to be a *basilisk* type, too, which meant the possibility of welts and stinging feet.

Lojón mumbled and the sound of a chuckle filtered through his hairy front. "They're not saying anything. Don't be sour just because you have to abide by the rules for once."

"Rules shmules."

"Very good, my lord."

Overlooking his manservant's mockery, Cund turned to his side and got a view of his mother, who was visible through a window.

No doubt doing one of her experiments...

She rarely went anywhere else these days, even within the castle itself, which was mostly beyond repair and couldn't even be accessed due to overgrowth.

There was no-one else.

Just them.

Sometimes he thought of the buildings being alive with activity as a mere myth, that it was always like this, and that she had lied to him.

Of course she didn't, but some days, he got angry. Angry at her, for not letting him go beyond. To see if there was anyone else.

Anything else.

She wouldn't even let him talk to the sisters most of the time. Even though they seemed friendly enough, she would scold and tug at his ear whenever she caught him sneaking into her lab.

He liked listening to their voices, as strange as they were. They came from some place he couldn't quite understand, almost like it was from some sort of door that was far away. They were scary at first, but they were nice to him, and even told stories about Tarinn at times.

It was more than what his brothers could do.

He still loved them though. They could be overprotective, but they were his family. They even saved him more than once, usually from a nasty fall.

Even if Mac *was* a cheater.

All four of them looked identical, save for their coloured necklaces that had their names carved in the back. They all had the same dark hair and sharp faces. The same skin tone and eyes. The same rigid movements.

Yet, over time, he knew that they had begun to develop their own identities. Maybe it was because he grew up with them and knew them so well. Or maybe it was because he came up with personalities for them all, much like his toys. Either way, he knew they each had their own quirks and ticks.

Kwenn was the oldest, and often seemed to stand back and direct the others almost like a leader.

Nuv was the most energetic. He would always be the first to dive into danger, and would even disobey Kwenn at times.

Gemma would have the most personality. Cund would see him play practical jokes on all of them, something which absolutely no-one else did. One of his favourites was pretending that his head had been turned backwards.

Mac was the inquisitive one. He often shadowed mother, and showed a higher enthusiasm for 'conversing' with the sisters. He was also the only one who demonstrated an ability to read.

All this without ever uttering a word. They could not. Their mouths were fake.

"Cund" Lojón said.

The young elven boy filled his belly with air, and closed his eyes.

"*Cundljósálfar*" he reiterated, with a sterner tone.

"What?"

"Get inside."

"Huh?"

Cund didn't quite understand what he meant. Was he *punishing* him?

"Get inside. *Now.*"

Lojón's manner had suddenly morphed. Goosebumps cultivated themselves on his skin, and he jolted up to his rear.

"What? Why are you say--

He saw him.

A man.

His brothers sprang to their feet, now noticing Lojón's heavy, cold tone. They all turned at once, their hips pivoting on squeaky ball joints.

There was a *man.*

Out of nowhere, he appeared. He stood a few metres away, silently observing them.

Cund's heart stopped dead. He stared dumbly.

"Cundljósálfar! Get inside *now!*" Lojón commanded.

The man was tall. He was dressed in a set of armour that was pale and scratched, and he had a billowing cape that was torn and singed. Feathers came loose from it and floated in the breeze, before burning away in flaming spurts.

Half of his elderly face was obscured by a cracked mask; its eerie porcelain features now dulled by a hard life.

His long grey hair fell freely down to the back of his knees, with much of it tied in decorative braiding.

A single, solitary emerald eye hovered over them all.

`"Who..." Cund stuttered, barely able to comprehend that he was seeing a*nother person* for the first time ever.

The man smiled and spread his hands, showing that he had nothing to hide.

"What... what are you *doing* here?!" Lojón yelled, pointing his metal finger at the interloper. "Don't! Don't come *any* closer!!!"

The man put his hands on his hips, and breathed deeply through his nose, as if relishing the fresh air.

"It's been a while, Lojón" he said with a soft, diffident voice. "How's things?"

"Leave" Lojón growled.

Cundl was frightened. He had *never* heard Lojón speak like this.

"*Cundljósálfar!!!*"

His mother was approaching now, faster than he had ever seen her move. Wearing a simple gown, she screamed and held the Water Sword in both hands.

"Mother?"

Her statuesque form was over him; her shadow wrapping itself around him.

"Mother" the man then repeated, not in mockery, but in a solemn acknowledgement of his own.

"Joner…" Queen Bean Si gasped. She shook violently, and the mere sight made the prince whimper in fear.

"Mum? What is *happening*?"

"Do what Lojón says, and get inside, now. Find the girls. They'll tell you what to do."

"*Mum?*"

"*Now!*" she cracked, her voice like lightning.

"Still a tyrant I see" Joner jeered, now walking slowly toward them.

"What do you *want*?!"

Joner stopped, and seemingly now viewed the four brothers for the first time. A profound look of both sadness and anger now crept across his deep lines.

"What… what *is* this? What did you *do*?"

"*What do you want*?" Bean Si reiterated, her sword now shining with an energy that made Cund's head spin.

"How did you get here? What *happened* to you?" Lojón appealed, as he stood in between the brothers and held them at bay.

"You hypocrites" Joner cursed. "You took them and you ripped them from their purpose. You created monsters… but you're good at that, eh, mother? I guess the apple doesn't fall far from the tree."

Cundl saw Nuv, who was eager to strike. He was frightened. For them. For Lojón. For his mother. And for the sisters, who were now vulnerable within the castle.

Joner? This... this is...

"No Joner..." Bean Si mewled, "... no, not again..."

"I'm not here to cause pain" Joner said stonily, now walking again. "I never wanted *this*. I'm not going to beat a dead horse. I'm just here to bring the girls back home. They deserve a *real* life, mother. You know this. They belong in Tarinn. I can see... I can see they've had an effect on you."

"Tripe" Lojón hollered. "You worked with them. You worked with the Pheekonshenee. And now, what, you're *remorseful*? You're just a sorry old man now, is *that it*?"

The queen raised a palm, indicating silence. "Lojón."

"Something like that" Joner admitted. "I... just want to make things right. I've seen all of this play out. Time is a bitch like that. Especially when you mess with it like I have... all because of my..."

"What?" Lojón said, ignoring his majesty's order.

"Anger."

Cund didn't know what was going on. A coldness crept into him, and he could not move his feet.

"I'm lost" Joner continued. "I can't tell where I am any more. I... I'm just here. Or there. My power. My life. It's cost me everything. I can't take the pain..."

His bright eye dripped, and he momentarily gained the youthful skin that revealed his handsome features.

"I need to do this" he quavered, his steps now stumbling slightly. "*Please. Mother*. No more. Just let me... just let me *do* this... just let me *take* them... they matter. They *matter*!"

Bean Si continued pointing the blade at him, but began to crumble.

"No. No more is right, Joner. You can't do this, my son. You *can't* do this. No more pain. No more *pain*..."

Cundl cried, and grabbed her gown.

She kicked him off. Violently.

"You're majesty!" Lojón decried.

"TAKE. HIM. NOW."

She was no longer herself. What little sanity she had left, was gone within a breath. The thread that Cundljósálfar coveted; the thread that kept her devoted to him, was now severed.

"I am righting this mistake! *Once and for all!!!*"

The prince yowled for her, but Lojón was beside him, and clamped him by the arm.

"Let's go! Now!"

* * *

Now unrestrained, Nuvummburtee lunged.

With no effort, Joner struck the machine in the head, sending him spiralling and skidding along the grassy knoll.

"So, this is where *they* came from?" he grunted, easily dodging Mac's piston like fists and implanting his own palm within his chest.

"Stay back!!!" Bean Si shrieked to her sons, as Kwenn and Gemma tried to follow up with their own attacks.

They immediately halted, allowing her to zip past them like a zephyr.

Swinging with mania, she tried to end him.

Unlike his battle with the king, Joner now possessed no blade of his own. Whether he had lost it or he refused to reciprocate, she no longer cared.

This was the end.

She would commit the ultimate sin. She would take the life of her child.

Joner refused her the satisfaction. He was like a tangential nightmare; unmoving, yet always outside of her reach.

Molten pain twisted her arm, and her bones felt like metal being eaten away by rust.

Vatn, just give me a little more time.

The Water Sword sprayed and splattered, and each drop ate away at her skin.

Joner saw the effect it was having on her.

"*This. This* is what I want to stop!" he moaned, as the acrid stench met his nostrils. "*Why can't you just accept this?!*"

She could not see. She could not breathe, due to the sobs collapsing her airways.

Joner zoned in on her wrist, and knocked the sword from her petrifying hand.

It almost brought her relief rather than pain, as she crumpled to the dirt.

This was enough for Kwenn and Gemma, who leapt after her.

She tried. Tried to tell them. To protect their brother. But words escaped her.

She was not allowed a final goodbye.

Enraged, Joner met their distance in a blink, and first kicked Kwenn in the torso. The force caused him to fold in half; as he skidded like a meteor and tore up the earth around his limp form.

Joner turned to Gemma, but was blocked again by Nuv and Mac, who were both mobile again, and were a blur in their simultaneous assault.

This still wasn't enough, as their 'creator' ducked and weaved with inhuman speed. He grabbed each of their arms in his own hands, and spun like a tornado, flinging them around like nothing. Both of their shoulders popped, and he put an exclamation to his brutality by smashing them together.

They fell into a twitching heap.

Joner barely had time to relish his victory, before Gemma jumped on his back.

His face warped into something grotesque.

"DAMN YOU ALL!!!"

Gripping a handful of hair from behind, he jerked upward, flinging his last victim over his shoulder and clubbing him downward.

Bean Si fell forward and reached out. She warbled something unintelligible; her twisted and swollen tongue begging for him to leave the boys out of this.

"This is what you wanted, *right*?!" Joner screamed. He raised his boot and began to trample Gemma.

Over and over, he was unrelenting in his fury and power. Shards of metal and skin flew upward and clinked against Joner's mask, and his mother could only watch in total loss and failure.

She was a failure. A failure to everyone she had ever known.

She deserved death.

Gemma's hand twitched to the heavens, begging for salvation.

Joner gave one final stomp to the machine's head.

Gemmadwyer stopped moving.

"You did this! *You*!!!"

Drool stranded from his gurning mouth, and he fell to his knees.

"You!"

He gasped and heaved, before grabbing his mother's face and pressing her forehead to his own.

"*You*!!!"

* * *

Kwennsefulass.

He heard her.

Vatn?

Kwennsefulass.

I can't move.

Yes. Yes you can.

I can't.

Yes. Yes you can!

The light shone into his ocular sensors.

It was there.

The Water Sword.

Crawl! Now! Save her!

Oh… okay. I'll try.

* * *

"Let me go! *Let me go!*"

Lojón pulled Cundljósálfar.

The prince was powerful. But the queen had been ready for this moment.

She knew. She always had this plan in place, for this very day.

The prince's powers began to nullify, thanks to the particle waves that emanated from the repaired Pheekon device.

It had to happen, otherwise the boy would've been unstoppable. He would've never left of his own volition.

He would've never left them to die.

They were here in the lab now. The sisters floated in their jars, as the gateway was flickering.

It would not open fully. It could not. Not without the Wind Shield.

But the way to Tarinn could be accessed through a crack in the door, thanks to Lojón and the privilege that was bestowed upon him by the gods.

This time, the Pheekons would not crack the whip. This was different; a move motivated by hope, rather than despair.

"I don't want to go!" Cund wept, rubbing his eyes and spasming with fear. "I don't want to."

"Listen to me" Lojón said, holding the boy's cheeks and wiping away his sparking tears. "You *can* do this, Prince Cundljósálfar. You are the last of the elves. *You.* Don't fail your mother. You have a duty now, right? No more playing. No more running wild. It's time to grow up."

"I don't want to! I... I..."

He began to become dozy, and Lojón himself resisted the urge to cry.

"Master Lojón... I can't..."

"Shush, boy."

He stroked the prince's silken hair, as he slowly sank to the tiled floor.

"Is... is the changeling ready?" Lojón murmured, looking to the sisters.

"Yes" an artificial voice from the speaker emanated. "It is... ready. The same genetic material as the prince. Based on arcane Dokkalfar rituals and enhanced by Pheekonshenee--

"Okay, save the lesson" Lojón stopped, as he looked into Cund's eyes.

He was out.

This was it.

"What... what about the regression..."

"It's ready" the voice confirmed again. "The prince will re-enter an infantile state, with human features. He will be genetically the same as the changeling. Twins, essentially."

"Good... good. And as for you and the boys..."

"Digitised memory fragments have been distributed. We... we will enter Tarinn in vessels of our own, and the brothers will follow. At different times – with as much leeway as the opening will allow. The guardian townships have been notified, and – saving gross negligence from the current descendants and/or unforeseen circumstances – we should find adequate shelter until our wards come and meet us. For the purposes of intelligence compartmentalisation, we will not divulge the destination of the prince and the changeling. No offense."

Lojón nodded, looking down at the sleeping lad that he cradled. "None taken... none taken..."

Would this work? Would any of this work?

He did not doubt his queen. He could not. He *dared* not. But... what would all of this lead to? Would the boy grow up and continue on the Aos Si? Maybe somewhere in the new world? Or would Joner find him, and everything would all be for nought? Or did the queen have another plan in mind? One that even *he* wasn't privy to?

Or... maybe the simplest answer was the correct one. That nothing mattered, as long as there was a future – a future of joy and prosperity.

His own memory would be altered irrecoverably by this. How much would he forget? This had never been done before, but he at least hoped he would remember his time before the war.

Happier times.

There was only one way to find out.

* * *

The Water Sword was a tidal wave of pure power.

The element swirled around Kwenn; engulfing his heart and zapping him with what Cund often described as 'pain'.

It was life itself, and it welcomed him.

His mouth was moving. He had lips. He had a voice.

"GET. AWAY. FROM. HER."

His throat tore apart and rebuilt itself. He gurgled and groaned, as he sprinted toward Joner.

"GET. AWAY!!!"

He swiped. It was clumsy and without any sort of technique whatsoever, but the sword compensated for this as it ripped the oppressive, weighty air with a razor-sharp dynamism that caught the omnipotent man off-guard.

Joner sucked in the crackling atmosphere through his ground teeth. He jumped backward in bonafide surprise as the amorphous tendrils sliced at his body, causing welts to spring up and burst in bloody pustules.

Kwenn kept going. Heedless of his own sense of preservation, he forged ahead and met Joner face-to-face, somehow making the man recoil as he raised his hands to shield himself.

"Vatn!" Joner clamoured. "Stop this! NOW!"

The pleading was not heard, and the blade made contact with his flesh, sinking itself into his shoulder.

This was the final straw for Joner. With a sound that obliterated the ears of all, he screamed with a madness that seemed to crack the world itself in two, as a quake concussed them all in its violent indignation.

The structural integrity of the Great Castle of the Leaf began to fail, and turrets collapsed in clouds of history.

Bean Si sighed slowly, with what little vitality she still had. Her legs were now broken, and she could only crane her head upward to see Joner stumble toward Kwennsefulass, who thrashed on the ground.

Dripping like rose blossoms, his essence fertilised the shifting sands, and he snatched the Water Sword from his quarry.

"A real boy, huh" he mumbled.

He seized Kwenn by his hair, and jerked him up to his knees.

"A *real* boy? Is that what you are?" Joner pressed hoarsely, his poisonous glare meeting the darting eyes of his copy.

"Answer me!!!"

"Leave… leave… him…" his mother eked.

Joner indicated to her. "You… you did this. Did *this*. You took them. You took them. The *don't matters*. *The emancipation of the sadness.* You took them, and you did what you condemned *me* for doing. But what you did was *far* worse. You made life without souls. You doomed them to non-existence. Just like the Pheekonshenee! 'Artificial intelligence' huh?"

He ran the blade's edge to Kwenn's cheek.

"Your 'real' children are not real at all!"

"That's not true… no…"

"Do *they* bleed, I wonder? Let's see!"

Joner cut. Deeply and slowly, taking pleasure in every moment. No blood.

"Just as I thought" he said humourlessly. He released his hold, before kicking Kwenn in the back and sending him into the mud.

He looked up, and met the blistered look of love from Bean Si.

"You… you *are* real…" she whispered.

They both closed their eyes, and went to sleep.

EPILOGUE

*K*wennsefulass.

"Kwennsefulass!"

"Huh?"

"You okay?"

Nuvummburtee stared him up and down. His skin was still red and slightly blistered, but he was otherwise fine. Cradling the Fire Helm underneath his arm, his eyes were sunken and pale, almost as if the Water Sword took some of the energy out of his own blue irises.

They ascended through the city, surrounded on all sides by twitchy guards and magi.

The massive elevator was loud and intimidating, making them all nearly lose their breakfasts in unison. The receding view of Keráan's lower levels – and the surrounding paleness of the Merca Lal Mountains – could be seen through the iron grating, as thousands of tiny flames got more and more condensed as they got further into the darker avenues.

Kwenn thought back to the fireflies of Gen.

"Yeah… I'm good" he whispered.

"I felt her" Nuv continued, staring out at the tops of the stone buildings. "Aodh."

The magi murmured amongst themselves.

Saumen shook his head. "Let's save it for the council, eh?"

Nuv kept staring.

* * *

The top of Keráan almost touched the heavens.

The council of the Sollikane was within a massive hall known as the *Discordium*, which housed several heads of the city and a few foreign dignitaries that ensured stable cooperation within Arlmai.

The Great Ring felt closer than ever before, as the anaemic silhouettes of the moons tried to be seen amidst the clouds.

It was substantially cooler here than down below, with the heat of the volcano trapped by city-wide instruments and diverted toward energy usage.

The black, marbled ground stretched outward into different administrative structures, a public garden and even an astrological platform that currently pointed toward the Floating Castle of Eelow.

Kwenn had tried to ask if Saumen knew anything about that particular wonder, but the old man refused to elaborate.

Signalled by jets of steam, they stepped off the platform. Public servants eyed them in surprise, but were wise enough to keep clear of the group as they were shepherded toward the largest building.

Curiously, they were not disarmed. Not that they could do anything with Kwenn's blade… but it was still odd. Keráan was an open-carry city, but the fact that they didn't bother confiscating the tools of the people that could've burned down an entire street spoke volumes.

Spoke *what* exactly?

"Hey, it's you!"

A small voice rang out. Melodious, it called from somewhere in the distance. They all looked around, and couldn't see the source.

"Hey! Up here!"

Puul was the first to see it. He pointed eagerly, and jabbed Ya'k, who was closest to him.

"There! What's that?" Ya'k called.

It was... a firefly?

How? When my mind went to them only moments ago...

No, it was too big to be an insect. Too bright.

Wings flapped in a blur, as a ball of light came down and floated in front of Kwenn.

"It's good to see you again!" it said, bouncing up and down.

It can't be...

"A fairy?"

"You got that right."

A man came toward the group. Incredibly tall, he wore a long brown coat that reached down to his dirty leggings. He wore a pair of gauntlets, which did not seem to get in the way of the smoking stick that jutted out from between his fingers.

His long, dark hair was tied up into a bun, and his disturbingly pale eyes adorned a face that was neither old nor young.

"Trebor!" Kwenn shouted; a little louder than he meant to.

"It's you" Saumen said sourly.

The fairy zipped back to Trebor, plopping itself onto his large shoulder like an obedient finch.

"He doesn't remember me..." it said with sadness.

Trebor ignored it, and continued toward them.

"Sire... I think it's safe to assume these are the folk you've been waiting for?" one of the magi queried.

"Sure is" he nodded. "Don't worry. I've got it from here."

Kwenn, Nuv, Panin, Puul and Ya'k looked around in complete puzzlement, as their detainers bowed and left.

Saumen continued to look grumpy, as the tall man carelessly flicked his narcotic away. "Good to see *you* out and about" he observed. "I thought you'd stay in your cave."

"Well, considering the fate of the world is at stake, I thought I'd do *something*" Saumen grumbled. "Like yourself, I take it?"

"I've been busy" Trebor shrugged. "I nearly died."

"Poor you."

"Trebor, what are you doing here?" Kwenn asked, trying not to be distracted by the fairy.

"Like you, the road led me here." He looked to Nuv and Ya'k, and tilted his head toward them in greeting.

They did the same.

"Damn, there really *is* another one of you huh? Joner... bloody hell..."

"You're one of the people" Nuv clarified, "who is part of this? You're one of the warriors who fought those wizards?"

Trebor scratched that back of his neck, almost embarrassed. "Yes. I was one of the idiots that caused all of this. Well... kind of. It's complicated."

"*Complicated*" the fairy returned mockingly.

He shushed it.

To be continued in Part Three...

ABOUT THE AUTHOR

Kris Godwin BA resides in the land down under, and is still in the throes of caffeine addiction.

https://krisgodwin.wordpress.com/

www.ingramcontent.com/pod-product-compliance
Lightning Source LLC
Chambersburg PA
CBHW070152120726
47909CB00001B/75